I0702032

THE FROG-EYED GOSPEL

Leslie DeBrock

2025

ISBN 9798218248840
Library of Congress 2023914012

Cover art by Chuck Harbaugh

Design and Typesetting by Wordworthy Media Services in Bellingham, Washington ~ www.wordworthymedia.com

To every frog-eyed one of us
whose received wisdom was
not enough.

Table of Contents

Prologue
The Fire of '58

On the shore of Lone Star Lake in northeast Texas, not far from the steel mill, there stands a row of cabins that overlook a swimming dock. Each cabin has eight or ten bunk beds, all of which are made as neatly as could be expected by preteen boys. Suitcases and duffel bags lie on the floor beneath the bottom bunks. In one corner a walled-off toilet and sink afford a pretense to privacy. No one is inside the cabins now. All the boys have marched out into the late afternoon heat, gone up the dirt road past the dock, past the rows of upturned canoes chained to the pine tree for the night. They've topped the hill where the mown parade ground spreads out with its flagpoles. They've crossed the field to the cafeteria where they've heard announcements and were led in prayer and then fed. Now it's almost dark and time for the vespers service. They've taken a short path into the woods to "the arbor," which is no more than a concrete slab with a tin roof supported by oilfield pipe.

There are almost sixty boys, ages nine to eleven, sitting in rows of steel folding chairs. They're waiting for the service to begin. They have been doing this every evening for the last four days, and this will be the last night of it. Tomorrow, Saturday, they go home.

The boys are puzzled that there is no adult present.

Someone, however, on this hot night, has built a bonfire as big as a station wagon in a clearing next to the arbor. There are logs the size of human legs piled up and blazing, throwing unwanted heat through the assembly. The boys murmur among themselves, wondering who built the fire and why. They become restless. The older boys dare to leave their chairs. They find pine cones and throw them at the fire, and then at each other. The more timid ones keep to their seats, expecting that tonight's preacher will show up soon and be angry at their irreverence. They've heard a different preacher every night, and they have no idea what this one will be like.

A tall thin figure dressed in black appears at the edge of the woods. "Take a seat, boys," he says in a smoky voice. "We're about to begin." He walks to the lectern and opens his Bible upon it and firmly smoothes the pages.

The boys settle and the preacher inspects their faces, shown in halves by the fire's light.

"Let us pray," he says and turns his face to the smoke billowing into the sky.

"Our Heavenly Father," he booms. "We are sinners, every one of us, and we know that sin must be atoned. Thank You, God, for loving us enough to send Jesus to atone for our sins. Thank You, Jesus, for coming to Earth, for toiling through a mortal life for our sake. Thank You, Jesus, for Your suffering and Your blood and Your death on the cross, and for offering us salvation from the flames of Hell that we so truly deserve. The Hell in which we would certainly endure eternity, but for the salvation that You freely offer.

"Lord, for the souls here tonight which You have already saved, we give our gratitude. But for those present here tonight who are still lost, and they know who they are, those yet unsaved and at risk of the flames of Hell, Lord, trouble their minds and spirits so that they are moved to accept salvation. Lord, make them realize the danger in which they dwell. If they die this night, their souls will suffer in agony forever without You as their Personal Savior. May their hearts be troubled until they find peace and salvation in Thee. Amen."

The preacher paces for a moment, bent forward with his hands clasped behind his back. He stops and regards the young faces.

"How many of you have some idea what Hell will be like?"

There is a tentative raising of hands.

"Most of you don't seem too sure. So I'm going to describe Hell for you.

"Hell is, first, the fitting place for sinners to spend their agonized eternity. And we are all sinners, the Bible says so. We're all guilty of sin." He points a gnarled finger over the crowd. "You all know the darkness in your hearts. In your minds." He paces and draws a deep breath. "The sinful, sinful thoughts you sometimes have."

He turns to the fire that pulses against the night. "I'm wondering. How close do you think you can get to that fire?" He pauses. "It's a puny comparison to Hell's heat, but let's do an experiment here tonight. How close to that fire do you think I can get? Twenty feet?"

He knows that most boys have no clear idea what twenty feet looks like, so he walks toward the fire and stops twenty feet from it. "This here is about twenty," he says. "It's hot where I'm standing here. I'm telling you it's really hot."

The boys' eyes widen. They wonder what this unpredictable man of God is going to do.

The preacher pauses to let the fire speak for itself. A log shifts and sparks spiral high into the dark. "I'll try fifteen feet. Anybody want to try it with me?"

Nobody does.

He takes three steps closer and grimaces. The boys watch.

"Hell is a lot hotter than this fire! And I can't hardly stand it right here."

A few of the boys look at each other. "Whoa," somebody says.

"TWELVE FEET!" He takes another long step. "AAAAAGH!" He jumps away and turned his back to the heat and runs away from it. Back at the lectern he yanks off his suit coat and waves it in the air. His face is flushed.

"That was painful, boys. And that's what's waiting for the unsaved sinner, only hundreds of times worse." He lifts up his Bible and jabs it with a forefinger. "Isaiah 66:24 says … 'The worm shall not die, neither shall the fire be quenched.' " He flips pages to another passage. "Here it is … Mark 9:43. Mark says that the sinner will go, and I quote, ' … Into Hell, into the fire that shall never be quenched.' Take a look at it, boys. Right here for you to see." He points to the flames. "Do you want to lie down in that fire? Do you want to sit in that fire? Do you want to breathe in that fire?"

He raises his voice to a shout. He shouts about lust. About the evil of touching one's own body "in the lust of the flesh." He uses the word "sex" as if the word is distasteful in his mouth. He wails about the sin of failure to honor one's father and mother. Taking God's name in vain. He goes on and on with gathering intensity.

There is audible sobbing. Somewhere a small voice is heard: "I want to go home."

The evangelist continues. "Luke 16:24. The rich man died and cried out from Hell, 'I am in anguish in this flame!' "

He jerks his head up from the page to glare out into the assembly. "How many times must God say it? You will burn in Hell if you are not saved. Now here's what you've got to do," he goes on. "God's own word makes it very plain. Give your life to Jesus."

He pauses for effect. "It's that simple. Jesus. The pure Son of God came to this Earth and DIED for your sins. All you have to do is say, 'Jesus, I am a sinner. Save me from my sins. I give my life to You.' "

He goes on to quote John 3:16 and other passages that offer hope. "Ask Jesus to save you now. Right now. And you will be welcomed into His arms on the Day of Resurrection to live in perfect bliss forever. But you have to take your first step. So, right now: everybody stand up. If you are saved already, then pray for those who are not. If you are not saved, and you know who you are, then walk away from your chair and come here to me and I will pray with you and lead you to Jesus."

A weeping ten-year-old steps into the aisle and goes to this formidable preacher and says, "I don't want to burn." The preacher says loudly, "Yes, thank You, Lord." Then to the child, "Just repeat after me. 'God, be merciful to me, a sinner.' Can you say that?"

"Yes, Sir," the boy replies and repeats the words, trembling, "God, be merciful to me, a sinner."

Other boys take courage and come to the preacher, some in tears, some shaking.

Eleven-year-old Peter Loucas stands where he is. Frowning. Breathing rapidly. Gripping the chair in front of him and wishing this to be over.

"Do you believe?" the preacher goes on. "The Devil makes you doubt. The Devil wants your eternal soul. The Prince of Darkness confuses your mind. Will you reject Jesus, who loves you and who bled and died for you? Jesus wants to save you. Let Him into your heart. Right now. Right now. Right now."

There is no hell like belief in Hell, and Peter Loucas believes in Hell and that he has offended God beyond all remedy. Such a terror makes him wish he'd never been born, yet there he stands in an undeniable and irrevocable state of existence.

He knows what his own sin is, and it is this: for over a year he has resisted being saved. He has sat through countless sermons in which the path to salvation has been laid out. He has stood, like he is standing now, listening to his pastor pleading for lost souls to come to Jesus. He understands that the greatest decision of his life is in his own hands, and that every moment of his life, from this point onward, is a risk of eternal damnation. Yet he resists.

He doesn't know why. He can't articulate that being saved is an adult decision and that he's not yet able to give up his childhood. He's not ready to give up his parents as his ultimate safety. He doesn't yet fully own himself and can't give himself away. His childhood vocabulary cannot express these things.

The terrible responsibility for his immortal soul, which he'd not asked for and at this moment does not want, compresses his mind into a state of abject dread. He is something more than his known self. He carries the heavy custody of a soul and the shocking responsibility of protecting it from eternal torment. His heart pounds and his sweaty hands clinch the chair back.

The preacher goes on with his cajoling. Peter, trembling with the weight of his non-decision, notices the moths and June bugs, neither sent by God nor in any way concerned. Attracted to the light, they fly into the flame. Their wings singe and they fall spiraling into the embers and are no more. Pete Loucas envies them.

Down at the lake, in the water, a young frog swims awkwardly with its vanishing tadpole tail and new little legs. Its shrunken gills are giving way to lungs that need air. It swims up from the dark and breaks the surface with its nostrils and eyes, and it tries to focus on the glare of the bonfire above but comprehends none of it.

Chapter 1
1965: A Curse of Providence

The Sabine River originates a little northeast of Dallas in what was, first, buffalo country, then cotton country. It meanders uncertainly over the blackland prairie of central Texas, gathering small creeks and tributaries until it becomes worthy of being called a river. It eventually turns southeast and leaves the black soil of the prairie and finds the red clay and pines, the hardwoods and gentle hills of East Texas before becoming the border between Texas and Louisiana. By that time it's laden with silt and carrying saucer-sized clots of crude picked up in its passage through the oil fields of the Woodbine Formation. The small town of Sabine Gap, five miles from the river on the Texas side, has been an oil town since 1932. Before the oil boom it had been a farming community with a feed store, a cotton gin and a bank. Several denominations of clapboard churches poked their steeples no higher than the pine trees.

By 1965, thirty-three years after the oil boom, the feed store was no longer the biggest building in town. Tinker Tool and Die, the Sabine Gap Hotel, and J.C. Penney's were bigger. The cotton gin, a corrugated tin building bigger than any other, now sagged abandoned in a weedy field not far from the railroad station.

Also by 1965, the oil money had paid for a fine new

two-story high school with Spanish style arches and tiled corridors. Pete Loucas was a senior there, expecting to graduate in another three months.

It was February, and while winter already had a worn-out feel to it, a blue norther let everybody know that it wasn't spring yet. On this particular day, Tuesday the 9th, it was damp to say the least. It was afternoon and the high school had just let out. The kids who had cars, oil money kids, threw their books in the back and revved their engines in the parking lot, seemingly unable to leave without the full attention of everybody in earshot. Quite a few kids, singly and in pairs, walked toward home, books under their arms, maybe holding hands if they were going steady.

If it had been a nicer day, Pete Loucas might have simply run the three miles home in his track shoes, but today he took the school bus. While it wasn't exactly raining, there was just enough water in the air to get clothes wet if you were out long enough. He stood against the half-wall of the bus shelter gazing at the weather, oblivious to the commotion of all the other students around him. He watched for the number 6 bus, intending to get aboard in time to get a seat if the elementary kids hadn't already taken them. Presently he saw it coming around the corner of the school, its broad wipers making slow sweeps across the glass.

Not only did he get a seat, he got one at the window. A lot of parents must have picked up their little kids on this wet day. Pete sat with his books stacked in his lap and watched droplets of water jerking their way down the side window inches from his face.

When the lineup was fully aboard, the driver levered the door shut and rattled the bus into gear. They pulled out onto the street, and Pete watched the town of Sabine Gap slowly pass across the window. Some cars had headlights on. People walked with their heads down. At the edge of town Ed's gas station sat with its pumps idle, and Ed was inside with his feet on his desk, talking to somebody on the phone.

When they were clear of town, Pete kept his eye out for a particular drilling rig. There was a new well going in at a pasture along his bus route, and his dad was on the crew. But when he came by the rig, he was puzzled to see that none of the crew was there. There was just a Railroad Commission truck where two men sat looking at some paperwork they were trying to keep dry under a black umbrella. All the equipment was idle at the platform. A pipe dribbled red mud into the slush pit. The tool shed looked to be locked up. Pete figured they must have broken a rod somewhere deep in the hole and had to quit early. He'd find out from his dad at dinner.

The bus lurched to a stop across the road from Pete's driveway. A bunch of cowbirds startled up out of the wet Johnson grass and flew into the woods, but Pete Loucas didn't see them. He was tall and so his head had been up near the curved ceiling of the bus. He had to duck his head and come out sideways, the stair treads being too small to accommodate his size-14 feet.

He crossed the road, gave a wave to the driver, Mr. Nolan, and then took care stepping over the cattle guard and onto the dirt driveway. With his head hunched down against the damp wind, he brought his books tight to his chest and broke into a trot.

Before he could even see the house Pete noticed a fresh set of tire tracks in the sand, which was unusual. He didn't expect his dad home this early even if the crew quit drilling early. They would usually spend the rest of the day in the shop doing some kind of maintenance or other.

The driveway curved around a stand of pines and down a gentle slope. It was from there that Pete saw a car parked at the house which he didn't recognize at first. When he was closer, he saw that it was Brother Deckert's Oldsmobile. He wondered why his pastor would be so far out of town at this time of day. Coming to dinner was his best guess, though it was a bit early for that.

Pete picked up his pace, leapt onto the front porch and pushed his way through the front door. "Hey Brother Deckert," he said cheerily. "You must have smelled something cooking."

Brother Deckert didn't smile, but stood solemnly and advanced to greet Pete. With a hand on Pete's shoulder, he said, "Hello Pete." He lowered his eyes for a moment and then brought his gaze squarely to Pete. "I'm afraid I bring very bad news."

Pete glanced around the room and for the first time noticed his mother, Lavena, sitting wet-eyed in the armchair. She glanced up at him, and quickly back down, offering no clue. She fixed her gaze on something beyond the floor.

Brother Deckert held his eyes on Pete's. "Pete, I have to tell you that your father was in a bad accident this afternoon."

"Oh." He waited. "Well, how bad? Where is he? Is he here or in the hospital or what?"

"No, Pete. Not here. Not in the hospital."

Pete held his breath for a moment, already avoiding knowing what he feared he would soon have to know. "Well … what happened? How did he get … ?"

Steadily, with an even voice Brother Deckert said, "I'm told that the men had just finished their lunch break. Your dad climbed the derrick and took his place on the monkey board. They said the swivel was on its way up. He reached out to take the end of the drill pipe and just seemed to miss it with his hand. It may have been the wind, but he just lost his balance."

"So he what, fell off?"

"Yes."

Pete was quiet for a moment, trying to think of another question to ask that might delay his knowledge, but concluded there was none. "So, he's dead?"

"I'm so sorry, Pete."

Pete stepped back and turned in a circle. He went to his mother and knelt where she sat. She looked up at him with a pleading expression, shook her head slightly and looked down again. Pete looked back to Brother Deckert.

"Where is he?"

"He's in Heaven now, Pete."

"No, I mean where IS he?"

"He's been taken to the funeral home."

Pete had driven by the funeral home hundreds of times, but he'd never been inside. He didn't really know what they did in there, nor how they did it. He had a vague image of a steel table and probably chemicals. His dad lying there with people working on him. It crossed his mind that he'd ask his dad all about it, but the absurdity of the thought quickly followed.

"I'd like to pray with you," Brother Deckert said.

"Okay," Pete said, mentally trying to catch up with events. He went to the couch and sat down, and Brother Deckert sat down with him.

Brother Deckert began, "Oh Lord, we come to Thee in a difficult hour of need. Please, Lord, bring comfort to Pete and Lavena Loucas in this hour of dreadful loss. Enter their hearts, oh Lord. Help them to find the wisdom of Your will. Comfort them with the knowledge of the resurrection to come. Place in their path the hope of an end to all grief and despair. Instill in them the knowledge, even on this sorrowful day, that Pete's father, Lavena's husband, he even now in this moment is at Your side in Your Kingdom, and that in due time they will be rejoined in Your Second Coming. The day will come that the graves will be emptied and the sea shall give up her dead.

Bless us, oh Lord. Show us Your path of righteousness. Give us strength and faith to live in accordance to Your will. We ask these things in Jesus' holy name, Amen."

Nobody moved for several seconds. Then Pete, feeling that it was incumbent on him to participate, said, "God, I just need to … understand." Then he said, "Amen."

Brother Deckert stayed with Pete and Lavena for about another hour. He read to them from the Bible. Revelation 21:14. "He will wipe every tear from their eyes. There will be no more mourning or death or crying or pain." Psalm 147:3. "He heals the broken hearted and binds up their wounds." John 14:1. "Do not let your hearts be troubled. You believe in God. Believe also in Me."

He asked if there was anything he could do, or anyone they would like him to call, family members perhaps?

"Just let folks at church know," Lavena said.

"Edna and Margaret in The Women's Auxiliary already know," Brother Deckert said. "They should be here any time now."

Indeed, about then they heard the rumble of a car coming across the cattle guard. Brother Deckert looked out through the Venetian blind and said, "Here comes Edna Muncie now. It looks like somebody's with her." He watched Edna's Buick roll to a stop and saw Edna and Margaret, both friends of Lavena's, emerge from the car with covered dishes of hot food in hand.

Brother Deckert went to the door to let them in. The women, holding baking dishes in one hand, gave him, and then Pete, one-handed hugs. Edna reached up to touch Pete's face. "I'm so sorry," she said. Pete nodded mutely.

As soon as they could put the food down in the kitchen, Edna and Margaret went to Lavena and put their arms around her as best they could with Lavena still in her chair.

When the women were established in the house, Brother Deckert led them all in a last prayer and took his leave, feeling a little guilty that he had the luxury of leaving this sad house. He drove away hoping that he would not soon have another day as difficult and painful as this one. He was already trying to compose words for the funeral he would have to preach.

With Brother Deckert gone the women took over the house. Lavena apologized weakly for the state of the kitchen and for the laundry in the hallway. Edna and Margaret assured her that their own kitchens were worse and hugged her and made themselves busy with the dishes and stove. They looked into Pete's face with their sad eyes and hugged him again. Pete half-heartedly returned the gesture. He didn't know how to act. He wanted their sympathy and resented their pity.

"I'm going out." Pete said.

Lavena looked at him as if she'd just realized he was there. "You're what?"

"I want to be by myself for a while."

"Where are you going?"

"Just the woods. I don't know. I think just out in the woods."

"Why?"

Pete looked at her. He had no answer. She had asked him a question and he felt that he must answer. He had never not answered her.

"Talk to God," he said, which might have even been true. "I'll be back."

Pete was aimless at first, knowing only that he wanted to get out of sight of the house. There was chain-link fence that kept cattle out of the backyard, and Pete would normally have vaulted over it, but this time he used the gate. He took the path downward toward the pond. He wished he'd put on his coat, but had no intention to go back to the house for it.

He could no longer see the house, and he walked faster. *Daddy's dead.* He visualized his father in his work clothes and tin hat. *I want that hat.* His stride lengthened and left deep heel marks in the sand. *I want my dad.* He began to trot down the slope toward the creek and the pond. *I want to ask him something. I don't know what, but something.* He began to run in earnest. He left the trail and struck out through the woods and underbrush. He ran harder as if, were he to run fast enough, he could catch his father's soul before it got away. He skirted pine trees and thrashed through sumac and wild grape. He leaned forward and threw his forearms in front of his face and broke through holly and briars. His shirt tore but he didn't care. Dead twigs and branches broke off before him. He was heedless of the possibility of poison ivy and copperheads as he leapt down a draw and crossed the creek at a narrow place. He ran up the other side of the creek bank, furious that he couldn't run faster. Furious that he couldn't fly. He stumbled and got up again and ran. His lungs burned in the cold air and his legs were beginning to fail him, but he wouldn't stop. He would never stop. Not ever.

He fell, got up and fell again and lay in the damp leaves. He rolled over and looked up at the sky. Sounds began to come from his chest that he'd never heard before. His breath fogged in the chilled air. Ugly tangles of pine and hickory partially hid the ugly sky. He wanted to pull leaves over himself and stay there forever.

"God's will," Brother Deckert had said.

Chapter 2
Mad at Jesus

At seven years old Beulah got mad at Jesus, and she told Him so. "You makin' me really mad," she told Him. "Sometime when I git big, I'm goin' git You back."

Reason number one was that her mamma had a heart attack and went to live with Jesus. The other reason was that she found out at school that Santa Claus was just made up. Beulah was getting so mad that she crossed her heart and hoped to die if she ever got fooled like that again. "Strike three, and You're out," she said to Jesus.

Her brother, Roscoe, was twelve. He was bossy to start with, and now that Mamma went to live with Jesus, he was worse. As for instance, Roscoe said she couldn't sleep in Mamma's bed no more. That was gonna be his bed from now on. He told her she could sleep in his old bed if she wanted to, or just stay on the couch.

Roscoe told her she had to start doing dishes. Just the little ones, but still. Beulah didn't want to do no dishes. Besides, Roscoe's cooking stank. It was usually just eggs and they was usually burnt. It got to where sometimes Beulah would sneak over next door to Clifford and Lummie's house and eat with them-all. Clifford and Lum had so many kids they ack like they didn't even know she was there. After the electricity went off in her own house, she slept over there sometimes.

The only time when Roscoe wasn't the boss was when the Tin Cup church ladies came over. On Sunday mornings especially, they came walkin' into the house like they owned it, and started to fussing about this got to be cleaned up. That's got to be put together. They's dirt all over something or other. They made her and Roscoe get up and get ready for church. There wasn't gonna be no laying out from church, they said. If it was just one lady it wasn't so bad, but if there was three of them, look out! They were lible to start trying to out-boss each other. But one thing for sure, Roscoe went to Sunday school and church if he wanted to or not, and so did Beulah. One thing good was that the church ladies started a collection and the electricity went back on. But Beulah was still mad.

Beulah and Roscoe's cousin, Prentice, he used to stay with them, but he went off to Korea when he was big enough. He got back from Korea not long after Mamma went to stay with Jesus. He moved back in with them and said Korea was a long way off, but Jesus was even more of a long way off than that, and nobody could go there until Jesus decided He was ready. He also said he was going to be like their daddy till they didn't need him no more. Beulah turned eight by then, and she said, "Does that mean Cora's gone be our mama?" Prentice just looked off somewhere and didn't say nothin'. Roscoe was still just twelve, but he said he ain't never had no daddy and he didn't need one startin' now. Prentice was strong though. He picked Roscoe up off the ground and held him up in the air and told him two things. He said, "There ain't nobody in your life ever again goin' be on your side like I am." Then he put Roscoe down and said, "You don't have to like it."

After that Beulah and Roscoe always got to school on time with some breakfast in their bellies 'cause Prentice cooked it, and he didn't burn no eggs. They quit goin' over to Clifford and Lummie's so much after that. Generally when they got home from school, Prentice, he was still working somewhere, but if he came home late, he'd have a sack of smoked pork or something. He'd get Beulah and Roscoe busy. "Beulah, you ain't too short to reach in that drawer and git us some knives and forks," or "Roscoe, we need some ice tea tonight. Go next door and acks Lummie can we have some ice."

Beulah, though, she still had troubles. Night haints woke her up yelling. She'd get in fights at school, and sometimes she didn't stay at school once she got there. At home she'd pitch a fork-id fit if Prentice put a stew pot in the wrong place. "That ain't where Mamma keep it," she'd holler. She'd bang her head on the wall so hard it scared Roscoe and Prentice too. Sometimes they'd get Lummie to come over and calm her down.

Prentice went from one job to another, doin' yard work mostly, until the time he got hired to dig out some old pipes at the wax plant. He must have done a good job, because they started calling him back and finally started working him regular. It was night shift lots of times, but it was pretty good money and about the best black-man job in town. Not like white folks, but still.

Roscoe seen his wad of bills one time and started in on him to get a car for them to go to town in, because Mamma's old truck was crowded in the cab, and he didn't like riding in the back. Prentice said he wasn't wasting money on no car. He said he was saving up, but he didn't say for what.

When Roscoe got bigger, him and Prentice got in more and more fights. "You ain't my daddy and you can quit akin' like you is." Finally when Roscoe was seventeen, he lied about his age and went to the Army. He went to boot camp and came back to visit once after that, all dressed up in his uniform. He said he was going to Hawaii for some more training and he was most likely going to Viet Nam after that. Nobody knew where that was, but everybody in Tin Cup came to see him. Them boys he was in high school with, they were all jealous. The girls were all sashay and smiles. When it was time to take Roscoe to the bus station they used Clifford's Pontiac. Roscoe was mighty proud.

Prentice stayed quiet like he was puzzling on something. He just shook Roscoe's hand and told him to be careful and write once in a while, and handed him a silver dollar. "This is for luck," he said. Then Roscoe got up on that bus. He waved at everybody out that back window, and that was the last time anybody ever saw him.

By that time Beulah was twelve. With Roscoe gone she was twice as mad at Jesus. She got to where Prentice couldn't do nothing with her. When she was in the eighth grade, the police got her for trying to steal beer at the Blue Top Grocery. In the tenth grade she quit school. After that Prentice didn't see her much unless she called asking for him to come get her from somewhere. Sometimes she wanted money. Mostly she just wasn't around.

Chapter 3
A New-dug Grave

At the Sabine Gap cemetery on the day before the funeral, a battered Chevy pickup with no license plates lurched past tombstones and monuments on the gravel driveways. It crossed a shallow ditch into the older end of the cemetery and circled behind a hedgerow to the machine shed where it stopped in a small cloud of its own smoke. Two graveyard men in soggy bib overalls climbed out. One of them, the fat one, chewed tobacco. The skinny one lacked the teeth for it. The skinny one, who smoked roll-your-own cigarettes, pulled himself up onto the driver's seat of a small tractor and started the motor while the fat one who chewed, collected two shovels and a green tarp and then seated himself in the front-end bucket of the tractor with the tools across his lap. The skinny one pulled a lever, and the fat one's feet came up off the ground. Thus situated, they travelled the lanes of the all-white part of the cemetery to the site of the grave they were to dig. The backhoe swung loosely behind them like an appendage of something prehistoric.

Early the next day, the day of the funeral, the church was very cool and dark inside. The only people there were Brother Deckert, laboring in his study, and two employees of the funeral home who were ferrying flowers into the sanctuary. The casket was already in place directly in front of the pulpit, but it hadn't yet been opened. The sanctuary echoed with the footsteps of the men bringing arrangements from the van parked at the side door. The door opened and closed repeatedly, reverberating through the building and alternately letting in a gray light or closing the room into semidarkness. When they'd gotten all the flowers inside, they arranged them on stands at the head and foot of the casket. Off to the side they distributed all the miscellaneous bouquets that had been given individually along with the signed sympathy cards. When they were done, they lifted one final wreath onto the lower half of the casket and centered it carefully. Lastly, they placed a stand at the head of the coffin, which held a photograph of the deceased, pictured in his Army dress uniform, silver wings of a paratrooper on the lapel. Then they released the catch and opened the top half of the coffin and made sure that the corpse was still properly arranged. They stepped back and surveyed their work. One of them stepped forward and rotated the wreath slightly and stepped back again. They exchanged a slight nod and went out of the sanctuary through a narrow door and a short way down an unlighted hallway to Brother Deckert's study. Brother Deckert came back with them to the sanctuary to inspect their work and give it his approval.

Brother Deckert was six feet five and weighed 225 pounds. For his height alone he might be taken for the man in charge. When he spoke his baritone voice confirmed it. His coal black hair was parted on the right, and his black horn-rimmed glasses gave him a scholarly Clark Kent appearance. He entered the sanctuary erect, barely clearing the door jamb. He scanned the arrangements while the funeral home men stood as if at attention. Brother Deckert nodded his approval and the two men went at ease. Then the three of them left together through the side door to the van where they shook cigarettes out of their packs and one of them offered lights all around.

"Did either of you know him—John Loucas?"

"I can tell from his picture in there that he was a paratrooper. Too bad he wasn't wearing his chute," one man said. Brother Deckert and the other man gave him a look, but otherwise ignored the comment.

"One of my kids and his kid are in the same grade," the other man said. "I've seen him from time to time. Talked to him once or twice. Didn't talk much. Real shame."

"No," Brother Deckert said. "He didn't talk much. And yes, it's a real shame."

"We better go," the other man said.

Brother Deckert went back to his desk and sat looking at his notes. The place and date of birth. The names of his parents. Military service. Masonic Lodge. Survived by. He would read the scriptures that he always read at funerals. Resurrection. Salvation. Reunited in Heaven. He privately thought it a wonder that such important things could be of so little comfort to a wife who's lost her husband. A son who's lost his father. Nevertheless, he would deliver his sermon as expected. He would extol the Christian virtues of John Loucas, though he'd known little of the man's heart. He would emphasize the glory of salvation and take the opportunity to encourage everyone to attend to their relationship to God. But Brother Deckert, aspiring to be honest with himself, sometimes found the words to be thin in his mouth. The bereaved would nod and thank him for his words of comfort, and perhaps the words would truly help. Church members would congratulate him on conducting a fine service, and he hoped that the service would be truly fine. He would do his best, but privately he was dissatisfied with what he was able to give.

Before the appointed hour, several deacons arrived at the church to make ready for the service. They sought out Brother Deckert who gave them the printed order of service that the funeral home men had brought. They spent a few moments looking it over. The ones who would usher chose their sides of the aisle. The two who would serve as greeters took their station at the front doors.

Soon the first cars began to arrive. People emerged in their somber Sunday best, oilfield men awkward in their shined shoes, wearing their Sunday suits on a weekday. Women heavy on their Sunday heels. They entered the building with a decorum that the occasion warranted. The church organist had begun playing something slow in a minor key.

By the time Pete and Lavena arrived in the funeral home Cadillac, the sanctuary was mostly filled. The two of them were ushered into Brother Deckert's study to wait for the service to begin. When the time had come, Brother Deckert led them in a short prayer. Then the three of them walked into the sanctuary together. Pete and Lavena went to their reserved places at the front, a few feet from the coffin.

Brother Deckert stepped up onto the podium and took his seat near the lectern. The low whisperings and murmured conversation ceased. A soprano and an alto from the church choir stepped forward and sang:

> When peace, like a river, attendeth my way,
> When sorrows like sea billows roll;
> Whatever my lot,
> Thou hast taught me to say,
> It is well, it is well with my soul.
>
> And Lord haste the day when the faith shall be sight,
> The clouds be rolled back as a scroll,

The trump shall resound
and the Lord shall descend,
Even so, it is well with my soul.

When they were done, Brother Deckert nodded his thanks to them and stood silently at the lectern until they were seated. Someone in the crowd coughed and cleared their throat.

"We come to the Lord's house for many reasons," he began. "Our reason for being here today is the saddest of them all." A few *amens* sounded in the room. "A man, a husband and a father, has been called to Heaven before his time, or so it seems to us." Brother Deckert went through the sermon he'd written, acknowledging the pain of loss and offering the comfort of anticipated reunion in the afterlife.

When he was done speaking, the ushers, beginning with the back rows, directed attendees forward to view the body. A few, as they passed by, laid a hand on Pete's shoulder or spoke softly to Lavena, and passed forward to have their last look at John Loucas in his coffin. Working from back to front, the whole assembly passed by the casket and paid their respects, had their moment with the deceased, and went out the front of the building to wait.

Pete and Lavena were at last alone in the sanctuary save for Brother Deckert and the funeral director who hovered in the back. They stood and approached the open casket. Lavena wept quietly. Pete trembled, his jaw clenched. After a few moments the two of them stepped back, and the funeral director came forward and closed the casket lid and latched it. The pallbearers appeared from the wings, ready to carry the coffin to the hearse. Pete and Lavena were escorted again to the limousine.

Pete sat with his mother in the newest, cleanest, most expensive car he'd ever been in. He watched, through the unfamiliar tinted glass, as the pallbearers brought the casket out the front door and down the steps to the hearse. Except for two, they were men he knew. Deacons who could be counted on. One was Tommy Thompson, who often went fishing with his dad at Caddo Lake. Or deer hunting. Another man whom Pete knew was Orney Yandell, who always called his dad when he needed his car fixed. He was the only one of the six who showed any emotion. Orney's eyes were wet and red. He wore the worst-looking shoes. Pete watched them all as they turned at the bottom of the steps and went to the open doors of the hearse. When the casket was in and the doors closed, the driver started the motor and crept forward. The limousine driver did the same and followed.

Pete watched the familiar landmarks of Sabine Gap pass by. The pipe yard with its stacks and rows of drilling pipe, wet weeds growing between them. The pumping wells in otherwise vacant lots. The barber shop with its spiraling red and white sign. Everything looked as it always had. Traffic on the street pulled to the curb out of respect for the dead and let them pass, windshield wipers waving at the light drizzle.

Pete tried to make sense of the last three numbing days since his father's death. He was convinced that this was part of God's grand plan, but how it was all supposed to work baffled him. He resolved that, if God wanted him to live through this experience, then there must be a lesson in it for him. It was incumbent upon him, as a devout Christian, to absorb it, and so he would. He thought himself man enough for that. But, at the moment, none of this was *well with his soul.*

In a few minutes they reached the entry gate to the cemetery and passed beneath the wrought-iron angels of the arch. At the gravesite a smaller crowd than before assembled under an awning. Two young men with white towels quickly wiped moisture from all the folding chairs. Again, Pete and Lavena were seated at the front. Again, Brother Deckert, in his most solemn and resonant voice, presided with readings from the Bible and ended with a prayer.

Amen.

The people began to mill about, conversing in low tones, ambling in the direction of their cars. The funeral director came to usher Pete and Lavena back to the limousine, and Lavena moved to follow him. Pete did not. He stood facing the casket, still on the blocks ready to be lowered as soon as everyone was gone.

"It's time to go, Pete," Brother Deckert said.

"He's not buried yet," Pete said.

Brother Deckert hesitated, then said, "They'll do that as soon as we're gone. It's time for us to go."

Pete took a step as if to follow Brother Deckert, but his legs stopped and would not move. "I ... I can't leave him here not buried yet."

Lavena shot Pete a look that said, *What do you think you're doing!*

Pete looked back at her and gave a helpless shrug. "I can't," he said.

The funeral director joined in with Pete and Brother Deckert. "It would be best not to be here when they fill the grave," he said. "It's something that loved ones need not experience."

Pete's face took on a pleading expression. "No. Y'all go wait in the car. I'll come when they're done. I ... I just ... Y'all just go on."

Brother Deckert said, "Listen, Pete, ..." but Pete interrupted, sobbing.

"I hate this, Brother Deckert. I don't know what God

wants out of this, but I hate it." He sobbed again, but went on. "And I have to see it through. I need to find out what God wants from me." He was breathing rapidly now, and shallow. "I can't find out if I don't go through the whole thing. I have to stay here."

The casket, still above ground, sat gathering small droplets. "Besides," he said, "How can I let my daddy be lowered into the ground without nobody here with him?"

"Pete, you don't want to do this," Lavena interjected.

"Yes I do, Mother." It was just like her to tell him what he wanted.

"But I can not," she said. "I've filled enough graves for a lifetime."

"Then you go with Brother Deckert," Pete said with as much gentleness as he could muster. "I'll come on later. You can all go on. Go home if you want to. I can run home from here."

"Not in those shoes," she said.

They were all frozen for a moment, disturbed and confused by this impasse.

Brother Deckert tried to mediate. "Now listen, Pete. There are some things …"

"I'll stay with him," the funeral director interrupted. "Maybe it's best to let the young man do it his way. He's brave. If it's what he's moved to do, he might always regret not doing it. Let's let him do it his way. I'll drive him home if you don't want to wait."

Pete was grateful for this unexpected ally. He looked into the man's face as if for the first time. A face he might never see again after this day.

"Alright. If that's what you really want, Pete," Brother Deckert said.

Lavena, bewildered, looked to Brother Deckert who said, "Okay. Okay. Pete, I'll drive your mother home."

When Lavena was in the car and the door was shut, the funeral director gave a signal to two workmen who had been waiting some distance away. They came and pulled the tarp off of the mounded dirt and took their places around the grave.

On signal the pallbearers lifted the coffin and two funeral home men pulled out the blocks. A fat man in faded overalls gave Pete a sidelong glance, but otherwise they all did their best to be invisible as they lowered the coffin into the hole. It rattled into the concrete burial vault and bumped bottom. The two men pulled out the straps, while other workers started gathering the folding chairs.

Pete heard a machine running and looked to see a backhoe lumbering up from the east end of the cemetery, a portly man sitting in the front-end bucket. It was driven by a skinny toothless man who drove up to the grave and got down, leaving the motor running. He hooked one end of a chain onto the lid of the vault, fastened the other end to the bucket of the backhoe and went back to the driver's seat. With the vault lid suspended above the grave, the fat man steadied its swinging and guided it into the hole. He climbed down to unhook the chain from the vault lid and, with help, climbed out.

"Are you ready to go now?" the funeral director asked.

"No Sir," Pete said, grateful to have this competent man beside him. "Not yet."

"Alright." He nodded to the skinny man, who hesitated, and so the funeral director nodded again. "I'm here with you," he said to Pete.

"Yes, Sir."

The motor revved and the bucket began pushing red clay into the hole. The clay resounded loudly against the concrete vault. Again and again the dirt rolled ahead of the machine until the sound became more muffled. In a few minutes the hole was full and the earth mounded over it. The operator looked at Pete standing there. He shook his head slightly and continued. He used the bucket to press the dirt down, then piled more dirt and packed that down until the force of it lifted the front of his machine. When he was done, he backed away from the grave and lowered the bucket for the fat man to climb into it. They lurched away toward the cemetery's machine shed, the fat man's feet swinging in the air.

Pete and the funeral director stood watching them go. The other workmen were gathering the chairs, carpets, tent and poles and carrying them to the truck.

"Are you ready?" the funeral director asked.

"Ready for what?"

"Ready to go now?"

Pete took several steps toward the raw dirt and regarded it for a moment. When he looked up again, he said, "I guess I'm ready."

A few minutes later the two grave diggers sat in the shelter of the machine shed, passing a pewter flask between them.

"That was damn strange, if you ask me," the skinny one said.

"What was strange?"

"Why, that kid. Him just standin' there watchin' us fill up the hole. Who was he, anyhow?"

"Well, I'm not sure, but I think we just buried his daddy."

"Damn. He's a looney one, if you ask me."

"He ain't no loonier than any of them that puts a casket in a concrete vault. That's what's downright crazy."

The skinny one sipped from the flask and wiped his mouth on the knee of his overalls. "What's crazy about a vault? Everbody that can afford one gits a vault. It preserves things longer."

"They just ain't thinkin', that's what's wrong. Think about this," the fat one said. "The Second Coming could happen any minute, everbody knows that, right? So just suppose we was havin' the Resurrection, and your casket was in one of them concrete things. You might not could get out."

"Shit fire, of course you could git out. Don't you think that the Lord Almighty could git you out. Why, the Angels rolled the stone off Jesus's tomb, didn't they? Pretty as you please."

"Yeah, but that was Jesus," he said. "The angels come there just for Him. And besides, all they had to do was roll it. At the Second Coming, though, everbody's gonna have their hands full. There might not be enough angels. You might git missed. Me? I ain't takin' no chances. No Sir. Not where Heaven and Hell is concerned." He took his turn at the flask. "That there is a serious matter."

"Well, damnation. Maybe they ought to just freeze-dry you and hang you up in the garage. That way you'd be ready." He took the flask back and drew a long swallow. "You just ain't got enough faith. But I guess Presbyterians is like that sometime."

"What?"

"You are a Presbyterian ain't you?"

"My daddy was, but I'm a Baptist. I changed when I married Shirley."

"Well there you are. You just go whichever way the wind blows. You ain't got no faith at all."

"You just hold on now. You got no right to judge me. What are you, some kind of Holy Roller? You think you know everthang!"

"All I know is, *Straight is The Gate and Narrow is The Way, and few there be who find it.* That there is scripture. I seen it for myself one time."

"You're just bein' sacrilegious. Give me back that flask! You done had enough."

Pete accepted a ride home from the funeral director, and Brother Deckert was still there when they arrived, but he left soon after. Lavena said that she hadn't slept well and was going to lie down for awhile.

"I'm going out in the woods before it gets dark," Pete said. But he didn't go to the woods. He changed into rough clothes and went out the door wearing his hunting jacket, but he got no farther than his dad's work car. He got in on the passenger side and sat looking out at the bare trunks and brown leaves of the woods. The only green was the holly at the edge of the clearing. The red berries and the damp leaves were reflected points of light.

"What do we do now?" he said aloud, whether to his dad or to God he couldn't have said.

Chapter 4
Lawman's Lament

Rake Connor hated it when his wife became difficult. "Belinda," he said. "It's time we brought that kid back here and knocked some sense into him." He sat with his elbows on the kitchen table, his fists at his forehead, talking toward his lap.

Belinda stopped pacing the kitchen and leaned against the refrigerator. "I don't know, Rake. He's never done anything like this before. Maybe he just needs time to settle down. For now we bail him out, read him the riot act and give him a chance to do better. Let's wait until the spring semester is over and see what his grades look like. You know he's a good kid. And smart. Maybe we know somebody down in Austin who can keep an eye on him. Let's not overreact."

She walked over to him and stood behind his chair and put her hands on his shoulders. "We just need to impress on him the seriousness of his situation. Make him understand that he owes you for bailing him out. Point out the danger of messing with drugs. You're certainly qualified to do that. Remind him that things like this can follow him even after he graduates, as far as getting a good job is concerned."

Rake shrugged her off. "Do you honestly think it's just a matter of saying the right thing to him, and then everything will be okay? He's got a record now. And I have to stand for reelection next year, remember that? Whoever runs against me is going to make hay of this, you can bet on it."

Belinda stepped back and folded her arms. "This is not the time for that, Rake! How can you be thinking about elections in the middle of this? Is that all you think of? Please just stop being sheriff long enough to be a father."

Rake slid his chair back and turned toward his wife. "Come on, Belinda. It's not like that."

"If it's not like that, let me see you turn off that goddamned radio! It sits there squawking at us even now, and you jump to it like it was God Almighty speaking from the clouds. It's like we have the whole county with us everywhere we go. I would like just once to …"

"I was a deputy before we married," he interrupted. "You knew that …"

"Stop it. Stop it. Just stop it!" Belinda walked to the sink and put both hands on its rim, leaning over it as if she might be sick.

Rake stood and went to her. He started to touch her, but thought better of it. "I just don't know what the world's coming to. I don't know what possesses kids to be hippies and disrespect the flag and burn draft cards and all that shit. I don't know why all the coloreds are having riots and *sit-ins*, whatever that is. The world is going crazy. Why can't everybody just do what they're supposed to? I don't know what Rake Jr. was doing at that demonstration. He's gotten in with the wrong crowd. It's high time for us to yank him right back out of it."

"Maybe he was just in the wrong place at the wrong time. Maybe he had nothing to do with …"

"BELINDA! He hit a fucking cop with the sign he was carrying. In most situations that could have gotten him killed. At the station they found marijuana in his pocket. He's not innocent. And it's a known fact that The University of Texas is filthy with that sort of scum. It was a mistake to send him there. We should have sent him to Stephen F. Austin, like I said in the first place. We might just do that yet."

The two of them were silent for a few moments, breathing deeply and trying to get their bearings. They made eye contact. Rake tentatively put an arm around Belinda's waist. "I'm going down there and get him. Three hours there and three back, plus whatever red tape I have to deal with. I'll leave first thing tomorrow. I'll have him here by suppertime. He'll be at SFA come next fall."

"No, Rake. He's not in kindergarten where we can just move him from one school to another. He's nearly grown. If you don't include him in the decision, it won't work. Maybe we can help him decide the right thing, but at his age, we can't make him do anything. This is going to be a process that we're not entirely in control of."

"I'm not sure of much, Belinda, but I'm sure of this: He needs to be showed who's boss when we're footing the bill. He'll go to SFA or he'll join the Army, or he'll stay in jail. I'll see to that."

"The ARMY! You've got to be kidding."

"I am NOT kidding. I served my country in Europe. I went in a kid and came out a man. It's exactly what all these war-protesting hippies need. Some discipline. And R.J.'s going to get a taste of it, and real soon."

The next morning, Monday, Rake skipped breakfast in order to be at his office for shift change. He notified his staff that he'd be gone for the day and put his senior deputy in charge, the one who was most likely to run against him come next election. Or the one after that.

By the time Rake got on the road, he was hungry, and he knew of a good place just outside of town to fix that. It was nine-forty-five when he pulled in to the Streamliner. He ordered chicken fried steak and hash browns. He looked around for the cute blonde waitress and was disappointed that she was not there. Instead the cook, the one that was obviously a queer, was there waiting tables on double duty. Rake wondered if he'd ever get the chance to arrest that faggot. For dodging the draft or sodomy or God knows what kind of pervertedness. At least Rake Jr. was no queer. He counted his blessings: "One!" he said aloud.

He ate his food, drank his coffee, paid the bill and left without leaving a tip.

Rake always found it relaxing to be on the road. It gave him time to think. The spring sun was warm. He passed through pine forests dense with undergrowth, sweet gums, hickory and a half-dozen kinds of oak in pale-green leaf. The cleared fields were turgid with new grass. He passed through small towns one by one, some with sagging mansions built before the civil war. The little business districts of hardware and feed stores, banks. Churches for whites and blacks. Rake thought of all the recent civil unrest. Race riots in Detroit. Students demonstrating against the Army of their own country. Burning draft cards. He was proud of his service in WWII, and had no sympathy for the freeloaders who shirked their duty. The country needed a real leader. Maybe Nixon would try again. Maybe Rake Jr. would come to his senses.

His road met up with the newly-built I-35. Rake marveled that there could be so much concrete on earth. On the outskirts of Austin he began to feel vaguely like an outsider. There were too many lanes in the roads and too many cars driving too close together. The people in the cars were all strangers to him, and likely strangers to each other. It got worse when he reached the campus of the University of Texas. He himself had gone to school in the small town of Nacogdoches where students had morals. Here in Austin girls wore halter tops and no bras. Their long straight hair hung down to their flower-decorated bell-bottoms. From behind, the boys looked like the girls with their long hair and flamboyant shirts. That is, until you saw the beards. Every cigarette looked to him like a joint, and was, maybe. All of it, Rake knew, was approved of by the pointy-headed intellectuals in the classrooms.

On campus he found the registrar's office and made it clear that Rake Connor Jr. was, as of that day, no longer a student at The University of Texas. In front of R.J.'s dorm he approached two capable-looking ROTC'ers and paid them too much money to help him move R.J.'s things from the dorm to the station wagon.

He went to the campus police department, introduced himself and asked about his son. They directed him to the downtown jail. Because of the drug citation, they told him, his son was being held there rather than on campus. Rake found the building long before he found a place to park. When R.J. was finally brought out to meet him, Rake informed him that he was coming home, or he was going back inside to await trial. With that understood, Rake paid the bail. They walked out of the building with Rake leading and R.J. following four feet behind.

The station wagon had gotten hot in the sun, so they drove with the windows down until they reached the I-35 on-ramp, where they put the windows up to hold the air conditioning. At Round Rock they left the interstate for US 79 and from then on had the reddening sun behind them. They did not speak until Buffalo where they bought barbecue wrapped in brown paper at a roadside joint. After that it was dark.

It was near midnight when Belinda saw the lights of the station wagon pull into the driveway. She'd thawed a steak soup and made cornbread and iced tea to put on the table on short notice. She relit the burner under the stew as soon as she saw them. Though the circumstances were unfortunate, she hadn't seen her son for more than six weeks, and she was glad she would see him tonight. She peered through the window again and saw the headlights go out and the dome light come on as the passenger door opened. She smoothed her hair with her hands, and then smoothed her apron. She heard one car door close and then the other, and footsteps approached the back door. She was about to open it for them when Rake Jr. burst in. Belinda opened her arms to hug and greet him, but he walked past her without speaking and went straight up the stairs and into his room and shut the door.

Belinda could have wept right then, but she composed herself. She ached to put her arms around her son, but she knew how to wait. When her husband came into the light of the back porch she said, "That bad, huh?"

"He'll come around. I'll see to that," he said. He stepped into the kitchen and hung his hat on the wall behind the door. "But it might take some time," he said.

Belinda sighed. "Well. I've got some supper ready. I bet you're both hungry."

"I could eat. It smells good in here."

Belinda went to the stove and brought out the cornbread, still warm in the cast iron skillet. The table was already set for three. "You want iced tea or coffee?"

"Tea if you've got it made."

"It's made."

She filled three glasses with ice and poured the tea. "You want to go up and tell R.J. that supper's ready?"

"I suspect it might go better if you do it," he said.

She raised an eyebrow and went up. She tapped on Rake Jr.'s door. "R.J.?" She listened and heard nothing. "Supper's ready, Honey. Come on down. And just so you know, we don't have to talk about any of this tonight. We can just have supper together and the hard stuff will still be here tomorrow. I expect we could all use a break from it for now."

She waited for a response, but got none. After a few uneasy moments she added, "I'll be glad to see you. In spite of everything I'm glad to see you, even if it's just for a little bit." She drew a deep breath and exhaled it, and went back down to the kitchen.

"What'd he say?" Rake asked her.

"He didn't say anything. It was like he wasn't even there."

"Well."

"Let's just leave him alone for awhile. It's worth understanding that this must be pretty hard on him too. We need to keep that in mind."

Rake leaned back in his chair and heaved a breath at the ceiling. "Leave it to you to take his side. He could benefit from a little more discipline and a little less *understanding* in my estimation."

"Listen to you. For God's sake, Rake, everything isn't about *sides*." Belinda had been about to sit down, but she now felt more like standing. "We're a family, and we're all on the same side. A little empathy would be in order."

"All I mean is, Belinda, I see things every day that empathy ain't going to help. This is one of those things."

Belinda stepped back from the table and went to the stove and stood facing it. "This is not one of those things," she said calmly. "This is our son we're talking about. We don't need a sheriff right now. It's not good when you bring your work into the house with you. Not in any sense of the word."

"I'm just saying, we let him go to Austin, against my better judgment ..."

"All right, all right. Maybe we gave him more freedom

than he was ready for. Let's just not get into blame. You yourself said that ..."

Rake slapped a hand on the table and nearly shouted, "I just mean that if we'd sent him to Stephen F. Austin like I wanted us to, he'd of been right there in Nacogdoches where it would have been easier to keep an eye on him." Rake calmed his voice to say, "There's just not so many communist influences in Nacogdoches."

"Who has said the first thing about communists?"

"You know what I mean. All those un-American protesters and hippies and draft-dodgers. It's a well-known fact that communists are behind all that."

In exasperation Belinda went on. "I don't know the first thing about un-American whatevers, and neither do you. It might enlighten us both to see what R.J. has to say for himself."

"Damn straight!" Rake pushed his chair back and stood. "Let's get him down here right now, and we'll hear his side of it, if that's what you want. He can come down here and face us instead of being such a coward hiding in his room like a damn fourteen-year-old."

Belinda stepped in front of him. "You are not going up there right now. We don't need confrontation. We need to calm down. All of us."

"You are not telling me where I can go inside my own house."

"Stop, Rake. We're all too wound up."

"Get out of my way!" he said. He pushed past Belinda and went up the stairs two steps at a time.

"R.J.! Come outta there right now. We're gonna get a few things understood."

Belinda stood at the bottom of the stairs, weeping into her hands.

Rake tried the doorknob and found it locked. "R.J., I'm countin' to three and coming in, door lock or not." He took a breath. "One!"

"Rake, stop. Please," Belinda blurted.

"Two."

Belinda sunk to her knees on the bottom tread of the stairs. "Three!"

Breaking a hollow-core door is an easy thing for a large man with previous experience at it. Rake found some gratification to be doing something he was good at. The door collapsed, and Rake strode into the room. He looked around, bewildered.

"He ain't here!" he shouted.

Belinda took her hands from her face. "What?" she said weakly.

Rake opened the closet. He looked under the bed. He went out into the other rooms of the second floor. "He did come up here, didn't he?"

Belinda made no effort to reply.

"Rake Junior!" he shouted. "He ain't up here!"

He felt a small breeze before he saw that the window was open. He stuck his head out and searched the darkness. The light behind him shone on the bent aluminum gutter under the window. He brought his head back into the room and walked slowly back to the stairs. He looked down at Belinda and said, "He's gone off. I can see he went out the window. He's gone off somewheres."

Back in the kitchen the two of them tried to think what to do. Belinda said, "I'll call Rory's mother. He might have gone over there. I can't think where else he would be likely to go, unless it's to Sheila's house. But they split up a long time ago."

"Alright," Rake said. "I'll put in a call to my office, and to the city police too. They'll keep an eye out for him. Maybe as a favor to me, there won't be any paperwork."

"Paperwork? Jesus!" Belinda said.

The next few days were excruciating for both Belinda and Rake. It gradually dawned on them that R.J. must have completely left town. No one they knew had seen him. They inquired with the registrar at U.T. and with the campus police. Running out of ideas, and having their hope worn thin, they began to direct their anxiety toward each other. A week went by. And then a month. Two months. Belinda's grief and worry settled into her heart and into the house like an unfriendly dog.

Rake took refuge in his work. Few dared to mention his son in front of him, but word got around. And around. With each circuit the story got seedier. The sheriff's son was a hippie. A drug user. A card-carrying communist.

Nobody said those things openly to Rake, but he noticed how people averted their eyes when they met him. How low-spoken conversations stopped when he came into the room. Sometimes he could override the mood with his big-voiced charm. Other times he just felt run down. He began to sort people into groups of either friends or enemies. The enemies were out to get him. This next election was going to be his hardest yet.

Chapter 5
Wicked Little Sister

Larry Henderson's second tour of duty in Viet Nam didn't go as well as the first. The fighting and casualties had gotten heavier every year since 1961. Larry got there in '63, and by the end of '64 he could see that the worst was yet to come. He'd reupped after his first tour, but he would not do it again. He'd be stateside in seven weeks if he could stay alive that long.

Back when he was in high school he'd been given a choice by a judge in Oklahoma: join the Marines or face prosecution and almost certainly go to jail. With his record, the sentence wasn't likely to be short. It was one of the ways small towns got rid of habitual juvenile delinquents: make them somebody else's problem.

The Marines suited Larry. It gave him a purpose and a place to belong. When he arrived in Viet Nam, he was one of 16,000 U.S. soldiers there. He did not become one of the 216 killed that year. By the end of 1965 there would be 200,000 American troops there, and 1,928 of them would die. Larry didn't need to know those figures to know that things were not going well. By the New Year of '65 he carried shrapnel in his body. His ears rang constantly. He'd forgotten what real sleep felt like, and he vacillated between a superstitious premonition of his own death and a swell of hope that he'd be shipped to California in a few weeks not in a body bag. He'd go home. Except he had no home. Not really.

Larry was at that seven-week point when a black man, a splib—Pfc. Roscoe Waters of Sabine Gap, Texas—got his legs blown off by a claymore that wasn't supposed to be there. Larry was the first to reach him and fumble for a femoral artery, yelling for a corpsman.

"My sister. You tell her. My sister," the kid said over and over.

"You'll tell her yourself," but he knew it wasn't true. "Tell her what?"

"You got ..." And that was all.

Black and white soldiers generally stayed away from each other if they could, but in that moment, Larry recognized the absurdity of war. Of race. Of life. It was an epiphany of sorts. A kind of emptying out. A forgetting of all definitions and an opening up to the humanity of everyone he'd ever seen scared, hurt, dying, laughing. Larry began to laugh. In the swoon of that moment Larry became someone he didn't know very well. He was amazed to find himself laughing, and that very fact struck him as hilarious. What did it matter that he laughed?

Two months later in the early spring of 1965, Larry landed state-side. He carried a silver dollar and the stolen tags of Pfc. Rosco Waters.

His first act after carrying his duffel off of government property was to get a car. He paid cash for a two-toned green '58 Chevy that looked like trouble in every sense of the word. Some previous owner had replaced the stock 283 engine with a newer 409 cubic inch V-8. It had high-lift cams, two four-barrel carbs and four in the floor. It was lowered in back and had loud dual exhaust that only smoked a little. The flashy spinner hubcaps and the red rolled-and-pleated leather interior gave it a kinky Christmas aspect, and so Larry dubbed it Jingle Belle, partly in mockery, and partly in honor of Hell's Belle, the CH-46 helicopter that had carried him so many miles over jungle. He drove the Belle to a 7-Eleven where he loaded a styrofoam cooler with Pabst Blue Ribbon, which he slid into the passenger seat. He wedged two cartons of Camels behind it.

At a phone booth he looked up gun shops. The addresses were meaningless to him, so he dialed for directions. When he hit on one nearby, he went there and came out with a Browning .45 caliber semiautomatic pistol, standard issue in Viet Nam to officers and machine gun crew, and 100 rounds of ammunition. In his car he loaded the pistol and laid it on the front seat where he could see it. As a weapon it was a pale shadow of the mounted M60 machine gun he was accustomed to, but it was a familiar sidearm. He'd lived for so long with weaponry that being without it left him feeling exposed and incomplete.

He stopped at a self-serve gas station to top off the tank and check the oil and tire pressure. The tires looked bad, so when he spotted a wrecking yard, at the outskirts of town, he pulled in to see what they had. Fifteen dollars later he had two matched, reasonably good tires in back, and the best of the original four on the front.

He drove across California without sleeping, compulsively imagining the landscape as seen from a helicopter, imagining what desert warfare would look like. Where he would set up a fire base. He drove for many hours, stopping only for gas or food at the truck stops. He followed Route 66 as far as Amarillo, Texas, and then dropped down to Lubbock where he caught Highway 80 East.

A couple of times he tried to rest, but he needed the sound

of his motor running. The best he could do was to pull in at a truck stop or a drive-in hamburger joint for fried potatoes. God, how he had missed fried potatoes.

Eventually he neared Grand Saline, Texas. He began seeing pine trees with underbrush. This land was less flat than before, and the highway rolled in low hills. Not long after that he reached Longview. It was in a wet county, so he stopped there, bought more beer and rented a room in a cheap motel off High Street. He stayed there two nights drifting in and out of an unrestful sleep. On the third morning he showered, shaved and put on fresh clothes. He bought breakfast at a place on Main. According to his map and his reckoning, Sabine Gap was less than two hours south on winding county roads.

He checked out of the motel and headed south on a narrow farm to market road, forested on both sides. Here and there dirt tracks penetrated the woods, just wide enough for a car to run into an ambush. He passed cobbled-together shacks squatting in clearings, tin-roofed and unpainted. Old cars and washing machines, rusting tractors and who-knows-what sprawled in the weeds. Little churches looking not much better. Once he thought he glimpsed a river off to his left.

Barbed wire fences separated grazing cattle from the spinning counterweights of pumping wells. He was in oil country. There were clearings in the woods where lay truckloads of drilling pipe, drilling equipment, and big duea-axle trucks with HALLIBURTON in red letters on the doors. Groups of oil tanks stood behind earthen dikes, some flanked by steel cylinders standing thirty feet tall with blue flames visible at the base. What they did, he had no idea.

At about one-thirty p.m. he guided the Belle onto Main St. in Sabine Gap and stopped at a Gulf station for gas. The attendant was cleaning his windshield when Larry asked, "I'm looking for a family by the name of Waters that lives here. A

Negro family. You happen to know them?"

"Naw, I don't reckon." He scratched his head. "You could try the phone book."

"You have one I could look at?"

"They's one in the office yonder. He'p yourself."

Larry went inside and found the greasy phone book, the thinnest he'd ever seen. There were three "Waters" listings, two of them on the same street. He took the book out to the attendant. "You have any idea if these are Negro families? The one I'm looking for had a son in the Marines."

The attendant brought the page close to his face and dragged a finger down the page. "Well, them two is on a street that ain't in Tin Cup. Must be the other'n."

"Tin cup?"

"Yeah. You know. Nigger town." He pointed down the street. "Go that-a-way and turn left at First Baptist. Another two or three blocks and you're there. There ain't no street signs, so you'll prob'ly have to ask around."

Larry paid for the gas and left. He turned at the Baptist church and two blocks later crossed the railroad and then spied another church. Emanuel Church of Jesus.

There were black women gathered under a spreading walnut tree, setting out wooden folding chairs and putting large bowls of food on a picnic table. When Larry pulled onto the clay parking lot, they stopped what they were doing. Two of them hurried into the side door while the rest watched him park his bizarre vehicle. He got out and walked toward them.

"I'm looking for Miss Beulah Waters," he said to the one who stood in front of them all. "I've got an address, but I don't see any numbers on the houses anywhere."

"If you lookin' fo' somebody fo' house work she ain't do that no more," the woman said.

"I was in the Marines with Private Rosco. I, uh, wanted to

pay a visit to his family."

The women glanced at one another. One of them said, "Go knock on that blue house down yonder. Where that chinaberry's at on the other side."

"Chinaberry?" Larry didn't know the meaning of the word.

"Chinaberry tree. That pale green one with the white flowers."

"That tree down there?"

"Yessuh. That chinaberry tree. Blue house."

Larry thanked them and backed Jingle Belle out of the lot and lumbered slowly to a pale green tree laden with white blossoms in grape-like clusters. He parked behind a used-up red pickup. A neglected bed of daffodils and hyacinths framed the stone walk to the front door. With a *here goes* that he might have muttered before battle, Larry approached and knocked on the front door.

Larry stood, preparing himself to meet the sister of Private Roscoe Waters. He'd rehearsed what he would say. *Hello. I'm Larry Henderson, and I served with your brother in Viet Nam. I was with him at the end. He said "tell my sister."*

There was a loud thump from inside the house, and surprisingly heavy footsteps approached the door. Larry was starting to imagine a heavy woman. When the door rattled open, Larry found himself looking at the bare chest of a sturdy black man. He adjusted his gaze upward to see the face of a man who'd obviously been sleeping.

"How can I he'p you, Suh?"

"I'm trying to find Miss Beulah Waters, the sister of Roscoe Waters. I was in 'Nam with him."

"You lookin' for Beulah?"

"He just said 'my sister.' I think her name is Beulah."

"Who said?"

"Private Waters." Larry hesitated. "Look. Uh, I was the

last one he talked to. When he got hit, I mean. Is this the right house? I can just go on if it's not."

A half-hour later Larry was seated on a weary stuffed armchair in what was still Minnie Waters' living room, though she'd been dead for several years. Prentice Waters sat on the couch where he'd been sleeping. The guarded beginning of their conversation relaxed a little, but only a little. Prentice remained cautious, as he would with any white man whom he didn't know well. In spite of Larry's apparent good intentions, Prentice was uneasy with Larry's disjointed train of thought. Just the sight of the car he drove would make anybody think twice about him.

"So, you was with Rosco when he died?"

"Yeah. We were just starting out on patrol. He tripped one of our own Claymores. Whoever left it there is prob'ly dead or wishes he was."

There was a silence of several seconds. Larry's right leg pumped like a sewing machine against the floor. He shook a cigarette out of the pack he kept in his shirt and for the second time offered one to Prentice.

"Thank you, but I quit using them," Prentice said for the second time. Larry lit his own and blew smoke toward the ceiling.

"So, I guess I should find his sister then. I want to give her his tags and this silver dollar and some other stuff he had in his gear. He didn't have much else of a personal nature."

Prentice held out his hand for the coin. "I give him this the day he left. "Beulah, that's her name," he said, turning the coin in his hand. He thought for a moment, deciding how much to reveal. "Beulah, she don't talk to me much. Who can say? It might mean something to her if you was to tell her yourself that you knew Roscoe. She took it right hard when he come home in that bag." He handed back the dollar.

"When should I come back?"

"Beulah, she gone be hard to find. She in lots of trouble since her mama passed, and then Roscoe. I don't know for sure where she's at. Sometime she come to me axin' for money." He glanced at the ceiling and back again. "I usually have a little bit, but I suspect she use it for booze. I reckon she into heroin. Now and then I run into somebody say they seen her with some man or other. They's a place out at the county line. A honky-tonk colored folks goes. The Bottle and Glass. I'm told she spendin' a lot of her time out there. I hates to think about it. It's a rough joint."

He paused and then continued, ruminating more to himself than talking to Larry. "First Minnie and then Roscoe, it broke something in her. Lawd. I reckon they ain't no end to the way peoples gets messed up. Roscoe was nearest she had to a daddy till I come along, but by then it was mostly too late."

There was silence again. Larry lit another smoke and, once again, offered one to Prentice. Prentice accepted it out of graciousness.

Larry drove back to the Longview motel and paid for three more nights. On the next Saturday afternoon he ate at Lube's Cafeteria and headed back to Sabine Gap. He stopped at the same Gulf station to ask about the Bottle and Glass.

A different man, very skinny in grimy blue coveralls, came out to the pumps. "Fill her up?" he asked.

"Ethyl," Larry said. "And where can you buy beer around here?"

"Sorry, Cat. You done left Gregg County. This one here is dry. The direction you're headed there won't be no more beer 'till you get to Pecan County. Six or seven miles to the county line."

"Is that where the Bottle and Glass is at?"

"The Bottle and Glass!" the attendant said. "You don't want to be goin' there." He looked at Larry with interest or suspicion. "That there's a nigger joint. You want to go some-place like Jo-Jo's if you want to drink or dance. Maybe git a little tail. Not no nigger joint. White man's likely to git his guts yanked out before he gits to the door."

Larry's first impulse was to grab the man by the throat, he couldn't have said why. But he kept his cool. "That's my busi-ness, not yours," he said. "Just tell me where it's at. It'd save me having to find out somehow else."

The man's eyes widened. "Alright. I'll tell you. Ain't no skin off my nose." He pointed down the highway. "Just keep goin' the way you're headed. When you get to the Tyler high-way, turn left. That'll take you to the county line. Out there, there's a whole bunch of liquor stores and honky-tonks. The Bottle and Glass has a little sign at the road. On the right-hand side. It sets back from the road down a gravel drive. No big neon or anything like that. Bouncers will meet you in the parking lot. There's serious shit in that joint, I'm just tellin' you."

"You sound pretty familiar with it," Larry said.

The man blinked a couple of times. "I'm just trying to he'p you out, Mister. I don't mean no offense."

Larry paid for the gas and left.

The sky was nearing twilight by the time he turned off the highway onto the gravel drive of the Bottle and Glass. There were already twenty or so cars in the lot. Cars of every descrip-tion from decrepit Fords and Plymouths with gaudy spinner hubcaps and added-on chrome mirrors, to one bright yellow Lincoln Continental as long as a house with the spare tire in a chrome kit on the back. Raucous music thundered in the low building.

Larry turned the Belle around to face the way he'd come in, and parked. He slid the 45 under the driver's seat, out of sight but reachable. He got out and closed the door and started to lock it, but on consideration decided to leave it unlocked, the easier to get back in. He surveyed the parking lot the way he might have observed a jungle landing site for a helicopter. Three black men stood near the building facing him. They were wide-stanced, watching him closely. The largest one took a long drag from a cigarette and tossed it aside.

As Larry approached, they separated slightly. "Good evening," he said.

They didn't answer.

"Uh, listen. I'm trying to find somebody."

"Uh-huh," the wiry one said. "We just bet you is."

"Look, I'm not trying to make any trouble for anybody. I just got back from 'Nam. A guy in my unit was Roscoe Waters. Had a sister named Beulah. I came to pay his family a visit. Beulah's brother, Prentice, told me I might find her here. Or find somebody who can tell me where she's at."

"He told you that, huh?" The three looked at each other knowingly.

Larry surmised that these two knew more than they wanted to tell. "I'll just go inside and ask around."

"You ain't from around here." The skinny one stepped into Larry's path and tilted his head. "Cause if you was from around here, you'd know that you ain't goin' in there to ask around." The three of them snorted and chuckled derisively. "This ain't your turf, Bro."

"I won't take long. I'll just ask around and then go."

"Let me 'splain somethin' to you. You go in and they might be objections. The kind of objections that gets the po-lice interested. It's my job to make sure the po-lice don't take no notice of thangs here. So if there's gonna be any trouble, let's us have it right here right now so we can drag your sorry carcass somewheres else."

Larry stepped back and drew a breath. "Let me show you something. I'm just going to take it out of my pocket real slow. He reached into the pocket of his jeans and pulled out Rosco's tags. "If she's here, and if you could show her this, I'd find a twenty in my wallet just as a way to say thanks."

The wiry one took it from his hand and read the name. Then showed it to the other two. They looked at each other and seemed to agree on something. The wiry one said, "My two bros here, they don't wont to be left out. You wouldn't want to leave them with bad feelings, would you?"

Larry dug in his wallet and came up with two twenties, a ten and two fives.

"I see if she's here." He took the bills, distributed them and turned toward the building.

Larry leaned against a pickup to wait. He lit a cigarette and offered one to the big man. "We got our own smokes," he said.

In a few minutes a skinny young woman came out of the honkey-tonk, staggering a little. A man came out behind her and shouted, "Get back in here right now!" When she kept walking he grabbed at her arm, but she shook him off. The wiry bouncer said something to the man, and he swore and went back inside. Beulah kept walking, jerking her head around as if looking for somebody. The big bouncer hollered, "Over here, Trixie."

"In there I'm Trixie. When I come out that door, you can use the name my mama give me."

"Ooo-hooo!" the big one said. "She got a mouth on her, ain't she?"

"Yeah, she famous for that mouth. Ain't you, Sugar? That mouth is yo' bread and butter."

"Fuck you," she said, and walked past him.

When she was close enough, Larry was about to speak to her, but she spoke first. "You was with Roscoe?" she said, bleary but wide-eyed. As if her brother might walk out alive from this strange white man's memory.

Chapter 6
Home for Sale

Near Longview, Texas, on the tarmac at Gregg County Airport, Gwynn Callahan stood on her toes to accept a good-bye kiss from her father. "Gwynn, you know I really do appreciate this."

"I know, Dad. I know you do."

"If you have any trouble, any at all, you can call me collect. At home or at the office, just call."

"Yes, Dad. You told me. I've got it. And I've got all the paperwork right here. The power-of-attorney documents, access to bank accounts and the safe deposit box, the mortgage papers, everything right here." She patted the thin briefcase her dad had just recently bought for her. "I'll call you anyway, just to check in and let you know how things are going. Don't worry."

"I'm not worried, Sweetheart. I just really need to keep a strong presence here at the office. At least until I've been here for a while. It just wouldn't look good if ..."

"I know Dad. I can handle it. It's just one thing at a time."

A few feet away the co-pilot shoved her suitcase into the tail hatch of the single engine De Havilland and shouted, "Last call for boarding: Tyler, Dallas. All aboard."

Gwynn picked up her carry-on, climbed the portable stair

and ducked through the doorway. Inside the plane she nodded to the six or seven other passengers, stowed her bag under the seat and sat at a window on the terminal side. She fastened and cinched her belt and looked out into the slanting sunlight to perhaps give her father a final wave, but he was nowhere to be seen. The co-pilot entered the plane, closed and fastened the door and hunched his way up the aisle to the cockpit. She sighed, relaxed into her seat and turned her attention to the activity in the cockpit where the pilots were checking instruments and speaking their arcane language into microphones.

The engine rattled to life, rough and coughing at first. The whole plane vibrated until the motor revved into smoothness. The pilots talked and flipped switches. Then the brakes released and the craft lumbered away from the terminal. Squares of sunlight coming through the west windows made a sudden march leftward through the cabin as the plane pivoted toward the runway, and then the squares vanished altogether. The motor set up a roar and gravity shifted, pressing passengers into their seatbacks. The plane rocked briefly and leapt into the air, climbed sharply and banked westward in a slow arc.

Gwynn pulled her blonde hair back from her face and looked down from her window. She was surprised to spot her father's car so easily. The long Lincoln was like no other in sight. A crawling black mark on the highway as if a felt tip were censoring something written there. The plane leveled and the car was swept from view, leaving her alone with the vast flat expanse of pine woods into the hazy distance.

They landed in Tyler and took on two more passengers. In another forty minutes they were at Love Field in Dallas.

In the terminal Gwynn found a bank of pay phones and made two calls as promised. The first to her father to let him know that she'd made it okay to her connection. He didn't answer so she left the message with his secretary who sounded very young. The second call was to her Grandma Rose in Oakland to let her know that her flight was on time.

She found her gate, took a seat and waited. At last she boarded the Boeing 707, settled in and waited some more while other passengers jostled, overhead bins slammed. Other seat belts clicked. The plane began to roll, bouncing too much for her to focus on her magazine, so she looked out the window at the dizzying machinery of aviation. It seemed to her that they must have taxied half way to California by the time they were positioned at the runway and cleared for takeoff.

She felt so lonely. A year ago she was in her junior year at Berkeley. She had a boyfriend, a smart sweet guy. They were getting to know each other. Would they still be together, she wondered, if she hadn't had to leave? She didn't ask him to wait for her, and he didn't offer.

The jet engines roared, tarmac lights sailed past her window, faster and faster still. It was beyond odd to be headed toward Berkeley. It was where she wanted to be. Yes, this interruption was only temporary. A year at most. But soon she'd be making the return trip to Texas, hurled again away from her dreams and possibilities. Her tears took her by surprise, and the harder the engines pulled, the more they flowed.

"Is this your first time, Honey?" A woman maybe ten years older than herself reached from across the aisle. "Don't worry. This is normal. We're doing just fine," she said, and patted Gwynn's hand.

The plane lifted. The lights of Dallas and Ft. Worth receded. Gwynn settled back for the long night while half the nation slid invisibly beneath her in the dark.

At the San Francisco airport, Gwynn claimed her luggage and caught a cab to her grandmother's house in Tilden Park near the golf course. The sun was not up yet. The cab driver carried her luggage to the front door, and Gwynn paid and tipped him in cash. As he drove away she stood for a moment breathing the salt air that drifted from the Bay.

Grandma Rose answered the doorbell in her bathrobe and slippers. "Come in, Dear One. I'm so glad to see you." She held the door while Gwynn brought in her suitcase. "What do you want first, breakfast, a nap or a shower?"

"A hug."

It was almost noon when Gwynn emerged from her bedroom and shuffled toward the smell of coffee. She could hear the faint clatter of dishes and the splash of water coming from the kitchen.

"Good morning, Brown Eyes," Grandma Rose said when Gwynn came in.

"Good morning, Brown Eyes." Gwynn repeated the endearment they'd shared since she was very small. She pulled back a chair and fell into it. "I was going to wash my face, but I couldn't find it. Can I have some coffee?"

"This is a little stale, but you're welcome to it. The percolator is set up for a new pot."

"I'll have a half-cup of stale, please, while I wait for the fresh."

An hour later the two of them sat in Rose's kitchen, still sipping coffee and nibbling croissants. Their breakfast plates were stacked next to the sink.

"Gwynn, Gwynn. Dear. You have every right to be disappointed. Even angry." Rose touched Gwynn's hand across the table. "I understand that much very well. But there's no help for it. You cannot change what you can't change. Believe me, if that were possible, I would have changed many things by now."

Gwynn gave a weak smile. "I know, Grandma."

"Your mother's death has been an ordeal and a loss for all of us. Nothing will ever be the same, and we must all accept it as best we can."

Gwynn suddenly felt ashamed for having taken her grandmother so much for granted. For being so self-centered. Of course Grandma Rose was grieving just like everyone else. She had lost a daughter whom she adored. "Grandma, how are you doing with all this?"

"All this?" She swallowed and turned toward the window. "I play bridge. I go to church. I put on music. I visit friends. I do have some lovely friends. But it's hard. Not just losing Ruth, but losing you as well with this relocation to Texas. I go on just as I must, and you must."

They were both silent for a long moment.

"Let me tell you something about your father," Rose said. She sipped her coffee and waited for her granddaughter's full attention. "I didn't approve of him at first, you know. He was from Texas, and he seemed rather incurious about the larger world. Oh sure, it was clear that he would do well professionally. But I wanted my daughter to have someone who, how shall I say it? Someone with more warmth. I thought he was a little self-centered, and I suppose he is. But over time, I did see him become a devoted husband and father. His lack of demonstrativeness does not mean that he doesn't love, and grieve, deeply. His way of handling loss is not your way, nor mine. But it is his. And it may take him quite some time to get through it."

She paused. "I guess that's true of all of us."

"But Gran, Texas? I'm a year and a half from graduating, Grandma. Couldn't he have … I don't know, waited until then before he took a job in Texas? I assumed that, when the end came for Mom, I'd at least be able to pick up college where I left off. I thought Dad would have wanted that. Instead, he drags me to Texas."

"It's just for now. After all, you may have needed a little time yourself. Were you really ready to get back to college right after she died? This might be easier if you can acknowledge that in some ways it suits your purposes too. Allow yourself this time to regroup. When you're ready to restart your studies, then do so, whether your father likes it or not. I think it's good that you're helping him out right now. I don't think you'll ever regret doing that. But your life is still your own."

Gwynn stood and walked to the front window and drew the curtain aside. "It's almost like he wants me to pick up where Mom left off. He's my father, and I want to be helpful to him. I know he hurts too. But this seems so one-way. What will I do in Longview, Texas?"

"One thing that I know about you is that you are intelligent. You're young and beautiful and smart, and you have people who love you, and that includes your dad. This is a big detour, but not the end of the road. Go to Texas. You don't really have any other good option right now. Be as helpful as you can, but also explore. Find things that interest you and pursue them. Stand your ground if the occasion calls for it. For now you have a lot to do. Your dad obviously trusts you to put you in charge of so much. I trust you too, and I know you can handle it. This process will be an education in itself. Take it on bravely and learn what you can from it."

Gwynn wiped her eyes. "I feel so alone with it all."

"Yes. That makes it hard."

"Gran, can I stay here? I mean just until I get the house sold and all that?"

"Well certainly. I thought that was obvious. Having you here is the one thing that I like about all of this."

"Can I use your car?"

"Only if you pick up a few things for me while you're out."

Two days later Gwynn went alone to the house she'd grown up in. Michael, her old high school flame, had offered to come and help. It was generous of him, but he'd started using a lot of drugs and was not at all dependable. The rest of her friends were away at college. In a different world. Besides, being alone suited her.

Stephen. Yes, she would love to have Stephen. What better time to have an older brother present? But there wasn't much he could do from Germany. Being alone in the house had one advantage. She had the freedom to be stunned. To scream. Cry. Slam doors without anyone's judgment or comfort. She was here to claim what she wanted to keep for herself and guess at what Stephen would want to keep, as well as her father. The rest would go into the estate sale, and then she would choose an agent and put the house on the market.

But first, this.

Eventually she must go into her parents' bedroom, she knew that. She would need to clean out her mother's make-up shelves. Flush the medications. There would be hair brushes, tooth brushes and ointments in wrinkled tubes and half-used jars. She would face these things, but not now. She would start in the kitchen.

Early afternoon light filtered through the backyard Monterey cypress onto the windowsill above the sink. The house had been shut for several weeks and had taken on an unfamiliar smell. The curtains were dusty. The empty refrigerator sighed like a ghost.

She turned on the lights and the sudden hard definition of the space was an assault. She turned them off again.

On the kitchen table was the bundle of un-made cardboard boxes, the packing tape and felt-tipped marker that she had bought before she and her dad went to Texas. She cut the binding strap, opened up the first box, taped the bottom and began to fill it with things to keep. For some odd reason, the first thing she thought of was the can opener. Not the electric one—her dad had already taken that one anyway—but the old one she remembered from early childhood. The one that had been used so many times to open cat food for Sugar and Spoon. She still remembered the first time she was big enough to open a can by herself. She'd opened all six cans of cat food, and the dogs ate ecstatically until they got sick on the floor. Gwynn opened drawers until she found that opener, and she put it into the box.

She gathered momentum and became more practical as if she were at a garage sale. It occurred to her then that she did not want to live in her father's new house in Longview. She would go to Texas, but she would have her own place, and she began choosing things to keep that she would need. A drop-leaf table and two chairs. A stainless pot and a skillet and old utensils from before the newer set that her dad already sent with the movers. There were towels that she would not sell but would keep for herself.

Later she braved her own room. The whole upstairs had been recarpeted and painted just a year earlier. Her mother had gotten sick right after the renovation, and these new colors were, in Gwynn's mind, the color of dying. She never wanted to see them again.

The little-girl quality of her old room took her aback. Her cheerleader's uniform and the spelling bee trophy. A picture of Elvis and a dried prom corsage. So much had changed since she lived here. She began to recognize herself as an adult with an adult's concerns. Childhood was over.

In Stephen's room she sorted through his civilian clothes, wondering what he would want to keep and whether they would even still fit.

She became paralyzed in her parents' room and went back into the hallway and broke into tears. She sat on the stairs with her face in her hands and wept aloud and blew snot into her hands and angrily wiped it onto the carpet. "I don't have to do this!" she shouted to no one. "I can't do it all."

Chapter 7
A Chat with the Man Upstairs

Lavena woke up early on her first Monday as a widow. She couldn't remember her dream, but she knew it had been a better world than the one she was waking up to. But wake up she must.

The funeral was done. Out of town relatives gone home. The refrigerator was amok with hot-dish leftovers, and the flowers were starting to wilt. Sympathy cards, having no real place to be, cluttered the coffee table and window sills. Laundry was starting to pile up. It being Monday, she would not need to open her beauty shop. At least that could wait another day. She lay in bed for a while but finally got up at around six-thirty and dressed.

By a quarter to seven the percolator was sputtering through the one thing it knew how to do, and Lavena was standing at the kitchen window looking for some kind of meaning out there in the woods. The bluejays testified to a religion she was not privy to.

She turned and went to wake Pete for school. Back in the warmth of the kitchen she poured two cups of coffee, and then, realizing her mistake, she poured her husband's into the sink and watched it waste into the drain. Bacon started to sizzle in the skillet that she didn't remember putting there. She tended to it, and thus began her necessary attention to the day.

After breakfast Pete walked out to the highway and caught the school bus for his first day back. The faces on the bus were the same ones he'd been seeing for years. He looked at them and wondered how many of them knew about his dad. He looked at a few faces closely, but couldn't tell by looking whether they knew. He tried to discern if anyone looked at all sympathetic toward him. No one appeared to pay him any attention at all. He felt that they should know. He wanted them to know. He wanted to shout out loud, *My dad was killed last week. We buried him on Friday!* He wanted to force everyone to know it. He wanted someone to publicly say, *I know your daddy was killed, and I'm sorry. I know you're sad, and I'm sorry.* He looked at the floor, letting the miles go by until the bus stopped in front of the school. If they do know, he concluded, they don't want to talk about it.

Walking into the building he was mildly surprised that he even knew his way around. But it wasn't the school building that had changed. It was him. On the way to his locker he met a pair of girls who were in his English class. He looked at their faces and wanted them to come to him. He wanted them to touch him and say they were sorry about his dad. They would never have talked to him before, but now … now it was different, wasn't it? Now he was singled out. But they didn't come to him. He saw one of them whisper to the other, and they lowered their eyes and walked by.

Since sixth grade Pete had felt that he'd been singled out in an extraordinary way. That was when God called him to preach. Since then he'd known exactly what his life was about. Since that long ago Sunday when he announced to the whole congregation that he was headed for the ministry, he'd been treated like an honorary preacher. By the time he was in high school he was accustomed to giving devotional messages to Sunday School groups, children and adults alike. He tended to view everything he did as preparation for, or temptation away from, God's calling. His father's death brought a new dimension to all that. Now, in addition to being the God-annointed one, he was also the kid whose father had been taken by God.

Today his classmates were giving him sideways glances, or maybe he imagined that they were. He couldn't tell. His friend Hank made strained attempts to be funny in order to cheer him up, but most others simply avoided eye contact. He couldn't find a way to pick up where he'd left off because he couldn't figure out what to pick up and didn't remember where he'd left off. But mostly he wondered why God had done this to him.

He went through that first day attending each class in turn. His teachers gave him make-up assignments. Most of them made a point to privately offer condolences. He was grateful that none of them said anything about his father's death being the will of God. He was already weary of that one.

By Tuesday it seemed to Pete that everyone had simply forgotten about *that accident* they'd all been talking about the week before. During P.E. class Pete threw himself into half-court basketball with a fury that allowed him to momentarily forget. Afterward in the shower he felt vaguely guilty for having forgotten. He supposed that his father was in Heaven by now. It was hard to be sure. He mentally sorted through the scriptures he knew by heart, trying to pin down whether a person went straight to Heaven or Hell the moment they died, or whether they were just dead until the third day. Like Jesus was. Or were they just dead until Resurrection Day? He found the scriptures to be somewhat muddled on the subject. Also, against his own will, he wondered about the current state of decomposition of his father's body. He quickly put those thoughts out of his mind, or tried to. He found that, although he could control what he did, he could not control what he thought.

That afternoon Pete didn't take the school bus home. The skies had cleared and the air still had a February feel to it. He carried all his books to his locker and left them there. He took out his track shoes and put them on. He tied his regular shoes together by the laces and slung them around his neck and headed out. He ran at a trot across the parking lot and off toward town. He used side streets to get to the railroad track where he could run on the crushed rock. The shoes he carried flopped against his chest but he ignored that. Almost relished it.

When he neared the cemetery he left the railroad tracks and headed for the wrought iron, angel-guarded gate and went through. He leapt onto the grass and threaded his way through the tombstones and finally stopped, panting, at the fresh dirt of his father's grave. There was no headstone yet, but there was no mistaking the place. He stood there breathing deeply, wiping sweat off his face with the sleeve of his T-shirt.

The area was littered with small clods of dirt and red clay. There were already tiny sprouts of St. Augustine grass.

Pete looked up at the sky as if to say something to God. The cumulus clouds might have hidden a throne, but of course God didn't have a throne in the clouds. Heaven was somewhere else out there, maybe in another dimension. "Thy will be done," he said aloud. "Thy kingdom come." His words didn't seem to carry.

Breathing more slowly now, Pete sat on the ground, cross-legged. He looked down at the bare dirt and visualized the casket a few feet below. He wondered if morticians had reset the broken bones. "God, help me understand how this is Your will." He glanced around as if someone might hear him. "If it's Your will, then there must be some benefit to it. Am I being tested? Is this a punishment? God, You know I want to be a preacher and spread Your gospel. Is that what this is about?"

He was sincere, yet his words seemed to fall to the ground. He sat silently until his butt started to feel cold. He stood and rubbed his back pockets. "Can You give me some kind of sign, Lord?"

He waited and searched the sky. There was no sign that he could recognize.

"Maybe later," he said to God. "Amen."

He regarded the wounded ground. The newly exposed clay that had lain hidden from the sun since earth's creation now lay naked and drying in the daylight air. Scattered around in the flattened grass. It struck him as obscene. "It seems to me that I deserve some kind of answer," he said, and he began the four-mile run home.

His breath began its familiar jogging rhythm. Inhale four strides, exhale three strides. He could do it forever. As he breathed deeper and settled into his pace he became aware of a dark place in his lungs. A dark thing there that didn't flow in and out with his breath, but lurked in the deep recesses of his chest. He could feel it sloshing like a pint of crude oil, poisonous and explosive.

He thought about God up there looking down, and he began to have dangerous blasphemous thoughts. "What did I do to You to make You so…? So mean." He glanced at the sky. "Come on! Say something!"

God didn't say anything.

Chapter 8
Can't Make Me

Mr. Horton, the geometry teacher, was a man who observed the world from more than one kind of angle. He noticed the intersections among people as well as lines on a page. He observed congruences or the lack thereof. On this particular morning he watched his students file into the classroom, taking notice of who looked like they had slept well or hadn't. Who looked hungry or well fed, whose clothes were clean and whether they fit. Pete Loucas particularly caught his attention. His socks didn't match.

"Pete Loucas," he said.

"Yes, Sir?"

"Dress code. Your shirt tail is out."

"Oh. Okay, sorry."

"And what's with the socks?

"What?"

"I beg your pardon?"

"I mean, Sir?"

"Your socks, Pete. They don't match."

"Is that in the dress code too?"

Mr. Horton half smiled. "No. I guess not. Not that I know of."

Pete faced the wall and tucked in his shirt before taking

his seat.

The bell rang and Mr. Horton went to the lectern. "Good morning, y'all. Time to cut the talk and get your homework out on your desk. We'll have a little question-and-answer before you hand it in." He allowed just a moment for them to settle.

"We all know, at this point, how to bisect an angle. Some of you expressed an interest in trisecting one. Did anyone in this class become the first person in human history to succeed?"

There was a little groaning and some laughter.

"I thought not. How many of you tried it?"

A few hands went up half-heartedly.

"Don't feel bad. I tried it too when I was your age. Feel free to keep trying." He stepped away from the lectern. "So. The business of last night's assignment: are there any questions?" He scanned the room.

"Loucas. I don't see anything on your desk. Get your assignment out. Why isn't it on your desk?"

"I don't have it."

"Did you leave it at home?"

"No, Sir. I didn't do it."

There was a brief low murmur in the room. Mr. Horton blinked a few times and ran a hand through his hair. "You didn't do it," he repeated.

"No, Sir."

He took a deep breath. "Why didn't you do it? What happened?"

"It just didn't seem important."

There were whispers in the room.

"Are you trying to be cute, Pete? Because, if you are, I am not amused," Mr. Horton said.

"I trisected a 135-degree angle, but that was the only one.

Well, actually I had to do it backwards. I made a right angle off a straight line, bisected the 90s and added one of the 45s to the other side. So I guess that doesn't really count."

"That's right. It doesn't count." Mr. Horton raked a hand through his thinning hair. "So the homework. Did you do any of it?"

"No sir."

"That's too bad. You know what the deal is. I explained it on the first day. What it takes to get along in this class. Do you remember what I said?"

Pete looked at the floor, wishing only that this would go ahead and play itself out quickly. "Yes, Sir."

"You turn in your assignments, and you will pass this class. You fail to turn in your homework, and you will get the paddle. We've been over this before, haven't we."

"Yes, sir."

"I don't get it, Pete. This is getting to be a habit, and I'm tired of taking up class time with this stuff."

"Yes, sir." Truth was, Pete didn't get it either. He felt that he should feel some remorse about not doing the homework, but he didn't. He just wanted to get on with this thing.

"Well don't just sit there. Get up here and put your hands on my desk." He opened a drawer and pulled out a board that was twenty-three inches long and five inches wide. It was wrapped in white tape at one end and shaped into a handle at the other.

"Do you remember how many times this makes? My recollection is that this is the third."

"Yes, sir."

That's three licks, then."

Nearly everyone in the classroom flinched, blinked or drew breath when Mr. Horton delivered the first firm pop to Pete's butt. Most were looking at the floor when the second one came. At the third pop, nearly everyone, including Pete, was holding their breath.

"Now let's get back to geometry," Mr. Horton said. "Get some paper onto your desk and pay attention to the lesson. And if you don't think it's important, pretend that you do."

That afternoon Mr. Webb, the track coach, stood erect at the starting line of the running track, a clipboard in his hand and a stopwatch on a chain in his pocket. Six boys were poised at the starting blocks waiting for his signal. He'd already noticed that one of the runners looked lethargic.

He signaled the start with a slap to the clipboard. Five boys leapt into a sprint, and one lagged behind in an uninspired lope. Immediately he whistled them all to a stop and waved them back.

"Loucas!" he shouted. "Get the lead out of your butt." He walked a circle around the whole group. "Everybody, get back to your blocks. Loucas, we're going to start over, and I want to see you in front when you round that first turn, do you hear me? I'm not running a day care here, and this ain't nap time."

Everyone but Pete laughed. Somebody hummed "Rock-a-Bye Baby," but Pete ignored it.

"Are you ready, Loucas?"

"Uh huh," Pete mumbled.

"I beg your pardon?" the coach said. "At first it sounded to me like you said 'uh huh' but I must have surely been mistaken. Would you repeat?" He waited. "Right now would do."

There was no laughter among the boys now. They glanced at each other and looked furtively at Pete and down at the cinders of the track.

"Yes, Sir," Pete said.

"Louder. I can't hear you."

"YES, SIR!"

Mr. Webb accepted this without expression. "Robinson, trade lanes with Mr. Loucas here. I want him where he can hear the start signal better."

"ON YOUR MARK!"

Once again the boys tensed. Mr. Webb thought that Pete looked a little better now. In fact, when he gave the signal, Pete took off with a fury. By the first turn Pete was a stride-and-a-half in the lead. But there was a flailing aspect to his gait, and it looked like he was meandering in his lane. *This is not good,* the coach thought to himself. *What the hell?*

Sure enough, when the runners made their first pass around the track, Pete, though still in the lead, was white around the lips and had red and white splotches in his face. *Oxygen debt,* the coach thought to himself. *Now he's overdoing it.* Midway through the second lap Pete lagged to second. Then third. By the time they passed again Pete was number five and six was gaining on him. As the runners finished the mile, the coach shook his head. Five runners had crossed the finish line and were catching their breath when Pete slumped across, barely able to stand up. The rest of the workout didn't go much better, at least for Pete.

After practice, when the team was in the showers, Mr. Webb stood at the windowed door of his office, looking out into the locker room, considering the upcoming regional meet. Pete had work to do, but he had been showing promise, and had been a hard worker. Until today. He hoped that today was just a fluke, but inwardly knew that it wasn't.

Pete was dressed and headed toward the door with his gym bag when Mr. Webb called out to him. "Loucas! You got a minute?"

Pete stopped at the exit and turned toward Coach Webb. "I know I didn't do very good, Coach." he said. "Didn't do what you been teaching me. I just… I don't know if I want to run track anymore."

Mr. Webb was taken aback by such a drastic leap from a short conversation. He didn't reply at first, but just watched Pete standing there with one hand on the door handle, gym bag in the other. Oddly stooped posture.

"Well, Pete," he said slowly. "Look. Why don't you come in here for a minute and set down. Let's see if we cain't get some clarity on what you want to do. I'd hate to see you quit."

Pete hesitated at the door as if neither option was agreeable to him, to go into the office or to go out the door.

"I've got some Ne-Hi orange in here in the fridge. You want one?"

"Alright."

The coach went to the little refrigerator, took out two bottles of pop, levered them open and handed one to Pete. "You WAS pretty sorry out there today. I know you can do better than that." He took a sip of his own drink. "As for quitting track, you'll have to make up your own mind. But one thing's for sure. Whatever you do, do it like a man. Stay in track and compete like a man, or stand up straight and look me in the eye and tell me that you want to quit. But own it. One way or the other. I just don't think you want to go through life with today being your last workout. Quitting when you're down sets a bad direction for yourself."

Pete sat, considering.

"Young folks sometimes don't think in the long term. Don't realize that the things they do, or don't do, can stay with you for a long time. Become part of who you are. I'd hate to see you have regrets."

Pete still didn't respond, so Coach Webb went on.

"I know life has been hard on you lately. But you've got to fight back. Not fight hard so much as fight smart. Now I admit, I have my own reasons for wanting you to stay. I think you've got a shot at regional in the 440. You're not bad at relay. You'd make me look good if you stay with it and work hard."

Pete sat looking at a spot on the coach's desk.

"Everybody has their ups and downs, you know. Don't let this rough patch; and yeah, I know it's a serious rough time. Just don't let it completely throw you. I didn't know your daddy, but I know he was a paratrooper in the war. He could obviously be tough. I doubt he'd want to see you give up. But you're the one who's got to decide." He stopped talking and waited.

Pete shifted in his chair, lifted the Ne-Hi a few inches off the desk and put it back down without drinking any. He started to speak, but only cleared his throat and looked toward the door. "Okay," he finally said. "I'll see you tomorrow."

"Alright. See you tomorrow."

Pete picked up his bag and went out, leaving the orange soda in a puddle of condensate.

Chapter 9
Both Shoes On

Lavena pulled into the church parking lot and backed into a space so that she could get out of her car on the leeward side. The wind was whipping low clouds across the sky like stampeding cattle. Brother Deckert's car wasn't there; nevertheless, she got out and went inside. A few steps down the dark hallway she knocked on his door. There was no answer.

She was actually relieved. It had taken her days to work up the courage to even come here, and now that she was actually at the church on a Tuesday afternoon, she felt conspicuous and trivial. She was afraid she was wasting Brother Deckert's time. He was probably busy with more important things, doing the Lord's work. Bringing lost souls to Jesus.

Heading back out she pushed the side door open, ducking against the wind, and scrambled back to her car. She sat looking out toward the street imagining that every car that passed by slowed to look at her. "People are gonna be talking about me," she said aloud. "Maybe already are."

Guess who I saw sitting outside the preacher's office the other day.

Oh, I know! She's really gotten pitiful. Such a shame.

She should just leave and come some other time. Or make an appointment. Did people actually make appointments to talk to their preacher? Maybe she should forget the whole thing. She'd been through this, over and over in her mind, and no, she could not forget the whole thing.

She picked up her Bible from the seat beside her, unsure why she'd brought it, except that she always brought her Bible to church. She thumbed through it but couldn't focus. A nearby oil well wheezed and groaned in a regular rhythm, massive and unfazed by the wind.

Hoping for anything that might help her calm down, she opened the glove box and took out a half-empty pack of Camels. They'd been her husband's. Lavena herself had never smoked except maybe one after dinner with him. She pressed the cigarette lighter on the dashboard and waited for it to click. When it did she tapped a cigarette out of the pack and put it to her lips. Then she felt even more conspicuous, and so put the cigarette back into the pack and put it back into the glove box.

She should leave. She fumbled in her purse for the car key, but her hand was shaking so that inserting it into the ignition switch took all of her attention.

"Lavena? Hi, Lavena, I'm surprised to find you here this afternoon."

Lavena looked up to find Brother Deckert standing next to her car. She put the keys back into her purse and looked up again. "I ... I was just ... I just dropped by to see if I could talk to you. But if you're busy I can ..."

"No no, it's quite all right. I've been at the hospital in Longview visiting some folks. You might know that Brother LeRoy is in the hospital. Had his surgery yesterday. He's doing fine. But come on in out of this wind before we get clobbered by a flying garbage can or something."

"Okay," she said vaguely.

Brother Deckert's study was a dark quiet grotto compared to the bluster outside. It had the aroma of tobacco, which she associated with men in general, and with her husband in particular. Her gaze swept the shelves laden with Bible commentaries and theology. She thought that Brother Deckert must be a very wise man.

Brother Deckert went to the chair at his desk and invited Lavena to take the stuffed armchair. The only sound was the muffled rumble of the wind and the faint metronomic whine of the oil well outside.

"How have you been, Lavena?"

Lavena took a deep nervous breath. She crossed her arms and then uncrossed them and put her hands on her knees. "I just." She looked out the window and then back to the minister. "I guess I just want to feel closer to God, and I don't know how."

"Don't we all," he said. He regarded her closely and took a deep breath of his own. He pushed from his mind that she was an attractive woman, not yet forty. He reminded himself not to allow unseemly distraction.

"Lavena, how long have I known you? A long time for sure."

"We started coming here when Pete was three. Fifteen years."

"Lavena, in all that time I've known you to be a good Christian woman. Devout. What do you think it is that keeps you from feeling close to God? Do you pray often?"

"Yes," she whispered.

"If it's not too personal, do you mind telling me what you usually pray about?" He waited for Lavena to answer.

"You don't have to tel …"

"I met John Loucas when I was 18 and he was 21," she blurted. Her words spilled out like pus from a wound. "He was the finest man I ever met. He had a job and a car. He got me out of that cotton farm. My daddy was a sharecropper, did you know that? But John had been places. Waco. Galveston. Even Dallas. We were in love and it was good. We got married in a civil ceremony and rented a house in Limestone County. Then the war came. He went away to training and then to England. After D-Day, I got a telegram: 'Missing in Action,' it said. But I knew God wouldn't let him die. I just knew it. I knew that God made good things come. So I cried for joy when I found out he was a prisoner of war. In Germany. I cried for joy that he was a prisoner, Brother Deckert. Now it seems like a funny thing to be happy about, but I was. I was happy.

"When he got home from the war, he found a house we could rent in Groesbeck out toward Waco. He got a job. I felt like God was being good to us again. When Pete came along, I was full of happiness. I was happy to be gone from that nasty farm with no running water. The wind blowing all the time. I still hate the wind. That old house full of me and my sisters in our flour-sack dresses—that was all in the past.

"We left Limestone County and came to Sabine Gap when John got the job with the drilling company. We saved up and got a house of our own. In another year Pete would be in college. College, Brother Deckert. I didn't even finish high school. Please don't tell anybody that.

"Then one day, just like that. John was gone. What I want to know is, why does God make things so good and then jerk it all away?" Her fists were clenched and her face was red. "We keep sayin' God loves us, but I don't see no love in that. How can I feel close to God?

"And now, in these last few months, Pete has become somebody I don't hardly know sometimes. The Devil is working on him too, I can tell. Maybe you noticed lately he finds excuses to miss church. He goes off into the woods and I don't know what he's doing or when he'll be back."

Brother Deckert held still and let Lavena pour out her sorrow and her fury. He watched her there, miserable and trying to compose herself. He knew scriptures he could go to. He knew a dozen things he could say, but the words felt feeble before they got to his mouth.

She began again, "Forgive me for saying so, Brother Deckert, but my prayers are empty. The Bible is empty. I'm sorry, but your sermons are empty too. At least to me. There's not enough Bible and not enough praying in this world to make this any good." She paused and said, "I guess the Devil has taken my heart."

They sat in silence for a moment. The wind thumped the windows. "I guess I better go," she said and stood up.

"Don't go yet, Lavena. Stay just a little longer." He picked up his Bible and thumbed his way to the Book of Job, and read aloud. He read words of comfort in the face of calamity. But he knew that the context missed the mark. He himself did not believe that God was testing Lavena in order to prove a point to Satan. He hoped that Lavena was comforted, but the abstract nature of the words bothered him.

Lavena glanced at the floor and back up to Brother Deckert's face. "What about Pete? Am I supposed to just let him ruin his life and set a path to Hell? I'd rather see him dead than have him go the way he's been heading."

"Lavena, don't …"

"You don't know what it's been like with him. He sasses me. He blasphemes the Lord. He skips school and doesn't do his lessons. Did you notice he wasn't in church Sunday? Well, he wasn't. One of my beauty shop customers told me she saw him at the Blue Top Grocery Store. Everybody knows they sell dirty magazines there. Teenagers get beer there. I don't know. I just don't know."

There was a short silence. Brother Deckert started to speak, but Lavena interrupted him. "You know what's going to happen. He may not even graduate this spring. Unless he changes his ways, there's no use him starting college. He'd fail. And if that happens, his draft is going to be 1-A instead of II-S and he'll go off to war. Edna's Roger already went to Viet Nam and now he's buried in the Sabine Gap Cemetery. I went to the funeral over at the Bible Baptist. Who did I see there? Madge Maples and her son Autry. He came back from Viet Nam, but he's in a wheelchair with a catheter bag hanging on the side."

Lavena put her face into her hands and allowed herself to weep briefly. She recovered herself and looked directly into the pastor's eyes. "Brother Deckert, I've already lost all I can stand to lose," she said, and turned her eyes toward the window. The oil well outside pumped on in its indifference.

Brother Deckert shifted in his chair and picked up his Bible and found Jeremiah 29:11. He read aloud to her, *For I know the thoughts that I have toward you, saith the Lord, thoughts of peace, and not of evil, to give you an expected end.* Then I John 4:18. *There is no fear in love, but perfect love casts out fear: because fear hath torment. He that feareth is not made perfect in love.* He closed the book. "Read Job," he said. "And when you're done, go right on into Psalms. I think you'll find comfort there while you get through this hard time. That's just what this is: a hard time. Remember that. You've had hard times before. You'll get through this one too.

"And Lavena, I will talk to Pete. He and I get along. He's a good kid going through his own hard time. I'll talk to him."

When Lavena left the church, she was glad that Brother Deckert would talk to Pete. Maybe he needed a man to set him straight. But she was as perplexed as ever. Fear and love and torment rolled in her mind like oil and water and blood. She drove back to her beauty shop and unlocked it. She went in. Presently a car parked in front and her next customer emerged, holding her hair against the wind. *Why does she even bother to do that*, Lavena thought. She put on her sturdy face and waited.

Lavena came home from work late. It was dark, but she could see in the headlights that Pete had not raked the leaves away from the house like she'd told him. She, herself, had put in a long day at the shop. She'd stopped at Brookshires on the way home where she spent as much as she dared on eggs, bread and two pork chops. In a few days she hoped to finally get John Loucas's last paycheck, which would mostly go to the mortgage. She also hoped for an insurance payment sometime soon, but the drilling company and the insurance company were passing her back and forth. The tombstone was ordered but not paid for. The VA required mounds of paperwork to qualify for the veterans' burial benefit. At least as a single parent of a minor child, she was qualified to receive twelve dollars a month from Social Security. That had started in March. The last one would come two months later when Pete turned eighteen. She was holding things together as best she could and had a lot on her mind. Pete could at least rake the damn leaves.

When Lavena came through the back door carrying her purse and the bag of groceries, she found the house dark. She flipped on a light with her elbow.

"Pete?" she hollered. She set the groceries on the kitchen table and dropped her purse onto a chair. "Pete, where are you?"

"In here!" he shouted back.

Lavena went into the hall and peered into Pete's room. In the dim light from the kitchen she could see him sitting at the back window. She turned on the light. Pete had his BB gun resting across the window sill.

"What are you doing?" she asked.

"Nothing," he said. "Shooting birds. Or was until it got dark."

"Why on earth are you sitting here in the dark? For goodness sake, get off your butt and make some iced tea for supper. You can set the table too." She went back to the kitchen and put the pork chops on the counter and the eggs in the refrigerator and slammed the refrigerator door a bit harder than usual.

She heard Pete coming down the hall, and something was odd about the sound of it. When he reached the kitchen door, she looked at him, cocked her head and said, "You've just got one shoe on."

"I can count," he said flatly.

"Are you getting smart with me? Don't you dare! Why are you wearing one shoe?"

Pete looked down at his feet and back up. "I was going to go barefooted, but then I couldn't decide."

The idiocy of the statement frightened her. "DECIDE!" she commanded. "Don't be crazy."

"Okay, but I'm not the crazy one."

Lavena blinked and took a deep breath. "Who IS the crazy one?"

"Whoever's in charge."

Lavena wanted no more of this conversation. She walked out onto the back porch and looked up into the trees, black forms against the last of the dying light. "What is wrong with him!" she said to herself.

She sighed and went back into the kitchen, struck a wooden match to light the stove. She spooned bacon fat from a coffee can into a cast iron skillet and floured the pork chops.

When Pete came back to the kitchen, she stepped out of his way while he got a saucepan, ran two inches of water into it and lit his own burner to make tea.

"The leaves need raking," she said.

"Yeah," Pete said. "I thought maybe I'd let them stay there."

Lavena turned and faced him. "What?"

"Yeah. I mean Yes, Ma'am. We keep raking them up and God keeps making them grow back and fall on the ground again. Maybe God's plan is for them to be there. Maybe it's a sin to keep taking them off for no reason."

"Why, that's the flimsiest excuse for not raking that I've ever heard. It's probably sacrilegious to boot. I'd be careful if I were you."

"No, really, Mother. I've been thinking about it. And I was thinking about not getting haircuts anymore, too. And stop shaving. Jesus had long hair and a beard. You can see that in all the pictures." Pete was seated at the kitchen table tying his shoe.

"Don't be ridiculous. You'd look like a hippie."

"Maybe if Jesus was around right now, people would call Him a hippie. Maybe for all intents and purposes, He was one."

"PETER LOUCAS!" Lavena shouted. "The very idea! I will not have that kind of talk in this house. If your father was here, he'd ..."

She froze. A long silence followed during which the two of them breathed deeply and avoided eye contact.

"Daddy might actually think about it," Pete said and went out the back door and vanished into the dark. He left the saucepan on the flame.

Lavena went to the door and turned on the porch light. "Pete?" she said, but he was gone. "You're going to get the belt," she tried to shout, but it came out weak. He was nearly eighteen. She wondered if she could ever whip him again, but she didn't know what else she could do.

When Pete was clear of the house, he headed for the back side of the garage where his father's work car was parked.

Someone had driven it home the day after the accident, and it hadn't moved since. He aimlessly opened the door and got into the driver's seat. The car smelled dusty with the faint scent of his dad's aftershave. His knee brushed the key fob dangling from the ignition switch. In defiance of everything in his life, he turned the key and pressed the starter button. Nothing. He tried the headlights. Then the horn. Still nothing. He simply sat, both frustrated and relieved.

Lavena was dutifully chewing a mouthful of pork chop when Pete came back into the kitchen.

"Hungry?" she said.

"Yes, Ma'am."

"I don't want any more of that kind of behavior."

"Alright."

"Let's make him proud of us," she said.

"Okay." Whether she meant his dad or Jesus, he didn't know.

Lavena was relieved that Pete seemed to have come around. She had neither the energy nor the heart to control him the way she felt she should. She relaxed a little when he poured tea into her glass and then into his own. He was wearing both shoes. One of them was tied.

Chapter 10
The Hand That's Dealt

Brother Deckert washed his face in the men's room and dried with a paper towel. He'd been in a budget meeting all morning that included two of the church's most prominent and outspoken deacons. They were good men, and they meant well, but they were certainly opinionated. By eleven o'clock they had hammered out a reasonable projection and all but agreed to replace the worn out shape-note Broadmann Hymnals with the more contemporary round-note version. A few of the old timers were unhappy about it and wanted to keep the musical notation they'd learned in their childhood. The change, to their way of thinking, was tantamount to abandoning the King James Version of the Bible. It was finally agreed that they would order the modern version for the congregation, but to include twelve of the shape-note version: one for each of the apostles.

With the meeting over and everybody more or less satisfied, Brother Deckert went to his study followed by the head deacon who plopped himself into the stuffed armchair and crossed his legs in a satisfied manner. Brother Deckert was ready for his bologna sandwich and iced tea. Maybe a quick nap. Hadn't they both had enough of talk and negotiation for one day?

"What's on your mind, Brother Deacon?"

"Aw, nothin' much. That was a mighty fine meet'n wasn't it? Mighty fine."

"It was," Brother Deckert agreed. "We got a lot done. Now I'm glad it's over. Aren't You?"

"Oh, yeah, I reckon. I just need to kill a little time before I get Janelle at work."

"Well, make yourself at home here. I've got some things I need to get to." He gathered his papers and started for the door.

"Oh. In that case I'll mosey on too. I'll see you Sunday."

Brother Deckert pretended some arrangement of his desk while the man left, then he phoned the church secretary and told her the minutes were in his hand, and could he drop them off for her to mimeograph them.

At last he turned the doorknob and opened his office door just as Pete knocked on air where the door had been. They almost collided.

"Pete! What a surprise," he said. "What brings you here this time of day?" He stepped back a little and regarded Pete. "For that matter, why aren't you in school?"

"I skipped," Pete said flatly.

Brother Deckert took a moment to let this sink in. "Why?" was all he could think of to say.

"I've been praying. Or trying to. I just felt like it was more important than school."

"Well, Pete? Don't you think there's enough hours in the day for both?"

"Can we talk? You got time?"

Brother Deckert mentally saw his sandwich and iced tea slide away. There would be no nap. He stepped backward from the door and laid the meeting notes on top of the other papers on his desk.

"Come on in. Take a seat there," he said, indicating a stuffed armchair that was probably still warm from the head deacon's behind. He had a good idea what this might be about, but wisely waited for Pete to do the talking. "What's up?"

Pete took the chair, glanced at Brother Deckert and away again, finally settling his gaze on the floor.

After a moment of silence, Brother Deckert prompted him. "Does this have something to do with your dad?"

Pete's words suddenly rolled out, as flat and sticky as tape. "Everybody says it was God's will. I guess that must be so. But I keep thinking, what was God's purpose? He must have a purpose, and I can come up with two things. Maybe because God called me to preach and I accepted the call, now He's preparing me. Maybe, because I'm gonna be a preacher. I have to go through this. Take this loss so that, when I have a congregation someday, I'll know what it's like when people come to me for comfort. Maybe I'm suffering so I can be better at helping others." He looked up at Brother Deckert. "Did things like that happen to you when you got the call?"

Brother Deckert looked into the face of this miserable boy. "Pete," he said. "To answer your question, no. My mother and father and my sisters are all still alive. I can't say that being called to the ministry has brought me any misfortune. As to whether God is preparing you for the future, I couldn't say. We have some scriptural comfort, and you and I have read those passages together.

"You should know this, though. This pain won't go away. Not ever. You live with it until it just becomes a part of who you are. That's all. You're not the same as you were before your daddy was killed. You won't ever be the same. How that fits into God's plan may not be known until you're an old man. Maybe not until we get to Heaven, and then you can ask God directly."

"I'm asking Him now," Pete said, and he turned his eyes upward and addressed Heaven. "God, why won't You tell me? Is this my training program, or is it punishment for something I did?" His voice was breaking now. "What sin have I done? Is it because … ?"

There was silence except for Pete's shuddering breath.

At length Brother Deckert said, "Pete?"

"Brother Deckert, is it because I touched myself?"

"Pardon?"

"You know. Jacked off?" he said, and burst into tears of shame.

Brother Deckert looked at Pete sobbing into his hands. He was perplexed at the ricochet of the conversation. He had an impulse to put his arms around Pete and hold him, but, out of propriety, he refrained. *So much suffering for all the wrong reasons*, he thought to himself.

"Pete, I assure you that that had nothing to do with your father's death. If that were the reason, there would not be a man alive today."

Pete laughed into his wet hands and took a deep breath. He accepted the tissue that Brother Deckert offered and blew his nose. He calmed himself and leaned back in his chair, looking at the ceiling to avoid looking anywhere else. There were hairline cracks in the plaster. "It says not to in the Bible."

"Yeah," Brother Deckert nodded. "Paul did address the subject. Remember, though, that Paul didn't even consider marriage a good thing. Paul was not God."

Pete considered this, distracted for the moment from his own grief and confusion. The idea that anything in the Bible could be taken in any way other than absolute was new and dangerous.

"But God killed that man, on the spot, when he spilled his seed on the ground. That's in the Bible."

Brother Deckert was still trying to align himself with this turn of the conversation. Nothing at seminary had suggested that counseling the bereaved could lead to a theological discussion of masturbation, but there it was.

"Yes. Onan," he said. "Pete, to truly understand the Bible, it takes a lot of study. We miss a lot when we pick a passage here and there to try to make a point. Most often the passages cited have no relationship to each other and sometimes no bearing on the subject at hand. We have to know the context."

Pete nodded without speaking, so Brother Deckert went on.

"This particular issue doesn't get talked about in sermons. As you can imagine, no preacher wants to stand before the congregation on Sunday morning and seem to be justifying playing with our wee wee."

Pete guffawed but kept his eyes on the ceiling.

"When that scripture was written, Pete, there was a Hebrew law that a man should make babies with his brother's wife if that brother had died without children. It seems that family heritage was much more important than marriage fidelity in those days."

Brother Deckert went to his bookshelf and selected a Biblical concordance. He thumbed pages. "Here it is, in Genesis. Thirty-eight verse eight. Read it when you get the chance. You'll see this in a different light."

He studied Pete for a moment and continued. "Look at it this way. We're taught not to steal. Not to lie. We have the golden rule. We know that we won't always be perfect. We make mistakes now and then. That's why we have Jesus. To forgive us." He paused. "So who are we that we should not forgive ourselves?"

Pete took this in but returned to his original point.

"So why is my daddy dead when there are so many useless, stupid men still alive?" He put his face in his hands and breathed heavily.

"I can only tell you this. Your father's death is not your fault. Nothing you did made it happen. No plan you have for your future caused it. I wish I could give you a better answer, but I'm not God, and I can't know His mind any better than you."

Pete looked at him.

"Does it surprise you to hear me say that? Just because I was called to preach doesn't mean I know any more than anybody else. We have to live with a lot of questions that will not be answered."

After a moment Brother Deckert said, "I'm going to repeat that. We have to live with a lot of questions that will not be answered. Not on this earth. So I'm going to tell you to forget the question of why. Put it out of your mind. It holds nothing good."

"If I can," Pete said.

"But what you must do is endure this. This is the hand you've been dealt. You have to play it and play it straight. That's your only way to thrive in this world."

When Pete left Brother Deckert's study, he felt somewhat less guilty and a great deal more perplexed. Later, when he read the passage in Genesis, he was astonished to think that God would kill Onan like that. Why hadn't God given him a more reasonable punishment and then another chance to do his duty? What God did to Onan was bad for Onan, but worse for the childless woman. And what a curious rule! And when did that rule change? Or had it even changed? Should his dad's brother be making him some half-siblings? He had to stop this line of thought before he went crazy.

Chapter 11
Baited with a Doughnut

Sabine Gap Baptist was Brother Deckert's first congregation, and, though he'd made some missteps, he was getting the hang of church politics. The two most senior deacons, Brother Wally and Brother Broussard, seemed to want authorship of every good idea, and no idea was good unless it was theirs. Leading the monthly deacons' meeting was a challenge for the young minister while these two old war dogs were trying to out-do each other.

He had an idea that he wanted to develop, and it would need to make its way past these two. The issue at hand was Pete Loucas and his faltering faith. Several church members had noticed Pete's change in behavior and commented on it. But it was Pete's mother, Lavena, who was most disturbed and most frequently in his office confused, agitated and seeking advice. He wanted to help in any way he could, but there was only so much a pastor could do. He'd been called by God, but he was not God. He did have an idea though, and he needed the deacons to work with him on it.

In pursuit of this plan, Brother Deckert made it a point to be outside the church and in the parking lot before Brother Broussard, who always arrived early on Sunday morning. He watched for Brother Broussard's Buick, and when he saw it enter the lot, Brother Deckert angled in that direction, pretending to be examining the cracks in the asphalt pavement. He was fifteen feet away when Brother Broussard and his wife emerged from the car.

"Wha-cha doin' Preacher?" Bob Broussard said. "Thinking about planting some onions out here on the asphalt?"

Brother Deckert looked up as if surprised to see him there. "Oh, I was just wondering if we shouldn't do something about these dandelions. They're kind of pushing up the pavement. Maybe we should do something before they rip up the whole parking lot."

"Yeah." Broussard stretched his back and tugged his pants upward with both hands on his belt. "That there can be a problem, them dandelions can." He walked over to Brother Deckert and shook his hand. Both men stood a moment looking down at the dandelions as if they held some deep theological significance.

"Tell you what," Broussard said. "I'll drop by this week with a gas can and dribble a little regular on 'em. That'll fix 'em for a while."

"Oh, well, that's a good idea Bob. Yeah, a good idea," Brother Deckert mused. "Much appreciated." He pulled a pack of Camels out of his shirt pocket and shook one out. "Say, you have a light? I left mine inside."

When his cigarette was lit and he'd taken a long pull, Brother Deckert exhaled and said, "Say, Bob? You and Shirley were pretty close to the Loucases, ain't that right?"

"Yeah, we had 'em over a few times. Played forty-two. No gambling, mind you. Shirley still tries to keep tabs on Lavena, things being the way they are. Why'd you ask?"

Brother Deckert studied the gutters at the eaves of the church. "I've been hearing things about Pete. I hope I'm not speaking out of turn about their personal business, but Pete seems to be taking things pretty hard, his daddy getting killed and all. I just wish there was something we could do to ... you know, keep him active in the church. Inside the Lord's fold, you know what I mean?"

"Yeah, I know. That was such a shame. The Lord works in mysterious ways."

"Well anyway," Brother Deckert said. "I guess I better get inside. He dropped his cigarette to the pavement and ground it with his shoe. "Thanks for taking on the dandelions. Maybe somebody will have some idea for helping Pete Loucas when we get to deacons' meeting Wednesday. I'm going to bring it up then. You gonna be there?"

"Yep. I'll be there."

That evening when the Sunday night preaching service had just ended and the congregation was mingling and exiting into the night, Brother Deckert made it a point to intercept Brother Wally on the front steps.

"It's a fine warm night, isn't it?" he said. "Makes me realize that the spring revival is coming right up."

"That it is," Wally allowed.

"Say, you got a minute? I want to ask you about something. I've been trying to think of ideas to make this revival special," Brother Deckert said. "Not too unusual, you understand, but just different enough to make people pay attention. Most especially the young people. High school kids in particular. We need to do everything we can to draw in the young folks."

"Yeah," Wally said. "You know, we will be having the youth gatherings in the social hall like we always do."

"That's true. We will be doing that. But if you can think of anything else, we might discuss it at deacons' meeting Wednesday. You know, I was talking to a preacher friend of mine when I was down in Beaumont. He told me they tried out an idea last year to give the young folks somebody that they can relate to better. I think they called it a Youth Pastor or something. One of their high school kids. Kind of an honorary thing I guess. I don't think he actually preached. Anyway, let me know if you think of anything. You usually come up with something."

At Wednesday's deacons' meeting all the routine issues passed on the first vote, but there was one item that didn't fare so well. Two of the oldest deacons were adamant that the new central air conditioning should only be used for the Sunday morning services. Sunday night and Wednesday prayer meetings were in the cooler part of the day. "It's fire in the pulpit, not ice on the pew that's going to get sinners to Jesus," one of them hollered. Pretty quickly there was wrangling about what temperature it should be set to. It seemed that negotiations could fall apart when Brother Deckert shouted.

"Gentlemen! This is what we're going to do. I'm going to call roll here. Everybody who has an air conditioner at home is going to answer me with the temperature they keep their own living room. If you don't have air conditioning, then just pass. And you're going to tell the truth here. We're going to average those numbers, and that average is the temperature we're going to set it at."

The men shuffled in their chairs and mumble agreement. The roll was called, and seventy-seven degrees was the result.

After that, tempers cooled. Brother Deckert congratulated Bob Broussard on his success with the dandelions, and then they moved on to finalizing plans for the spring revival. They unanimously agreed to call the evangelist Douglas McPherson, who was gaining some fame in the region, to do the preaching.

When they were ready to adjourn, Brother Deckert brought

up a non-agenda item: his concern for Pete Loucas. "I'm afraid the boy is in a real, adult-sized crisis of faith," he said.

Bob Broussard was quick to join in. "Me and Shirley have been talking about that some. She talks to Lavena from time to time. Pete has been skipping church lately. Skipped school some too. There ought to be something we can do to draw him back into the fold. He needs the Lord's comfort right now more than he realizes." When he saw that he had everyone's attention, he went on. "We've all known Pete since he was a little tyke. Is there anybody here that hasn't heard him lead a prayer or give a devotional in their Sunday School? Satan works hardest on the devout, and Satan is finding him vulnerable in this time of loss. We need to pray for him, and pray for his mother too. It was a dreadful loss, John Loucas getting killed like that. It's a lot to overcome."

That was the opening that Wally needed. He'd been incubating the idea of a youth pastor ever since his conversation with Brother Deckert three days ago.

"Brother Broussard, you're absolutely right," he said. "Now is the time for us to step up. We've just been talking about our spring revival, and it just might be an opportunity to give young Pete a purpose. What if we was to have an official duty for him in the revival? We want to draw in young people. We could have us a Youth Pastor. Make it official. Let him lead the opening prayers and sit up on the podium with the preachers. If he'll do it, that is. When we print the flyers, we could have his picture on it right there next to Rev. McPherson."

"Pete Loucas would be just the one," Broussard replied. "He's always been a good Christian. Devout. I doubt he's ruined his reputation yet. He might could be a good Christian witness."

Everyone in the room looked at Brother Deckert to gauge his reaction. Brother Deckert nodded somberly as if this were a new idea to him. The idea picked up steam. Another deacon noted that Pete was respected at school. "He don't play football or nothin', but he does run track. That counts, don't it?"

It was generally agreed that running track indeed counted, and that Pete was their choice. By the end of the meeting the position of Youth Pastor had been vaguely defined, and Brother Deckert was commissioned to approach Pete with the proposal.

When the meeting was adjourned and everyone had gone, Brother Deckert stood on the front steps of the church enjoying his last cigarette of the day. He was pleased and hopeful, and more than a little bit proud of himself for pulling it off. He was sure that Pete would accept the proposal. Sometimes a battle can go well.

Brother Deckert rose early the next morning. He dressed quickly and stepped out the back door into the faint suggestion of dawn that bloomed in the east. He wasn't often up this early, and he was surprised to find his car covered with dew. He found a clean rag on the back porch and went around wiping the windows. It was a beautiful morning.

Few people were around at that time of day. He loved the comfort of the seats in his Oldsmobile, but as he settled into that luxuriance, he became uncomfortable in his mind. Self-doubt began to stalk him like a vague scripture that could mean anything. *Lord, sometimes I wish You'd make Your way more plain,* he prayed silently. *How can I be sure that this is Your direction and not some odd-ball idea of my own?*

After about twenty minutes he reached the driveway to the Loucas place. He didn't drive in toward the house. He wanted to catch Pete alone. So he turned the car around and backed slowly and quietly over the cattle guard, turned off the lights and the motor and lowered a window and lit a cigarette.

The sun was just up by then, and already he felt the warmth. After a few minutes he saw Pete in his rear-view mirror, walking head-down at a determined pace toward his bus stop. Brother Deckert leaned over and pushed open the passenger door.

Pete stooped and gawked into the open door. "Brother Deckert? I don't want to be rude, but what in the world are you doing here this time of the morning?"

"Hop in, Pete. I wanted to catch you before school. Something came up in deacons' meeting last night that I need to act on right away. I'll explain while I drive you to school."

"Well," Pete said doubtfully. He backed himself into the car seat and knocked the sand off his shoes against the door frame. "Am I in some kind of trouble?"

Brother Deckert seized on the question. "Only you know if you're in trouble. You're not in any trouble with me. Otherwise, I couldn't say, other than what you've already told me about. But this isn't about any of that. I just came here to prophecy to you. You ever been prophesied to before?"

"Come again?" Pete wasn't sure this was going to be any better than a lecture. "Are you predicting that I'm not going to graduate? I will, you know."

Brother Deckert started the car and pulled out onto the paved road. "Prophesying isn't usually about predicting the future," he said. "The prophets spoke truth to those who needed to hear it. When they spoke prophecy to kings, that's the part that got into the Bible. I am here to tell you some truth that you may not want to hear and offer you a path. That's what prophets do." He looked over at Pete and grinned. "Sorry I forgot my long white robe and shepherd's staff. Didn't really have time to grow a long beard this morning, and I can't find my sandals."

Pete began to smile.

"Also my donkey died. My ass, actually."

Pete snorted and relaxed just a little into the smooth acceleration of the Oldsmobile.

"Pete, I think you've let your dad's death throw you off track. You've been skipping school and church. Your mother is beside herself about your behavior. Your faith is a shambles and your Christian witness is in disrepair. I'm here to show you what you need to do to get back on track and probably become closer to the Lord than you were before."

"Oh," was all Pete could think to say.

Brother Deckert told Pete about the deacons' meeting and their decision to ask him to be Youth Pastor. He said he needed his decision right away, because the flyers needed to be printed. "Pete, you're going to be Youth Pastor in this revival. And your spirit is going to be revived more than anybody else's. I'm sure of it."

"Sounds like I don't have any choice."

"Right. You really don't. You can think of me as Jonah's whale. I'm swallowing you up and I'm going to spit you out into the service of God."

Pete suddenly noticed that they were not headed toward the school. "Hey! Where are we going?"

"Doughnuts," Brother Deckert said. "The Streamliner is out this way. You wouldn't mind a doughnut before school, would you? Cup of coffee? We can do that and still get you to school by the time the bus would have got there."

Pete's head was spinning. "Alright," was all he could say.

At the Streamliner they took a booth at the front window. Brother Deckert ordered two doughnuts and two coffees from a young, very pretty blonde waitress. He'd seen her before, and by her speech, he knew she was from somewhere else. Pete stared out the window, preoccupied with the strangeness of the morning.

Brother Deckert resumed the conversation they'd been having in the car. "You know, Pete, Satan works hardest on those who are closest to God. I think that's why you've been having such a hard time. But you're about to embark on a remarkable journey."

The young woman returned with their order. Pete glanced at her quickly and looked away. The sun was lighting the tops of the pines on the other side of the road.

"We agreed last night on who to call to preach the revival. I think you'll like him. Ever heard of Douglas McPherson? He's been getting kind of famous."

Silence.

"This is a good doughnut, Pete. You should try yours."

"How much time do I have to decide?" Pete asked.

"About being Youth Pastor? Oh, about fifteen minutes. Like I said. We have to print the flyers, and you have to get to school."

"Well, what does a youth pastor do? What does it even mean?"

"I don't know, I've never seen one. Been kind of wondering myself. We'll invent it together. But I do expect that you'll start the services. Either lead the opening prayer or call on somebody. You'll have a chair up on the podium next to mine. If something comes up that you want to say, you can say it. We'll meet with the evangelist before every service for prayer. We'll work it out. Let the Lord guide us."

Brother Deckert looked at his watch. "I guess we better get you to school. Doughnuts probably doesn't qualify for excused absence."

Chapter 12
Biding Time

Gwynn watched the two of them walk out of the Streamliner into the morning sun. She hadn't heard much of what transpired between the preacher and the kid who was with him, but what she did hear amazed her. *Revival.* She hadn't realized that people still did that. The job Gwynn had found allowed her to be a fly on the wall in this strange part of the country.

As she turned away toward the kitchen a spear of reflected sunlight flashed at the front window. She looked up to see an old red dilapidated pick-up roll off the highway onto the gravel. It was one she recognized. Even through the closed window she could hear the grinding of gears as the truck down shifted and lurched around behind the cafe to take a parking spot near the coloreds' window. Even though she'd seen this several times, she still shook her head at the very idea of a separate window to serve Negroes in back.

She carried her tray into the kitchen and stepped around to the back window through which she watched the truck bounce to a stop. A tall, slightly stocky black man stood up out of it. He slammed the door hard, but it bounced open again. He grabbed the open door in both hands and lifted mightily, rocking the truck on its springs. Then he slammed the door again and it stayed. He sauntered toward the order window, glancing up at the sky now and then.

"Good mornin' Miss Gwynn," he said. He faced her, smiling, but did not make eye contact. He was wearing very greasy coveralls but was fairly handsome for all that. Gwynn guessed him to be about thirty-five.

When she'd first seen him, she'd tried to engage him in casual conversation, but he seemed afraid of her somehow. She did learn that he worked nights somewhere nearby, firing boilers. Something to do with the oil field. Since that time, she'd seen him every week or two, and brought him his breakfast on a paper plate, which in good weather, he took out to the picnic tables where Negroes could sit. "Good morning, Swat," she said. "Pancakes and eggs this morning?"

Looking near her, but not quite at her, he said, "Yes, Ma'am. And a little bacon too, if that's alright."

"Of course it's alright." She said it with a smile, but in her heart she was embarrassed and outraged that she, at twenty-one years of age, received such deference from a man fifteen years her senior. It was an affront to her own dignity, as well as his, to be serving this man at a dingy back window when there were plenty of seats inside. She was not used to this kind of thing, and furthermore, she had no intention of getting used to it. The sooner she could get back to California and finish her degree, the better.

Swat dug deep into a pocket of his coveralls and brought out two one-dollar bills and two half-dollar coins and presented them to Gwynn. He appeared not to know how much money he'd given her, and she would have almost believed it, but now suspected that this was an act. She just didn't believe that Swat was dumb or ignorant.

She made his change. He dropped a nickel and a dime into the tip jar.

Gwynn gave his order to Danny, the fry cook, and turned

toward catching up on clearing and resetting the tables, saving her thoughts for later.

That night she wrote a letter:

Dearest Stephen,

You can tell from the postmark that I'm not in CA anymore. I'm also not living in Dad's new house. I'll get to that later.

He gave me power of attorney so that I could sell our old house and take care of the business end of closing bank accounts etc. He's thrown himself into his new job to the exclusion of everything else. Well, almost everything else. I'll get to that later too. I'm not even sure he has room in his head to miss Mom. Sometimes I think he's not even aware that she's gone.

I stayed with Grandma Rose when I was in Oakland. She sends her love. I had to keep reminding her that you're in Germany, not Viet Nam. Every time there's something on TV about American casualties, she's scared all over again that you're one of them.

It was very hard, going through our house, deciding what to sell, what to keep, what to throw away. I hope it's okay that I let your bicycle go in the estate sale. I kept your ROTC uniform. I swear, when I went into the house to start sorting things, I broke down and cried when I found Sugar and Spoon's food dish. Such a simple thing. Getting to Mom's sick room was harder. The cushions she needed and the toilet chair. All the IV supplies and medicines left over. I shipped everything that I kept back to Dad's place in Texas. I was so alone. I should feel lucky that the Army let you come home at all before she died. I'm so glad you were here to help with planning the funeral. But now I miss you terribly.

When I was with Grandma, I all but promised her that, when you get out of the Army, you and I will stay in her carriage house and finish our education at Berkeley. Actually, that's not such a bad idea. Think about it, will you? I'll promise not to be a little brat if you'll promise not to be a shit.

For now though, I'm stuck here in capital "E" East Texas. I started out staying in Dad's house. A mansion actually, with a full acre for a backyard. I guess he thought I was going to play "lady of the manor," and I did actually give it a shot. But it didn't take long for me to have enough of that. It made me wonder what life was like for Mom as his wife. Just taking care of everything about the house while Dad did his thing with his career. It just wasn't working for me. When he brought a lady friend home for drinks, and she was still there for breakfast, that was the last straw. I hired him a housekeeper and a gardener, and I told him I was moving out. He begged me to stay. We have a compromise for now. He's bought a little cottage on Cherokee Lake not far from Longview, and I'm moving into it. He says it's a good investment, but I think it's his way of keeping me from heading straight back to California. So I still see him fairly often with the understanding that I don't want to meet any of his "friends," male or female. I didn't like it when he tried to fix me up with one of his new colleagues. AS IF!! I'm not going to get involved with one of these cowboys and start making grandchildren for him! He's also suggesting that I transfer from Berkeley to a little college here: Stephen F. Austin State College. Can you imagine?

Even though Dad would be willing to support me here in Texas, I've taken a job at a little cafe outside of the big city of Sabine Gap. It's called the Streamliner. I will forever be more respectful of waitresses after this. It's an education in itself. The people here are nice up to a point. I just don't get how they think.

But I am saving money. Even though I think Dad would pay for me getting back to Berkeley, I don't want to have to be totally dependent on him. No bargaining power in that. I might need to be ready to pay my own way by next fall.

So really. I intend to be ready to move by the time you're discharged. Our housing will be covered at Grandma Rose's, and it would be a great place for you to get your feet back on the ground in civilian life. You'll have the GI Bill too. I would love so much for us to be students together.

Write me when you have time. And drop a line to Grandma Rose. She'd be thrilled.

Love you, big brother,
Gwynn

Chapter 13
Seven-Day Revival

Pete anticipated his mother's vehement objections, and he was prepared to slay them. "Mother, I need to use Daddy's car for a few days. I'm pretty sure I can get it started."

Lavena was just out of bed, still in her house coat and slippers and not quite finished with the dreams still swimming just behind her eyes. Pete's declaration threw a twist at her that she hadn't reckoned on. Her husband's work car hadn't been moved since the day he died, and allowing it to move at all meant saying goodbye to him in yet another relentless detail. She wanted to put it off, and she scrambled for the logic to support her denial. Surely, given Pete's recent behavior, she could find plenty of reasons to say absodamnlutely no.

"Just what makes you think you need to use that car? We can go anywhere we need to in the one we're using."

"I have things I need to do after school. I don't think I'll be done by the time you leave the shop. You'll need to drive yours home, and I'll come home later." Pete had just set her up for her first objection and he was ready for it.

Lavena filled the percolator at the sink and was about to scoop Folgers into the basket. "I doubt you have so many important things to do that some of them couldn't be done tomorrow. You can get my car after school and then pick me up at five. What do you need a car for anyway?"

"That's just it. I've got to meet Brother Deckert and a few deacons at the church at five-thirty after they've got off from work."

Lavena put the percolator down and reached for the coffee can. "What do the deacons want with you?"

Pete drew a breath for the kill. "Didn't anybody tell you? I'm going to be Youth Pastor for the revival. I've got to get the flyers from the print shop and then meet them to talk about who's going to put them up and where. Sort of divide up the town. We'll also knock some doors and urge people to come to meetings. Maybe do a little witnessing for Christ." He gave this a short moment to sink in. "I won't be late though. Probably home by seven."

Lavena was slack-jawed. "Well, Honey! I had no idea. What's a Youth Pastor?"

"We're still working that out. But the deacons voted on it last week and called me to the position. So I agreed to do it. I'll be involved in the services somehow. I gave them a school picture to use on the flyer."

"Why, Peter Loucas, that's … wonderful!" She sat down at the kitchen table with the Folgers can still in her hand. "I'm so glad to know this. Why didn't you tell me before?"

"Well, I guess I was still thinking about it. Kinda wanted it to be a surprise. Anyway, Brother Deckert wants us to meet at the church."

"Well, I am just so proud of you! Stand up here and let me give you a hug."

He stood tall.

Mr. DeShazer at the print shop slid one sheet from the sheaf of flyers for Pete to inspect. Pete was awed to see the heading with its photograph of Brother Deckert, the evangelist McPherson and himself. His own name was in bold letters along with the names of the two preachers. He was both amazed and embarrassed to see his name on an equal footing with the grown men. He didn't feel that he'd earned it, but there it was.

Right away he started distributing them: Rexall Drug, Sabine Gap Hardware, Brookshires and Piggly Wiggly. All the while he wondered how long it would be before his classmates would see them and what they would think. Would they say anything to him? Would they be impressed? Would they think he was strange? He was certain that some would think him strange.

Driving his dad's old Plymouth gave him feelings of both connection and loss. Already he was taking his role seriously. Feeling grown-up. He wished his dad could see him, and wondered if maybe he did. Some people said so. In any event he didn't feel so angry. So lost. He still missed his dad terribly, but now felt that he had a purpose he could rise to.

He parked on Main Street in the center of town and went from one business to the next, asking permission to display one in their window. Most were willing. By the time businesses were closing that afternoon, he'd reduced his stack by twenty-three. The rest he would hand over to Brother Deckert, and adults in the church would distribute the rest in nearby communities. Whiskey Creek, Pirtle and Red Oak.

Just before the lunch bell on the last Friday before the revival started, the principal allowed him to use the microphone in his office to make an announcement to the whole school. His palms sweated when he walked into Mr. Horton's office. He scooted awkwardly around behind the enormous oak desk. Mr. Horton showed him how to hold the button down while he spoke. After fumbling with it for a moment, Pete held down the black button and read from his prepared announcement.

"Hello everybody. This is Pete Loucas. I just want to take a minute to invite everyone to the spring revival at West Sabine Baptist Church. It starts this Sunday morning at eleven, and will meet every evening for the rest of the week at eight o'clock in the evening for the preaching service. After each service there will be a youth gathering in the social hall for food, music and games. I will be there, and I hope to see you there too. Everybody is welcome. Thank you."

Pete took his thumb off the black button and handed the microphone back to Mr. Horton. He was almost dizzy as he walked a little too fast around the desk toward the door. He bumped the edge of a filing cabinet hard enough to leave a bruise on his upper arm, but he tried not to show it. He stopped in the hallway to watch students rushing out of classrooms for lunch. He was amazed to think that he'd just spoken to them all.

The following Sunday morning the revival was officially underway. Pete put on the only suit he owned, with his one white shirt and clip-on tie. The suit was dark blue. Dark enough, it had been decided a few months before, to wear to his dad's funeral. It still fit him, but just barely. He arrived at the church early to meet the two preachers for a pre-service prayer in Brother Deckert's study.

Entering the study Pete was reminded of recent conversations he'd had there with Brother Deckert. He'd been in a very different frame of mind then. He felt good to look around at this space dedicated to books and contemplation and know that he was becoming a legitimate part of it. There was *Barkley's Bible Commentary* in seventeen volumes within reach of Brother Deckert's chair. *Mathew Henry's Commentary* and *The Sermons of Billy Sunday* higher up. The room smelled of books, leather and tobacco.

The evangelist hadn't arrived yet, so Pete and Brother Deckert had a moment to greet each other and acknowledge their camaraderie. Pete had never felt so grown up.

After a moment the study door opened, and Pete saw Brother Douglas McPherson for the first time. He wasn't a big man, but he stood at his full height. He wore a perfectly fitting suit with a paisley tie over a shirt that wasn't quite white. It was more of a light purple. It had never occurred to Pete that a dress shirt could be anything other than white. Pete tried to estimate his age but found it difficult. Brother McPherson seemed like he could be in his fifties, but his facial complexion was clear and smooth. It was as if he'd applied makeup.

Brother Deckert welcomed him in and the three of them shook hands. Pete noticed a contrast between the handshakes of the two men. Brother McPherson's hand felt limp and humid. Only the fingers made contact. Brother Deckert's was far more generous and engaging. The three of them filled the small room. Besides the desk and its chair, there was a small couch and an armchair, all of which left just enough floor space for Pete, Brother Deckert and the visiting Brother McPherson to kneel on the floor in prayer.

It gave Pete a heady sense of pride to pray with them as an equal. And later when they walked into the sanctuary it made Pete a bit nervous making his entrance. It helped a little to see the three armchairs on the podium, knowing that one of them was for him.

The two preachers went to their own seats while Pete was first to the lectern. He tapped the microphone. "Can you hear me?"

People in the congregation nodded that they could. Pete looked across the crowd and recognized most of the faces. There were many smiles and nods of encouragement.

"I want to welcome everybody to the Lord's house this morning." Pete scanned the audience and stopped on a familiar and dependable face. "I'd like to ask brother Carl McGrath to lead us in our opening prayer. Stand now please and let's bow our heads before God."

Thus the event began. It would last for seven days. That night Pete met again with Brother Deckert and Brother McPherson. He was a little less giddy than he'd been during the morning service, and a little more observant. He noticed, but granted little importance to, Brother McPherson's hair. Every hair was in place. Pete wondered how and where a man could get his hair to look like that. He'd seen women come out of his mother's beauty shop with the same hair-sprayed effect. But McPherson could certainly preach, he'd give him that.

On the second night, Monday, Pete felt vaguely uncomfortable looking at Brother McPherson's hands. The fingernails were perfectly even, clean and a little too long. There was no evidence that they were useful for anything beyond being admired, especially with the outsized diamond on his right middle finger. It far outshone his wedding band. Pete noticed but brushed it off. Brother McPherson's gripping story from the night before still echoed in his mind. It had been about the lost sinner who had passed up a final chance to be saved. The sinner had felt the Holy Spirit tugging at his heart strings, but he'd hardened his heart and left the church unsaved. That very night his car stalled on the railroad tracks. After the impact, the poor sinner's brain slid out "like a piece of liver" and the lost soul now burns in Hell. It was a convincing story. Pete did admire the way Brother McPherson could deliver a vivid sermon.

It was Thursday night, when the three were meeting for prayer, that Pete began to feel consciously disturbed about Brother McPherson. Pete arrived at the parking lot at the same time that Brother McPherson did, and saw him sweep his sky-blue Cadillac into Brother Deckert's marked parking space, seemingly excessively self-possessed behind the wheel. Pete waved to him, but McPherson hadn't noticed. He got out of the car and paused and placed his hand on the hood as if the paint itself were evidence of God's favor.

Pete tried to imagine himself in that stance, and could not.

Later when they were in Brother Deckert's study, Pete listened to the enunciation of McPherson's prayer. He sounded exactly like Billy Graham on television. The pacing and phrasing were the same. But where Billy Graham sounded authentic and sincere, McPherson's voice sounded vain and in love with itself. Condescending. It certainly didn't sound like a humble man addressing his God. Pete muttered under his breath, "I imagine you'd take God's parking place if He had one."

"What?" McPherson said.

"Nothing."

For the duration of the revival Pete joined other church members in the afternoons to knock on doors and urge people to come to meeting. He visited a few whom he knew and for whose souls he felt concerned. For six consecutive nights Pete opened the meeting and briefly addressed the congregation. Several times he delivered the opening prayer himself. But with each day Pete became more disturbed by Brother McPherson. By the end of the week, Pete harbored a secret dislike of the man. He wondered if Brother Deckert had noticed any of these same things, but didn't have the nerve to ask him.

Another, more important thing troubled Pete. It was the very fact of his dislike for the evangelist. It was near to blasphemy to disapprove of a man whom God Himself had called to service. Preachers became what they were because God had called them to His work, and they'd responded. Pete himself had felt the call and had announced it publicly. How then could he feel such hostility to a man of God who was doing the Lord's work? Pete had no answer for this, and he knew that he wouldn't have an answer anytime soon. But he also knew it was a question he couldn't leave alone.

On Saturday morning the three men met again for prayer before they went out again to make contacts in the community. Brother McPherson's prayer included the words, "… and Lord, I thank You for all the souls I've saved …"

Pete couldn't let it go. When the praying was done, Pete said, "Brother McPherson, you haven't saved any souls."

"Well of course I have. Quite a few of them right here in your own congregation. They've been coming here for a while, but didn't get saved until I came along."

"Brother Deckert's been getting them ready for quite a while. Then you came along and Jesus saved them. Not you."

Brother Deckert interrupted. "Yes, we all know that it's Jesus who saves. And we're all working together to advance the kingdom of God. Praise the Lord."

"Praise the Lord," Brother McPherson repeated.

It was the last day of the revival, and Pete couldn't have been readier for it to end. He'd put out a few more flyers after the morning meeting and was back home before noon. It was already getting hot. It being Saturday, his mother would be home early from work. He felt agitated and unfocused without knowing why, and in an attempt to dispel his agitation, he did the one thing that he knew his mother would most appreciate. He put on jeans and a T-shirt and went out the back door and down the steps and pulled the lawn mower out from under the porch.

It was soothing to push the mower back and forth in straight lines across the lawn. The drone of the motor and the rhythm of his stride and breath was enough religion for the moment. Seeing the shredded grass flying from under the mower and the smooth even surface of the mown grass behind him was enough purpose. He fantasized Brother McPherson being cut to pieces and spat out with the grass clippings. Sweat dripped from his eyebrows and chin. He felt that he could mow forever, and he completely disappeared into it.

Still, the predictable evening stretched ahead of him like a sticky sheet of flypaper. He would dress and go to church and open the service. He would endure McPherson's sermon with its probably-not-true lurid tales of sin and damnation. He would watch McPherson's right hand rise in dramatic gestures that best showed his diamond. Afterward he would stand with the two preachers and shake hands with nearly every attendee as they left the church. A third of the women would express their sympathy once again about the death of his father, and tell him again something about God's will and His mysterious ways. Pete would once again watch classmates pass by him with sidelong glances, escorting girls to their cars and heading out to the Dairy Queen or who knows where.

Something in him balked. Maybe it was the death of his father. Maybe it was a few too many sympathetic gazes. Maybe it was the hormones of a chaste eighteen-year-old. Maybe it was the strain of maintaining belief in things that didn't really add up. Maybe it was simple spring fever, but Pete Loucas realized, rather than decided, that he could not force himself to attend one more meeting of this revival. Not even this last one. Never mind that he was officially the Youth Pastor. Never mind that it would enrage his mother. Never mind all the questions he'd be asked by people whose business it was not.

Never mind that he would disappoint Brother Deckert.

That was the rub.

Pete shut down the throttle of the mower and grounded the spark. In the silence that followed he felt the energy drain from his legs. He dragged the mower back to the house and put it away and sat on an upturned bucket in the garage with his face in his hands. He didn't know what he would tell Brother Deckert. He only hoped that there would be some future explanation. Some reasonable sense he could make to explain himself. The only thing he was sure of was that he was not going to church this night.

When his mother drove up to the house, the sun was already slanting through the pines. Pete had finished the lawn, and as a ploy, he kept himself busy with other chores. He imagined that being on his best behavior would help defer his mother's suspicion. He took laundry from the washer and hung it on the line while his mother started dinner. He made a noisy show of putting the gas can away that he'd left in front of the house. He went into the kitchen and took the garbage bag from under the sink and grabbed a few newspapers from the basket in the living room. He carried these to the burn barrel where he built up a fire of papers and put the garbage on top. He stood watching while the flames caught and swelled, transfixed by the smoke rising faster. The flames grew to a hot bright orange and burned clean.

When Lavena called him to supper, he went into the kitchen, washed his hands with dish soap and dried them on his shirt. A pitcher of tea, still hot from brewing, sat on the counter. He took down two tall glasses from the cupboard and filled them with ice that he chipped with a pick. It fractured and popped when he poured the hot tea.

Lavena was already dressed for church. At thirty-eight she was still a youthful and good-looking woman with black hair and intense green eyes. Pete could remember hearing her laugh with his father that she was deficient in the boob department. They had often embarrassed him with their banter. Their obvious affection. And now, as he watched her tight-fisted grab into the silverware drawer and her quick steps between the stove and the kitchen table, Pete knew that her grief was as raw as his own. Knew that they both sought the line between grief and anger.

"It's getting late," she said. "You'll have to eat quick and get ready. I've got to get there for choir practice."

"You go on without me," he said. "I'll come later in Daddy's car." It was a daring proposition, and Pete chewed slowly awaiting her response.

"We're not burning gasoline in two cars when we're going to the same place. Why on earth say such a thing?" She sat with her fork suspended eight inches in front of her mouth, lips slightly parted as if to say more.

"I've got just enough time to do this math homework."

"Homework! You don't have to do that now. It's Saturday night. You can do it tomorrow after church. Or before church if you get up in time."

"Mother, I just want to get it over with. I hate math. I've been stewing about it, and right now, I think I know what to do. I want to do it before it gets away from me. I'm trying to catch up at school, and if I knuckle down right now, I can at least get the math done. I can do history tomorrow." Pete almost believed himself.

His mother hesitated. It was true that Pete's grades had dropped since his father's death. They'd had arguments about that. She grudgingly relented. "Well, alright. Get busy on it. I'll see you at church."

As soon as Pete heard his mother's car going over the cattle guard, he flew into action. He was going frog gigging. He was going to have the solitude and silence that he'd begun to crave. There would be no man-made commotion in the night-time tranquility of the river bottom.

He jerked on a pair of cut-off jeans and put on some old sneakers without socks. In the garage, next to his dad's fishing tackle, he dug out a flashlight and the spring-loaded frog gig on its ten-foot pole. He took the jumper cables and the salvaged headlight from which his dad had made a hand-held spotlight. He found the roof rack and screwed it onto the drip rail of the car.

He used well-rehearsed balance and leverage to load his 11-foot aluminum john-boat onto the rack and tied it down using the bowline and trucker's hitch his dad had taught him. He remembered the snakebite kit, bug repellent, drinking water. He hastily made a sandwich of white bread and bologna, working quickly as if his plans were fragile. Any interruption or second thought could completely derail him.

Satisfied that he'd overlooked nothing important, he got behind the wheel, pulled the choke three quarters of an inch, pressed the gas pedal halfway and released it. When he turned the key and pressed the starter, the flat-head motor clattered to life and revved.

Pete's legs were quivering with adrenaline at the audacity of his stunt. Under the urgency of this adolescent escape, the old car slewed sideways in the loose sand of the driveway. It rumbled over the cattle guard and laboriously accelerated on the highway, gears shifting and shifting again, the racket of it fading into the cooling air.

Chapter 14
Frog Gigging

Once he was on the road, Pete realized that he'd best avoid driving through town, so he took a right turn onto the less travelled Pentecost Road, and then a left on Goforth. Once he'd crossed the Marshall Highway, he knew that there was little likelihood of being seen by anyone he knew.

Twenty minutes later he turned off the pavement into Sinclair Camp where oil company families raised their kids and their gardens. He gazed at the houses with their lit windows, imagining men sitting down with their children and their wives. Men who were still alive.

Just past those houses the road went steeply down onto the flood plain of the Sabine River, which during spring floods could be more than a mile wide. The whole flat expanse of it was injured here and there by oil wells. Every drilling site had its old slush pit, now filled with water and growing cattails. Each well sat on an oil-soaked elevated berm on which nothing grew. Narrow oil-topped roads meandered to each well in a maze-like complexity that one must learn in daylight in order to navigate at night. The flatness of the land was naturally pocked with ancient meander scars and other inexplicable holes of water, isolated and lonely. A spot known as Clear Lake was one such two-acre pond, and this time of year it was alive with all creatures of water, mud and grass. It was full dark when Pete steered the Plymouth onto the packed earth berm of a flowing well at the water's edge.

He turned off the motor and the headlights. Silence and darkness swept over him like an ocean. He sat still for awhile, allowing his eyes to adjust. The cooling engine ticked away like a syncopated clock. The world of daylight, time and dogma drifted a universe away.

He and the place gradually became accustomed to each other. The crickets were the first to resume. A lone frog croaked somewhere on the banks. Another frog took courage and answered.

Pete quietly opened the door and stepped out onto the bare ground. Stealthily he released the binding on the boat and pulled it off the car, heaved it to the water's edge and set the bow afloat with the stern on the bank. Reflected starlight showed ripples spreading over the water. He went back to the car and opened the hood, disconnected the battery and took it out. He carried the battery to the boat and set it gently in the middle. With the jumper cables he connected the battery to the spotlight. The high beam shot directly into his face and left him momentarily blind. Feeling foolish, he disconnected it and stood in place until he could see again. Then he finished loading the boat with the tow-sack, snake-bite kit and his frog gig.

Night voices filled the air. Crickets. Frogs. All in their individuality of voice, direction and distance. The far-off yapping of feral dogs known to roam the area. A screech of an owl in the woods near the river. The constellations wheeled overhead, unknowable and silent as God. The daytime sun swung below his feet like a one-way pendulum, illuminating some foreign world.

Pete set the spotlight into its bracket in the bow and re-connected the battery cables. The spotlight skimmed the water and illuminated the banks. He waded to the bow and tied the painter around his waist. With the boat in tow he eased out to thigh-deep water, feeling the muddy bottom one slow step at a time. He reached for the gig, sprung open the jaws and weighed the shaft in his hand for its balance point. He brought his concentration to the hunt while time itself found an alternate axle on which to roll.

The beam rocked and swayed over the ripples, and fearsome insects flashed through it, briefly illuminated. Reflective eyes of critters, amphibian, insect and mammal, shone out of the darkness. Pete's own shadow projected large against the willows.

Pete waded silently through the dark water managing his balance on the uncertain bottom, balancing the gig lightly, moving toward a likely pair of eyes. The spotlight kept the frog transfixed. He inched nearer until he could thrust the gig.

He jabbed, and the jaws snapped. The frog kicked at the air as Pete brought it to his hands. He pulled the tow-sack over the frog and gig, and pulled the jaws open. The frog dropped mutely into the wet burlap. He returned the sack to the bottom of the boat, rebalanced the gig, oriented the light and scanned the shore again.

Time dissolved while stars swam their formations through the sky. Frogs gathered in the tow-sack as if of their own accord. The shoreline rotated like a mud clock. More than once Pete saw the black undulating swim-stroke of water moccasins as they went their way on the surface. Nothing was there that did not belong in that two-acre universe.

A sound broke the spell. Pete straightened and gathered his awareness of the larger world. He'd heard something akin to a howl or a sob. Maybe human, maybe not. He stood still, listening. Not owl. Not dog. Not whippoorwill. He heard it again, and it jarred him back into the world of time. He cupped his hands to his ears. There was a far-away motor. Voices.

He brought his watch to the light and saw that it was late. Without stealth he pulled the boat back to the car. Using the flashlight he restored the battery to its place under the hood, careless now of his own noise. He shivered, having become cold and a little afraid of the dark.

He heard it again. This time it was definitely human. Singing? No. Pleading.

He calculated the distance and direction of the sound and thought it to be further down by the river, maybe 300 yards, maybe a half-mile. When he had everything loaded and secured, he debated whether to head for home or to ease down toward the river to see what was happening. It was most likely teenagers drinking beer. Maybe someone he knew. He got into the car and headed slowly toward the river.

He stopped on the riverbank near a pumping well that sat on a platform projecting over the river itself. He killed the motor and headlights and got out and stood listening again. With the flashlight he walked out onto the platform and looked up and down the river. The wheeze and moan of the well was the only sound.

Then, to his right, headlights appeared through the trees on the other side of the river. He switched off his own light and watched them bouncing nearer. They stopped a short distance down river. There was muttering and the opening and shutting of doors. Flashlights levered in the dark revealing only nonsense. Pete watched as figures passed through beams, casting outsized shadows against the underbrush.

He positioned himself behind the well and watched as best he could with the uneven lights swinging in front of him.

Occasionally the beam of a flashlight crossed a standing torso or a pair of legs. There was pleading, "Ya'll don't need to do no more."

"Shut him up."

A dull thump like a mattress struck by a bat.

"… blood on your shoes."

"Help me … cinderblocks …"

"… rid of them shoes too …"

Then came the splash of something large hitting the water. Pete heard the ripples reach the near bank.

Someone said, "It's done. Let's get out of here."

Pete had heard enough. He backed away from the well, keeping low. After a few yards he stood and ran toward his car. He tripped on a briar and fell crashing into underbrush. A light beam passed over him back and forth, searching.

"Who's over there?" somebody shouted. "Hey!" he shouted again." Then in a friendlier tone, "Come on back, buddy. We got some beer over here. Come join the party."

Pete stayed on the ground and crawled through the grass while lights searched the woods above him. After some time they gave up and drove out of the maze of paths. When he reached his car, he started the motor and backed out to the road without lights. He didn't turn them on until he was well away.

Pete headed back to town driving hard. The wind drag on the boat was formidable. He hoped that whoever was at the river couldn't catch up with him, and he doubted that they could. They'd have to go all the way back to the highway and cross the bridge. He figured he had at least a ten-minute head start. For that matter he didn't think they would try. And besides, how would they recognize him? He was just a guy driving through the middle of the night with a boat on his car.

He slowed a little and considered what he should do, and kept coming to the same conclusion, though he didn't like it. If he hoped to ever live with himself, he must go to the police. When he entered the city limits of Sabine Gap and passed under the first streetlights, he slowed to the speed limit. A new anxiety crept over him. In the remote darkness of the river bottom it had been easy to believe that he was witnessing a murder. Now, in the lights of town, driving on clean pavement, it seemed less real than a bad dream.

He parked in front of the police station and sat for a moment gathering his wits and listening to the cool-down ticking of the motor. Two officers came out the front door and lumbered down the concrete steps. At first he thought they were coming out to meet him, but they only glanced at him, raised eyebrows to each other and walked past to their own squad car. Pete watched them drive away and considered doing the same.

When they were gone, he got out of his car and, in his wet shoes, went up the steps and through the front door. Two people sat behind a counter engaged in a conversation that went on for some time. A bell sat on the counter, and after some consideration Pete decided to ring it.

"We see you," one of them said. "What do you think, we're blind or something?"

"Sorry," Pete said and waited, wishing he could just walk out and go home.

After several minutes, the larger of the two men got up and put on a cowboy hat and went out, bidding his partner a good night. The one remaining looked at him and said, "Shift change. So what can I do for you?"

Pete couldn't think how to begin. "I heard and partly saw some people killing somebody," he said.

The cop behind the counter eyed him for a moment, evaluating the kid in front of him. "You heard and partly saw," he said flatly.

"Yessir."

"And you come here to make a report."

"Yessir."

"How come you didn't just phone?"

"It was down in the river bottom."

"When?"

"Thirty minutes I guess."

"Couldn't you of waited for Monday?"

The question put Pete off balance. "Well. I guess I could, but I thought you'd want to go catch them. The ones that did the killing."

"Where was this again, at the river? This thing you heard and partly saw?"

"Just down from Sinclair Camp. Straight down from there there's a platform well. They were on the other side of the river from that."

"And you're thinkin' that we're just gonna jump in our cars and go tearin' out of town lookin' for killers? The ones you heard and sort of saw."

Pete felt even more ridiculous than he had feared he might. "I just thought it would be good to tell you as soon as possible."

"Answer me this. What was you even doing out there? In the middle of the night?"

"I was frog gigging at Clear Lake. That's when I heard it firs…"

"Show me your driver's license," he interrupted.

Pete reached for his wallet, but he'd taken it out of his cut-offs hours ago. "It's in the car. I'll go g …"

"You stay right where you are. Is your name Peter Loucas by any chance?"

"Yessir. How did you know?"

"SELLERS!" The man shouted toward the hallway. "I THINK THIS ONE'S FOR YOU."

"WHAT?"

"COM'ERE. THIS MIGHT EXPLAIN SOME THINGS."

A minute later Pete was seated in Officer Sellers' office, trying to give a coherent account of what he'd witnessed.

"I think the one throwed in the river was a nigger," Pete said.

"And just why do you think that?"

Pete swallowed. He felt dizzy and slightly nauseous. It was one-thirty a.m. and he was tired, hungry, thirsty and dirty. The chair he sat on seemed designed for discomfort with its low armrests and flat oak seat.

"I said why do you think that. Answer me, son."

"I heard somebody say 'Shut up, coon-ass.' "

Officer Sellers leaned back with a snort. "That's it? That's it? You heard somebody say 'shut up coon-ass'? Why, I call a white man a coon-ass ten times on a typical Sunday. That don't mean nothin', Coon-Ass."

Pete shifted in his seat. "One of them sort of sounded like a colored man when he said, 'Oh Lawd, oh Lawd.' Like that."

The florescent light hummed. Heavy feet thumped the wooden floor in the hallway. There was laughter somewhere.

Officer Sellers slowly leaned forward again, elbows and fists on his desk. "Son. Do you know it's against the law to make a false report to law enforcement? Because, you know what? I don't think anything happened except for inside your addled brain. Did you see anybody do any throwin'? No. You heard something splash. They could have been dumpin' old tires. Did you see anybody at all? No. You saw flashlights, or so you say."

Sellers' face turned a deeper shade of red. "I got two things I want to say to you, son. Naw. I got more than that. First off, you didn't actually see a goddamn thing but some flashlights on the other side of the river. That much you admit. Second thing. Whatever it was, it happened in the river bottom, and Sabine Gap Police ain't got no jurisdiction out there. Out there it's Sheriff Connor's problem, so you're wasting my time. Third. If it wasn't somebody dumpin' trash, it was prob'ly a bunch of drunk teenagers chuggin' beer in the woods. If they take their drinkin' to the river, that's fine by me. Not my problem.

"But you know what would be a problem for me? It would be some wet-behind-the-ears dickhead getting people riled up about some killing that didn't happen. The next thing you know, there'd be the N-double-A-C-&-P nosin' around and making trouble. After that would come them Freedom Riders or whatever they call theirselves. Sabine Gap is a peaceful town, and it's my intention to keep it that way."

He pushed his chair back and stood up and brushed the front of his uniform. He turned his back to Pete, his gaze on the city map that hung on the wall. "Let me tell you something. I know who you are. You want to know how I know? Last week while I was getting my hard-earned few hours of sleep, you want to guess who knocked on my door and woke me up?" He turned and faced Pete. "It was a pair of your holier-than-thou busy-bodies handing out pamphlets about some revival." He put his hands flat on the desk and brought his large face forward. "And guess whose picture was on the front of that pamphlet. Yeah, that's right. You. Right there between them two preachers, all three of you looking like Jesus warmed over. Grinnin' like a jack-ass eatin' briars. So tell me. What were you even doing down at the river? Wasn't you supposed to be whooping it up for Jesus?

"Go home, son. Git out of here. Take two asprins and forget about calling me in the morning.

"I said, Go!"

Before Pete could react, Sellers said, "Wait! One more thing. Your mamma's been looking for you. She's been calling ever' half-hour since I come on duty. Five or six good cops with better things to do have been out looking for you. If I ever have to hear your name or see your face again, you'll be wishing you were somebody else. Git goin' and don't you stop even if I tell you to."

Pete stood to go. His whole body felt heavy, and his feet seemed to belong to somebody else. He found the front door and went out and stood a moment on the top step. He fumbled with his car keys, hands shaking. The street was empty except for his car. When he got behind the wheel, his leg trembled so that he could barely operate the clutch. He backed out of the parking spot and headed through town toward home, wishing he had somewhere else to go. The clock at the bank read 2:11.

When he crossed the cattle guard into his own driveway, Pete could see through the trees that lights were on in the house. He parked beside the garage in his usual spot, got out of the car and closed the door quietly, for what futile reason, he couldn't have said. The tow-sack of frogs was in the floor on the passenger side. He had no stomach for gutting and cleaning frogs. He lifted it and untied the knot and dumped them out onto the ground where they righted themselves and sought direction. He left them to their fate and went inside

Lavena stood braced against the kitchen countertop as Pete opened the back door. "Where in the H. E. Double L. have you been? Do you know I've had the police looking for you? What can you possibly have to say for yourself?" She paused.

"We're going to start with a whipping, and then you're going to tell me what possessed you to skip church and then come waltzing in here after two a.m. For starters you can give me your belt."

Pete almost did what she said, but caught himself. For the first time ever, there was a difference between the two of them that could not be mended, not by obedience, nor by whipping nor apology. Until this moment he had always had some way to appease his mother. Make her pleased with him. Proud of him, even if proud for the way he took his punishment. For the first time in his life he knew that resolution was not possible.

"I'll explain it the best I can, Mother. But I don't want to give you my belt. And whipping won't do either of us any good." He surprised himself with these words. He half-slouched, afraid of what he'd just said. He started to speak again, but she beat him to it.

"I'll be the one to decide about that. You'll give me your belt, and you'll do it right now!"

Pete pulled the back door closed behind him and moved slowly to the kitchen table, sat down and looked up at her. "You could whip me with a belt, or not. It really wouldn't matter one way or the other. There's worse things than whippings."

Lavena was momentarily speechless. She mentally scrambled for some new leverage.

"Mother, do you remember the last time you whipped me?" Pete said. "I was fifteen."

"What's that got to do with anything?" The shift unbalanced her.

Pete, for his part, felt caught in some non sequitur to be talking about whipping, of all things. This was far afield from the issues of the night, but he continued nevertheless. "I heard you and Daddy talking about it afterward. I heard you tell him you didn't feel right about it. I heard him tell you that you'd over-reacted, and that was the truth. I knew then that it was my last time to be whipped. There won't be any more." Pete felt as if he'd just walked onto a stage with neither costume nor script. His actions seemed not to be his own, those of an animated circumstance that made decisions without him.

Disbelieving, Lavena said, "Any more what?"

Pete was sitting, and Lavena was standing. Nevertheless, Pete looked directly into her eyes. "Whippings."

"Peter Franklin Loucas, I am going to split you apart at the seams until you are right with God and right with me. You'll right this minute …"

"Mother."

"… get out of that chair and …"

"Mother."

"… put your hands on the counter to …"

"MOTHER!"

She stopped talking and looked at him blankly.

"Mother, there are things that can't be made right." His voice broke into sobs. "Why are we even talking about this? It has nothing to do with anything. Something happened tonight that's … I don't know. It's hard to explain. I have to do something. Somebody has to do something."

"Do something about what? You're not making any sense. Who have you been with, anyway? I hope it wasn't that …"

"I was by myself. I wanted to be alone, so I went by myself."

"Went where?"

"Frog gigging."

Lavena stopped breathing for a moment. "Frog gigging? You went frog gigging?" She shook her head. "Explain this to me, and it better be good."

"There's nothing good about it." Pete put his elbows on the table and his face in his hands. His eyes were closed, but he heard his mother pull a chair out from the table and sit down.

"You lied to me."

"Mother, I hate that preacher."

"What?"

"But that's not even important either. I heard somebody getting killed. Out there in the river bottom." With that he openly wept. He heaved so deeply that he felt he would vomit. He wept for the murdered man. He wept that McPherson was alive while his father was dead. He wept for the change occurring between himself and his mother. For his vanished childhood and ominous future. He pulled his T-shirt to his face, blew snot and wiped tears.

"Have you been drinking?"

Pete had to laugh. "No, Mother. You know I haven't been drinking. Jeez." He got up and went to the bathroom where he took a long pull of toilet paper and blew his nose again. He washed his face and went back to the kitchen and sat down.

Lavena watched him. She was exhausted and confused. "The police called and said they found you."

"I found them, they didn't find me. I stopped at the station before I came home."

"What in the world have you gotten yourself into?"

"I was down below Sinclair Camp. Clear Lake. I kept hearing hollering down toward the river like somebody was in trouble." He told her the story. She listened without interruption.

When he was done, Lavena drew a deep breath and said evenly, "I've been worried sick. I had no idea where you were. I called the police, and I called the hospital." Her voice quavered. "You have exposed yourself to the Devil and he has enrolled you in his work. It's your own fault. You failed to be with God's people in God's house tonight." She closed her eyes for a moment. "You've played the fool, and now you have a fool's troubles. As far as that goes, your troubles are yours and you can work it out with God. As far as the police go, if something bad happened, it's none of your business. The police can handle it. It's what they get paid to do. There's nothing you need to do about it."

"Mother, I heard a man begging for his life. A Negro man. I heard him say he had children. Then I heard him get thrown in the river, right in front of me. Maybe there was a reason I was there. Maybe God wanted me to be there."

"That's crazy talk, and I won't listen to a word of it!"

"Maybe God wants me to bear witness. Wants me to do something."

"Do something like what?" she demanded.

"The police didn't believe me. They're not going to do anything. They didn't want to know about it. Maybe I should tell somebody at the newspaper."

"Oh, no!" she said emphatically. "Don't you dare get mixed up in something you don't know anything about. Even if something did happen. No. Especially if something did happen, you could wind up having those people after you. Me too for that matter."

Lavena stood up from the table and went to the sink and turned to face Pete. "Listen. I go every day and unlock that beauty shop. Women come in and I talk to them and wash their hair and twist their curls. I get them out from under the dryers and brush them out, and they give me three dollars and I start on the next one. The phone rings and somebody makes an appointment. That's why the lights come on when you flip the switch. If you start getting involved in racial stuff, and word gets around, that telephone on my wall will stop ringing. That is, unless it's somebody threatening to burn my shop down. And that's just what they'd do to me. There's no telling what would happen to you."

Pete picked up a salt shaker from the table, looked at it

and put it back down. "I thought you were braver than that. I thought you had more faith in God."

"Faith in God," she said flatly. "I wasn't the one who went frog gigging when he should have been in church. Listen to me, whatever happened probably happened for a reason. If a colored man did get killed out there, it's probably because he did something he shouldn't have. He could have been a rapist. That sort of thing doesn't happen to coloreds who know their place."

She got up from the table. "It's been a hard night. I'm going to bed. I suggest you do the same. We will be going to Sunday School and church in the morning, do you understand me here?"

Pete nodded.

"That preacher may not be your favorite, but church is not the preacher's house. It's God's house."

Lavena went to her bedroom, closed the door, and wept. Until that night she had managed her despondence over her husband's death. She'd felt that she was able to be a mother to Pete. She could do it for Pete, for herself and for Pete's father. Now she felt overwhelmed and inadequate.

Since girlhood she'd armored herself against grief. But this night had threatened her with the loss of her son, and the thought was unbearable. On some level she knew, but would not acknowledge to herself, that a part of him was indeed lost to her already.

Chapter 15
Oil Finds Water

Pete slept three hours or so, if it could be called sleeping. Dreams of tangled vines and mud. Wheels with no traction. Impersonal snakes crawling in his pant legs. When he woke up it was barely light. He tried to go back to sleep, but finally he admitted to himself that he would sleep no more.

He got out of bed and rummaged in his closet for a fresh pair of jeans and a button-up shirt. He crept to the makeshift shower in the utility room instead of the one in the bathroom, so as not to wake his mother. The shower hadn't been used since the last time his dad came home from work. After showering he lathered with his dad's brush and shaved with his dad's razor.

He was so agitated that he could hardly get dressed. He paced constantly and had to make himself stop to put on his socks. He was hungry, but the idea of cooking or even eating repelled him. He didn't want to be alone, but his mother was the last person he wanted to be with. He paced from room to room. The car keys lay on the kitchen table like a dare.

While dawn pushed against the windows, an inclination blossomed in his mind. He examined his wallet. Four dollars.

It would be a daring extravagance, but he could think of no other way to survive the next hour. He picked up the keys and went out to the Plymouth and headed directly toward the Streamliner.

Gwynn was also awake early. Her work for her father in California was done. The house was sold. Furnishings shipped. Assets transferred. Now she was back in Texas, but no longer in her father's house. The little cottage on Cherokee Lake was her home now, and instead of being in college, she was waitressing. If the cafe were inside the city limits of Sabine Gap, it would be required to be closed on a Sunday morning. But it was located just out of town, and Gwynn would be there for the six a.m. opening time.

From where she lay she could reach the window curtains which she drew back to gaze out over the vapored surface of the lake. She would not have guessed that Texas had so many birds. At the moment everything outside was quiet except for the tentative pleep of a robin. But within the next few minutes the pre-dawn filled up, one critter at a time, with so many chirps, tweets, chitters, warbles, screeches, caws and toots that she could hardly differentiate among them.

Texas was such a foreign country to her. She sometimes caught herself trying to calculate an exchange rate for her dollars. The Bay Area was so far away in every respect that it took on the substance of an old movie she'd once seen. Her former college friends were strangers to her now. People of another race. Here in East Texas there were no freeways to take you anywhere, whether to mountains or to concerts, Mexico or Canada. She could not smell the vast Pacific Ocean that stretched beyond imagining to all the places a freeway couldn't go. She no longer encountered the variety of people who ranged from professors of statistics at Berkeley to the dreadlocked street musicians with steel drums and fire in their eyes. She never even saw so much as a bag lady with her shopping cart and her story of woe.

She got out of bed and went to the bathroom and turned on the shower, letting it run until hot water arrived from some distant part of the house. Her only mirror was the full-length one she'd bought at Sears in Longview and hung on the wall herself. She stood in front of it while the water ran. She was lovely, and she enjoyed knowing it. Ever since she was a young girl, she'd accepted her own beauty the way she'd accepted the friendly sun, the country club her parents had belonged to. Birthday parties at Golden Gate Park.

She examined her eyes, a little blood-shot and sleepy, but a rich dark brown. The smooth skin of her neck and shoulders seemed light-complected despite the tan. The tan lines of her swimsuit were still visible around her breasts, though she hadn't worn her bikini since leaving California. She wondered if she might never wear one again. She evaluated her breasts, thinking they could be a bit larger. She ran both hands over the vertical crevice of her navel and across to her hips. Was she gaining weight? At twenty-two was she past her prime? From the side she admired her red-blonde pubic hair, fluffed forward in a springy handful. In her face she could see a replica of her mother. She must have looked very much the same when she was young.

By the time she was in her car and on her way to work, the optimistic sky was showing off its colors. The car actually belonged to her brother, an orange Karmann Ghia that had been a common sight on the west coast, but in East Texas it drew stares. Driving his car made her feel closer to her big brother. He would want it back, of course, when he got out of the Army, but it was hers for now. Whenever she happened to meet other Volkswagen owners on the road, they flashed their peace signs and waved their camaraderie. Other drivers were more likely to give here a slack-jawed unfriendly stare as if the car itself were evidence of subversion.

She arrived at the diner to find that Danny, the fry cook, was there ahead of her. He usually opened up, but being rather obviously a queer, he preferred to stay in the kitchen away from the customers. He was safer in the kitchen.

Waitressing at the Streamliner was no dream job, but at least it gave her an income of her own and put her among people. It made her less lonely, and it was a good vantage point from which to apprehend this alien culture. She enjoyed the short conversations with locals. She marveled at how, like children, most of them unquestioningly accepted their world at face value.

The breakfast customers were mostly workmen in big cowboy hats or the metal hardhats of oilfield roustabouts. She watched them emerge from pickup trucks, some of them emerging boots-first. Some hat-first. Others butt-first, dragging their huge bellies after them, finding their balance, hitching up their britches and ambling toward the front door of the cafe.

It amused her that, to the men who came in alone, or at least without women, she was temporarily their woman. Whether imaginary mother or lover or both, they claimed her with their eyes. Some men in their loud-voiced, big-hat machismo came on to her lewdly. Others silently and guiltily leered from the darkness of their own minds, although most were simply sweet in their warm good will. She developed a knack for deflecting unwanted advances and defusing their innuendos and double-entendres. A few men made a try at bringing her to Jesus. Their reasoning, she suspected, was that if they could persuade her to be saved from Hell, her gratitude would make her favorably disposed to love them. Their neediness filled the room.

Such was the curse of beauty in a sexually repressed world. She could no more let her guard down among them than a sparrow could roost with hawks. The Streamliner job and her mother's wedding ring allowed her an arena of safety. If necessary she claimed that her husband was in the Marines and would soon be coming home on leave.

Pete had never before in his life gone to a cafe by himself. When he turned into the Streamliner's gravel parking lot, he felt shy about it. He imagined that everyone was watching him. When he pulled open the glass door and went inside, there were three men at the counter, smoking and drinking coffee. An elderly couple sat at a booth near the window. Pete chose the empty booth next to them.

He put his forearms on the table and looked about. The lady facing him gave a faint smile. The three men at the counter conversed among themselves in low tones, smoke rising in front of them.

Out the window Pete saw a dirty pick-up truck loaded with pipe and tools: obviously the men's. The '59 Ford with clothes hanging in the back was the elderly couple's, traveling from some place to someplace else. He looked back at the truck and wondered if it had been in the river bottom. He looked at the men and wondered if they had killed anybody lately.

"Good morning. Coffee?"

Pete looked up into the most beautiful face he'd ever seen. He did remember vaguely seeing her before, but he'd never SEEN those brown eyes. Blonde hair to the shoulders and skin like peaches and cream. An innocent inch of cleavage above the top button of her blouse. Pete's eyes involuntarily shot back down to the table in front of him. "Yes, ma'am," he said to the flatware in front of him.

She turned one of the cups on the table right-side-up and

poured. She took a menu from under her arm and laid it next to the coffee.

"Cream?" she said.

"I think it is," he said, and then blushed at his own nonsense.

She reached cream from a nearby table.

"Oh, uh ... no, I don't use it."

"Oh," she said. "Then I'll come get your order when you're ready."

Pete furtively watched her walk away toward the kitchen, ashamed to be so captivated by the musculature of her calves. The backs of her knees.

He could tell from her speech that she was from somewhere else. Right then he wished that he was from wherever that was.

Chapter 16
My Real Name's Prentice

Prentice Waters woke up alone in his hot little house at four-thirty in the afternoon. He still slept on the living room couch even though his Aunt Minnie was long dead. The house was his now, for all practical purposes, but it still felt like hers. All of her little shelves were still on the walls of every room, even in the narrow hallway and the bathroom. Shelves made of odd boards and pieces of plywood, scraps of a neighbor's pine flooring, or a length of shiplap she'd found somewhere. Some were supported by tenpenny nails driven into the wall, or by salvaged angle brackets or perhaps a hand sawn piece of 2x4 toenailed into place, none of it exactly level, and all of it without regard for the red-barn patterned wallpaper. Every shelf was laden with figurines. Tiny squirrels frolicked on ceramic tree trunks, stallions reared, owls sat blinkless in gathering dust. A green glass bear fished in a green glass stream next to a ballerina on pointe.

An oscillating fan the size of a dinner plate wagged this way and that, stirring the hot air. Prentice lay watching it for a moment. He didn't get up right away, but rather waited for his dream to dissipate. Korea again. The unimaginable cold. Trying to drive the ambulance, its steering wheel missing. Turns of hopeless direction. In the back, blood leaking from stretchers onto the floor and then into the frozen ruts beneath. He was tired of that dream.

He stretched his eyes open wide, shook himself and sat up for a moment. He leaned forward over his feet, stood and made his way toward the bathroom, canting his shoulders to avoid knocking against the shelves in the hallway. The bathroom had only the pink toilet and a rusty metal shower. He turned on the cold water and slowly fed his body into the spray, gasping with the shock of it.

At five-thirty he stepped outside onto the freight pallet that served as a side porch. He nodded toward Clifford, his neighbor who stayed with Lum and her several tykes. The air carried the smell of crude oil baking up out of the blacktop street and from the fire dikes of the nearby oil tanks. As he walked under a chinaberry tree, his shoes popped the ripe droppings into a yellow goo. The hammer of sunlight struck his face and arms as he rounded onto the street. He turned toward the sun and led his long shadow westward past Emmanuel Church and then a few shacks beyond. When he got to the house with the purple front wall, he stepped around a dusty car, walked inside without knocking, dropped $1.25 into the Ball jar on the upright piano and went on into the next room.

Three men and a woman were already at the table eating thick slices of ham, mashed potatoes with red-eye gravy and turnip greens.

"Hey, Swat," the woman said. "We been afraid you miss your supper. I know you ain't cooking for your own self." Alice was her name.

Prentice took a chair without speaking. Presently Ruby, a portly woman, came from the kitchen, put a plate before him laden the same as the others, and beside it, a very large glass of strong, sweet iced tea. She gently slapped the back of his head and went back into the kitchen without speaking. Beyond a slight hint of a smile, a bare tightening of the lips, he ignored it.

Alice said to him, "Swat, we been missing you in the choir this summer." Her companion bobbed his head up and down, his mouth being full.

"I'll be back directly," Prentice said. "They gone' shut down production at the plant sometime soon. Then we'll be working some daytimes. Maybe get Sundays off."

"Cora been asking about you. She say she gonna cook up some o' her jelly roll when you get back into the daylight." At that the two men guffawed through their mouthfuls.

"Cora didn't say no such," Prentice said. "Besides, Cora too skinny. She break, I git ahold of her."

"Cora ain't the kind that breaks." Alice regarded Prentice for a moment. "You better look again, Swat. That's all I got to say. Look again."

"Why y'all so itchy 'bout me finding a woman? Ya'll ack like I'm some kind a pistol gotta be stuck in a holster."

"Yeah. Maybe that pistol ain't loaded no-how," one of the men said. The others put their forks down and leaned back laughing.

Alice, unfazed, shouted into the kitchen. "Ruby! Hey, Ruby!"

"I ain't got no more tea ready," came the response.

"Naw. Ruby, what you fixin' tomorrow?"

"Tomorrow? It's gone be chicken tomorrow."

"Hear that, Swat? You go up the road there and tell Cora she don't have to cook at her house tomorrow, 'cause you paying for her chicken. You got the money somewhere, 'cause you shore ain't spending none. You got the best paying nigga job in town and you still driving Minnie's old truck. Ain't no woman gone ride in that thang."

"Alice, with you here to instruct me, what I need with another woman?" Prentice said.

The room erupted in laughter.

About then Ruby came out of the kitchen carrying banana pudding. It was a thing of beauty inside a vanilla wafer crust, and a meringue with caramel beads gleaming on the top. For a while there was only the sound of forks on plates. Hot coffee spilling into cups as Ruby made her rounds.

Alice backed off but not for long. In a more somber tone she asked, "You heard from Beulah?"

"She comes around for money sometimes. She say I'm living in her mama's house, I can pay her rent. So I give her some." After a deep breath he said, "I reckon she spend it on booze and them no-account mens she stay with."

There was general head-wagging around the table.

"It's a shame," Alice said. "Ya'll was a good family when you and Roscoe and Beulah was kids. You and Beulah was the sweetest things. Minnie was a saint on this earth. I'm glad she don't have to know about Beulah getting to be the way she is."

"Beulah straighten out one these days," one of the men offered.

"Maybe," Prentice said. "Maybe Beulah straighten out. Maybe Roscoe gone come back from Viet Nam saying 'It was all a big mistake. See? It's me. I'm home'."

"Aw, Swat. Don't be like that," one of the men said.

"Be like what? Her mama gone. Her brother come back in a body bag. She kicked out of that white high school just as soon as it integrated. That's a lot to come around from."

"She still got you, Swat. You all she got now."

"Oh, boy," Prentice said, and applied himself to his banana pudding. He blew his coffee and said, "All I can think to do is go down there to the Bottle and Glass and crack some heads and drag her outta there. Then what? She go to Sunday school while I go to jail?" He shook his head. "They's a dark side to everybody and everything. I seen it in Korea. Roscoe seen it in Viet Nam. Beulah seeing it right here in Sabine Gap. Oh, excuse me. I meant to say Tin Cup. Sabine Gap is for white folks."

"Swat! Calm yourself down." The older of the men at the table addressed Prentice firmly. "You think there's anybody here at this table who don't know that? Git ahold of yourself. We all been dragged through the dark side of this world. And we all have seen redemption in unexpected places. The onliest place redemption cannot happen is in a bitter heart. So git ahold of yourself. When Beulah is ready to be redeemed, she gone need you to still be there. Be patient."

"Patient," Prentice mused.

Everyone ate silently for a time. Ruby came out of the kitchen with her own dinner on a plate, pulled out an empty chair and joined them at the table. She cut off a bite of ham and put it in her mouth and then stopped chewing. She looked around at the somber faces. "My, my, was the puddin' that bad?"

Chapter 17
What Can a Deacon Do

By the first week in May Lavena was scared that the Devil had completely taken her son. Ever since the spring revival he was more erratic than he'd been before. More disrespectful and disobedient. He almost never went to church. The school notified her that he was skipping classes, and his grades were so low that he might fail to graduate, which had serious implications. If he didn't get into college, he would lose his II-S draft classification. The daily news was full of Viet Nam, body bags and flag-draped coffins. Pete's misbehavior was more than just an inconvenience that he could make up in summer school. It was potentially life-and-death. It was potentially Heaven and Hell. The idea of Pete drifting away from God, not getting into college, being taken into the Army and maybe killed and, unthinkably going to Hell, was unendurable.

She worried. She prayed, and sometimes felt that she might cry. But she must not ever cry, for if she started to cry she would never stop.

For a while she resisted an impulse to talk to Brother Deckert again. She'd already bothered him enough, and he'd done all he could do. Besides, she was the kind of woman who could take whatever life threw at her. She wasn't a whiner. She wasn't a weakling widow who went crying to the preacher every time she felt blue or every time she wanted a caring man to look into her face.

Or every time her son lost his soul.

But no. She must try everything. She talked to Jesus. "Everything to Him in Prayer," the hymn went. Lavena prayed but after a while she could think of nothing more to tell Jesus. There was nothing that He didn't already know. But the thing was, Jesus never said anything back. Even though she feared that she was a pest to Brother Deckert, she reasoned that, if people could talk to God over and over, it should be okay to talk to His preacher. Jesus had His say in the Bible, and that was pretty much that. Only Brother Deckert could say anything back.

She vacillated until the day she was giving a shampoo and set to Babette Klein. Lavena was twisting and pinning curls onto the rollers on Babette's head when she said, "So I hear Pete has a new girlfriend. Quite a cute little number, I hear."

"Oh?" Lavena tensed but remained casual. Alert.

"Well, Lavena, surely you must have met her by now. What's she like? I hear she comes from California."

Lavena tried not to appear clueless. Tried not to reveal too much.

"Well, she's very nice, and she seems to be a good student," she faked.

"Oh no, Lavena. You're thinking of somebody else. This girl isn't a student. She works out at the Streamliner. She's a little older of course, but you know young people these days. The old rule of the boy being older than the girl doesn't seem to apply anymore. I have to say that a younger man would be okay by me, if you know what I mean." Babette laughed as if she and Lavena were sharing a joke.

Lavena nearly fainted.

When her noon break came and no one else was in the

shop, Lavena, trembling, dialed Brother Deckert's number. The phone rang and rang again. It rang some more. Lavena hung up. In a way she was relieved that there was no answer, but her mind was no less troubled.

She blocked out a Thursday morning in her beauty shop schedule. When the day came she left home at eight as if she were going to work, and in fact did go to her shop. With no appointments to attend to, it was a place of refuge. She sat in one of the dryer chairs, praying and talking to herself. At nine she picked up her car keys and went out the door.

She parked next to the church and went in the side door near the pastor's study. The corridor there was always dark and cool. She walked in the dim light to the office door and raised her hand to knock, but stopped. She could still turn around and get into her car and drive away. And then what? After hesitating, she went ahead and knocked twice.

"Come on in!" came the familiar voice. "It's not locked."

She pushed the door open and was greeted by Brother Deckert's earnest face. Going into his office again felt a little like repeating a grade in elementary school. She hadn't been there since before the revival.

"Mrs. Loucas! Good morning. A pleasant surprise to see you this morning." Brother Deckert indicated a deeply upholstered armchair and invited her to sit. "Would you like some coffee? It's still pretty fresh," he said, pointing to a thermos that sat balanced on the window sill.

"No, thank you." She clutched her purse in her lap.

"Well, I hope you won't mind if I have a cup. I usually have some this time of the morning. So. How are you getting on? Is business doing okay?" He started with small talk, feeling for that opening that would bring them to her reason for being there. Did she need anything. And finally, "How's Pete?"

"I'm worried about Pete." She didn't want to tell Brother Deckert about the girl at the Streamliner even though it was the biggest thing on her mind. She stuck to safer topics. "His grades have fallen again. Even worse, I'm afraid. He's so sassy with me. We had a real blow-up last night when I asked where he'd been. I don't know where he goes. When I ask, he either won't tell me or he makes up something he thinks I might believe. He's skipping school. I'm truly afraid he won't graduate."

Brother Deckert thought for a moment. "I thought he was doing better. He seemed to be better during the revival, although it's true that he didn't show up that last night. I've been meaning to ask him about that."

In truth Brother Deckert was as mystified as Lavena. He'd been hearing things about Pete himself. Though he'd never mentioned it, he still remembered Pete's troubles after his father's death, and then that curious revival night when Pete had failed to show up. But he'd been under the impression that Pete was improving. For now he listened to Lavena and let her be his concern.

Lavena talked herself out and then sat silently with her hands in her lap. Brother Deckert observed her posture, her deep breathing. Her fierce eyes. "It's like he's gone back to the way he was before the revival, only worse," she said.

Brother Deckert didn't pray with Lavena that day. He didn't offer her any scriptures to read. She'd already read them all anyway. "Lavena, I will talk to him. I know how to find him, and I will talk to him the way a father would talk to a son. Just know that I may need to let our talk be just between me and him. But I will tell you as much as I feel that I can when it's done. It may take a little time."

That same day Lavena made an appointment at the high school to talk to the principal and some of Pete's teachers. When she went there, she felt awkward driving into the parking lot of the school, driving past the students' cars, many of which were newer and fancier than her own. It took all the courage she could muster to be there, since she herself had not graduated from high school. It was painful to walk among such youngsters whom she considered more educated than herself. She called on the Lord for strength.

The meeting was in a small conference room with a round table. When they were all seated, Mr. Horton, the principal, opened the meeting and stated his concerns. He held a typed sheet of paper in front of him and peered through his bifocals. "Well, it looks to me like Pete Loucas's grades have dropped off a cliff. And, what's it say here? He's been cutting classes? Yes. Well. I'm very concerned that, if his behavior doesn't change, we can't graduate him, that's for sure. Maybe if he goes to summer school." He looked around the room. "We're here to see if we can find a way to get him back on track, is that right? Who's got an idea?"

The room was quiet until the biology teacher spoke up. "In my class he's not passing, but he's close. I'd say maybe a high D. I could give extra credit for that owl that he shot early last fall. He did a pretty good job of stuffing and mounting it. He donated it to the science lab, and we still have it there. The extra credit could push him over the top if he'll just come to class."

The English teacher, whom Lavena knew to be Pete's favorite, thought it might be an idea for him to write about what was disturbing him. She could give him compositional credit, which should bring him up to a passing grade. "But," she insisted. "I can't do much if he doesn't show up and do the work."

The school counselor said that she'd already called Pete into her office on several occasions to discuss his falling grades and spotty attendance. She said that he had always been polite, but agitated. She thought there seemed to be more than the death of his father at play here, and that Pete was fixed on the idea that he had witnessed a murder. He'd said that the police threatened to cite him for false statements if he bothered them anymore. She also noted that Pete had tried to talk to her about race and about religion, which as a public school employee, she was not prepared to discuss. He'd also brought up questions about evolution. "It's all quite a muddle in his mind, I think. He's taking on some big questions."

Everyone looked to the biology teacher, who squirmed a little and said that, yes, he had mentioned evolution briefly in class, and that Pete had asked more questions about it than most students do, but that he, the teacher, had sought to de-emphasize it.

Lavena glared at Mr. Horton and said, "You let them teach that here?"

Mr. Horton responded that students need a little preparation for the ideas they would encounter in college. They needed to be exposed to the academic view of the world.

Lavena slid her chair back and told them all that they would be more help if they read and believed their Bible. Soon after that the meeting ended inconclusively.

Brother Deckert, meanwhile, went back to his deacons for help. "I thought we did pretty well the last time," he told them in their meeting. "Back in the spring when we made Pete Loucas the Youth Pastor, he did really well. It was good for him. Now, in a few weeks' time, Pete Loucas is going to be out of high school. I hope. I think it's important that he not be left with too much time on his hands. You know, have no clear direction. And it would be good for him and his mother both if he had more than some run-of-the-mill part-time job. We know he knows how to work. Several of you have hired him in the past to mow your yards and stuff like that. But now he needs more than that. So ask around. Look around. Let's try to help him get a good job for the summer. One that will keep him busy in a good way and also pay him a better wage than he'd get ushering at the Texan, or taking orders at the What-A-Burger. I imagine their finances are kind of hard for him and his mamma."

Brother Carl McGrath said he knew someone who was making a real good living selling Kirby vacuum cleaners. He could find out who Pete would need to talk to.

The room was silent until Bob Broussard said that he was friends with the superintendent at Petroleum Dehydrate, Hank Grizwald. They were going to shut the plant down for maintenance and would need a few more hands to dig trenches and thread pipe and such like. It would be temporary, but the pay was good. Everybody but Brother McGrath agreed that it sounded like a pretty good idea for all they could tell. Bob agreed to talk to Hank and let Brother Deckert know what he had to say. Brother McGrath muttered that he still thought selling vacuum cleaners was a good idea.

Chapter 18
Sweetness with a Burn to It

Pete allowed himself to be convinced to attend classes for the last six weeks of the school year. None of his teachers wanted to fail him, and nobody thought that he would benefit from failure.

So he went. He didn't run track, and he didn't do assignments. He showed up, and his presence allowed the school to graduate him, partly out of hope, partly pity and partly relief to be done with him. When graduation day arrived, Pete didn't attend the ceremony.

He'd lined up a few yards to mow for pocket change, but other than that, he spent time in the woods hunting squirrels out of season and fishing in the ponds without a license. People sometimes saw him at odd hours running along the road in his cut-off jeans and track shoes.

Inwardly Pete thought of himself as a modern-day John the Baptist, dwelling in the wilderness. He sometimes talked to his dad, and sometimes he prayed, but he wanted no Sunday sermons. He figured he'd already heard every sermon that there was to hear and had preached a few of them himself. There was a hole in him. It was hard and round. An empty place that bullets would bounce off of.

There was a day in which he had the lead role in the movie of his life. He could see himself onscreen as he put his .22 rifle in the car. He drove toward the river like James Dean. He stopped frequently to gather discarded whiskey and beer bottles. He piled them into the floor of the Plymouth. At the river he passed Clear Lake, small and green in daylight. He went straight to the well platform on the river where he'd been on the last night of the revival. The ordinariness of it was stunning.

From there he saw clearly across the river to the dirt track on the other side where the other vehicle had driven its terrible cargo. It all seemed so small and un-mysterious, like it could have been just a bad dream. Maybe it didn't happen. But it did.

Wishing Gwynn to be watching his screen performance, he put two bullets in his mouth and one into the chamber of the single-shot. He threw the bolt forward and pulled back on the firing pin until it clicked. He spun one of the empty bottles as far upstream as he could throw and quickly drew a bead on it as it floated by. The shot missed by an inch. Very rapidly he drew the bolt to eject the empty shell, pulled one bullet from his teeth and reloaded; closed the chamber and pulled the pin, aimed, fired. This one, too, missed. The bobbing neck of the bottle shrank into the distance while he fired the third time, and the bottle rounded a bend out of sight.

"I'm better than this," he said aloud. He said it again, louder. "I'M BETTER THAN THIS." A fragment of his voice echoed from the far bank.

He picked up another bottle, this one with a Wild Turkey label. A dribble of brown liquid rolled in the bottom corner of it. Pete sniffed at it tentatively, a sweet smell. Forbidden.

He poured it into a puddle in his palm and dipped a finger for a defiant taste. A sweetness with a burn to it. *So that's what whiskey tastes like*, he thought.

He reloaded, his mouth as well as the chamber and threw the bottle spinning over the water. This time he willed himself toward precision. He fired and the bottle burst into shards and was gone. He dared another question. *I wonder what sex is like.*

Chapter 19
The Wax Plant

"Wax plant?" Pete said.

"Yes. You know that place. Right by the railroad where it crosses Goforth. It's on the right if you're headed toward town. You've passed it a hundred times. Just turn in there and go straight along the tracks. The office is the tin building right in front of you. Talk to Hank Grizwald. Everybody calls him Griz. Brother Brousard knows him from high school, and he's already put in a good word for you. But you better get out there before somebody else beats you to it."

"Does he go to our church? I don't think I know who he is."

"Griz? No," Brother Deckert said. "His wife's a Holy-Roller, so he goes out there. You've probably never seen him. Don't worry about that. Just go there and tell him you know how to work hard. You don't have to know pipe-fitting or anything. You'll just be helping, and they'll tell you what to do. Pay attention and put your back into it, and you'll do fine. It'll sure pay better than Brookshires or the What-a-Burger or just about any other summertime job you're going to find. A lot more regular than mowing yards. By the end of the summer you'll be well-set for college."

"Well," Pete said. "I guess I could go out there straight from here."

"Here's a better idea. Be out there at seven tomorrow morning. It'll show him you know how to get yourself out of bed. And here, I want you to take this. It ought to be enough to get you a good pair of work boots at Penney's. Wear them when you go out to the plant. He might just put you to work on the spot. You can repay me out of your first paycheck."

Pete held the twenty-dollar bill with something akin to reverence. "What if he don't hire me?"

"Then you can wear out those boots mowing my yard for the rest of the summer," Brother Deckert said with a wink.

At six-forty-five the next morning Pete turned off Goforth Road onto the graveled and rutted driveway of Petroleum Dehydrate. It paralleled the railroad track where a line of five black and dirty tank cars sat, ponderous, spewing steam from hoses attached to their undersides. There were already three vehicles parked at the tin shack straight ahead of him. One was a battered International Harvester pickup with no tailgate and no license plate. It sat crooked on mis-matched wheels. A dusty black Pontiac was next to it. The third was a gleaming rose-colored Cadillac. Off to the right a beat-up red pickup sat by itself.

Pete parked next to the International and went to the paint-peeled door of the office, while two men, one black, the other white, watched him from the doorway of a low tin building a hundred feet away.

Pete had barely gotten inside when a sandpaper voice said, "You Pete Loucas?"

Griz was about fifty years old and as many pounds overweight. His thinning hair was an unnatural jet black.

"Yes, Sir," Pete said.

"Here." Griz thrashed around in a deep drawer of the desk, which was hardly visible under the clutter. "Here," he said again when he'd found what he was looking for. "Fill this out. You got a social security number yet? It don't matter. You can get one."

Pete took the paper and looked for a surface to write on and a fountain pen to write with. He spied a ball-point on the floor which he picked up and tested. There was a chair, but it was covered with papers and notebooks, so he knelt on the floor and used the wall to write on, shaking the pen frequently to keep the ink moving.

Presently two other vehicles arrived and parked near the office. Pete could hear voices outside and the sound of steel hitting steel, a scraping noise of something heavy being dragged. The sustained ring of pipe rolling on its dunnage.

He handed the paper back toward Griz, who was thumbing a thin phone book and seemed not to notice him. "Here's this," Pete said.

"Just put it down. Go on. You work out there, not in here in the office. You ain't that educated yet."

"So, I'm hired?"

"Yeah, so go find Heck."

"What?"

"Heckle. Go find him."

He went outside to look for Heck. The Pontiac was just leaving, and a black man was getting into the red truck. It started on the third try and rocked its way down the driveway in a thin cloud of the Pontiac's dust. Pete followed the sound of commotion behind the office.

When he rounded the corner there were two men carrying a 20-ft. length of 4-inch pipe and laying it up on sawhorses next to a pipe threader. One of them looked at him and said, "Get a shovel out of the tool shed and dig us a trench from that pump yonder over to where we already dug that hole."

"Where's the tool shed?"

The man gave him a slack-jawed look that said, *how dumb can you get?* "Can you see that little building over there by the big one?"

"Yeah, I see it."

"Well that's, the, tool, shed. Do I need to tell you what a pump is too? It's that thing the size of a wheelbarrow next to the tank yonder. Start digging there. I presume you know what a shovel looks like."

For the next two hours Pete dug. The sun got higher and hotter and the morning's breeze wore down to nothing. Not knowing exactly what was needed, he began with a shallow trench, as straight as he could manage from the two points. He could always make it deeper if needed. He noticed he was the only one without a hat.

At nine-thirty they all took a short break for water and smokes, sitting on discarded lumber in the shade of a raised 500-barrel oil tank. "What do they call you?" the older of the two men said.

"Pete. Pete Loucas."

"I go by 'Heck'. That there's Jeckle. Them's Loper and Tiny."

Jeckle gave a quick nod.

"That trench you dug, if you can call that a trench, has got to be a foot deeper and twice as wide."

"Alright."

"And pile your dirt neater all on one side. The way you're spreading it around we'll need a truck load just to fill the hole back up. There's gloves in the tool shed. Find you some that ain't too wore out."

By bits and pieces, Pete began to understand what this wax plant did. Sludge and sediment from the bottom of oil tanks throughout the southwest was brought in by tanker truck and railroad car. The plant processed the slop into a crude black paraffin which was then shipped out by rail. Where it went from there and why remained a mystery to Pete.

The biggest chore of this maintenance shut-down was the replacing of rusted pipe through which the finished wax would be pumped into a mansion-sized storage tank, and from there into steam-heated railroad cars that came in rotation on the siding. Every pipe had a smaller pipe running through it. This smaller pipe would be pressurized with steam to keep the wax hot and liquid for pumping.

In this manner Pete passed his first two and a half weeks at Petroleum Dehydrate. Every morning the same two men came up from the boiler house. The white man got into the Pontiac and drove away, followed by the old red pick-up driven by the Negro. Heckle and Jeckle showed up, opened the tool shed, and the three of them dragged out the pipe threading equipment and digging tools. They put on their gloves and tin hats. The sun rose above the boiler house, hotter day by day. Pete never saw Loper or Tiny again, and nobody mentioned them.

Pete occasionally asked a question about this or that. "What's that thing there?"

"Pump," Heck grunted.

"What does it pump?"

Heck let his arms go slack and looked up. "You're the one graduated from high school. You tell me." He turned back to the pipe threader and seemingly spoke to it. "We need some more two-inch. Go down there to that flat-bed and bring the rest of it up here."

Glad to do something besides dig, Pete went to the lopsided International. The key was in it. He drove it down past the boiler house, past equipment and structures he couldn't name.

When he reached the pipe yard, he found a twenty-foot flat-tired trailer laden with pipe of different sizes. He sort of knew what two inches looked like, so he set to work transferring what he hoped was the right size pipe from the trailer to the pipe rack on the pickup. He was glad to be working out of sight of Heck and Jeckle, even if only an hour.

By early June, Pete's wrists, neck and ears were nut-brown. His hands and arms were still winter-white owing to the gloves and overalls that covered the rest of his body. The days were getting hot in earnest, and all the men at the wax plant ate salt tablets like candy and drank water by the quart. Griz always stopped at the ice plant and brought a block for the 10-gallon water can. Like the others, Pete began to take a perverse pride in his toughness against the heat and his aching back and weary arms. And against the sometimes fierce banter among the men. Heck and Jeckle competed to invent the cruelest hilarity, usually at Pete's expense.

"Frog gigging? You had a night to fool around, and you went frog gigging?" Heck straightened from his work at the pipe threader, leering around at the group. "Shit fire, if I had a night off like that I'd be after some pussy, how 'bout y'all?"

"Hey," Jeckle put in. "Leave him alone. If the kid likes frogs better'n he likes pussy, that's his business. It's a free country ain't it?"

"Yeah. Anyhow, I reckon frog pussy is prob'ly about right for Pete's dick, ain't that right, Pete."

At first Pete had no response. He just kept winding the lever arms on the pipe cutter, wishing he had a comeback. His face was already too red to blush. "I don't know," he finally said. "There's frogs out there too choosy for any of y'all to have any luck."

———

It was on Friday, June 10th that Griz called them all together. "We're gonna be starting up next week. Monday if everything goes right. Heck and Jeck, you two are gonna be on days with me. Monroe and Tiny are coming back for swing."

"Who's taking graveyard," Heck asked. "Loper and Swat?"

"Loper had a heart attack, and he ain't coming back," he said in a firm manner that invited no further questions, and flatly left it at that. He sent everybody back to work except for Pete. "Loucas, you come on in the office for a minute."

Pete dropped a glove and picked it up. "Now?" he asked.

"Yes, now, if you can spare the time."

Griz turned away and headed into the office. Pete followed at a brisk pace behind him.

Griz was talking before Pete's eyes could adjust to the indoor light. "I gotta put you on nights. As I already said, Loper had a heart attack."

Pete absorbed the meaning. "When do I start?" was all he could think to ask.

"Eleven o'clock."

"Monday through Friday?"

"No. Not Monday through Friday. You think you're workin' at the bank? Every night. It takes three days to shut this plant down, and about the same to start it up again. So when we get it runnin' it stays runnin'. I'm shoot'n for Monday to have us back into production." Griz looked at Pete over the top of his glasses. "Set down," he said.

Pete moved a lunch pail out of the only available chair and sat.

"Here's the thing. I'm kind of in a spot here. Swat there knows how to handle the boilers and just about anything else out here. You, on the other hand, don't know jack-shit. All the same, I can't have no nigger being boss to a white man, know what I mean? All hell would break loose. So you are going to replace Loper as operator. You get a raise. Swat's still the boilerman, but he'll show you how to do most of what you need to do. You get what I'm saying?"

Pete nodded as if he did.

"Now Swat there," Griz went on, "he's a good nigger, and he'll make sure everything runs all right, but you have to keep him in his place. You got to make sure he says 'sir' to you when he talks to you, you hear me?"

"Yes, Sir."

"That might not sound important, but it is. Besides that, now and then you have to tell him what he's got to do, and I'm going to help you out with that. Monday night I want you to tell him to do up the laundry. Just tell him that. He knows how to take it from there. That ought to get you through the night. Rule number one. Don't you ever let him sass you. You're just a kid and wet behind the ears, and I'm afraid you could let him get the best of you. I've had to fire him a few times already, just to teach him a lesson. I don't want to have to fire him again if I can help it. I don't want to have to fire him just because some kid like you let him get out of hand. There's white men who'd like to have his job, and he knows it. There's also white men that know it. When you get right down to it, he's about the best man I've got. Works hard, does things right. Keeps his eyes open. And he's a veteran. That counts for something in my mind. But he's still a nigger."

Pete's head was swimming. "What do you want me to do?"

"It ain't a lot. I'm gonna show you now how to keep the log. When the still is running, you'll keep track of the tops tanks and the finish tanks. Stuff like that. Now and then you'll pump into the railroad cars. Switch them before they run over. Blow out the lines. But that won't come until we're up and running. On Monday Swat will show you how to run the boilers, probably just enough pressure to run the blow-barrels for the laundry."

"Run the what?"

"Blow-barrels. That's the laundry. You'll see. You can sweep the lab, or better yet, tell Swat to do it. Yeah. Swing shift might leave you some pipe to thread for day shift if they don't finish everything up. We won't start the still until at least Sunday. Don't mess with any of the operation without Swat knowing."

It hadn't occurred to Pete until that moment that, when the plant was running, it would run seven days a week. Working nights would mean sleeping days. Seven days would mean missing at least some church services. Any social life would have to end by ten-thirty. But he'd get a raise. Exactly how much he didn't know.

"Well, go on," Griz said.

"Go where?"

"Back to work. I'm not paying you to stand there."

Griz had a different conversation with Swat. Rather than call him into the office he walked down to the tool shed and banged on the tin siding with a wooden hammer handle. Swat looked up toward the noise and, seeing Griz, came toward him wiping his hands with a fragment of greasy towel.

Griz offered Swat a cigarette, which Swat accepted out of the necessity to come across as subservient. "You heard what I said about Loper?"

Swat had heard, but said "No, Suh," so that Griz could say it again. "Sump'in happen to Mister Loper?"

"He had him a heart attack this morning right before he left the house."

"Law!" Swat acted surprised.

"That kid that's been helping on days, Pete. He's taking Loper's place. For obvious reasons I can't let you do it. So here's the thing. I'll explain everything I can to him. How to keep the log and all that. I don't want him screwing anything up out here, and I don't want him getting hisself or anybody else hurt. Do you get my drift?"

"Yes, Suh. I'll watch over him."

"He's still the boss."

"Yes, Suh."

"As long as nothing goes wrong, then I don't have to do any extra paperwork. I really don't like extra paper work, you understand me?"

"Yes, Suh," Swat said.

Griz turned back toward the office. Swat watched him for a moment and then continued his search for the right pipe-threading die in the tool shed.

Chapter 20
Dinner with Daddy

When her phone rang Gwynn knew it had to be her father. No one else ever called. But instead of answering "Hi, Daddy," she simply said, "Hello?" She could at least pretend for a moment that she *might* have a social life.

"Hi, Baby. What'cha up to?"

She pulled the phone cord around from behind the toaster, set the base on the kitchen table and took a seat at the window facing the lake. "Hi, Daddy. Tuesday is my day off, so I'm just catching up on things. I started a letter to Grandma Rose. I owe her one. Mostly I'm staying inside where it's cool. Are you at work?"

"Yeah. Meetings all day. But I guess that's what they hired me for. It's about time they put a chemical engineer into administration around here. I can help them understand the practical side of depreciating capital equipment. The accountants know the write-offs, but I know what works. Anyway, enough of all that. I don't see you much since you moved out to the lake. What say I take you to dinner tonight?"

In the way that private thoughts can sweep by in the slimmest of moments, Gwynn calculated that she was probably getting this Tuesday invitation because her father had been otherwise occupied on the weekend. He may have even just now found out that one lady friend or another couldn't be with him tonight. Hence this invitation. This was becoming her role with him: to fill the gaps. He wanted her nearby and available, and had gone to considerable trouble and expense to arrange it so. It was on his insistence that she'd moved with him to Texas, and she had felt then, so soon after her mother's death, that she owed it to him in his grief. In truth the arrangement suited her to some degree. She needed time for her own grief. She wasn't ready to go back to college. She would be soon, though. Of that she was certain. Words between her and her father on the subject had become testy, and she wondered if he planned to offer some new enticement at dinner tonight to get her to take root here in East Texas. She hoped this wasn't going to be another introduction to one of his single colleagues.

With that thought she said, "Will it be just the two of us this time?"

"Absolutely," he said. "Just you and me and good food. I found this really nice Cajun place over in Kilgore, of all places. Johnny Case's. Ever heard of it? Ever had Cajun food?"

Gwynn laughed. "No, I can't say I have. Don't they eat turtles and stuff?"

"No, no. It's not like…well, maybe. I don't know. But there's other stuff too. You can get a steak there if you want. This place has a reputation from Dallas to Shreveport. First class. You get a chance to dress up really nice instead of just your jeans and sneakers. It's in Gregg County too. You can get drinks there. It'll be good to see you."

"It sounds nice, Daddy. But I work tomorrow. Early. I don't want to be out late."

"Dinner at six. You'll be home by nine. Sound good?"

"How do I get there?"

"No, Baby. I'll pick you up at five-fifteen."

Getting ready to go out, Gwynn felt agitated. She couldn't

decide what to wear. She hadn't worn any of her evening clothes since before her mother died. She hadn't been on a date either. Going to dinner with her father wasn't a date, but she had some of the same jittery first-date feelings.

She took several outfits out of her closet, still in the dry-cleaner plastic. She pulled out a cardboard box of shoes. There were shoes she'd forgotten she had, and there was jewelry somewhere if she could find it.

She berated herself for being so flustered. It was just her FATHER, for Christ sake. When she began talking aloud to herself, she thought she must be neurotic. Unfocused, she went to the mirror and fussed with her hair, back to the bedroom to compare shoes and outfits, and paw through the earrings and necklaces, some of which had been her mother's. She considered hosiery, checked the colors of lipsticks and eyeshadow, all the while pacing from room to room.

At last she sat down on her bed and put her face in her hands. She wept for a moment, then took a deep breath and calmed herself. Drank some water. Slowed down until clarity began to come.

Everything is different, she thought. *I don't know how to dress because I don't know who I am anymore. I don't know how to relate to Dad.* Then she spoke aloud. "Maybe this is what it's like to grow up. Why should I be so bound by what he wants from me?" She said the words aloud to let them sink in.

She scanned her bed, now covered with skirts, blouses, dresses, shoes. The urgency of moments ago was gone.

"I need a new perspective," she said, and to emphasize the point to herself, she went out the kitchen door and down the sloping lawn to the dock and boat house. At the end of the dock she turned and considered the house, looking at it as if for the first time. The little kitchen window. The carport. Oak and pine trees shading all. "I've got plans to make," she said.

She went back inside and chose a pair of newer tight-fitting jeans. She picked out a turquoise western-style blouse with mother-of-pearl snaps and a burgundy bandanna at her neck. Her long blonde hair would occasionally reveal the Hopi-inspired silver earrings. For the first time ever, she wished she had cowboy boots, but a nice pair of heels would do just fine. This was probably less formal than what her dad had in mind, but she knew she'd turn heads. She was in the mood to turn heads. Especially her own.

She stepped in front of the full-length mirror again and looked at it backward over her shoulder. "Howdy y'all," she laughed. Then she laughed some more. "I ain't really from around here, and I ain't stayin' long neither. Y'all just appreciate my nice looking butt while ye can."

It was obvious from the parking lot that Johnny Casey's was an upscale restaurant. The pavement was clean and the cars parked upon it were nothing but the best. Cadillacs and Lincolns, shiny and black. One yellow Corvette stood out like a canary in a flock of ravens.

When they reached the front door of Jonny Casey's, Gwynn's father reached out to open it, but it opened itself before he touched it. A rush of cool air scented with cayenne and seafood swept around them. Before their eyes could adjust to the indoor light, a mature woman's voice welcomed them with, "Y'all come right on in. Will it be just the two of you?"

"Yes. A reservation for Robert Callahan."

"Oh yes. Your table is ready, Mr. Callahan. Right this way."

They followed the elegantly-dressed black woman past a cloakroom in which Gwynn noted a dozen or so very clean cowboy hats in hues from black to white with one purple one standing out. They were led to a window table and seated in upholstered chairs. The linen napkins were embroidered with red crayfish, and the silverware was gleaming and heavy. In the garden outside, carp and catfish circled a fountain in resplendent promenade. The waitress handed them menus of faux leather. They were picture books with marbled end sheets, and most of the listings featured words in French.

"We have some wonderful appetizers this evening. Is there something I can start y'all off with?"

"Two gin and tonics," Robert said.

"Uh, I'll choose a wine," Gwynn interjected. "What do you suggest with frog legs? I presume that they're on the menu." Her father's eyes widened in surprise.

"Indeed they are, and any red wine will suit so long as it's not too sweet. We have an excellent five-year-old Cella Lambrusco that I can recommend."

It was Gwynn's turn for a raised eyebrow, but she said nothing except to order the frog legs and the wine.

The waitress, either mis-apprehending or ignoring Gwynn's intent, took both orders: gin and tonic for Mr. Callahan and a full bottle of Lambrusco for his escort.

"I'll have those right out along with dinner rolls. They're just coming out of the oven."

A short time later Robert was into his second G&T. Gwynn sipped her wine. Little frog bones were piled on a pale blue dish between them. There was a lull in their small talk.

Robert held his drink at eye level and looked into its bright refractions. "What prompted you to choose frog legs? You were pretty quick with that."

"Curiosity, I guess. There's a kid who's started coming out to the Streamliner fairly often for breakfast. I once asked him how his car got so muddy in this dry weather. He said he'd been frog gigging. People do that I guess."

"Does he eat them?"

"He says he does."

"You like him?"

Gwynn put her hands down on the table and leaned back. "Dad! I told you. He's a kid. He's a bit young."

"Sure. 'A bit young.' You meet somebody you don't like, you don't say 'He's a bit young'."

Gwynn laughed. "Okay. Yeah. He's a sweet kid. Naive as hell. But he asks a lot of questions." A momentary faraway look came over her. She leaned forward again. "He even asked me one time if I believed in God. Can you imagine that?"

"Yeah, I get that a lot. The first question people around here ask is 'What church do you go to?' People wanting to convert me I guess. Was that what he was doing? Trying to convert you?"

"No, I don't think so. I think it was more like he was trying to decide something. Interested in another point of view. The only thing he's tried to convert me about was frog legs. Now at least I can say I've tried them."

Robert chuckled. "Yep. I can tell: you like him, young or not."

"Daddy, quit it! My love life, if and when I ever have another one, is none of your business until I decide it is."

"Okay, okay. I'm sorry. I'd just like you to be happy. Meet somebody. You just don't meet the right kind of people at that Streamliner place. You could get a better job if you were to try. If it's waitressing you're into, and I doubt that it is, this woman serving us here makes a damn sight more money than you do out there on that God-forsaken highway to nowhere."

"The people are interesting."

"Yeah, I just bet they are. Roustabouts and shit-kickers. Occasional truck driver. You meet them all out there. I just don't understand why you won't take a position at Eastman Kodak. I could make it happen. You could have a good career there."

Gwynn bristled. "What you want is for me to marry one of

these string-tied Texans and start having grandchildren. Move into a five-bedroom house a block from yours."

"No, no I …"

"Yes you do! It comes out every time we talk. Every time you have more than two drinks. And it doesn't matter how many times I tell you. I'll be happy when I go back to Berkeley and finish my degree. And, by the way, I'm switching from home economics to pre-law. I'm getting clearer about what I want to do. I've just needed this time." Her voice caught. "Just some time, you know. Since Mom …"

"Yes. I know." He reached for her hand. "And I'm glad you were willing to come here. I like having you nearby, even if we don't see each other that much."

They were quiet for a few minutes. The waitress came to check on them and went away.

"Our family is a wreck right now. Mom gone. Stephen in Germany. Grandma Rose is the only one still in place."

"Have you heard from Stephen lately? I know he writes to you."

"Not for a while. But there is something that you may not know. Stephen is actually considering giving up his military career. He's serious. There's a good chance that, when this tour is up, he'll be getting out. He's been very lucky so far. He's talking about going back to college for a business degree. And, Dad. We're both talking about rooming at Grandma Rose's. He and I can at least be family again, whatever that will mean. We … Maybe someday you'll come back too."

Robert sat staring straight ahead, tight-lipped. "I never thought you, of all people, would be so ungrateful," he said evenly.

Gwynn fixed her gaze on him. "Ungrateful?"

"Yes, Gwynn. Ungrateful. After all I've done for you here. Paying your expenses to move. Giving you that house at the lake to live in for FREE!"

Gwynn was stunned. She suddenly yearned for her mother in a way that she had not recently done. She longed for the way her mother could always shine a precise light on vague circumstances. Gwynn was afraid of her own rising anger, that it might rob her of logic and self-control. She felt unsafe to allow herself to feel as betrayed as she actually felt.

She slid her chair back from the table and leveled her eyes at her father. Her voice trembled when she said, "Dad, let me refresh your memory. This whole Texas thing was entirely your doing. You didn't discuss it with me, Stephen or anybody else that I know of. I dropped out of school when Mom got sick. I helped you and Mom as much as I could, and I'm glad I did that. After she died and you took this job, I came with you because it was what you wanted. I went back to California for you and sold our Berkeley house. OUR HOUSE! It was my home too. You insisted that I come here, and in truth I needed a break, but I could have stayed with Grandma Rose. In fact she would have appreciated it, but I thought you needed me more.

"But that morning when I was making breakfast for the two of us, and it turned out to be three. When that...that woman came out of your bedroom, NO. Don't interrupt me. I don't even WANT to remember her name. That was the last straw, and I told you so. THAT'S when you got the house at the lake. It was your way of keeping me around for you to call on whenever you don't have a date. A better offer."

Gwynn paused. "Daddy, you've chosen to come here for your own reasons. You grew up here. I get it. But I'm going back to California for mine. I'll stay with Grandma Rose with or without Stephen and finish my degree and build my life. But it won't be here in Texas."

"Grandma Rose, Grandma Rose, Grandma Rose," he blurted. "She never did think I was good enough for her precious daughter." He was becoming much too loud. "Precious, precious, precious. Nothing's good enough for Preh-shuss," he sang to the room. "Now she's put'n these high-um-mighty plans …" He waved his open hands on either side of his head and fell silent.

Tears formed in Gwynn's eyes, and she wiped them with her napkin. "Daddy stop. Please. You've already had too much to drink."

Their entrees arrived at that moment. The waitress was professional and gave no indication that she saw anything amiss. Gwynn and Robert straightened themselves and gave every possible indication that everything was fine.

"I believe you, Sir, ordered the T-bone rare and the lobster, and for you, madam, the catfish." As per policy but against her better judgment, she added, "How are your drinks? Are you ready for another, Sir?"

"Yes, thank you," he said for the room to hear.

"Shall I pour for you, ma'am?"

"No thank you."

The waitress placed their food in front of them and left. Gwynn excused herself from the table and went to the ladies' room. She looked at herself in the mirror and remembered how she'd felt just a few hours before. How she'd primped and meticulously chosen what to wear. It all seemed so pointless now. Pointless to even be in this strange part of the world. She tended to her make-up, took a deep breath and returned to the dining room.

The two of them ate perfunctorily, hardly speaking. Robert, when he did speak, was slurring noticeably. Mid-meal he ordered another drink. At that, Gwynn excused herself again, went to the maître d', and asked her to call a cab, and to please just quietly signal her when it arrived.

Some minutes later, she saw the cab pass by the window.

Then the maître d's signal.

"Dad," she said. "You've had too much …"

"Wha' jew mean, I …"

"Hush. Just listen. You need to go straight home from here. My cab is outside. I'm going now. We'll talk when you're sober."

Before he could respond, she stood and walked briskly toward the front door. "GWYNN," she heard him shout. She was inside the cab before the cabbie could get out to open the door for her.

"Go," she said. "That way. I'll give you directions." She didn't look back.

Chapter 21
Night Shift

Pete hadn't counted on having to work nights when he took this job, and he couldn't say he liked it. *Men love darkness rather than light because their deeds are evil*, kept cycling through his mind. He was a world away from anything he could have imagined. In daylight, before the plant started up, it was simply a rusted and run-down conglomeration of tanks, pipes and pumps. In the dark under the burden of actual production, it was nine acres of Hell's back campus. Lights were few, and where they were present, they served mostly to blind the eyes. The roar of the still in the middle of the place overpowered sanity.

The still was the centerpiece of the whole operation. It stood next to the pit like a rusting church of Satan, a towering volume of flame enclosed in steel, foreshadowing a dreaded Hell to come. It burned and purified oilfield sludge and contamination. A steam-powered peristalsis pushed the black slop through intestines of 4-inch schedule 40 pipe, back and forth through the flame.

Don't you touch anything about the still, Griz had said. *You don't know enough to do it any good, so leave it alone. If the charge pump quits, tell Swat. If it springs a leak in there, shut off the gas and run like hell. Naw,* he'd added. *Forget the gas. Just run like hell.*

The pit was an unpaved gouge in the ground the size of a large swimming pool. At odd hours of the night, semi tanker trucks crawled off the road and over the cattle guard into the plant where they circled and backed up to the hole to disgorge their petroleum dregs. When those deliveries arrived, Pete stood in the fumes and collected samples from the outflow of the truck and signed the bill of lading. That was as close to the still as he cared to get. He could feel the heat of it against his skin and the roar of it in his chest.

The separator stood at what was considered to be a safe distance from the still. It was eight feet in diameter and thirty feet tall. It injected chemicals, which no man there could pronounce, to remove salt water and a jelly-like kerosene they called "tops." This was pumped to the tops tanks to wait for dark when, away from the eyes of the Railroad Commission, it was let loose into the creek.

Steam-heated pipes kept the black wax liquified into the finish tanks. At intervals these tanks were pumped into railroad cars, which then rolled in and out on the siding that paralleled the plant entrance. The cars sat there now with their steam umbilicals spewing in the dark, ponderous and dripping on the creosoted ties. Nearly everything at the plant that wasn't black with a patina of wax, was red with rust.

Throughout the plant and at random intervals, wafts of leaking steam drifted through the night like sheeted ghosts. Leaking steam, above ground and below, gave evidence of the general shoddiness of everything. Various pumps, their valves and packings in all states of patched-together disrepair, strained at their work.

A stone's throw from the still, across a span of black-soiled purgatory, was the boiler house, a low and rusted structure of corrugated steel, built years ago by no man competent in his trade. Inside this building three boilers, horizontal cylinders as tall as elephants and twice as long, screamed like jet engines. The steam was kept near a targeted 307 degrees Fahrenheit; 60 psi. The pressure pushed outward from there in all directions, through rattling and hissing pipes, powering everything that moved or breathed in that toxic and combustible world.

On his first night shift Pete crossed the cattle guard at the plant entrance and assumed an unearned air of competence. Heck was in the office getting ready to leave. As soon as Pete walked in, Heck grabbed his lunch pail and headed for the door. "She's all yours," he said, and he got into his car and drove out. It was the first time Pete had ever had mixed feelings about seeing Hector go away. He was alone out here with Swat.

Swat didn't say much. He was quiet in the way of someone who carries more wisdom than he could possibly explain to a fool. Much of the time he seemed to be thinking about something somewhere off in the distance. He did his work. In fact he made it a little too easy for Pete. He also surreptitiously watched. When Pete adjusted the water input on a boiler, Swat followed not long after, to have a look for himself. When Pete climbed a ladder on the side of a railroad car, Swat was somewhere nearby casting sidelong glances. After a while it became unnerving.

Toward the end of his first week Pete was in the boiler house, which was illuminated by a single 60-watt bulb dangling from the ceiling. He stood at the firebox of boiler no. 1, his face close to the sight glass, intent on it as if divining absolute truth from ambiguous scripture. He could not see the water level line in the tube, which meant one of two possible things. The boiler could be seriously low of water, in which case pumping in more cold water could cause the boiler to crack and explode from the thermal shock. Or the boiler could be so full of water that it was in danger of losing useful pressure, which would drag the operation of the plant down. In such a case the movement of product through the still would slow to a dangerous point. The fire in the still would have to be brought down to avoid an explosion there. At his feet the charge pump dragged its opposing pistons, doggedly forcing water into the boiler, one hissing stroke at a time. The fire box below threw a flame the size of a Volkswagen into the boiler's innards.

Looking carefully at the light refracted through the tube, Pete determined, he hoped correctly, that the glass was full of water rather than empty. To be safe, insofar as safety could be had, he turned down the gas to reduce the flame, and with a gloved hand he turned the pump's steam supply valve a minuscule five degrees to the right to slow down the action. Then he stepped to his right and turned sideways so as to move crabwise between the two boilers, thereby reaching the blow-off valve at the back. He found the valve lever at the bottom rear and put his foot on it and shoved it down.

The building was instantly infused with oily vapor, a fog that made it impossible to see his own hands. Scalding excess water roared out the back of the boiler, shot through a gap in the siding provided for such purpose, and flew out into the dark. Pete wondered. If he had been wrong about the sight glass, would he have lived to hear the commotion?

After a considered moment he felt for the lever and tugged it back up. Then he made his blind way back to the sight glass and waited there for the fog to clear. He was careful to touch nothing with his bare skin. Touching the boiler or a steam line would instantly make a blister. He, and everyone else who worked there, carried such blisters in various states of healing on their elbows and forearms and faces. In the fog he brought his eyes so close to the glass that he risked touching it. He found the water line, visible now, but still high. He slowed the pump with another quarter turn of the valve, opened the gas valve to the firebox and felt his way to the door and out into the night. "I'll get the hang of it," he said to himself.

He took off his gloves and looked up where the stars wheeled their determined path, reticent to reveal any true locus of Heaven. Hell on the other hand was everywhere illustrated. Working seven days a week meant missing a lot of church, which he didn't mind. What church or preacher or prayer could more exactly stand proxy to his religion than the dangerous and uncertain ground where he stood?

It was two-twenty a.m., lunchtime on graveyard shift. He crossed the truck turnaround to look for Swat. He found him standing at the blow barrel, a 55-gallon drum standing on end on cinder blocks, open at the top and filled with water. A hose connected at the bottom blew steam that hammered wildly as the bubbles slapped to nothing in the cold water. The plant's laundry was Swat's regular chore. He was dumping great clumps of Tide into the cauldron. A heap of all shifts' work clothes, crusty with wax and dirt, lay at his feet like some Devonian beast dragged up with the crude.

Pete shouted above the racket to get Swat's attention. When Swat turned, Pete made plate and fork motions to signal "lunch."

Swat responded with a lifted chin. Which can be a complicated gesture.

Pete turned and walked toward the office, considering. Between good friends a lifted chin indicates an affirmation or conspiratorial mood. Delivered with a smile, it's a light-hearted agreement. Between strangers it can be slightly adversarial unless accompanied with a smile. Between adversaries it's an open acknowledgement of the adversity, particularly if one lifts the chin and then looks away with no smile, offering no further engagement.

So far, Pete and Swat had spoken only when necessary. There wasn't much that needed to be said. But Swat's lifted chin troubled him.

Pete was first into the office. He was supposed to be first. He got his lunch out of the refrigerator and sat in the chair at the desk. The lone reason to eat in the office was that it had an air conditioner. Other than that it was dim, cramped and cluttered.

Swat came in carrying his lunch, causing Pete to wonder if, as a Negro, he was allowed to put his lunch in the fridge with white men's lunches. Swat sat on the folding chair. As the two men ate, silence was third party to the room. The air conditioner rattled in the window.

Pete chewed his sandwich and sipped his coffee. He considered what boss-like thing he could say. "You gonna get all that laundry in one load?" It was a useless question. It made no difference whether it took one load or ten. With the plant running at full production there was always laundry to do.

"I expect," Swat said.

Swat finished eating and left the office first, which as a black man, he was obliged to do.

Pete turned to the east window and, in the way that a man lost at sea might look toward land that isn't there, he looked for signs of dawn. He wanted to go home and to bed. Instead, he went back to the boiler house to check the sight glasses and pressure gauges. Number one was getting a little low, so he increased steam to the charge pump. Boilers two and three were little changed.

Over the next ten days Pete became more accustomed to being awake all night and sleeping during the day. Brother Broussard called him and said he'd bought himself a new air conditioner and that Pete could have the old one for five dollars. He could pay it out of his next paycheck. Pete bought it and took it home and wrestled it into his bedroom window. Having it there made it much easier to sleep through the heat of the day.

Griz came out to the plant early that payday morning to give Pete and Swat their checks as they got off shift. Pete accepted his envelope and took it out to the Plymouth before ripping it open. He sorted the check from the stub and looked at the total. His first paycheck from the plant was only for the last three days in that pay period. He'd taken that check home and showed it to his mother, who was thrilled. He'd opened his own bank account and deposited ten dollars, keeping the rest to buy gas and pay Brother Deckert back for the work boots. Two weeks later he got another check, this time for eighty hours. After taxes he had just over a hundred and twenty dollars. But now that the plant was running, he was drawing night shift premium at operator scale while working seven nights a week. That was a hundred and twelve hours plus overtime for the weekend shifts at a full dollar and a quarter above minimum wage. His paycheck rivaled those of his dad. He sat with the check in his hand. The bank wouldn't be open for another two hours.

His mother was up and getting ready for work when he got home. She walked into the kitchen in her robe, looked at him and said, "What are you grinning about this early in the morning?"

"Oh, nothing," he said. He felt protective and private about his new affluence. "What time does the bank open?"

"Nine o'clock, why? Did you get paid?"

"Yes, Ma'am. Every two weeks."

"How much was it? Let me see," she said. "Where's the check."

"I left it out in the car," he lied and hoped that the envelope wasn't showing in his back pocket.

"Well, how much was it?"

"I forgot."

Lavena decided not to push it further. "Well, you owe me that twenty I gave you for gas. You'd better save the rest."

"Yes, Ma'am," he said, disappointed at the boredom of such a prospect.

After Lavena left for work Pete went to shower in the utility room. It was a room his dad had added onto the house and where he shed his dirty clothes and cleaned up after work. It was Pete's to use now.

Pete undressed and took a bar of soap from the bathroom. In the shower another bar sat untouched and dried out in the soap dish: the last one his father had used. Pete couldn't bring himself to use that one. He wondered if it was crazy for him to want to preserve it? Pete did sometimes think that he must be crazy. He would certainly tell no one about the soap.

When he'd showered he put on fresh clothes and drove to the bank. He got there before it opened and had to wait for nearly ten minutes. He sat in the car watching people come and go. The druggist walked past, keys in hand, and opened up the Rexall and disappeared inside. The lights came on.

There followed a sight that made the hair on his neck stand up. It was Beauford Antwiler, that no-good creep, going into the pharmacy. He was jerking along a girl of about eight, one of his own kids. The girl had bruises on her skinny legs, and she lurched behind her father, looking sad and fearful.

Pete's vision turned yellow. His heart raced and his breath came in shuddering gulps. "WHY!" he sputtered. He caught himself and said more quietly, "Why is that asshole alive, and my daddy's dead?" Then he glanced around, hoping nobody had heard him and that nobody saw him now, weeping in his car. Or heard him say "asshole."

On his next shift at the plant at about one-thirty in the morning, Pete was coming down from the tops tanks when he heard the blast of an air horn. He looked out toward the road to see a truck slowing toward the plant entrance. Actually he couldn't see the truck at all, but the red and amber running lights brightened the night like a horizontal Christmas tree. The tractor pivoted onto the cattle guard and rumbled across, drawing its tanker trailer behind. Pete walked out to the black pit and stood there while the rig circled and stopped. A set of bright spotlights on the back of the tractor came on shining toward the rear. After much grinding of gears the rig backed up to the pit and stopped where Pete stood. The driver climbed down from the cab, papers in hand.

"Another beautiful night the Lord hath made," the driver said, advancing toward Pete. Then he stopped abruptly. "Where's Loper? He's usually the one that signs on nights."

"Loper had a heart attack. I'm taking his place."

"When was that?" he asked in astonishment.

"Weeks ago. I guess you didn't hear about it."

"Well." He gave Pete an appraising look. "Ain't you a young'un. You ain't twenty-one yet, are you? Naw. Eighteen, though, I bet. I strictly stick to the law. It ain't nothing personal. Strictly stick to the law. Mostly. Besides, young'uns cain't keep their mouth shut."

Pete stood slack-jawed trying to make sense of the man, who had already turned back to the cab of his truck.

"Cindy," he hollered through the open door. "You can stay in the truck. Loper ain't here."

There was the faint sound of a female voice saying something back.

"Naw, he's dead. Heart attack." He turned toward Pete. "He's dead ain't he? Loper?"

Pete shrugged and started to speak.

"Okay, maybe not dead, but he ain't here. So you can just stay in the truck. But hand me that … naw, the other one. I said the OTHER one. Yeah." He tiptoed reaching into the cab and came down with a white envelope, which he stuffed into the back pocket of his overalls.

"Business first, that's what I always say. Let's dump this shit in the pit. Hey, that rhymes. Shit in the pit. Poet and don't know it."

Pete climbed to the top hatch of the tanker, the driver attached an extension hose to the spout at the back of the trailer. When Pete had verified that the tanker was a full one, he shouted down, "OKAY."

The driver pulled the lever on the gate valve and a six-inch stream of heavy black liquid shot out horizontally and splashed into the pit.

"Back in a minute," Pete said. He walked around front of the truck and headed to the lab for sampling vials. When he came back, he did as Swat had instructed. He clamped the vial into a foot-long handle and held it to the stream. If there was water in the load, it would be at the bottom. He gently collected a sample for analysis in the lab while the splatter of petroleum sludge soaked into cuffs of his coveralls and coated his rubber glove.

"It's a honest load," the driver said. "You get what you pay for." He nudged Pete with his elbow, "And there ain't nothin' you cain't git if you're willin' to pay for it."

Pete just nodded. He brought the full vial into his own grip, wiped it with a rag and put a rubber stopper in it.

The two of them stood there next to the semi. It would

take close to an hour for the trailer to empty.

"Magazines?" the driver said.

"What?"

"Do you want any magazines? They're used, but still pretty damn good if you get my drift. Big discount."

"No. I gotta go. Give a honk when it's empty."

"Don't want none? Young boy like you. You ain't some kind of homo, are ye? You don't look like no homo."

"I gotta go," he said.

Pete glanced up toward the cab when he came around the front of the rig, but the woman, Cindy, was nowhere to be seen. Could have been in the sleeper.

The nearer it came to quitting time, the more Pete felt the cash in his pocket. Almost radioactive. Possibilities swam through his head. He could buy a box of bullets and go to the river, except he'd have to go home for his .22. Late in his shift as the dark began to fade toward light, his mettle started to rise. The prospect of going home began to feel to him like a jail sentence, though he'd feel guilty not to be there for his mother. He knew that he should be more available and accommodating to her since the death of his dad. But the more clinging and controlling she became, the more he wanted to get away from her.

When the idea of going to the Streamliner for breakfast first occurred to him, it rang in his head like a bell. He had the money. He had the time. If he ate at the cafe, his mother would be gone to work by the time he got home. The prospect of a mere "Good morning" from the waitress, Gwynn was her name, thrilled him.

On a pretext he went into the office just before the day shift workers arrived. He was almost trembling when he picked up the phone and dialed.

"Hello?"

"Hi, Mother. It's me."

"What?"

"Griz needs me to stay another couple of hours. One of the day shift people won't be here until later. So I won't be home for breakfast."

"Oh. Okay. But won't you get hungry? I could wrap up some toast and sausages and drop it by on my way in."

"No. Uh, Griz is bringing some doughnuts, he said he was. That'll hold me over."

"Where's Griz getting doughnuts? Surely he's not driving to Longview!"

"I don't know. Maybe they're left from when he was there, or something. I don't know. So anyway, you don't need to make me anything." Pete wished he'd said that Griz was bringing biscuits and sausage. Leftover cornbread. Anything.

"Who is it that's not coming in? Why aren't they coming on time?"

"Uh, Hector I think. A doctor's appointment I guess. Does it matter? Griz wants me to stay."

"The doctor's office doesn't open until nine. Is Griz there now?"

"NO! I mean, no. He phoned a while ago."

"What did he say when he phoned?"

"I have to go, Mom."

"I hope this doesn't happen a lot."

"I have to go."

"You need to sleep."

"Bye, Mom."

"Okay. I'll see you at supper. Be sure to get some sleep."

"Bye."

By the time Pete hung up the phone his whole body wanted to run. He wanted to run and run and run until—until what, he couldn't say. Just run.

Chapter 22
Joy in the Morning

Gwynn didn't know what it was that woke her. The bark of a dog somewhere across the lake. An owl, a raccoon or maybe a possum at the trash bin. She didn't hear anything now. Perhaps it was her own unremarkable dream of someone, she didn't know who, was trying to parallel park a very long car on a crooked curb. No matter. She shifted under the cover and readjusted her pillow. Pulled up the sheet to cover her exposed ear. She waited for sleep that seemed to wander the room, not quite landing anywhere.

She usually avoided looking at the clock, but this time she yielded to the impulse. It was 4:47.

With a weak groan she pulled the sheet over her head and turned onto her side with one hand under her head and the other between her thighs. The bed felt good.

A small breeze rattled the oak leaves outside the window, and a light pop from something, probably an acorn, hit the roof and rolled down. Gwynn sighed and uncovered her eyes to look toward the window. There might be light. No. It was too early.

Maybe she slept a little. Thoughts and half-thoughts mixed and matched. Nonsense and profundity, hilarity and sorrow, all half-formed and swirling on their own, without regard. Her college boyfriend swam by riding his motorcycle under water, looking straight ahead toward something she couldn't see.

She hadn't thought of him for quite some time. Thinking of him now gave her a brief pang, but she couldn't really say that she missed him anymore. When a thing like that is over before it begins, it's completely over. Gwynn thought it was surreal, the way a person could be falling in love, could anticipate a life that depended on that love, only to have it all vanish into … into what?

She drew her hand from her thigh to her belly and pressed it there. Drew a breath and pressed harder. It felt good to press hard against her own insides. To reach for a part of herself that only she could know.

There came a faint pink flash against the window. She was quite sure she'd seen it. A moment later a confirming roll of thunder far away. Far away. She lay there listening for the first birds, but there were none yet. Maybe she dozed again.

The breeze outside picked up. Through the open window it reached her face. The oak outside seemed to be coming awake with her. More acorns hit the roof and made their tiny drum roll toward the gutter. Another flash, closer this time, followed by a rattle of thunder, followed in turn by large, scattered rain drops. Gwynn got up to pull the window down, but changed her mind and opened it wider, the better to hear the wind.

She got back into bed and pulled her pillow into her arms, stroking it as she might stroke a lover.

She was awake now. No denying it. The whispers in the oak became urgent. The wind. The wind.

By then she knew what she was doing. She turned onto her back with both hands pressing her abdomen. Press and release. Press and release. She drew a hand up to lightly brush her breasts, and then back down. There was no hurry. Both hands swept the insides of her thighs.

She turned again to her side and reached down to her feet and massaged the soles. Spread the toes apart, moved up and squeezed her calves. Her breathing became slow and deep, at times in synch with the sighing of the trees. The smell of rain was in the air, and thunder rolled again. Her thighs of their own accord pressed against each other. She brushed her hair back from her neck and stroked below her ear and down to her breasts again. She touched a nipple the way one might touch a cake fresh from the oven to test its doneness.

Her pleasure became her purpose, her intelligence, her strength. She accepted without creed that pleasure could be as instructive as suffering. Pleasure became who she was, and she moved vigorously as if blown by wind. The rain came down hard and then harder yet. Torrents washed away all the dust and detritus, sorrow and dissembling from the roof and the leaves and her spirit. Sweet moisture of authenticity soaked into her skin and into the ground, nourishing the roots of resolve. Gwynn gasped, then shrieked with the power of it. The power she claimed for herself. "Yes," she breathed. "Yes."

Just as suddenly as the rain had come, it stopped. A sudden silence. Another momentary shower scampered over the roof and quickly died. Faded to nothing. Leaves dripping.

Gwynn lay for a moment, her breath slowing. Her heart climbing down from a mountain, amazed at the mystery that a human body could give such pleasure to itself. It was the only thing keeping her alive against the constraints of this place where she was stranded.

Chapter 23
White and Black

It was still only June, but Pete felt like he had been working nights for half of his life. In spite of the maintenance they'd done during the shutdown, the plant was a rickety mess of steam leaks, core-pipe leaks, loose-jointed steam pumps and rusty tanks. There were temporary clamps everywhere on pipes of all sizes. Even the pit was so full of its own sediment that it could hardly hold the load of the tanker trucks that filled it. At boiler no. 1 the push-rod packing of the charge pump was so worn down that water continuously spit onto the ground. Worse than that, a thousand feet away from the boiler house, there was so much blow-by around one of the cylinders of the finish pump that it forced out a spray of hot black paraffin on every back-stroke. When they were pumping finished product into a railroad car, it took a constant watch to keep the leaked wax from hardening on the reciprocating valve cams, causing the pump to stop completely and just sit there sputtering goo.

The temperature at night was in the 90s, and even hotter inside the buildings. Hottest was the boiler house. The only respite was in the office where the window-unit air conditioner ground up the heat as best it could. It was a relief to go there for lunch breaks, and just as much a relief to get away from the snarling grind when lunch was over.

Pete had just finished eating and left the office to put his belongings in his car. He had three railroad cars to fill with finished product before his shift was over at seven. The first one was already filled and capped, and he had a good start on the second.

To get the third one ready he hefted the three-foot crescent wrench and carried it at his waist, shot-gun style, out toward the tracks. He knew his way there in the dark, so the flashlight rocked loosely in his back pocket. At the car he felt his way to the ladder and climbed up with the 30-pound wrench in one hand. He gained his balance at the top, spread his feet over the curve and went to work loosening the eight top-hatch nuts. The bolts were as big as his thumb. He fitted the wrench to the nuts one by one and leaned into them as much as he dared. For lack of a good place to stand he could turn a nut only about a third of a turn before having to reposition the wrench. It was tedious and heavy small-step work, standing on the round top of the car. His ankles grew tired along with his forearms. Most of the nuts came up smoothly far enough that he could swing the bolt down off the dome cap, but some of them were rusted in place, or even worse, cross-threaded. The fifth nut on this car seemed to be just that. In any case he couldn't budge it. He tried bumping the wrench with his hip, careful of his balance lest it pop loose and send him flying. After four or five bumps it moved slightly. A few more bumps and he could swing the wrench with arm strength.

This being the third tank car of the night, Pete had already climbed up and down fifteen or twenty times. Up to open the hatch, grab the goose-neck rope and tie the pipe down at the dome. Down again to switch the pump from the previous car to this one. Blow out the line to the previous car with steam. Then climb the just-filled car to close the hatch, flip up the bolts and tighten the nuts. Down from that one and up the next to insure that the wax was flowing as it should. Climb again periodically to check on the progress, and when the car was near full, leave room to blow out the line without over-flowing and then on to the next car. He was starting to wear out.

The last top-hatch nut was worse than the previous one. He leaned against the wrench beyond all caution. He climbed down and brought back penetrating oil. He went again for the blowtorch and tried heating the nut to make it expand, all to no effect.

He balanced the wrench on the dome lid and gave his arms a rest. He felt his way back to the ladder, climbed down and marched back to the tool shed to find a cheater pipe. If he didn't get this car opened up soon, car no. 2 would be full, and he'd have to stop the pump. He needed somewhere to put the wax. The short line from the finish tank to the railroad cars had no steam core, so stopping the pump would mean having to blow out all the line with steam. It would make an already long night even longer.

In the tool shed he found a 4-foot length of 2½-inch pipe. He figured that it should give him enough leverage.

Back at the railroad car he one-handed his way up the ladder carrying the pipe, fitted the wrench onto the nut and slid the cheater over the handle. He gave it a shove. He could feel the wrench handle flex with the force of it. The nut didn't budge. Pete was getting annoyed.

He pulled the cheater off the wrench and pitched it out into the dark where it rang once and rolled. Back on the ground he found it with his flashlight and carried it back to the tool shed. He was developing an attitude. He searched the area where the pipe-threading equipment was set up. On the ground, oily steel shavings sparkled in the light, and some of them cut into his boot soles and stuck there in small clods. He searched until he found a seven-foot scrap of pipe, long enough, he figured, that something would have to give.

He couldn't climb carrying that pipe, so he leaned it against the side of the railroad car, climbed halfway and then worked it upward until he could hoist it up onto the car. Steadying it with his right hand, he finished the climb and stood there heaving and catching his breath.

He gripped the pipe at about its midpoint and slid it over the wrench handle. Hand over hand he worked his way to the opposite end and established tension against the nut. He pushed as hard as he dared, and it seemed to him there was a little give, though he didn't hear or feel anything pop loose. Since there was no footing to push further, he repositioned the wrench for the next push.

Two repositionings later, when the bolt twisted in two, it didn't happen suddenly. There was no snap. Just silent imperceptible separation. At first Pete thought that the nut was turning. But the bolt had finally broken, and the wrench was no longer anchored to the dome. The weight of the wrench slid off the dome, banged the top of the car and dropped off, dragging its end of the pipe off into the dark. At first Pete resisted. He tried to hold his end of the pipe and keep everything level, but the darkness was disorienting, and the leverage against him was too great. He felt the wrench fall, strike the top of the car and gain momentum, pivoting downward and behind him. The flashlight fell from the dome, spun away and went out.

Pete let go of the pipe as it swung down. A second later he heard it ring like a dull bell in the dark below. He fought to regain his balance and almost succeeded. But his left foot had stepped too far over the curve of the railroad car, and his center of gravity was somewhere in the air around him.

He spun and belly-flopped onto the steel dome with his arms stretched upwards, hugging the curve as best he could.

His feet hung uselessly. He slid slowly at first. The black grime was almost enough to stick him, but it would never give enough traction to climb. He clung with everything he had, including his face. As his descent accelerated he felt the warm oily grit transferring to his right jaw and cheek. Temple. Ear.

He landed on his feet, but his right ankle hit the edge of a cross tie and twisted. Throwing out his hands to break his fall, he hit the crushed rock with his palms. Finally, on his hands and knees, the damage done, Pete eased himself down and lay there for a moment taking stock of himself.

Then, partly out of defiance and partly out of denial, he stood up and went to the ladder and climbed back up. There was a slickness in his right palm, which he knew must be blood. Nevertheless, he opened the hatch, drew the gooseneck pipe to the dome and tied it down. He climbed down, limped to the pump and turned on the steam to blow out the line to the previous car. He switched the pump to fill the current one, and by then he knew it was time to face what had happened. The swelling and pain were just beginning.

Swat was in front of the headlights of the company pickup shoveling a ditch when he heard Pete's wrench and cheater hit the ground. He didn't know what it was, but he knew it didn't have the sound of a thing done on purpose. He stood for a moment but heard nothing more. He made to continue his work but stopped again, replaying the sound in his mind. He could see nothing in the direction it had come from. Not even a flashlight. He stomped his shovel upright in the ditch, grabbed a flashlight from the truck and walked toward the sound, sweeping the dark with his light. Against a waft of steam he caught the momentary silhouette of someone limping toward the tool shed. He tacked in that direction.

"Mister Pete, what done happen to you?"

"I tripped. I'm alright."

"Ain't you got no flashlight?"

"Prob'ly busted. I'll find it when it gets light."

Swat trained his light on Pete's torso and saw the thin line of blood drizzling from his fingers. "Hey, uh … Mister Pete. Let's go in the lab yonder and have a look at you. You walking funny and it looks like you might of sprung a leak or two."

"I'm alright."

Swat carefully calibrated his obsequious tone. "Just the same, let old Swat have a look. I'd be worried bad if I don't just get a look at you in the light."

"Okay. But first, you go take a look into car two. I just blew the line. If it's full enough you can batten the dome."

"All right. Yes, Sir. I'll do just that." He gave Pete another once-over, avoiding shining the light into Pete's face. "I'll be back directly."

Pete got to the lab ahead of Swat and went to the sink to start cleaning the battered skin of his hands. The bleeding had slowed to an ooze, but the cuts were full of oily grit. His right ankle no longer wanted to bear his weight.

Swat came in and first looked at Pete's hands since that was where he first saw blood. He rummaged in a cabinet for a moment and found a bottle of Johnson's Baby Oil. "Here," he said, turning to Pete. "Use this. It'll soften that grease so you can wipe it off. Then you can use soap and water." He looked at Pete's face and had to stifle a guffaw. He took a moment to control himself. He gained a sober expression and started to speak, but he burst out laughing instead. When he could breathe again he said, "I'm sorry, Mister Pete. But this side of your face is plumb black." He sputtered into laughter again and said, "Mister Pete, you ain't likely to ever again look so much like me as you do now.

"I'm sorry. I don't mean to laugh at you." He bit his lower lip and squeezed his eyes shut. "Here. Wrap this around your hand until we can get to it. What done happened to you?" He led Pete to a chair while Pete tried to explain what happened.

"First thing, Mister Pete. I'm gonna shine this light in your eyes just a bit." He quickly did so, checking Pete's iris response. "That's good. Now hold your head still and follow my finger with just your eyes." He drew a cross in the air. "Yes, good."

He pulled a low stool in front of Pete and sat on it facing him. "Let's get that boot off and check out your foot. Prop it right here." Swat unlaced the boot and gingerly pulled it off, watching Pete's face for signs of pain. "I believe you sprained that ankle. Draw me a circle with your big toe." He watched. "That ain't no circle. Try again."

"No," Pete said.

"Yeah, I wouldn't neither. It's already swelling and changing color. I'm gonna find something to wrap it with and then maybe get some ice. It's good we getting to this right away."

Swat took a roll of gauze from the first aid box and began wrapping Pete's foot and ankle. His movements were swift, sure and neat. Pete, meantime, worked with rags and mineral oil to get the grease off his face. The cuts on his hands were minor, but they were in a troublesome location.

When Swat finished wrapping the ankle and tied off the gauze, he said, "How 'bout your hands?"

"It's mostly just the right one. Skinned up mostly. But Swat, that car is still filling up, and it's been a while since I looked at it. You better go check on it. See how much time we got till we have to blow out the line."

Swat looked at his pocket watch. "Yep. I expect I better do that." He reached into the first aid box and drew out a brown bottle. "Here. Use this peroxide and let it clean out your hands. I'll go take care of the pump. Blow it out if necessary, or maybe just slow it down enough to let day shift get it."

Prentice Waters left the lab and worked his way through the dark while a feeling of dread bloomed in his chest. Vague at first, it took shape slowly. Like a hole in the ground dimly seen in weak light. It gained definition as he walked the footpath, flashlight in hand, toward the railroad cars. There were rules in the world that nobody had thought of yet, and Swat sensed that he had just violated one. If the rules were undefined, then so was the punishment for breaking them. He'd become too familiar with Pete. Isolated in this world away from the world, he'd trusted Pete too much too soon.

Words he'd heard as a child came back to him. *A white man may think he's your friend, but you got to know better. Another white man raise an eyebrow, and he'll drop you like a hot potato.*

"I'm a damn fool," he said aloud. Thoughts swarmed like bats in the dark. *I should have called Griz. What if Pete's got a concussion that hasn't presented yet? Maybe he ought to be checked out in the emergency room in Marshall or Longview. What was I thinking to even be touching a white man? You don't even shake hands unless the white man hold his out first. It don't matter if what I did was perfect. In fact perfect is worse. Damnit, in Korea I got to where I could tend a wound in a ditch or under a jeep or hanging upside down in a tree. Doing that here could get me hanging right-side-up.*

He trembled from adrenaline. His legs wanted to run. He was scared and angry. Angry at himself and angry that he felt so trapped. At the moment, though, he didn't have time to think or feel. In a few minutes he'd be back in the lab with Pete.

Pete was gingerly wiping his face with gauze and mineral oil when Swat came back in. "Everything alright out there?"

"I slowed the pump way down. It won't need checking again for another hour. Prob'ly Griz and them can wrap it up when they come in. I checked on the boilers too. How you faring?"

"Alright I guess. Kinda starting to hurt."

Swat drew two deep breaths and set his eyes on Pete. "I got to get that wrap off your foot. It might do more harm than good. I never should have done that."

Pete was perplexed. "Why? You did it perfectly. It looks like a doctor did it. I was going to ask where you learned …"

"Mister Pete, just prop your foot back up here on this stool so we can …"

"No. That doesn't make any sense."

"We should get you looked at by a real doctor. And I better get this stuff offa you before …"

"Before what?"

For a moment neither of them spoke. Pete watched Swat's face; his pinched eyes and clenched jaw. Realization seeped like blood into gauze.

"You don't want day shift knowing you can do that."

"Mister Pete, I …"

"Stop calling me 'Mister'. I'm just a kid. You don't have to call me 'Mister'. "

"Yes, I do. I might forget sometime when other folks is around. I cain't let nobody see I done this on your foot. It could make trouble for both of us. There's ways things have to be done, and messing around otherwise always gets somebody hurt. Now, I'm going to shut my goddamn mouth and undo this gauze. Then I'll tell you how to wrap it back yourself. The job's gonna look ugly, but that's the point. And if somebody says, 'who wrapped up your foot?' you can say you done it yourself, and it won't be no lie."

Though his hands were shaking, the man began to unwind

the gauze, turn by turn. It accumulated into a convoluted bundle in his hands, which, when it was entirely free, he handed over to Pete.

"Now. Git ahold of the end of it and with one hand hold it there and go around a couple of times right there, that-a-way. Not too tight just yet. Yeah. That's right. And Mister Pete. If nothing ever gets said about me having anything to do with this, then that's probably best for both of us."

"Like this?"

"No. The other way. Yeah, like that."

Engrossed, the two of them applied themselves to the care of that injured flesh while pale light, unnoticed, touched the east window.

Chapter 24
That Kind of White Boy

At a quarter to seven, before any day shift showed up, Pete hobbled out to his car and waited. When Griz arrived, Pete told him that he had to go home in a hurry. "Mama needs help moving a hair dryer in her shop," he said, all the while hoping that Griz didn't look too closely into the car and see his wrapped foot.

"Well, alright," Griz said. "I guess Swat can report on your shift. "Anything I need to know?"

"Naw. The railroad cars are ready to go except for the third one. It'll need to get the line blowed out before long."

"Alright. Go on, then."

Driving home Pete operated the gas pedal with his injured foot, but had to use his left foot for the brake. Pretty soon he got the hang of the clutch-neutral-brake routine whenever he had to stop. He made it home, hobbled in for breakfast and afterward, over his mother's objections, drove himself to Dr. Nicholson's office.

"You say you wrapped this yourself?" The doctor was cutting away Pete's gauze. "Pretty damn good for an amateur. Who showed you how to do that?"

"My daddy did," Pete lied. "He knew how, and he showed

me and Mama when he sprained his ankle one time."

"Humph. I reckon you're a right good learner."

"Thank you. Seems like there's always something to learn that you didn't expect," Pete said, more to himself than to the doctor.

"Well. With that attitude you'll go far. I predict that."

"Go far," Pete muttered to himself, wondering in what direction.

Pete left the doctor's office with a new wrap on his ankle, a crutch under his right arm, a small bottle of codeine tablets and instructions to stay off his feet for three or four days.

Mid-afternoon he called Griz at the plant and told him he'd sprained his ankle chasing a possum off the back porch. Griz told him to come on in to work. Swat could do everything that had to be done. But it was the law that he had to have at least two men on every shift. There couldn't be nobody out there by theirself.

The next few nights at the plant were excruciatingly boring. Pete spent most of those nights in a cobbled-together Adirondack chair next to the lab building. Swat ran an extension cord out a window and set up a task light so that Pete could read if he wanted to. But the light mostly attracted bugs, and the reading material was mostly trashy magazines brought from hiding around the plant. Pete was too shy and private for the porn, so he dozed some and hobbled around some and gazed up at the stars a lot. By daylight after the third night he was almost frantic for something interesting to do, and the most interesting thing he could think of was breakfast at the Streamliner, a place he'd become very fond of.

He almost trembled with anticipation as he made his one-legged drive out to the highway. He looked forward to the waffles, hash browns and bacon, hopefully served by that sweet looking waitress, whose name was a constant echo in his mind. He might even get a little extra attention for coming in on a crutch, which he did, as it turned out.

A week or so into July Pete woke up to a peculiar orange light in the bedroom. His first thought was that the house was on fire. He opened his eyes and, seeing that it was not, closed them again. He tried to stay with his dream. An arousing and disturbing dream of clear skin and yellow hair, offering sensuous pleasures yet fraught with obstacles of shame. In it the Streamliner sat motionless without wheels on a railroad track while he, standing on the cross-ties, receded backwards into a dark and ominous distance as if drawn away by a great locomotive of suction.

He roused himself, leaned from the bed, lifted a slat in the venetian blinds and looked out, measuring the changes in the weather. Sunlight from the west made garish refractions through a cloud bank. Everything that should look green, the trees, the grass, looked the color of apricots. He ambled to the air conditioner and turned it off and opened the other two windows in the room. The breeze blew in the smell of coming rain. He might have heard thunder.

He pulled on his trousers and walked stiffly into the kitchen. The house was empty and quiet, and Lavena was not yet home, which meant it must be Thursday. She kept later hours in the beauty shop on Thursdays. On the kitchen counter he found the instructions she'd left him for supper. There were thick slices of ham to fry, and leftover cornbread and pinto beans to heat up. Simple enough. He walked shirtless out onto the back porch and sat on the steps to contemplate the sky. The strange colored oaks and pines swayed and whispered. He looked at his healing hands, front and back, as if he'd never seen them before, taking a small pleasure in his own disorientation. It could be any time of day, any day of the week. His own body could be his, or it could belong to someone else. Someone he didn't know. He didn't want the feeling to go away.

He'd been on his best behavior lately, at least as far as Lavena knew. What she didn't know was how often he went to the Streamliner, and why. She also didn't know about his growing respect for a Negro man. Having his preoccupation with Gwynn and his job at the plant, he needed no further declaration of independence. At least not yet.

By the time Lavena got home he had the table set and iced tea brewing. The leftovers were steaming, and the ham was in the pan. In moments they were at the kitchen table talking about the weather, although what was most on their minds was the absence of John Loucas. The two of them were joined in their longing for him, though neither of them mentioned it. Each imagined that they were protecting the feelings of the other.

At ten-thirty Pete went out the back door into the dark with his lunch pail in his hand. Pink flashes and low rumbles of thunder rode the breeze. The hope of rain was still only that. Just a hope. It was a sky straining to burst, but it could not.

He drove past houses, some with lights on, some without, imagining the people inside. He felt a dreadful longing. There would be husbands and wives in their beds waiting to hear the first heavy drops of rain. There would be children asleep, or not, secure with their parents in the house, the world arranged as it should be. He wished to be such a child.

When he got to the plant, the swing shift men were ready to leave. The foreman gave Pete his briefing. Tops tank no. 1 was filling and would need to be switched before long. He went out to his car and drove away, pulling dust into the air behind him. Pete looked out the office window and watched it swirl around the receding tail lights.

Swat was already there and repacking the stem of a gate valve. Pete took his clipboard to the lab and picked up a rag off the work bench. With a flashlight in his back pocket and a steel tape reel in his hand, he headed down the path to the tops tanks to take his own measurement. As he climbed the steel stair, he stomped the treads just to hear them ring. When he'd gained the catwalk, he stood there, 25 feet above the ground, and surveyed the dark world. The catwalk spanned the battery of tanks, leading from one top-hatch to the next. From that vantage Pete could see most of the town of Sabine Gap, and even beyond it to large stretches of the flat East Texas night. Looking southeast toward the Gulf he could see pink veins of lightning shooting through folds of a low cloud bank. He watched, listening for the music of thunder. He thought again of Gwynn. She'd be in her bed now. Gazing in the approximate direction of Cherokee Lake, he raised an arm and pointed across the world between them, trying to guess her exact direction, but his arm was a poor compass. He wished she could see him there on the tanks, in the wind, in the dark. He imagined himself heroic, doing a man's work in the night.

Trees swayed over the far-away streetlights of Tin Cup and Sabine Gap, making a Morse code effect. If he knew the code they might tell him something.

He opened the hatch of the first tank, turned on the flashlight and propped it to shine toward his hands. He held the dangling weight of the steel tape over the hatch and let it drop. It didn't take long to hear the echoing splash when it hit the slop. When the reel went slack, he began winding it back up, watching for the wet line to come up out of the dark. When he saw it, he held the tape directly in the flashlight beam and squinted at the numbers. He wrote them down and checked his watch: 11:45 p.m. He folded the rag around the tape and reeled it in, cleaning it as it came up.

With no. 1 being only about two-thirds full, he'd normally make the switch at about one-thirty. He had the option to switch now. It might save him having to do it in the rain later on. But that would also mean that he'd have to switch back to no. 1 and finish it off. Since there was no sure thing, he left the tops running as he'd found it. He'd come back in an hour, rain or not.

He considered the lightning. Statistically a tank gets hit by lightning only a few times a year. In most of those strikes there's no explosion, and the tanks just burn in place. But when explosions did occur, they were the talk of the county. Everyone in that part of Texas had driven out into the oilfield to watch such a fire, or to gawk at the aftermath of a blast.

Pete lingered up there, thinking back thirteen years to when he was five. He'd been asleep in his bed when he was awakened by a boom that shook the walls. Orange light pulsed through the windows and made the world appear to vibrate. His mother swept him up from the bed before he'd had time to be afraid. She carried him to the living room where his father stood watching out the front door window. The light made all the world look afire. His father took him and held him up to the window where he could see the road in front of the house, the grass all around, and further back, the roiling cloud of smoke shooting up from the earth. Everything was lit with the same glare, and the vibrating atmosphere pulsed in his chest. Heat pressed into the house through the door and windows. Fire trucks and men with large helmets and big water hoses gestured and shouted. One of the two oil tanks, the tanks that had always been there just like the road had always been there, lay crumpled outside of its fire dike, twisted and smoking in the dark. The other tank stood in its own place inside the dike, surrounded by flame. It appeared and disappeared in the thick smoke. Ever since that night it was the vision that come to mind whenever the preacher spoke of Hell.

Pete shook himself back to the present. He reminded himself that lightning always strikes elsewhere. Except when it doesn't.

Standing there looking over the sleeping town, wearing a man's work clothes, doing a man's job, Pete had a sense of childhood being a thing of the past. Like he'd never felt it before, he sensed himself to be an adult with adult ideas and concerns. It both pleased and frightened him. He knew that nothing would ever be as it had been when his dad was alive. He saw two imminent possibilities. He could start college in the fall, or he could be drafted into the Army. There was little in between for able-bodied males his age. He had doubts about his academic strength for college. High school hadn't ended well. As for the military, he thought of his father who had been a D-Day paratrooper. He doubted just as much that he would have that kind of courage.

The weather was changing fast. By the time he got back to the office the freshness of the cool front hit his face like a soothing wash. So welcome after the weeks of heat. The thunder was close enough that he could hear it. Like God's own breathing.

He went inside and recorded his notes before going down to the boiler house, where he checked the gauges and sight glasses. The steam pressure was slightly down in boiler no. 2, though not significantly. He reduced the steam to the charge pump to lower the water and turned up the gas to increase the flame. All this according to his blind reckoning.

At the leeward side of the lab, he found Swat seated on

a cobbled-together stool, scraping pipe threads with a wire brush. Pete positioned himself so that no light shone directly on his face, the better to observe the sky, and he saw no stars at all. A cloud bank rode blasting wind across heaven, flashing and eager for purgatory.

All across the grounds of the plant, tatters of leaking steam romped like things alive through shards of light. There was a bang when an empty acetylene cylinder fell over and rolled. He went to it and lifted it and propped it firmly against the building.

Lightning struck near enough to make him jump, and the wind gained intensity. Some isolated pellets of hail banged on the tin roofs and walls.

"Mister Pete!"

Swat was silhouetted against the lab. Behind him a spume of dust the size of a man swept into a pool of light, hesitated and went on. There followed an eerie stillness like a raised hammer, and then the fierce blow of compressed atmosphere.

"Mister Pete, let's us get outta this wind before we get clobbered with a flying crowbar or something."

"Yeah, we better. Let's go to the lab. Any other place around here is likely to fall in on us."

"Ain't that the truth! Me, I'll get our lunches outta the office if that's alright. We could least-wise have a little coffee."

Pete still wasn't used to being called "Mister."

They were in the lab when the first heavy round of hail pounded the metal roof. It soon gave way to raindrops the size of nickels. Pete looked out through a dirty window above the work bench. Lights flickered inside the lab and out, and pools of water formed under the light poles. Sheets of the tin roof and walls rattled and flapped against their nails, threatening to take flight.

"It's like being inside a snare drum in here."

"Yeah, I'd say we go somewhere else, but there ain't nowhere else to go," Swat said.

A lightning strike outside the window blinded them, and the thunder was like canon fire. Both men were wrapped in the same awe and fascination. Pete noticed that Swat, a black man, was apparently enthralled by the wonder of it the same as himself. Simultaneously he marveled that he would ever have thought otherwise. They opened their respective thermoses and poured coffee.

The two of them watched in silence until Swat shouted above the noise, "Mighty good thing you switched them tops when you was out yonder."

Pete didn't move for a moment. "I didn't switch them," he said.

" 'Bout when you think they need checking again?"

" 'Bout now."

They both stole glances at the slicker suit hanging by the door, dusty from long disuse.

Swat spoke next. "Well, these here shoes too good for gettin' full of wet clay. I'll find me some rubber ones aroun' here somewhere."

"What for?" There was a hint of challenge in Pete's tone.

"Go out and gauge them tops. Prob'ly switch them tanks."

"I'm supposed to do that. Switching tops is my job."

Swat gave a laugh. The kind of laugh that changes the subject or avoids it. "That's alright," he said. "Ole Swat'll get out there and take care of it. We ain't got but one slicker."

Pete had to respond quickly, as Swat was already making a motion toward the rain gear. "That ain't your job. It's mine."

Swat stopped and fixed his gaze on the window sill in front of him.

"Mister Pete, you ought'a just let me do it this time. Besides,

Griz find out I let you go on them tanks in this lightning, he gone fire my black ass. He done it before for less than that."

Wind shook the building and rain fell. Thunder roared. Both Pete and Swat were aware that, while they were having this discussion, the tops pump was blindly doing its work.

"Why would Griz do that?"

Swat was caught in a bind. "I ain't supposed to say nothing about this, but it was bound to come up. So I'll say it outright. Griz give me a talkin'-to when we started up the plant. He say you to get hurt, or even do something where you might could, and he find out, he's gone have my hide. He find out you climb them tops in this lightning …"

Pete let this sink in. "So that's why you've been watching me all the time."

"You could say."

Pete set his coffee cup down on the window sill and stood. He limped past Swat to the door and picked the slicker suit off its nail. Swat watched him knock off the dust.

"Please give me that, Mister Pete. Please."

"Griz don't know what nobody tells him," Pete said, and shoved an arm into the slicker.

"I know it ain't likely," Swat said. "But you get lightning-struck, my ass is in a sling."

"You get lightning-struck instead of me, and you ain't got no ass."

"Mister Pete …"

"I'm not telling Griz nothing."

The two faced each other through a two-breath silence. Then Pete said, "Griz also gave me a talking-to." After that he didn't know how to continue.

"I'm listening," Swat said.

Pete wished he'd kept his mouth shut. "He told me I better act like a boss, even if you do know more about this plant than

I ever will. He said I better not …" He couldn't go on.

"Better not what?"

"Ruin you."

"Ruin me," Swat repeated.

"You know, let you get …"

Neither one spoke for several long seconds. The wind shook the building, and there was the sound of something falling, metal on metal.

" 'Uppity nigger,' he mean."

Pete's only response was silence.

The storm was having its way with the world and the tops tank was filling. Both of them knew it.

"I'm not telling Griz anything," Pete said and put his other arm through the sleeve of the slicker and started fastening the snaps. He turned the door knob and the wind immediately kicked the door open.

Swat stepped in front of him. "You not telling Griz nothing tonight," he shouted into the wind. "Maybe not tomorrow. What happens someday you get pissed off at that goddamned Swat? Next month, or next year. What's Griz gonna hear then?"

A silence followed that made Pete dizzy with its overload of realizations. He was angry that a black man was arguing with him. He was ashamed of his own racial objection. He was sympathetic to Swat's situation and angry at Griz for putting them both in it. He felt helpless to untangle it. Pete was most comfortable when he knew how to please everybody. At the moment he didn't know how to please anybody. Not even himself. At the same time he felt the power of being white. It was the only time he'd ever had power over a grown man. With that power it seemed that there was no possible right thing to do, which frustrated his high opinion of himself. He surrendered to his rage.

"Swat. It won't matter," he shouted. "If I was to get it in for you and try to get you fired or in trouble, it wouldn't make any difference, would it?" He threw his arms out, palms up. "I can tell Griz whatever I want to, anytime I want. True or not. And Griz? He'll believe me, or pretend he does. You know that, and nothing's going to change it." He stood there in the open door with the wind blowing rain into the lab. Tears came down his face. "But I'll tell you this, Swat. I am not telling Griz a thing. Not one thing. I'm not that kind of white boy. I guess you'll just have to trust that. We both have to trust that." His voice broke, but he recovered enough to say, "The tops tanks are my job, and we're wasting time."

Pete struck off into the dark toward the tanks, not remembering to pick up a flashlight. Swat swore under his breath and followed him in his overalls, shining the flashlight ahead of them both.

Chapter 25
Frog-Eye

A week went by. The fury of the storm was spent, but the rain continued off and on. It had been a demanding night so far. A tanker truck arrived at twelve-thirty with a load of raw sludge for the pit. Pete took three samples while it poured out of the spout at the beginning, middle and end of the pour for Griz to analyze. The truck driver, on the way out, hit and broke a power pole. It was still standing, but it was splintered at the three-foot height and it appeared that the power line was now holding up the pole. Pete had to call and wake Griz, who came out at two-fifteen to appraise the situation and take insurance information from the driver.

All the while the rain came and went. Pete had put on a slicker early in the shift but took it off when the first shower stopped. The rain started again, and he was unsure where he'd left the slicker and was too busy to look for it. His coveralls were damp and uncomfortable by the time the tanker was empty.

At a quarter to three the tanker was gone, Griz had left, and Pete and Swat were tired, wet and hungry. They found dry coveralls in the lab closet and changed clothes in each others' presence. Pete couldn't resist looking at Swat's body. It was a greater expanse of black skin in nearer proximity than he'd ever seen before. For his part, Swat appeared unselfconscious and nonchalant. Once they'd gotten themselves dry and dressed, they wordlessly got their lunch pails form the refrigerator and, because it was raining, headed for the office.

Pete turned on the air conditioner and cleared some space for them to sit and spread out their food. They ate in silence until Swat noticed Pete rubbing the pad of his thumb with his index finger. He realized that it was something he'd seen Pete do many times. "What's wrong with your thumb?" he said.

Pete, suddenly conscious that he'd been rubbing a wart there, said, "Oh this? It's nothing. Just a wart. It's been there a long time."

Swat thought for a moment. "I can take that off for you. I'll do that soon as we're done."

Pete drew an apprehensive breath and held it a moment. "I don't know. It ain't no bother."

"Welp. I knows how. I done lots of 'em. My granny taught me how. She was a hoo-doo over in Grand Coteau on the Louisiana side. She could cure might-near anything."

Pete didn't exactly know what a "hoo-doo" was, but his imagination sped through visions of sharp objects, smoky candles and bat blood. The New Testament warned in no uncertain terms against dealing with sorcerers and witches. He didn't know how to respond to this apparently well-meaning man whose hoo-doo grandmother taught him to cure warts.

"It ain't no bother," he said, stalling for time.

Swat went on, "You go out yonder and get you a piece of pine about this size," indicating the dimensions of a table fork. "It can be a board or a old stick or a limb. That don't make no never-mind. It just got to be pine. You go ahead on. I ain't gone look, cause I cain't know where it come from. I wait here."

He sat looking at Pete expectantly.

Pete shifted in his chair for a moment and then, partly to

get away, stood and went out into the damp night. Finding a piece of pine wasn't hard. Plenty of saplings stood in the weedy areas of the plant. He high-stepped through the tall weeds as if there might be a way to walk that didn't get the cuffs of his coveralls wet. He found a four-foot sapling and shook the water off. He used his pocketknife to slice off a finger-thick branch. Having gone this far into the scheme, he shrugged and went back to the office. His legs were tired and he was ready to sit down again.

Swat took the stick from him at the door and without ceremony barked it into a garbage can with his own knife and shaped it into an approximately square bar. The scent of pine sap filled the office and seemed to take away some of the tiredness of that hour.

"How many warts you got?" Swat asked.

Pete looked at his thumb as if he needed a fresh count. "One."

Swat cut one notch on an edge of the stick. "Gimme yo' hand."

Pete had to make a final choice. His acquaintance with Swat was about to change, one way or the other. Either go along with this, or refuse. He extended his hand, and let Swat hold it palm up in his left. His mind was effervescent with all the things he'd been told about Negroes: *they're dirty, they carry diseases, they carry the curse of Ham.* But he'd already seen Swat expertly wrap his ankle, and nothing bad came from that.

With his right hand Swat drew the pine stick lightly down the axis of the thumb exactly across the single wart. "Now," he said, "I'm gone go out yonder and bury this here stick somewheres. Don't you watch me, cause if you see where I put it, this ain't gone work." Then he went out the office door and was gone.

Pete stayed where he was, still smelling the pine in the air and on his hands. He ate another Oreo out of his lunch pail and sipped black coffee. Presently Swat was back, and Pete watched his movements putting his things away, trying to detect something of mystery, but it was just Swat matter-of-factly putting his things away.

"Now that's done, I go check on them boilers again if you want me to."

"I could walk down there alright."

"You already been on that foot too much. I'll take care of it."

Pete watched Swat stand and straighten himself and go out the door, and then his dim image pass by the office window on his way to the boiler house. "There's a lot I don't know about him," he muttered to himself. "I should pray about this when I get home."

Pete didn't pray about it when he got home. In fact he didn't even go home at first. As quitting time approached, the eastern horizon began to glow gray, then brightened into an orange and yellow spectrum ricocheting in the clouds. Any evil that might have been done in the night seemed insignificant against such a dawn. Pete's mood became expansive, but with a loneliness that fenced it in. Or was it horniness? Or was there a difference?

When he left the plant at five after seven, he knew exactly where he was going. He went out the driveway to the road and, instead of turning left toward home, he turned right and headed for the Streamliner.

He felt guilty for leaving his mother to have breakfast alone, but he relished the fact that he wouldn't have to face her scrutiny. When he did get home, she'd be gone to work. In the meantime, he'd have the simple pleasure of this small adventure. It didn't hurt that he might see Gwynn's smile. So what if she was a little older? He could still enjoy her company.

As for the wart, Pete didn't think of it again until about ten days later. He was waking up at home in the late afternoon and absently rubbing the bump on his thumb with his forefinger when he felt something unfamiliar. He turned his hand to have a better look and discovered a ruler-straight line of white dots under the skin arranged along the axis of his thumb straight through the old wart. They varied in size, the two largest next to the original wart and graduating to lesser size like tiny pearls. They exactly described the path where Swat had drawn his stick over the skin.

Over the next few days the spots gained definition and at last presented themselves to be a string of new warts. If Pete had suspected some association with Satan before, he was certain of it now. He let it ride for a few days, only to see the new warts continue to grow.

He didn't know what he should do about it. *If thine eye offend thee*, the Bible said, *pluck it out.* Should he cut off his thumb? Pete had been constructing a theology of his own ever since his father's death, and this episode was becoming a part of it. It was more than two years ago that he'd announced his call to be a preacher. He genuinely felt that God had something for him to do on earth. Something more than simply being a good Christian mechanic or carpenter or fireman. Since that time, he'd considered everything that happened to him to be preparation for a life in the ministry. The death of his father was, to him, if not some Jonah-like coercion, then at least an experience God wanted him to have. He expected such lessons and was attuned to them. He wondered what he was to learn from these warts. He imagined them creeping over his body until he became a thoroughly warted evangelist, warning the world away from Satan.

Pete didn't say anything about it to Swat. If they got bad he'd go to the doctor. He'd talk to Brother Deckert. He'd talk to God.

One night Pete and Swat stood under a pair of flood lights unloading lengths of 3-inch pipe from a flatbed trailer. It had been brought in during the day shift and needed to be unloaded next to the tool shed, ready for repairs during the next shut-down. Pete and Swat stood at each end of the pipes rolling them down a make-shift ramp and stacking them on layers of 4x4 dunnage. The work wasn't conducive of conversation, so Pete was surprised when Swat hollered, "Mister Pete. That wart gone from yo' thumb yet?"

Pete didn't answer while they took their respective ends of another pipe, maneuvered it to the ramp, and rolled it down in sync. The dull ring of each pipe had exactly the same tone as the last one. They took another pipe. Then another. The tone rang, and rang again. Pete still didn't answer.

"Mister Pete?" Swat said again. "That wart you had. It gone now?"

"Well. Naw. It ain't gone."

"That cure didn't do nothin'?"

"Maybe it didn't do nothin'."

Pete didn't say any more, and Swat didn't ask, at least not right then. They were finished unloading the trailer and worked their hands out of their sweaty gloves and wiped the sweat off their faces.

Swat said, "Can I see your thumb?"

Pete held it out under the light like a dare.

Swat's eyes widened. "Oh. Uhh huh. Mmmmm. Well." Swat looked into Pete's face. "I half suspicioned that, Mister Pete. I wish you'd a told me."

"Told you what?" Pete asked.

"Nothin'. You prob'ly didn't know your own self. You

didn't look where I buried that stick, did you? No, I didn't think so. Yeah. I kinda' suspicioned."

Pete was getting a little spooked. "What are you talking about?"

Swat glanced into the shadows behind the trailer. "It's hard to 'splain," he said. "My granny over in Grand Coteau, when she learnt me the cure for the warts, she told me, 'It ain't gone work for them what got the frog-eye'. That's what she said. Said frog-eyed folks can be hard to cure."

"What in the world is frog-eye?"

"Well, I knew you was gonna aks me that." Swat took off his cap and wiped the top of his head with his palm and frowned at Pete with his black eyes. "When I was little I went to stay with my granny, I asked her that same question, and she told me this." Swat put one foot up on the trailer and rested his forearms on his knee. "The Frog. He don't start out as a frog. He starts out as a tadpole. Got him a tail to swim with. Ain't got no legs yet. Cain't git up onto the bank. He have to stay in the water all the time. He moves through water. The water bears him up. The water touches his skin everywhere, all the time. The light that comes to his eyes comes through water. If he smells anything, it's in the water. The water holds all that he knows or ever hopes to know. The tadpole swim around down there all the time, pickin' at the mud where the fishes and snakes going to eat him if they can, but he'd be happy just to stay a tadpole.

"But when he grows a little bit and his tail it starts to disappearin', he thinks *Where my tail go? How'm I suppose to swim without no tail?* Other tadpoles say 'what's that bump you got on you there? You look like you growin' something on your sides.' He say, 'I ain't growin' nothin'. What you talkin' about?' He denies it as long as he can. Then one day he git little legs and he's still confused, because he don't know what they for.

But they grow and they grow. He cain't swim as good like he used to when he had a tail. Got to use them legs. And then he get to where he cain't breathe right. And some of the other tadpoles make fun of him. Some of 'em git mad at him. And he had him some gills when he started out, but they disappearing just like the tail disappearing. Now he got to get some air to breathe or he gonna die.

"You hear me? He got to breathe air, or he gonna die. This don't make no sense to him yet. This beginning to make any sense to you yet?"

Pete's face began to flush, but he said nothing.

"So them legs," Swat went on. "They grow and grow and get stronger while the tail disappear. The gills disappear and some lungs grow. And that kind of thing keeps on till one day a catfish come after him and gonna eat him. So before he know it, he jump out of the water up onto the bank where the catfish cain't get him.

"When the catfish goes away, the frog set there on the bank thinking what just happened?"

As Swat went on, Pete put his fists in front of his mouth and began to tremble, but still he said nothing.

"Up there on the bank, that's when the frog knows that he's got to quit calling hisself a tadpole, cause he ain't one no more. He a frog. He set there on the bank and look around at a new world. They's new dangers in the new world same as the old. But now he has hisself two worlds he can live in. Sometime he go back in the water if it suits him. He still know his way around down there. Sometime he float at the top of the water and ain't nothin' sticking up but them two eyes and a little bit of nose. He can see two worlds, up on the bank or down in the water. Them tadpoles that's still down below, they say, 'What you doin' up there?' but he cain't 'splain it to them. They ain't no way to 'splain it. He just got to go on being Frog, because he cain't be nothin' else. Some of them tadpoles, they get mad at him. They tell him 'You gonna make trouble up there in the air. There's evil everywhere outside the water. You get out of the water, you gonna die. Ain nothing good gonna come out of this.'

"The frog, he say 'y'all don't understand. You keep growin' and you'll be up here too, just like me. But that just makes them tadpoles madder. All them tadpoles that used to be his friends, they all hateful to him now."

Pete wept quietly, making every effort not to show it.

"Some peoples is like tadpoles. Some peoples ain't. Some peoples stay the same their whole lives and never see up on the bank. Sometimes frog-eye be a blessing. Sometimes a curse. That all depend. But my granny say that's what it mean having the frog-eye. It mean they can't help but see what most folks can't see. But she say that her hoo-doo don't work on peoples that got the frog-eye. They got to find their own way and their own kind of hoo-doo."

When Swat stopped talking, Pete was breathing heavily. Tears coursed down his face camouflaged by the sweat. Swat's words had given him a new way to recognize himself, and the new recognition was both welcome and terrifying.

"What about you? You have frog-eye?"

"My granny say I did."

Pete was trembling. He felt naked as if truly seen for the first time. He finally managed to say, "What about these warts? What happens with them?"

"I don't know, Mister Pete. I guess you got to live longer than them warts do to find out. Just like the tadpole got to live long enough to be a frog. Not everybody lives that long."

Chapter 26
Midnight Bash

"Hey Swat. Did you ever notice that right around this time of night when we sit down to eat, it seems like a lot of cars go by? I wonder why that is."

"Closing time," Swat said.

"Huh?"

"Two o'clock. All the joints and honkey-tonks closes at two. It's the law. Everybody has to get in the car and go someplace else to conclude their drinking. Or maybe just go to somewhere and sleep it off."

Pete looked again toward the road where another pair of white headlights came from the left and became red tail lights going right.

"You think they're all drunk?"

"Maybe."

Pete sipped his coffee and thought of all the newspaper stories he'd seen about collisions in the night. So often around two-thirty in the morning. He would pay more attention to that in the future. It seemed that a big fact had been right before his eyes and he'd never recognized it. He wondered how much more he was failing to see. How many clues he was missing.

There was one question that Pete wanted to ask Swat but had

never dared, and even if he had dared, he wouldn't have known how to begin. It was about the night he'd been frog gigging, heard the violence at the river and gone to the police. The episode still haunted him. Ever since that night Pete had begun seeing Negroes in the community, not in the old way, but also not yet in a new way. It was the new way that eluded him, and Swat was his only window. Even the best windows face only one direction.

He wadded up the wrapper of his sandwich and tossed it into his lunch box. "Want a cookie?" he asked Swat.

"That's alright," Swat declined.

Pete leaned forward and stood up, surveying the sky. "I wonder how many stars there are out there."

"A bunch, I reckon," Swat said. "I read in a book one time that there's more of 'em than there is grains of sand on this earth."

"I wonder why God made so many. Seems kind of wasteful."

Swat chuckled. "Like they say, we'll understand it better by and by."

"You think there's other people out there? What if Jesus had to go to every one of those stars and die on a cross to save the ones that live there?"

"That would be a lot of crosses and a lot of nails. You'd think Jesus would git mighty tired of it after a while." Swat shook his head, suppressing a smile. "Dang, Mister Pete, but you ask some of the dangdest questions."

"I'm gonna ask you another one," Pete said, and swallowed. His mouth was suddenly dry.

"Let 'er rip."

Pete took a deep breath and began. "Last spring was there anybody you know of that went missing?"

Swat frowned, trying to imagine where that question was coming from. "Say some more, Mister Pete. So's I get some idea what you mean, 'missing'."

"You know. Somebody you might know of who went out one night and then never was heard from again?"

"What makes you ask that?" Swat could tell from Pete's tight voice that something was bothering him. "Did something happen last spring that makes you think somebody I might know went missing?" Swat froze momentarily in his own thoughts. Vaguely remembered visions of his daddy's cafe burned to cinders. Neither his mama or daddy ever seen again. "Tell me what you talking about."

Pete wrestled with his own tongue. He began to sweat. "Throwed in the river. I couldn't see, but I heard it. I was on one side of the river and they were on the other. I tried to tell the cops. There never was anything in the paper. Not that I saw. I never heard anything else about it. I'm sure it was … But maybe I was wrong. I don't know. I just thought somebody got killed and nobody would know what happened to them, and every time I try to tell it I start to feel crazy because nobody … nobody ever …"

"Mister Pete. Slow down. Just slow down a minute. Take a deep breath. Here, you want some water? Just say a little bit at a time. This was last spring? That what you said? Okay. Right. It was spring. And .. ?"

Pete took a sip of water. "Yeah. I was frog gigging down by Clear Lake. I was by myself, and …"

Pete told it. Once he got started, it rolled out of him, sometimes in excitement, sometimes in sobs. When he'd finally told the part about the police station, he stopped and brought his mind back into the present. Breathing more slowly he looked at Swat to gauge his reaction.

They both remained silent for a long moment.

"No," Swat said. "I don't know about anybody that went missing. If it happened the way you think it did, it wasn't nobody I know. It's a troubling story and it troubles me and you both. If it happened like that, it could have been somebody not even from around here. They could have been from somewheres else.

"But I will tell you this. Whether that really happened that night or not, what you saw was a true thing. People disappear. Sometimes it's people running from trouble. Sometimes it's trouble catching up with them. You might not have seen what you thought you saw, but it's still a true thing."

Swat gazed into a far away past. "A true and fearsome thing," he said.

It was about a quarter to three. Pete picked up a flashlight and tested it. "I guess I better check on … something."

Pete walked out into the dark, and as soon as he was far away enough not to be heard, he allowed himself to break out into sobs. The safe and orderly world he'd always known was in shambles.

He walked down to the tops tanks and took the readings, more out of a need to be alone than out of necessity. When he was done, he set his things next to the hatch on one tank and walked to the next one. He backed his butt up to it, hopped up and sat. The waning quarter moon was climbing out of the east. He was sure he heard some kind of animal in the weeds outside the fire dike. Possum. Armadillo. Skunk. Could be anything.

A car came down Goforth Road at a high rate of speed. Long before he could see it he heard the loud and angry roar of it. When it came into view, it was traveling much faster than any of the others had been, and to Pete's surprise, it slowed as it approached the cattle guard and turned in toward the plant. A pair of double headlights swung in through the gate and bounced into the driveway. By the lights alone Pete could tell it was a '58 Chevy. It crawled in slowly, illuminating the parked railroad cars one by one as it passed. The headlights were mis-aligned, and the exhaust was so loud that Pete could hear it over the rumble of the still. Pete moved to the end of the cat-walk where he could see better.

Swat appeared from the direction of the tool shed and vig-orously approached the car, shielding his eyes from the head-lights with one hand and carrying something in the other, a wrench or a length of pipe. He was leaning forward into his steps as if ready for combat.

From the catwalk Pete watched, dumbfounded, as Swat stepped in front of the moving car and swung at the two headlights on the driver's side. The lights went dark in turn. The newly one-eyed car rocked to a stop. The passenger side door opened and a very skinny, very black girl lurched out and stomped her way to Swat and began punching his chest with her fists. Swat grabbed both her wrists and marched her back-ward and put her back through the door she'd come out of and closed it. He stood there, apparently talking, but Pete couldn't hear a bit of it.

Meantime the driver's door opened and a white man got out, advancing toward Swat and shouting. When the man was close enough, Swat landed a single punch to the man's stomach. The man doubled over and staggered back, holding his abdo-men with one hand. He flopped back into the car on his own.

Swat followed him and pushed the driver's door shut. He stood there as if explaining something to the driver, bumping the top of the car with his fist as he did so. Then Swat stepped away from the car and started back toward the tool shed with the bearing of a man who had just unplugged a toilet. He stopped once and looked back at the vehicle, which was now backing out the driveway. When it got to the road it went its one-eyed way into the dark, much more slowly than it had arrived.

Pete didn't know what to do, neither as a boss nor as an

ally of Swat's. For that matter, he didn't know if he should be afraid of Swat.

He would feel cowardly if he did nothing, but he could think of lots of reasons to do nothing. Whatever had happened had passed. Whatever harm came or would come from it was none of his business. He hoped. What good would it do to call Griz in the middle of the night? Calling the police would be laughable, he knew that now. He wasn't sure he had the nerve to demand an explanation from Swat.

His legs trembled and his knees felt week as he descended the stair from the catwalk. As a stalling measure he went by the boiler house to check the pressures and water levels.

An hour and a half later Pete got his thermos and went to sit outside the lab. It would be getting light soon. He figured that Swat had had time to calm down, but was still uneasy about bringing up what he'd seen. As was customary at that hour, Swat came around with his own thermos.

With a dry mouth Pete managed to say, "Who was in that car that came in awhile ago?"

"You seen that, huh? It was just somebody that don't have no business here."

Pete thought for a moment. "Will they come back? I think I've been seeing that car around town lately. It's hard to miss."

"I think I persuaded 'em not to come back. Naw. Not if they knows what's good for 'em."

Pete gathered his thoughts and courage in equal measure. "I saw you knock out the headlights. And hit that guy."

"They was drunk. They likely hopped up on somethin' besides. I already told both of 'em never to come here. Not ever. This time I made sure they understood it. I made it so they didn't have but one choice: try to get home without bein' stopped by the police for a missing headlight and driving drunk."

"So you know them?"

He took a deep breath and exhaled toward the sky. "Mister Pete. You don't have to worry about none of this. And if nobody ever hears about it, I'd be beholdin'. Most especially, Griz. He won't tolerate no drunk niggas comin' round here. They ain't no quicker way to get me sent down the road."

"One of them was white."

"Uh huh. That just makes it worse."

Pete considered the logic of that. Nothing about those two looked like a white man driving the maid home, which was the only way Pete had seen blacks and whites in the same car.

"What if they get stopped by the police, and they tell the police on you. Would the police tell Griz?"

Swat sighed to gather his patience. "Mister Pete: a nigger girl and a white dude all drunk in a car that got whiskey bottles rollin' around. The police won't give a doodley-damn who broke the headlight." Swat laughed out loud. In a deep voice he said, " 'Sir, as soon as you're sober enough to assist us, we want to apprehend the perpetrator of your broken headlamps.' " He roared again with laughter. Pete managed to laugh too.

"Aren't you afraid they'll gang up on you later?" Pete's courage rose up from some place he hardly knew. "And who were they anyway?" He paused. "Maybe it's none of my business, but it almost is. What if I run into them myself sometime. What if I'd been out there filling a tank car while you were patching something at the boiler house? Just fill me in a little."

"He showed up at my house one time, that white guy. Woke me up." Swat considered how much to say. It might be best to satisfy Pete's curiosity.

"When I come back from Korea, my Auntie Minnie had just passed. Her two children was still staying in that house on their own mostly, except for the church and some other folks in Tin Cup. So I come to stay and took 'em over. Sort of their daddy. They ain't have nobody else. That girl you saw was one of them kids. Beulah. The other one, Roscoe, he didn't make it back from Viet Nam alive. Since then, Beulah, she been into drugs and who knows what. That guy she was with tonight, he showed up in town a while back saying he knew her brother in Nam. Her brother that got killed there. So this white guy, he come here on some kind of mission of his own. He seemed reasonable at first. He as much as told me he got no family and nowhere to go. He came hunting for Beulah, and when he found her, it seems like drugs and Beulah is the best he's got. Them two been gettin' worse and worse. Sometime Beulah come to me for money."

Swat poured the last drips from his thermos, screwed down the top and gently set it on the floor beside him. He bit his lower lip and drew a deep breath. "What you saw was a drug addict girl. A cousin of mine that I do what I can for her. There just ain't much I can do. She probably in a tight for money. That other one, he a shell-shocked soldier just out of Viet Nam. He can't figure out if he wants to be a white fuck-up or a black African one." He sighed. "Them two busted souls have fell into the same heap, trying to get through their God-forgotten lives. Lord help me, sometimes I wish he'd leave and take Beulah with him. But Beulah's mama was like my mama too, and since she passed, I do what I can." He looked directly at Pete and then looked away. Then back again. "If I had any gumption I'd just go off somewhere and get away from that whole bunch. Not even tell nobody, 'cept for one, where I'm gone. Make my own self disappear."

Pete listened. He put his last Fig Newton in his mouth and chewed. "I kinda' know what you mean," he mumbled to himself. Then to Swat, "Except for who?"

"Nobody. Never mind."

Chapter 27
A New Regular

On the afternoon of July 4th, a series of loud explosions jarred Pete from his daytime sleep. He didn't know what it was, and he leapt from bed before he was even awake. He stood in dazed puzzlement next to his bed. BOOM! He went to the venetian blind and lifted a slat to look at the thermometer he'd put outside the window. It read 102. Spooked cattle were running from the direction of the road and heading toward the woods behind the house. Boom! A car horn honking. Faint shouting. "Must be some fool throwing cherry bombs out of a car," he muttered to himself, and he flopped back onto the bed. The clock read 4:48. Each detonation seemed a little more distant than the previous. Boom, boom, boom off into the distance.

His mother had asked him to be up by five to be at the July 4th church potluck, and he'd said okay. It seemed odd to him, but July 4th had fallen on a Sunday. At this moment Pete didn't want to go anywhere, neither the parade in town nor the church service. The predictability of the patriotic sermon was mind-numbing. Even his dad, a former paratrooper, had been a little standoffish about flag-waving. The past few months had jarred him with two deaths. The pomp and ceremony felt like a denial of every recent torment. Nearly everything about it seemed trivial. Furthermore, the murder he'd witnessed at the river, and surely there was nothing else to call it, had been treated as trivial by everyone who should have cared about it. The revival and its prissy preacher had just about pushed Pete over the edge. He didn't feel like waving flags or bowing for rehearsed patriotic prayers.

In the kitchen he found a note from his mother:

> When you get to the church you can find me with the Broussards. Afterwards we'll have ice cream and watermelon and play 42 at their house. The Gentrys and Deckerts will be there too. See you when you get there.
>
> Mother

"I'm not going to any of that," he said to himself aloud. He clenched his jaw and stiffened his shoulders. Because he was not yet a man, his resolve required defiance. "I'm not going to the parade either. I'm not in the mood to watch boy scouts carrying flags, and I don't need to be entertained by fire trucks. I don't give a rip who the Crude Oil Queen is. I'm not going to any stinking parade, not to the church, and I'm not going to sit around with the Broussards or any other old people playing dominoes."

He opened the refrigerator and stood staring. There was leftover iced tea. Bologna. Wonder Bread. It was enough.

He sat agitated on the back porch eating his sandwich and watching the sun sink behind the woods. "I want a girlfriend!" He tried to think of somebody he might call, but couldn't think of anybody who wouldn't be about as boring as the parade. There was Gwynn, of course, but she was so far out of his league that he could only spare himself the humiliation of rejection. Every other girl he knew was interested in little more than Twiggy or the Beatles, or even worse, who's going steady with who. The triviality of everything was driving him mad.

He did hold out hope that religion would save him. Give him a purpose. But religion had become its own tangle. All that he'd been taught about what was good or evil was turned on its head. His only tangible relief for the moment was in running.

So he ran.

He still had his cross-country shoes. He put them on and jogged out to the road, turned away from town. He ran to simply penetrate space, but before long even the space oppressed him. Fields, trees, cattle, oil wells, repeat. He could run all day and get nowhere other than where he was.

A blast of wind took him by surprise. The sky showed a possibility of rain. He took some comfort that the weather itself appeared unsettled.

At the plant that night Pete felt so isolated that he didn't even want to talk to Swat, who never judged him or told him what to think. He usually just listened whenever Pete rambled about the things stewing in his head. But Swat was also often silent in the way of somebody who knows a lot more than what they're saying. Pete felt vaguely shamed by that knowing silence, and he wanted to avoid it. So he went, as he sometimes did, to the tops tanks down by the creek. There he could stand alone on the catwalk and think.

He went through the rigamarole of gauging the tops, and then he laid his clip board next to the hatch and gazed outward into the dark. The breeze lifted and rattled the pages. In one direction Pete could see faint lights from a Louisiana community far in the distance across the river. On impulse he clambered up off the catwalk and stood on the steel top of the tank itself. It pleased him that it was dark, and that there was no guardrail. He walked daringly around the unguarded circle feeling certain that he could fly if he chose to. In the far distance a Roman candle sent flares up from the invisible ground.

At this hour someone was still awake sending their tiny patriotic prayers toward the sky. It was nearly four a.m.

Even though he was tired, a chemical energy filled him. He couldn't hold still. He hopped back onto the catwalk, picked up his clipboard and reel and went down the stair to wander the grounds of the plant. He checked the boilers more often than necessary. He used a frayed and rotten broom to sweep spider webs from the corners of the boiler house. With a rag he wiped grime off the boilers' sight glasses. He abandoned that and went out to the pit where he picked up rocks and threw them at the armored side of the still, just to hear it ring against the roar.

Quitting time finally came. The thought of going home and to bed was unbearable. There was, of course, the other place he could go.

Gwynn stood at a booth making change for the two men who had just finished breakfast when she saw Pete's black Plymouth turned off the highway onto the gravel. Few such old cars were kept so clean. It stopped in the shade of a pine, and the boy got out. Or was he a man? Lately she'd been trying to decide.

She went back through the swinging doors to the kitchen where Danny was standing at the griddle watching pancakes rise. Bacon sizzled its vapors into the air around him. Gwynn sighed at the dumb simplicity of the menu. Bacon, eggs, hashbrowns, pancakes, coffee. If you could cook those without burning them and had some processed cheese on hand for the occasional omelette, you could feed the multitudes. She heard the front door swing open and then close. The previous customers were leaving just as Pete came in.

"Sit anywhere you like, Pete. Looks like you have the place to yourself."

Pete chose the booth at the window that overlooked the

highway. Gwynn poured coffee before he was settled in.

"Here you go. Coffee black. No cream. No sugar. And you like it a little stronger, right?"

Pete smiled up at her. "Someday you'll make some lucky man a good waitress."

Gwynn sputtered a short laugh. "And someday you'll make some lucky waitress a good tipper."

Gwynn looked around at the otherwise empty dining room. She reached across to an adjacent table and picked up another coffee cup and poured one for herself. "It was a busy first hour. Mind if I join you for a minute?"

Pete did not mind.

She slid into the booth and joined him gazing at the brightening morning. They shared a moment of stillness. It was quiet inside the cafe except for the hum of the ice machine and Danny clattering in the kitchen. Outside the weather was building again. Wind whipped the trees and rain started to fall. There was thunder.

"It's good to have some quiet after listening to the boilers and the still all night."

Gwynn stirred sugar into her coffee. "How long have you worked there, anyway?"

"Just since school was out, but it seems like forever."

"Do you like it?"

"It's okay. Pretty good money." He pursed his lips. "Nights is cooler than day shift. Pays a little better. I get tired of the seven-day part."

She let that sit for a moment before asking, "How long do you think you'll work there? Is it going to be your career?"

"No. Shoot. Not my career." Pete was stumped as to what was true about his career. He didn't know how Gwynn would take this, but he gave it out anyway: "Since sixth grade I've intended to be a preacher. Honestly, I don't know anymore. I've got some things to figure out.

How about you? You like being a waitress?"

"Humm," she said. "I can say this. I will never be rude to a waitress again." She sighed. "No, I'm going back to Berkeley as soon as possible. I've done about all I can do for my dad here."

There was a bright streak of lightning and a wall-shaking boom of thunder.

"Wow," Gwynn said. "That was pretty close."

"Close enough," Pete said, and while he was saying it another flash lit the room. Again, the thunder hit and rolled away while bullets of rain struck the window.

"My, my," came a voice from the kitchen. "What IS going on out there?" Danny came out to the front window to look at the weather.

"It's getting kinda wild," Gwynn said.

Danny stood next to Gwynn with a hand on her shoulder. They were both leaning toward the window, awestruck by the fierceness of the wind.

"The weather can change in a hurry," Pete said.

Both Gwynn and Danny turned to look at him as if they'd forgotten he was there.

"Oooo," Danny said. "Who is this string bean that keeps coming around?"

Gwynn poked him on the arm. "Not your type, Danny. You know that."

"Well." Danny shrugged. "He does look young. Probably jail bait anyway."

"Danny, everybody is jail bait to you. Honestly, hadn't you better rein it in a little. Be careful."

"Oh, you are cruel, Honey. Too cruel." Danny returned diffidently to the kitchen.

Gwynn turned to Pete. "Don't mind him. He just loves to tease."

Pete held his coffee a few inches from his face, his eyes a little larger than they'd been a minute before. "Uh, that's alright."

Danny shouted from the kitchen, "He's probably hungry. Why don't you ask him what he wants? Probably not on the menu, though."

"DANNY!" Gwynn shouted back.

Pete blushed. To change the subject he said, "I've never had French toast. Is it something they eat in France?"

"I've never seen it in France, but if you like pancakes, you'll love French toast. Especially with a little cinnamon on it."

"What is it exactly? Wait a minute. You've been to France?"

"Yeah, a couple of times with my family. It's bread dipped in egg batter and cooked like a pancake. Want to try it?"

"Sure. I'll try it." He turned pensive for a moment. "My dad was in France once, but I don't think he liked it much."

"Why not? What did he do there?"

"He parachuted into St. Marie Eglise a few hours before the Invasion started. Within a day he was a German prisoner."

Gwynn took a moment to wrap her head around this spinning conversation. "Anyway, what do you want for breakfast? I should get your order going."

"French toast and sausage."

Gwynn, without getting up, bellowed toward the kitchen. "DANNY! PETE WILL HAVE HIS USUAL. POACHED QUAIL EGGS, PASSION FRUIT COMPOTE AND SALMON ROE ON RICE CRACKERS!"

Pete spewed coffee onto the table. A wild guffaw came from the kitchen.

Danny appeared at the kitchen door. He put one hand on his hip and pointed at her with a spatula.

"Young Lady, God is still trying to make up His mind how He's going to punish you for your wise-assed-ness."

"Oh, I'm sorry," Gwynn said. "I meant 'French toast and sausage.' It just came out wrong."

"Well thank goodness. We're out of salmon roe, and they don't spawn again until October."

They laughed and glanced at Pete, who looked up, smiled weakly and turned toward the window.

"Danny doesn't mean any harm. We just get a little stir crazy sometimes doing the same thing over and over. I hope we didn't make you feel bad."

"No. It's alright."

"You know, when nobody is in here, we kind of act out. Virgil would probably fire us both if he knew what we do sometimes."

"Well. He won't find out from me."

They were interrupted by the sight of a green '58 Chevy that roared into the parking lot. It revved and spun out two donuts in the gravel, throwing up clots of mud and stone, some of which sprayed the side of Pete's car. Then it roared back onto the highway and went back in the direction from which it had come.

"Jesus!" Gwynn said. "I was afraid he was coming in here again."

"You know that car?" Pete asked.

"I know all I want to," she said. "Thank goodness Virgil, he's my boss, he was here when they came in the last time. I wouldn't have known how to handle it. Or …" She paused. "Maybe if Virgil hadn't been here, there wouldn't have been anything to handle. I don't know. Things get weird here sometimes."

"What happened?"

Gwynn scrunched up her face. "Well, in the end, nothing really. At least the way it started it would have been nothing where I come from." Her cup trembled a little as she sipped her coffee. "He had a girl with him. She was a black girl, that was the thing, I guess. Virgil wouldn't let me serve them. If I was them, it would have made me mad too. But I thought the whole cafe was going to erupt into a bar fight. Virgil asked them to leave. Politely, if such a thing could be called polite. Anyway, the girl looked scared and headed for the door. The guy grabbed her and told her to stay. And just like that," Gwynn snapped her fingers, "four or five oil-field types were standing next to Virgil, looking ready to fight.

"The guy looks at them and says something to the effect of, 'Any day of the week, one on one, I'd gladly feed you maggots your own dicks.' Then he backed his way to the door and went out."

She pointed to the parking lot. "I guess he just needed to come back and make a point."

Pete sat blinking. Hearing a young woman as lovely as Gwynn so unabashedly say the word "dick" had him distracted. "What happened after that?"

"Well, Virgil called the sheriff to come out here. His name is Rake. Ever hear such a name? Rake Connor. Handsome, I don't mind saying. But boy! He was outraged. He said he'd gotten other complaints about those two. I guess I should probably call Virgil and let him know he came back. It's a little scary."

"I've seen them before too. They came out to the plant one night. They know the guy I work with on nights. He knocked out one of their headlights and made them leave."

Gwynn put her face in her hands rubbed her cheeks. "Nothing against you, Pete, but I hate it here. I can't wait to leave Texas."

Pete didn't know what to say.

Gwynn changed the subject. "Have you ever heard of miscegenation?"

"No."

"Well, I had to ask. It's when a white person and a Negro have sex together. Apparently it's against the law in Texas. I'd never heard of that. But the scary part to me was that this sheriff guy, when he was here he looked straight at Danny and said 'Miscegenation is every bit as illegal as sodomy.' Danny turned white and went back to the kitchen. Since then Danny's been kinda jumpy. I think he's scared."

"You mean Danny's a queer?" Pete didn't know if he'd ever seen a queer before.

For a half hour that morning Pete was the only customer in the cafe. Gwynn seemed entirely comfortable and friendly toward Danny. Pete, on the other hand, wondered if it was immoral to be friendly to a queer. He even wondered if it was okay to be friendly with Gwynn. In the last few minutes he'd heard this sweet intelligent girl say "dick," say "piss" and take God's name in vain. She apparently thought it should be okay for blacks and whites to mix. Did that make her un-Godly? Did Danny's homosexuality make Gwynn someone whom he should stay away from? Would people suspect that he was a homosexual himself if he were seen being anything less than hostile? So many things to consider!

With Gwynn still sitting at his booth, Pete shifted in his seat and raised his eyes enough to look at her. "I know you told me once where you're from, but tell me again."

"Yeah," she said. "Oakland."

"Oakland?"

"It's near San Francisco. In California."

"I've heard of San Francisco."

Gwynn suppressed a snort and asked, "Have you always lived around here?"

He was embarrassed by the answer, so he didn't answer it.

"Do they have queers there, in Oakland?"

"Of course. Are you kidding me?"

Pete felt ridiculous and didn't want to talk about it anymore.

"What made you move here to Texas?" he asked.

"My dad took a job at Texas Eastman. I came here with him. For now."

"Just you and him? Didn't your mother come too?"

All humor passed out of Gwynn's face. "No. She died about six months ago."

"Oh. I'm sorry. I didn't mean to …" Pete felt his own eyes start to fill and resisted it.

"No. Don't apologize. It's alright."

Neither of them spoke for several seconds. Pete swallowed and said, "My dad got killed about that same time. What happened to your mom?"

Gwynn's lips pressed into a tight straight line. She looked at Pete and simply said, "Cancer."

After a slow breath she said, "What about your dad?"

"Fell off a drilling rig."

"I'm sorry, Pete." There seemed not much else to say. They turned away from that subject, but both of them sensed that this confidence they were sharing would likely continue.

When Pete had finished eating and paid the bill, he didn't want to leave. Gwynn refilled his coffee. He drank it slowly, but when some other customers came in, he stood and headed for the door.

"Come back soon, okay?" Gwynn said. "We'll behave next time, I promise."

"No we won't," Danny shouted.

Pete pushed the door open against the wind. "I enjoyed the Waldorf salad," he shouted back, and left.

From that day on, Pete thought about Gwynn when he woke up, when he went to bed and most of the time in between. He thought about Danny too, mostly thinking about how he should think. Gwynn and Danny didn't seem afraid to say the wrong thing. Or to think the wrong thing. Maybe Gwynn wasn't afraid to DO the wrong thing. There was an enticing thought. Pete began that day to spend daring moments imagining the wrong things that Gwynn might not be afraid to do. And why did the Beach Boys wish they could all be California girls? Thereafter he went often to the Streamliner with the intent of finding out.

The next day, when the lunch rush had run its course, Gwynn was helping Danny with the cleanup. She was stacking dishes into a rack for the dishwasher. Danny rolled the mop and bucket out of the closet.

"Danny," she said as he passed by her. "What is it about men?"

The bucket stopped rolling, and Danny leaned on the mop handle, looking at her with raised eyebrows.

"I mean, they all act as if they want something from me. Sure, sometimes it's obvious. The ones that leer and make lewd suggestions about what's on or off the menu. But even the well-behaved ones, almost all of them, look at me, almost pleading, some of them. Or they glance at me and look away as if they shouldn't have glanced, but because of some kind of need, they can't help themselves."

She stood straight and faced him. "What makes me such a big deal to them? Is this just my imagination? I'm sorry, Danny. I don't know if you can answer any of that. I'm sorry I …"

"It's alright. I know some people wouldn't call me a man, but I can answer at least part of it," he said.

"Oh, Danny. I didn't mean it that way. Please believe that. It's just that I've never felt any of that needy furtiveness from you. Maybe I'm asking you to explain something that you've never experienced any more than I have. If you don't want to get into it I underst…"

"It's okay, Gwynn. I do understand at least some of it. I did grow up in this Bible Belt after all, with fundamentalist parents. Not exactly conducive to good mental health, but I survived. It makes one observant. Sometimes I look at people and I know exactly what's going on in their heads, or at least think I do."

Danny rolled the mop bucket to a corner and leaned the mop handle against the wall. He turned back to Gwynn. "Back to your question about men; there are some things you already understand if you think about it. Like, when you were little, who was it that always cooked and served food in your house while you grew up?"

Gwynn swallowed. "My mom."

"Exactly. To some of the men, and women too, who come in here, you're their mom for the time being, whether they realize it or not. Or the mom they wish they'd had. The kind of mom that could get a good Oedipus complex going."

Gwynn laughed.

"No, I'm serious. They come in here wanting to be babied. They want to have a more useful puberty. They want to kill their fathers and marry you."

"Wait. This is getting a little deep, don't you think?"

"Maybe. Who can say? But here's something else that I think rings true. Most of the men who come in here are working men who have wives at home. Kids who misbehave and a dog that craps in the driveway. Their wife wants them to do more of one thing and less of something else. They come in here and find you: a beautiful young woman who's in a good mood, or at least pretends to be. They imagine what it would be like to wake up in the same house with you every day. It's a fantasy they don't even know they have. But they can't take their eyes off you.

"And as for the religious ones, they have an added layer of guilt. They can't just come in and enjoy you for who you are, because they're not supposed to enjoy you in the first place. I could quote you some Bible on the matter, but I won't."

Gwynn rolled her eyes. "I guess you just about explained it all."

"No I didn't," Danny said. "Some of them just want to fuck you."

"DANNY!"

"Oh, you know it's true, Baby. So please. Don't you go all prudish on me here. It's not lost on me, or anybody else, that you're a different kind of girl."

"Different?" She shoved the loaded dish rack toward the washer and set an empty one before her on the counter. "What do you mean, 'different'?"

"What I mean is, the first time you came here, when you saw me for the first time, you already figured out that I'm a queer. But you didn't react. You just said, 'Hi, Danny,' and shook my hand and that was that. And my queerness has just been an ordinary thing between you and me ever since.

"Just like a lot of people look at me and know that I'm homosexual, they look at you and know that you don't carry the same limitations as most people around here. And in their addled little sex-deprived minds, they fantasize that you're free for the taking, if they were only free to take."

Gwynn frowned. "You're kinda creeping me out here, Danny."

"The world can be a creepy place, Honey."

Chapter 28
The Tree of Knowledge

He dreamed of her when he slept. He thought of her in the late afternoon and through the long nights, and he was conflicted about her when he got off work in the mornings. Every day when quitting time came, he wanted to go straight to the Streamliner, but he had barely enough gumption to exercise a little restraint. His frequent breakfasts there were eating into his paychecks. He hardly cared about that, but he did have sense enough to know that going there every day would be creepy. He tried to calculate a reasonable frequency that would allow him to see Gwynn as often as possible without making a spectacle of himself. Occasionally he was frustrated that he got nothing more than breakfast and a thinner wallet. After all, Gwynn didn't work seven days a week. He kept a mental log in an effort to piece together her work schedule, but he could make no sense of it. Did her schedule change week by week? Did she have some kind of four-on, four-off rotation? Did she just take random days off now and then? There were times that she was there, but the cafe was too busy for him to talk to her. On those days he had to labor over his eggs and hash browns and watch her go from table to table, apparently enjoying talking with everyone in the room but him. Watching her laugh with other men made his face burn. There was nothing for him to do but go home and do his best to sleep.

He wanted to find some way to take his relationship with her to something beyond his own imagination. He could ask her out for a date, but it would have to be an early one. His work hours made for a tighter curfew than he'd had in high school. Then there was the fact of their age difference. He didn't know exactly, but he figured her to be three or four years older. Would he be able to live through the humiliation if she treated him like a kid? A kid with a crush on his teacher. Besides all that, Sabine Gap was a small town. They would be seen together and talked about, if they weren't talked about already. There were obvious differences between them. She had been a college student, and not just at Panola College, but at Berkeley, for crying out loud. An important place that was often in the news. Pete considered Gwynn much more sophisticated than himself, and there was some truth to that. Two months ago Pete had been a high school kid, and nothing much had happened since then to change the fact.

But he liked her. It seemed that she liked him. Once in a while they had moments of genuine conversation. In that open and confident way of hers, she told him how much she missed her mother. How she worried that her brother, who was in the Army in Germany, might be sent to Viet Nam. She'd put her hand on his when he told her about his father's accident. When he revealed that he might be a preacher one day, she said simply that she didn't believe in God in that way. She'd been so forthright that he was left to wonder what other ways there might be to believe in God.

In mid-August Griz put out the word that the plant was running out of raw material and would shut down in about a week or two. There would be no more deliveries to the pit for now. He said that he was putting in a bid for some tanks down near Houston, but the cleaning out of those tanks wouldn't get started until probably late September at the earliest. In the meantime he'd have to lay off everybody except for a few who would go on days for repairs and maintenance. He'd try to keep the ones with families. Pete, of course, would go since he was going to start college anyway. Obviously Swat would be laid off. Heckle and Jeck would go on nights to keep one of the boilers going, and Pete and Swat could work the week-end nights if Heck and Jeck wanted a night off. The ones who were to be laid off would get a hundred-dollar bonus if they'd please keep working until the actual shutdown. Swat would get seventy-five.

Until that news came, Pete hadn't had the luxury of imagining a day off. Now, with an end in sight, impatience set in and vibrated in his every nerve. When he drove, he drove too fast. When he ate, he could hardly stay seated. During those last remaining nights at the plant, he couldn't stand to be alone, but followed Swat, talking in a stream of consciousness.

"I've got nearly $900 saved up. That's tuition and books for nearly three years. Of course I have to get some clothes, and there's gas and groceries, but I'll be staying at home, so that won't cost anything. I wonder what I'd have to pay for an outboard motor? I could get a used one. That way I could get around on Caddo Lake. I used to go there with my dad. Stayed at Johnson's Landing. You know where Johnson's Landing is at?"

Swat did not know where Johnson's Landing was at. Swat was amazed at all the things he didn't know. He did not know if girls minded riding in an old car, even if it does run good and doesn't stink. He didn't know what size outboard it would take to pull a water ski, and he didn't know how far it was from Sabine Gap to Galveston. Yes, he thought maybe Galveston would be a good town to have a date but was probably too far away for a first one. No, he'd never been to the state fair in

Dallas, nor did he have any good ideas for where to go dove hunting when the season opened in September. Swat was starting to entertain the notion that he might not know anything useful in this whole wide world until Pete said, "You think I should join the Army?"

"Why would you want to join the Army?"

"Well, you were in the Army, weren't you?"

"I was," he said. "But I thought you was going to college, not the Army."

"Yeah. I guess. I just don't know if I can even sit down in a classroom anymore. Maybe it would be better if I just join up. Get it over with. If you join instead of get drafted, you get more choices about what you do."

"You get choices in the Army as long as you choose what they tell you."

Pete had no answer to that. "At least then I'd get the GI Bill to pay for college when I get out."

"There's a lot could go wrong with that plan."

"Yeah, I guess so."

"Mister Pete, I ain't your daddy, but if I was, I'd tell you to take a powder and calm down."

Pete's spirits ran high in those last days at the plant. As the end neared, his thoughts of Gwynn grew bolder. He had no knowledge of anyone else she was dating, which amazed him. In the next nine counties there was nobody else like her, and he couldn't live with himself if he didn't make some kind of advance. Then he saw in the Sunday paper that *Doctor Zhivago* was showing in Longview.

It was a true grown-up movie, and Longview wasn't too far to drive. If they saw the early feature they could still get a hamburger afterward and he could make it to work on time. It was about the most sophisticated entertainment that he could conjure. At least it wasn't another dumb Elvis or Beach Boys movie.

He procrastinated until the shutdown came in the last week of August. Pete worked his last night shift and drove home, not even sure what day it was. He showered, had a small breakfast with Lavena before she went to work, then tried to sleep for a few hours. He gave it up just before noon. He was hungry, and there was no question what he was going to do about it.

He yanked on fresh jeans and a clean T-shirt and his newest old shoes and headed for the Streamliner. He brought the old Plymouth sliding to a stop in the parking lot and bounded up the front steps and through the door. He scanned the room and was sorry to see that there were so many other customers. The lunch crowd. He hadn't thought of that, but he wouldn't let it deter him now.

Gwynn was standing at a table and writing on her order pad when he came in. She saw him and smiled. Pete took a stool at the counter.

Gwynn greeted him briskly. "Hi, Pete. Looks like your favorite booth is taken. Coffee?"

"Iced tea."

When she brought it, he wasted no time. "Want to go see *Doctor Zhivago* with me? It's on in Longview."

Gwynn glanced around the room. Then she said the words that every date-asker dreads. "Oh Pete, that's so sweet of you."

Pete felt his innards sink. He waited for the *but*. In an instant he became as subdued as he had just been enthusiastic. *What an idiot. I'm doing this all wrong. I wish I could just run out the door and start over.*

"But I have another idea," she said. "I can't talk right now though."

He was dizzy with relief. At least he hoped he could be

relieved. He breathed deeply while Gwynn zipped around the cafe. He generated worlds of possibility out of his only clue. *I have another idea.*

He sat at the counter long after he had finished his chicken fried steak. He drank glass after glass of tea while he waited for the noon crowd to dwindle. Danny came out of the kitchen a few times to help her gather dishes and clear tables. He never spoke to anyone, and he never served. Pete knew some of the patrons. A couple from church at one table. In a booth, the father of a girl he'd once dated. Finally Gwynn got a break.

She slid a tray down the counter toward him, loading dishes as she went. When she got to Pete she pushed the loaded tray back toward the kitchen door and came to Pete with a wet towel in her hand.

"Hoo!" she said and pushed a strand of blonde hair from her eyes. "This has been quite the morning."

Pete was thinking, *what's your idea, what's your idea, what's your idea,* but he only said, "Yeah. I was about ready to start clearing tables myself."

"You don't want any more tea, do you? Say no."

"No."

Gwynn wiped small circles on the countertop. "Can you drive a boat, and do you like to water ski?"

Pete blinked. "I can handle a boat. I've done a little skiing. But I'm not really very good at it."

"That's not what I asked. Did you *like* it? Was it *fun?*"

"Yeah, it was pretty fun. I fell a lot. I think I could get the hang of it with practice."

"Falling can be fun. Or at least funny," Gwynn mused.

"I could provide funny, I guess. But I don't have that kind of boat, do you?"

She raised an eyebrow. "I do. I think. Or at least, my dad does. I'd like to try it out, but I can't do it by myself. So do you want to do it with me?"

Pete was slack-jawed. He told his mouth to say, "Yes," and he was pretty sure he heard it do that. "When?" he asked.

"How about this afternoon? You teach me to drive the boat, and I'll teach you how to do a spin."

"I imagine your daddy might want to do that part. Teach you how to drive it."

"Oh no," she said. "I doubt he knows how. He's never there anyway. The boat came with the house."

"Huh. Somebody just left a boat and motor and skis when they sold the house?"

"My dad said it was a 'distressed property.' A repossession."

"Huh. And it's just a regular outboard?"

"Yeah. I guess that's what you call it. The motor clamps on the back. And there are skis in the boat house."

"Right." Pete's head was getting crowded with ideas, images and considerations. He'd presumed that he'd be at home this afternoon. He might need to let his mother know that he wouldn't be there for supper. Or would he? Better to tell her no and then show up unexpectedly, than to have her expecting him and then not show up. Simultaneously he conjured an image of Gwynn in a swimsuit. Then he considered the hopelessness of preserving his own modesty while wearing one. There was already a bulge in his jeans that was only hidden because he was sitting on a bar stool. Gwynn was still talking, something about stopping at the grocery store on the way home. They could meet there and he could follow her in his own car. He wasn't taking in a word of it. He was thinking of how to get into his house to get his swimsuit and out again without his mother extracting a thorough explanation. He decided to stop at Penney's and buy one rather than risk it.

For logistics' sake, he had to ask Gwynn to repeat much of what she'd just said. The important part was that the two of them would meet at Brookshires parking lot at two-forty-five, and from there he would follow her to her place on the lake.

"One more thing," Pete said. "I need to use your phone."

Gwynn let Pete come behind the counter to get to the phone on the wall. He dialed and waited several rings, his breathing shallow.

"Hi, Gina? This is Pete. Is my mother still there? No! Uh, no don't call me back. I'll wait. No really, I don't mind waiting."

He waited. He didn't want her to know he was calling from the Streamliner.

Finally. "Hi, Mother, it's me. Me and Eddie are going to go rabbit hunting down at the river. Maybe do something afterwards, so I won't be home for dinner."

"Yeah, I'll be careful. I'll come in quiet if I'm late."

"Okay."

"Okay."

"Yeah, okay. Bye."

He hung up and took a deep breath. He knew that she knew he was lying. And he knew that she knew that he knew it. He could live with that.

He left the Streamliner and went to the bank and withdrew $25 from his savings. From there he went to Penney's and was looking around for swimsuits when he heard a woman's voice.

"Why hello, Pete. It's been so long since I've seen you that I would swear that you've grown," she sang.

"Mrs. Broussard! Uh, hi." Pete looked around desperately. "Do you work here?"

"Why, yes I do. I haven't seen you at church in a coon's age. Where on earth have you been? I haven't hardly seen you since the revival. Where have you been keeping yourself?"

Pete mentally sorted through a world of hypothetical possibilities, seeking the straightest line toward an early end to this conversation. But two things were already clear; this was going to take some time, else his abruptness would become front-page news of the day at Sabine Gap Baptist. The other was that the peculiarity of his hurriedly buying a swimsuit this late in the season would make page two.

He negotiated his way through Mrs. Broussard's inquisition until he could reasonably say, "So, uh, where do you have the swimsuits?"

"Swimsuits? Oh my, swimsuits have been off the show floor for over a week now. I don't know if we'll even have any. Not until next spring. Can you wait until then?"

"I was hoping to get one today."

Mrs. Broussard put a hand on Pete's shoulder and looked into his eyes. "Of course. You've worked all summer and haven't even been able to go swimming once. And now you've discovered that last year's swimsuit is too small. I hope I can help. We may still have some in the stock room. I'll go and check."

"Thank you. I appreciate it."

"Do you want the boxer kind, or that skinny kind?"

"Boxer!" he said, a little too quick, a little too loud. He gave her the best smile he could manufacture. "The boxer kind."

"That's right," she said, as if complimenting him for a correct answer. She squeezed out a smile of her own and disappeared into the stock room.

In a moment she returned. "I found one," she announced triumphantly. "This will fit you too. You want to try it on?"

He didn't want to try it on. He paid for it and started to leave, but stopped. "I should get a button-up short-sleeve shirt."

She led him to the sale rack. He chose a pale blue. His mother had told him once that blue brought out the color of his eyes. He paid again and left.

It was easy to spot Gwynn's orange Ghia in the Brookshires parking lot. He parked where he could watch for her to come out. He glanced around, more uneasy than he needed to be about the prospect of being seen by anyone who knew him. He turned the radio on to KLIF in Dallas and slumped low in the seat. Dion sang *The Wanderer.* The Shirelles sang *Soldier Boy.* Pregnant Mrs. Yandel with her brood, the youngest with a thumb in its mouth and dragging a loaf of bread, passed so near that he could have spoken to her, but he did not.

At last Gwynn came out followed by a package boy carrying two brown bags. Pete gave a small wave. Gwynn returned it with a smile that made him curl his toes inside his shoes.

Gwynn tipped the package boy and got into her car and started the motor. Pete cranked the Plymouth and followed her out onto the street. He felt very self-conscious.

Finally they were out of town and heading toward the lake. The road was all but empty, and the sun was bright and hot. The landscape opened into hay fields and clearings where cattle grazed. Barbed wire fences separated fields and woods. Gwynn was driving more slowly than Pete would have preferred. He trembled with anticipation.

Passing through the countryside he could hear the occasional blue jay in the woods and smell the windrows of hay baking in the sun. Crows dotted the fields pecking for mice killed in the haying. The road dipped into a creek bottom where the air was momentarily cooler. Pete loved the beauty of God's creation, but he hardened himself against thoughts of God. His morality hadn't room for both God and Gwynn, and today it was Gwynn who was real to him. He envied Gwynn for her apparent lack of misgivings and second thoughts. He chastised himself for his own feelings of guilt, and also for daring to presume that there would be anything to feel guilty about. After all, nothing had happened yet between himself and Gwynn.

The Ghia slowed and turned right onto a narrower black-top road. Pete followed fifty yards behind. The woods grew thicker and the terrain began to roll. They passed an old un-painted house with an enormous oak shading the front. A crone sat on the wide sloping front porch with a bright bowl in her lap, a bushel basket on the floor beside her chair, likely shelling peas. A plaster Little Black Sambo in a broken straw hat fished off the top step with his two-foot pole. The woman nodded, and he nodded back.

At a crossroads they turned to the right again, skirting two sides of the house on the corner. Fishing poles hung in the rafters of a carport and an outboard motor lay in the yard. Mourning doves lifted off the wire fence and sailed over the field. Pete slowed and watched them until they reached the woods and were gone.

At last the lake came into view, barely, down through the trees. It disappeared again and then reappeared. Gwynn came to a near stop, made a hard right turn and descended a hundred yards on a sandy track, which divided then into two driveways. Gwynn veered to the right, and Pete followed. She parked under a cement-floored and tin-roofed carport near the back door of the cottage. Pete pulled up behind and got out.

"Well, this is it," Gwynn said, lifting a grocery bag out of the Ghia. "Home sweet home."

The house looked old and small. The white shiplap siding was blistered and peeling. The steep roof was randomly shin-gled in patches of gray, brown and green.

"You live here all by yourself?"

"Yeah. Weird, huh? Sometimes I wonder how I got here. It's like I got on a wrong train. Now I have to figure out how to get back."

Pete picked up the other bag of groceries and followed Gwynn through the back door and into the kitchen. "You've told me some of it. Coming from California with your dad, but why this house?"

Gwynn talked as she put items into the refrigerator. "It got too … I don't know. Strange. Living with my dad. I told him I was going back to California, but he really didn't want me to go. Long story short, he bought this as an investment and said I could live in it for free if I would stay a year." She stood up from the fridge. "He wants to tear it down and build a new house here. I think he imagines me and my brother moving here, starting families and having picnics here or something. Honestly, he's not thinking straight. And I don't know if I can last out a year."

Pete's eyes went to the wine bottle on the counter top. Three quarters full. Being well-versed in the evils of alcohol, he'd never tasted wine. Nor beer, for that matter, three bottles of which sat in the refrigerator. Gwynn was exotically worldly.

They made bologna sandwiches for a late lunch. Gwynn offered beer, and Pete accepted, beginning to imagine himself a little worldly too. He couldn't distinguish the beer buzz from the sheer headiness of simply being there.

Later as the afternoon heat reached its four-thirty peak, they changed into their swimsuits in separate rooms and went out the back door to the boat shed. Pete couldn't manage his eyes. Gwynn's swimsuit, fairly modest by swimsuit standards, was nevertheless a two-piece. Pete's eyes jumped from her navel to her face, from her face to the bit of revealed cleavage. From her bust to the sky. He turned away to gain some control of himself and reminded himself to breathe.

Gwynn meanwhile was pulling life vests and a pair of skis out of the cupboard in the boat house. "All this stuff came with the house when my dad bought it. Some of it looks use-able. Here. This one ought to fit you pretty well. I'll take this one." She handed him a kapok vest.

Pete looked at the boat where it swayed gently. "Kind of mossy on the bottom. We ought to clean it up some."

"Do we have to? Can't we use it like it is? I'd rather do chores another time."

"Sure. But does this motor even run?"

"You're asking me? I guess we'll find out."

She handed Pete a dusty pair of skis and turned to untie the bow line. When her back was to him, he watched her. The sight of her hair over her shoulders, of the curvature of her waist and hips, of her sturdy legs and smooth ankles and feet; it was enough to make his knees weak. In a daze he stepped into the boat and stowed the skis. Fortunately he'd had enough experience with boats that he could busy himself. He checked that there was gasoline in the fuel tank, and there was. There appeared to be no water in the bottom. He connected the gas hose to the motor and squeezed the bulb to pressurize it. He released the catch and lowered the prop into the water.

"Ready?" Gwynn asked. She had released the lines and was holding the painter in her hand.

"Give us a shove," he said.

Later Pete would remember the sound he'd heard just then. A light scraping against the hull. A faint sibilance as if the bottom of the boat were brushing over reeds. But something about it was wrong. The rhythm was off. It didn't match the momentum of the boat itself. He half-heard it, but being oth-erwise occupied, ignored it.

Gwynn meantime crawled onto the small deck of the bow and clambered down to the forward seat. "You need me to do anything?" she asked. "You'll have to tell me if you do."

"You might just pick up a paddle and be ready in case we drift back toward the dock before I get this started. You can fend us off and keep us pointed at open water." He pulled out the choke and put the throttle in start position. He wrapped the starter rope around the flywheel and gave a strong pull. It didn't fire. He tried twice more with no success. He opened the choke just a little and tried again. Still nothing, not even a cough.

A light breeze was in fact drifting them shoreward. When Gwynn reached to the bottom of the boat to get a paddle, Pete heard that rasping sound again. He glanced from the motor to the darkness under the covered bow, but his attention was still on the motor. He kept working, pulling hard, and finally the motor coughed twice. On the next pull it sputtered to life, running rough and setting up a vibration that shook the entire boat.

Gwynn screamed and jumped up onto her seat, flinging her paddle off to starboard, looking like she might jump out of the boat and follow it. That's when Pete saw the snake, a cottonmouth maybe three feet long. It charged out from under the bow, apparently rattled into panic by the vibration of the hull. It went quickly over the gunwale and into the water and, with its zig-zag stroke, headed back toward the boat house. Gwynn, in a panic of her own, had already flung herself as far from the bow as possible, rocking the boat violently as she went. Pete immediately shut off the motor.

With both of them in the stern, the bow lifted high in the air where the breeze caught it and swung them around toward shore.

"It's gone. It's gone," Pete said.

Wide-eyed, Gwynn said, "I'm sorry. I just …"

"It's okay. You did what anybody with any sense would have done. But we better kill it if we can. It's headed toward the boat house, and I don't think you want to be surprised by it again if you can help it."

They both saw the snake veering into the shore grass near the dock.

"Okay." She took a deep breath. "Okay, we'll go back. But I threw the paddle. What now?"

"Short of swimming for it, which I'm reluctant to do right now, I have an idea that might work."

Pete went to the bow and gathered the painter in a coil. He threw it to starboard so that it lay over the floating paddle. Gently he pulled it back to the boat, got a hand on it and paddled them back to the dock. Gwynn, proving that she wasn't helpless, climbed out and tied them to a cleat.

"Do you have a hoe, or a shovel? Maybe an ax or anything I can use to kill it. Big rocks, if it comes to that."

"There's a shovel in the carport." She shivered. "I have to go get it, don't I?"

"Or you could stay and look for the snake."

"Yeah. Right." Trembling, she stepped barefoot from the dock to the grass and went across the lawn, head-down and jumpy. Pete watched her, thinking that under different circumstances it might be a comical sight.

He kept the paddle in his hand and crouched on the dock where he could get the best view into the reeds. He remained very still, watching and listening. When Gwynn came back from the carport with a garden shovel in her hand, he raised his palm toward her and put a finger to his lips. When she stopped, he gave a thumbs-up.

They waited. The trees whispered. Blue jays argued off in the woods somewhere. Gwynn kept a sharp eye on the ground around her. Pete kept his watch at the water.

It was Gwynn who saw it first. She waved her arms and then pointed toward the opposite side of the boathouse, jabbing her forefinger toward it.

Pete rose quickly and, also barefoot, crept paddle in hand in the direction she indicated.

Pete had seen bigger water moccasins, but this one was big enough. It made its way rapidly toward the house, and he had to run to intercept it. He halted its progress with the boat paddle. The snake coiled for a strike and launched at the blade.

"Bring the shovel!" Pete shouted. There was no more need for stealth. Gwynn handed it to him and stepped back. Pete held it in both hands, leaning forward with the shovel blade inverted in front of him. He stabbed at the snake, aiming just behind the head, and after several tries, cut a significant gash about three inches behind the head.

Pete sparred with the snake while it alternately coiled to strike and stretched to flee, apparently hindered very little by the deep wound behind its head. When he finally managed to get it pinned under the shovel point, he took care not to lose his advantage. He pressed down hard and rocked the shovel side to side. The snake's white mouth involuntarily stretched open, exposing the fangs. Its body coiled and writhed frantically against the back side of the shovel. At last the head came free of the body. Pete stepped back and watched. For more than a minute the heavy body of the snake coiled, lifted, rolled, twisted, thumping the ground, leaving bits of blood in the dry grass and leaves. Eventually it slowed.

Pete pointed at the severed head. "Be careful of that," he said to Gwynn. "It's still dangerous."

Gwynn was in tears. She'd never before witnessed any creature's death, nor the kind of violence that had just played out in front of her, nor had she experienced the kind of immediate danger she'd just been exposed to. She walked to where Pete stood with the shovel still in one hand. "Hold me," she said. "Just hold me for a minute."

Pete let the shovel fall and allowed Gwynn to wrap her arms around him, her face to his chest. Slowly he relaxed and put his arms around her shoulders and held her tighter while she sobbed. He was struck by how small her body was. He felt it inappropriate that he should have an erection under the circumstances. But standing there barefooted, bare chested in his swimsuit with Gwynn pressing against him, there was no help for it.

After a few moments she released him. "I'm sorry," she said. She wiped her eyes and cheeks with her palms. "I must look a mess right now. I just …"

"You look beautiful," he said. "You always look beautiful."

She gave a weak smile. "I'm okay now. It's just that. I've never …"

"It's alright. You don't have to apologize. If you weren't pretty brave, you'd be in the house, in the bed, under the covers right now, not standing out here with bare feet."

Gwynn gave a shuddering laugh and sniffed, wiping her eyes again. "Wow," she laughed. "That was really something."

"Yes it was. At first there, I thought you were going to jump out of the boat."

She guffawed. "So did I. Oh my god." She laughed another sob, and cried a little more. "Have you killed snakes before?"

"A few."

After a moment Pete said, "We don't have to ski. We can go back in the house and …"

"No. I want to go out. At least go out in the boat. At least that."

"Okay." He looked at the snake's body still slowly rolling. "I better get rid of the head so it can't cause any harm. Then we'll give the boat another try. Second time's the charm."

"Yes," she said. "Try again."

He scooped up the gaping head with the shovel and carried it to the far side of the boathouse where he dug a small hole and buried it. He came back and picked up the snake by the tail and carried it, just barely flexing now, feebly trying to rise up. On the dock he swung it, rope-like, out into the air. It twisted and splashed and sank. He wiped his hands on his new swim trunks. "Crawdads and turtles will take it from there," he said.

They were vigilant to say the least as they launched the boat once again. The outboard started easier this time.

As they pulled away, Pete looked back and noted the landmarks for finding the way back. He started out slowly, familiarizing himself with the handling of the boat. How well it turned. How well it took waves passing over its own wake. In open water Pete advanced the throttle and made a few lazy loops. Gwynn looked back at him from her seat near the bow and flashed a brilliant smile. The wind took her hair in all directions, and they both laughed.

When they were well away from the shore and stumps that they might drift into, Pete cut the motor back to idle, and they puttered along at trolling speed. "You want to swim?" he asked.

"I don't know," she said. "What about snakes?"

"They won't be out here. They hang around the shore. They like the cattails and reeds. Bushes. Things like that. Besides, they swim on the surface. They'd be easy to see."

That sounded reasonable enough, but Gwynn didn't think her legs were ready to respond to reason when it came to climbing out of the boat and into the water. She still had the shivers from what she'd seen that afternoon.

"It's getting kind of late. The sun will be down past those trees in an hour or so."

Pete killed the motor and let the boat drift.

"Why did you do that?" she asked.

Without a word Pete stood up on his seat, dropped his life vest and cannonballed overboard.

Gwynn shrieked and burst out laughing. When he surfaced, she shouted, "Oh my god! I had no idea you were going to do that."

"HOOOO-Boy! Come on in. The water's great." He rolled face-down and swam a few strokes away from the boat.

Before he turned around he heard the splash as Gwynn dove in. In a moment she was there beside him.

"I'll race you back to the boat," she said.

"GO!" he shouted, and got the jump on her by half a length. As he began to pull away from her, she grabbed his foot and pulled him back. He laughed and got water in his mouth and started to cough. She swam by him. He made a grab for her foot, but she twisted away.

"Beat ya!" she yelled.

Laughing and gasping for air, they treaded water together. They splashed at each other and played a made-up version of tag and hide-and-seek around the boat, changing the rules to their own advantage whenever it suited them. Pete dove out of sight and came up quietly on the other side of the boat.

"Pete?" she said. "Pete, where are you?" The first hint of panic was in her voice. "PETE!" she yelled, panicked in earnest.

"I'm over here,"

"Where? Where ARE you?"

"I'm here. I'm here." He swam back to her, sober now.

"Damn you!" she said. "Don't do that to me. It's not funny."

"I'm sorry. It was a bad joke."

Gwynn held to the gunwale of the boat with one hand and wiped water from her face with the other. "I guess I'm just jumpy after that snake. Shit. Did you swim under the boat?"

"Yeah, I won't …"

"It's alright. I'm okay now." Her brown eyes looked into his. "Let's both do it."

They counted three and went down and under the boat and came up on the other side. They treaded water there, their foreheads touching. "Let's go make dinner," she said. "I'm getting hungry."

"Fine by me. But you mean *supper.* Those sandwiches we had were *dinner.*"

"Sheesh," she said. "Texans!"

They swam to the stern to climb in. Pete watched Gwynn lift herself, marveling at her grace. Her wet hair clung to her neck and shoulders.

Gwynn took her seat near the bow, picked up two towels and pitched one to Pete. "Don't start the motor just yet," she said. "Let's just look at this for a minute."

They sat still, catching their breath, gazing toward the west. The sun was low, and the sky was taking on pale colors. Chickadees far away in the woods gave shape to the silence.

"It's like a Rorschach," she said. "Those trees reflected upside down in the water."

He had to ask what a *roar sack* was, and when she explained, he wondered if there was anyone else in the county who would know such a thing. He moved forward to the middle seat, reached out and took her hand and pulled her to him. They sat side by side. Silent. Watchful. "Roar sack," he said again.

"Let's go."

He started the motor, put it in gear and slowly advanced the throttle until the boat lifted and planed over the water. The wind against their faces was cool now. Pete reflected on his weeks at the wax plant. It was incomprehensible that this lake and the wax plant, where he'd been less than twenty-four hours ago, could be on the same planet. He felt like a new person in a new world, and he hardly recognized himself in it.

As soon as they were in reach of the dock, Gwynn grabbed a plank and pulled them in. She climbed out, painter in hand. They secured the boat and put the gear away in the boat house. Walking gingerly and barefoot across the grass toward the house, they were alert for movement in the grass, but neither of them mentioned the cottonmouth.

"I want to shower the lake water off," Gwynn said when they were inside. "You can too if you want. It'll feel good to get dry clothes on."

While Gwynn was in the shower, Pete listened to the water splashing, and to her occasional gasp and moan of pleasure. It made him dizzy.

When she came out, she wore a burgundy tank top and an ankle-length light cotton skirt, the likes of which he'd never seen. It was ornately printed in more colors than he could count.

"It's from India," she said. "You see a lot of these on the West Coast."

"It's beautiful."

She spun around for him to admire and then turned her attention to the kitchen. "I put a towel out for you. I think there's still plenty of hot water." With a mischievous grin, she said in her best imitation Texas drawl, "Ah'll git supper a-go-in."

Pete wanted to touch her. It was true that they had touched before, but the touching had been of a purpose. Playing in the water. Comfort while the snake died. He'd never held her for the express purpose of the pleasure of touching. He stood, paralyzed, watching her, wanting to fold his arms around her. In that moment he would have gladly died for her.

She turned and saw him standing there. "What? Aren't you going to shower?"

"Yeah," he said and started to move.

"What?" she said again, puzzled.

"Nothing. I was just …"

When he didn't speak, she said, "Well. Go on. I can handle things here until you get back."

Pete closed the bathroom door and, with relief, took off his swimsuit. He was starting to ache from the erection he'd had most of the day. He didn't know if Gwynn intended to have sex with him, but he knew that he would soon explode, one way or another.

He puzzled out the peculiar shower controls and got a good warm spray going. With the water running over his head and shoulders, he tried to remember if he'd ever been naked in anyone's house he wasn't related to. The mere fact of being where he was stimulated him beyond his ability to bear it. Thoughts of sin still crossed his mind, but he had already made a decision: if Noah, Abraham, and King David could do the things they'd done and still reach the kingdom of Heaven, he was pretty sure he had nothing to worry about. If Gwynn was willing to make love with him, he would do it. He was ready to face what future regrets might await him.

Dried and back into his jeans and new shirt, he came out of the bathroom and found Gwynn pressing hamburger patties into shape. "What can I do?" he asked.

"How about opening that bottle of wine on the counter there. The opener's in the top middle drawer. And then maybe get the charcoal lit in the grill?"

"I'll light the charcoal first. Let it get started."

He brushed behind her on his way out to the car port. As he did, he placed a hand on her shoulder. She turned her head toward him and gave a quick smile and turned back to her work.

He trembled slightly as he dumped charcoal into the grill, doused it with lighter fluid and set the match to it. He stepped back out of the fumes and watched the flame spread. The coals started to glow orange around the edges. He sensed himself falling into that burning ring.

He drew his attention away from the heat of it and returned to the kitchen where he opened the drawer and pawed around in it for a moment. He picked up what looked to him like a long nail that had been twisted into a helix around a pencil. It had a rack-and-pinion operated by two side handles. Uncertainly he held it up. "Is this it?"

"Yeah, that's it."

"How do you work it?"

Gwynn blinked. "Just twist the point into the cork," she said and shrugged.

Pete looked back to the opener and the wine bottle. He did as she said, and was somewhat enlightened to see the side handles of the opener swinging up as he twisted.

"What kind of opener do you use?" she asked.

"I don't have one." He twisted a few more turns. "Never seen one before," he muttered, more to himself than to her.

"Wow," she whispered to herself. Aloud she said, "I put two wine glasses there on the counter," pointing with her elbow.

Pete got the wine open and poured two short-stemmed glasses to the top. He placed one of them on the counter within Gwynn's reach. She wiped her hands and lifted it carefully. "Cheers," she said. "Here's to not getting bitten by snakes." She delicately clinked her glass to his and took a full swallow. "Mmm."

Pete nodded and sipped from his own glass.

"Have you never had wine before?"

He winced. "No." He paused. "There's lots of things I've never had before," he said.

"Oh?" Gwynn looked at him with one eye, the other obscured by her wine glass. "What other things haven't you had?"

The color of Pete's face approximated that of the Shiraz. "Beer. Whiskey. Caviar," he said, and was silent for a moment. "I've never ..." His voice failed him. His mind told his voice to speak, but it refused.

"What?" She took her wine glass from her face and looked at him directly. "You okay?"

"I've never ..." He swallowed and took a deep breath. "It just comes as a surprise to me, Gwynn, that you even want me for a friend. Beautiful girls are generally out of my league. I don't know what I have to offer someone like you."

"Hey, take it easy. We're just a couple of people enjoying each other. And what do you mean, 'someone like me'?"

"You know. More educated. More sophisticated. A little older and more experienced." He looked her in the eye. "You could have any guy in the county. Me, I'm just out of high school. I've got no money to speak of. I live with my mother. I see the guys that come in at the Streamliner. They can't take their eyes off you. They have new cars. Probably boats and houses. They go to Austin and Dallas or New Orleans just for the fun of it. They ..."

"Stop it!" she said. "Just stop that. Pete, do you think I don't know that? What I also know is that most of them have the latest *Playboy* under the seat of their pickup with its fantasy California girls. They look at me and what do they see? The surfer girl, free and easy. They see escape." She gestured toward the whole wide world. "Escape from this ... from the Bible Belt mentality that makes them so pent-up and weird. They don't know who I am, and they don't want to know. Their leering just makes me feel lonely."

"What's Bible Belt mentality? You make it sound like some kind of dumb."

"Not dumb, Pete. Just narrow. Deep down I think they know. I think you know. There's a wider world than what's contained in the Sunday sermons they hear. It's frustrating. But I don't want to talk about them. I'm talking about you.

"Pete, we're friends. You held me this afternoon when I needed it. You just held me. Do you know how rare that is? Most of those guys you're talking about would have had their hands in my swimsuit while they had the chance. But you just held me and let me go when I felt better. You're different from them."

"Not that much different," he said. "I just didn't have the nerve."

She guffawed. "I don't believe you."

"Believe it, Gwynn. My eyes have been glued to you all day. All summer for that matter." He stopped, afraid he'd said too much. "Anyway, I really like you, Gwynn. You're different from anybody I've ever known."

"I like you too, Pete. And I know you've tried to hide the way you look at me. So here's a little secret. It's kind of cool to be looked at by a guy who's able to see me. I'm glad you like to look at me."

"Sex," he said. "I've never had sex. Not just whiskey and caviar and that stuff." He looked away, took a breath and looked back at her. "Right now I just want to grab you onto my lap and put my face in your hair. I ..."

Gwynn smiled at him, and her forehead wrinkled in sympathy. "How about for now, we think about having some dinner. I mean *supper.* I'm starving.

Pete picked up his wine glass and took a sip larger than the first. "Okay," he said. "To our friendship," but he found the term discouraging.

After a moment he said, "I guess I've been pretty lonely myself."

Gwynn put the raw hamburger patties onto a paper plate, and wiped her hands on a paper towel. "Which are you the most right now: lonely or hungry?"

"Horny."

"HA! I would have never guessed."

They looked at each other for a quiet moment.

Gwynn slid her hands down the sides of her long skirt and said, "I wouldn't dress like this for just anybody, you know. Still, let's just take it one step at a time." They were silent for a while, working side by side in the small kitchen.

Pete went to the carport to check on the grill. The coals were glowing red, and the grate was smoking lightly. He looked out at the sky and it was indigo. Vermilion clouds lay on the western horizon across the lake. He stuck his head into the kitchen. "You've got to come see this," he said.

She came to the door and stood there, a step higher than Pete. She put a hand on his shoulder and leaned out. "When I leave here, there will be a few things that I'll miss."

When I leave here. The words stung him every time he heard them.

"The grill is ready. Let's cook 'em."

When the patties were done, Gwynn lit two candles and turned out the kitchen lights. Pete refilled Gwynn's glass and made a little headway on his own.

They ate ravenously, and the wine ushered them into a realm they'd not shared before. Gwynn was lovely in candle-light.

They finished the hamburgers, one for Gwynn and two for Pete. They relaxed into their chairs, discussing sealing wax and cabbages and kings.

"So when I make jam and pour the melted wax to seal the jar, that wax comes from that place where you work?"

"It could. It would need some more refining. But I guess there must also be other wax plants in the country."

She changed the subject. "What do you intend to take at college, have you decided?"

"I thought I'd decided. I've been planning to be a preacher since I was in sixth grade. Now I'm not so sure."

Gwynn heard that as if it were any other career decision. She had no knowledge of preachers being "called by God," nor of the angst that would come with refusing the call.

"What do you think you might do instead?"

Pete shrugged. "I don't know. How about you. What were you majoring in?"

"Present tense," she said, more to hold the claim on her own intentions than to inform Pete. "AM majoring in. I thought I might teach home economics. Get a teaching certificate. Now I'm starting to think about law. Maybe work for a non-profit. Or even go into politics. There are so many people who need that kind of help. So much injustice. Being here has given me a lot to think about."

"Like what?"

"I keep thinking about this man that comes to the Streamliner sometimes. I think he works nights like you do. He has to come to the back window, no matter what the weather is. If it's too foul to eat at the picnic tables, he sits in his old truck. He deserves better than that."

"What color is his truck?"

Gwynn was almost offended at the non-sequitur. "What difference does that make? He's not allowed to come in and sit at a table like everyone else. I just hate that."

"What color is his truck?"

Gwynn gave an exasperated sigh. "It's red, okay?"

"I know him. We work together at the plant."

"Swat?"

"Yep. I'm his boss. At least on paper. Right now we're just working weekend nights keeping the boiler running since the plant is shut down. That's partly why I don't know about being a preacher. I'm not sure I agree with my own religion. I want people to be saved, but I don't think the people at my church can be my guide anymore."

Pete regretted where the conversation had gone. He wanted to get closer, much closer, to Gwynn, not talk about religion. "I saw you got ice cream. Feel like having dessert?"

They got up from the table and Gwynn brought out bowls. Pete scooped ice cream and opened a jar of spiced peaches. Gwynn brought the flashlight, Pete loaded a tray of everything else, and they went out to the dock. They sat side by side, their feet dangling over the water, and leaned against each other while the stars finished filling the sky. They talked some until Pete gathered his nerve. He reached an arm around her, pulled her to him and kissed her on the neck.

"I'm not sure I want it to come to this, Pete," she said.

"Nothing has to come to anything you don't want it to come to." He dropped his arm and took her hand and held it. "But if you don't stop me, I'm probably going to do it again."

He did it again, and she didn't stop him.

After a time they were harried by mosquitos. Gwynn stood and took Pete's hand and pulled him up. "Let's go inside," she said.

They stepped across the grass, across the very place where the cottonmouth was killed. Neither of them spoke of it, nor of the blood that must surely have dried there.

In the kitchen they put down their dishes and turned off the flashlights. Gwynn lifted Pete's shirt and put her arms around his bare middle and pressed her face against his chest, feeling how good it was to have skin on skin. He stroked the back of her head and put a hand in the curve of her waist.

"I don't have any kind of birth control," he said. "Do you?"

"Yes," she said. "I've put in my diaphragm. It's very sweet

of you to ask."

"I thought you didn't want it to come to this."

"Yeah." She swayed her head. "But I did, actually."

They went into Gwynn's bedroom and kissed their way past his prohibitions, past his shyness, and past his shame. Gwynn unbuttoned his shirt and he shrugged it to the floor. He found how to unfasten her halter top, and he kissed her neck and shoulders and breathed the gentle musk of her arms. They lay on her bed and held each other belly to belly, pressing hard against each other, kissing and breathing deeply.

Pete pushed all the thoughts of sin out of his mind, or tried to. All the sermons about the evils of sex swarmed around in his head, but he pushed them away and allowed himself this transgression. They separated long enough for Pete, with his back turned to Gwynn, to work out of his jeans as quickly as possible. He was embarrassed to be seen with his erection.

He hadn't realized how desperately he yearned to hold and be held. He trembled as he pushed Gwynn's skirt down past her hips and over her knees. Gwynn kicked it off and pushed it aside. She stroked the inside of his thigh, and when she touched him, when she wrapped her fingers around him and gently squeezed, he came immediately.

Shame, despondence and humiliation rushed over him and overpowered the pleasure of his orgasm.

"Oh no, no. I …" He silently convulsed. "I'm so sorry," he groaned, and made a motion to get out of bed.

"It's okay. It's okay," she said and pulled him back. "Pete, it's your first time. It happens to everybody. It's no big deal." She did her best to soothe him, ignoring the spreading slickness on the sheet. She held him to her. "It's alright. Just be still and hold me."

They lay together. Pete wept briefly.

She stroked his face. "We'll try it again," she said. "Just

wait. Second time's the charm. You'll see."

It didn't take long. The pleasure of touch was still there. Pete may have slept for a moment. After all, he'd hardly slept in the last twenty-four hours. But when they began to move and their bodies filled with pleasure, their blood ran high once more. Pete was more confident, encouraged by Gwynn's resilience and passion. Her durable good will.

For her part, Gwynn remembered the wonder of her first fumbling discoveries. She vicariously enjoyed Pete's astonishment alongside her own pleasures of sex after so long.

He entered questioningly. "Yes," she said, and drew him to her. They disappeared together into another world, sweat mixed with sweat. Breath with breath.

When their passion was spent, they lay together, their conjured world melting away, the created world to returning, they laughed.

"See?" she teased. "I told you ya." Pete laughed too, embarrassed. He kissed her and stroked her neck and kissed some more. The second time was indeed the charm.

Chapter 29
Cauldron Bubble

"Rake, Honey. I know being sheriff is a hard job, but honestly, it's not like you to let such petty nonsense get to you like this." The toast popped up, and Belinda snatched it out hot and started spreading butter. Sausage patties sizzled on the stove. "Will you please just sit down and stop pacing? Your eggs are about done."

Rake went to the table and swung his leg over a chair back and sat. Belinda poured a warm-up into his coffee and went back to the stove to flip the eggs.

"The thing of it is, it's the little stuff that adds up," he said. "Little stuff tilts things in one direction or another. I know it's not against the law for a white man and a Negro woman to be in the front seat of the same car, but the way things are going, it spells trouble that we don't need here in Kickapoo County. I'm willing to make concessions. You'll notice I didn't say 'nigger'. I can start sayin' 'black people' if that's a help to anything. And I'll concede to you that most of the 'black people' in the county are God-fearing folks who understand how things work around here. They know their place. What I've got a problem with is this outsider. He comes roaring into East Texas driving that bastard California-plated car of his. For some unknown reason he takes up with this nig …, 'black young lady,' and now everybody's got to see them two parading around like David and Bathsheba. Next thing you know, somebody's going to beat them up, or worse. Then I'm going to have to find out who done it and charge them for doing something that shouldn't of needed doing in the first place. And come election time, folks are gonna be wondering whose side I'm on."

Belinda put Rake's plate down in front of him and went back to the stove to fill her own. She sat down at the table and spooned some jam onto her plate. "People around here can't possibly have any doubt about whose side you're on," she said. "Your last election was a snap, and this one will be too."

Rake groaned and said, "I'm afraid you might be wrong about that. Word's getting around that Beeler is getting his ducks in a row to run against me. It looks like the coroner is backing him. At least that's what I hear." He shoveled half of an over-hard egg into his mouth and barely chewed it before washing it down with coffee.

"Beeler's running and Liam's backing him? After all you've done for them? Why?"

"Oh, hell, I don't know. Maybe he's still got a kink in his tail about that church bingo thing last year. Who knows?"

"Well, that wasn't your fault."

"I know. But the point is, this time, people are going to have to decide who to vote for. Last time it wasn't a hard decision, but this time it is. All the gossip about R.J. isn't any help. You ought to see how everybody stops talking when I come in the room. I'm not as oblivious as people think. I hear the talk. Some of it at least. 'Did you hear? The sheriff's kid was doing drugs. Run off to be a hippie! Connor don't even know where his son's at.' People think I'm coming apart. Treat me like I'm delicate. Either that or I'm the enemy. They're not just talking about R.J. There's this loud green Chevy with California plates roaming the county with a shave-headed white guy in Army fatigues and a … black girl in the front seat with him. Not the back, mind you. If she'd just sit in the back, folks could at least pretend to think she was the maid. So if they're doin' all that in the daylight, God knows what they do in the dark. And I'm going to bust them the first chance I get. Miscegenation might not be a crime in California or New York, but it still is in Texas."

Belinda scoffed, "Oh, yeah. I can see that. When was the last time that law was brought to trial? I can't think of a quicker way to brew some trouble. That story hits the *Dallas Morning News*, and you'll have every freedom-rider and NAACP-er in the South heading straight for Sabine Gap. You better think that one over."

"Shit," Rake said and leaned back in his chair, face tilted toward the ceiling. "Well. Maybe I can convince them to go somewhere else. Maybe I can make it so they don't like it around here anymore."

"Who is this black girl? She ought to know better."

"Well, she's a piece of work herself." Rake leaned forward on the table. "I'm in a position to know that the city police have been dealing with her for five or six years. Since she was in junior high. Petty theft mostly. Lately she's spent a lot of time out at the Bottle and Glass. Prostitute probably, but nobody cares what nig … They don't care what happens out there, so long as it stays out there. That's where she works, if working is what you call it." He raised his pitch and leaned back again. "What I don't understand is why a U.S. Army veteran would stoop to that. When I came back from Europe, we were proud. We got jobs and started families. This asshole is a disgrace to the Army and the nation he supposedly served. I'd like to rip that Army jacket offa' him and stick it where it don't fit."

Belinda put her hand on his and looked him in the eye.

"I'm more concerned about you than I am him," she said. "Leave this guy to stew in his own juices. He won't hang around here for long. As you said, somebody will persuade him to leave. It doesn't have to be you. When he goes, maybe he'll take her with him. They'll be somebody else's problem. Somebody else."

"And if he don't?"

Rake let his own question simmer. *If he don't?* He had another card he could play, if people wondered whose side he was on. He wasn't the only one in the county who was bothered by another matter. Swat Waters. Sure, he said all the right things, but you could tell he was thinking trouble just by the way he walked. Somebody ought to tell him he's not in the Army no more. And Griz out at the plant was probably paying him too much. Griz ought to hire somebody white to work out there. Some folks found it very irritating.

If he was to do something about all of that, then there'd be no doubt whose side Rake Connor was on.

Chapter 30
Higher Education

Pete and Gwynn slept and woke with the dawn and made love again with relish and urgency, the way the starved begin to remake themselves.

Afterward, when they lay spent and splayed in the sheets, Gwynn put a forefinger to Pete's chin. "I'm afraid I have to go to work." She rolled away from him, or tried to. The tangled covers bound her. Pete laughed and groaned and took up the task of freeing them from the knots they'd made in the sheets. Her revealed buttocks were a marvel, but he was depleted and could not have begun to make love again even though he craved it already.

"I'll make you some breakfast," he said.

"That's sweet, but I don't have time. Anyway, I'll get a chance to eat at work. Danny will see to it. And you don't have to rush. Just lock the back door when you leave."

Those words were like a floor falling from beneath him. *When you leave.* There was nowhere else on earth he wanted to be, but he would have to leave.

It was nearly ten o'clock when he got to his own driveway, rumbled over the cattle guard and came to a stop at his own house. When he set the handbrake and turned off the motor, a peculiar mood came over him in the silence. He sat in the car for a moment letting the sensation reveal itself. He'd always called this place home and never questioned it, but just then it didn't feel like home to him. He didn't belong. Not here. He felt a moment of panic as if he were treading deep water somewhere with neither boat nor shore in sight. There were monsters in the deep, and he was helpless against them. His heart raced and his breath was hard until he forcibly pushed away his panic. Gwynn. The only thought strong enough to hold him in place.

He got out of the car and went in the back door.

"So how did the rabbits like your new swimsuit?"

It was Lavena standing at the kitchen sink facing him like a gunfighter.

"What?" Pete was startled. How had he failed to notice that her car was there when he drove in? She should be at work by now.

"Oh, but you don't look like you've been rabbit-hunting, do you?"

"No." He knew it was true. How'd she know about the swimsuit? he wondered. It didn't take him long to figure that out.

"Tell me where you've been, and it better be good."

Pete shifted on his feet, the screen door still ajar against his back. He tried to think of something to say that wouldn't stick in his throat.

"Answer me," she commanded.

"I'd rather not." It was the only honest answer he could give.

"Well then let me tell you where you've been. Do you think nobody's noticed how much time you've been spending at the Streamliner, and why? But I really never thought it would come to this!" She slapped the countertop with an open hand. "I presumed and hoped and prayed that you'd come to your senses before things went this far." She pointed to a chair at the table. "Sit."

Pete edged into the kitchen and took his usual place.

"You, young man, YOU will, as of this minute, stop going to the Streamliner, and you will not see this California floozy again. Whatever you've started there is over, do you understand me?"

Pete's ire rose against her slander of Gwynn. "She's not a floozy," he said.

Lavena stood over him in striking distance. "I beg your pardon?"

"I said she's not a floozy. She's intelligent and kind. More so than anybody else around here."

"How dare you! Let me make something clear. I know who to talk to, to get her fired from there and keep her from getting any other job here in this town. I also hold title to that car you drive, and I can sell it anytime I choose."

Pete was feeling more defiant by the minute. "Sell it then!" he said. "Daddy's car. You go ahead and sell it. I have enough money to buy it back. Either that or get another one. I'm old enough to buy my own car, and I've probably got more money in the bank right now than you do." He trembled and tried not to think of the ramifications of what he was saying.

Lavena was on her heels. "I'll pretend I didn't hear that. You'd better pretend you didn't say it."

"I'll pretend nobody said anything," he said.

After that day Pete and his mother coexisted in an unsteady truce. He continued to spend as much time as he could with Gwynn but tried to do it in such a way that Lavena could, if she chose, pretend not to know about it. Lavena, for her part, tried to strike a balance that allowed her as much control over him as possible without driving him away. She began to regret that he'd earned so much money over the last three months. It gave him too much independence.

Most of the time Pete and Gwynn spent together was in the afternoons after she left the Streamliner, and before Lavena got home from work. It kept the peace between Pete and his mother, but also left Pete resenting the constraint.

It was Gwynn's day off, and Pete had driven out to the lake as soon as his mother had gone to work. They were lying on towels on the dock, catching the September morning sun.

"Hey," she said. "Have you registered at Panola College yet?"

"I've got till tomorrow," he said. "I'll register in the morning."

Gwynn rolled to her back and sat up hugging her knees. "Isn't that the last day? What if your classes fill up? Didn't you want to register early? Get the schedule you want?"

"Yeah, I guess." He regarded her foreshortened face from where he lay. "I can see up your nostrils," he said.

She ignored that. "You are going to register, right? If you don't, you're cannon fodder."

"I don't need two mothers," he said.

Gwynn groaned and closed her eyes against the glare on the water. "I wish I was going back to school tomorrow. I'd be graduating next spring if I hadn't had to leave." She sighed.

"What if I don't?" Pete sat up beside her and playfully pulled at the top of her swimsuit and tried to peer in.

She slapped him away. "Stop it! What do you mean, 'what if I don't?' " She cocked her head, waiting for an answer.

"Maybe I ought to just join up and get it over with. I barely got out of high school alive. The idea of sitting in a classroom makes me want to start running and never stop."

"Don't you dare sign up!" Without another word Gwynn stood and started toward the house.

"Hey, where you going?" he called.

She went inside and let the screen door slam. Pete lay back on the dock and closed his eyes against the sun. Ever since his summer of working nights, he had a new appreciation for the sounds in the daytime air. He lay listening to the jays in the woods and far off crows, waiting for Gwynn to come back out of the house. When she didn't, he rose and went in to find her.

"Gwynn?" The house was still cool and shadowed. "Gwynn, where'd you go?"

She came out of the bedroom and faced him across the kitchen. She had changed out of her swimsuit and wore jeans and a blue cotton blouse. She had a fist around her hair behind her head and was working a band around it for a ponytail.

"Pete, my brother has been very lucky. In the Army, I mean. He was in ROTC. Pretty gung-ho. His deployment was to Germany, and he's been there the whole time. It's worked out well for him. But President Johnson is drafting for Viet Nam, not Germany or Japan. That's where you'll go if they draft you or even if you join up. My gung-ho brother says that he'd desert before he'd go into that disaster. You have no idea what you'd be getting into."

"Well, Viet Nam is where the enemy is. You're talking like a war protester or something."

"The enemy? Who in their right mind thinks that the Vietnamese are any threat to us? It's a messy, pointless war, and the only real thing about it is the blood. And you're right. I have been a protester."

"You have?"

"Yes, I certainly have."

"At Berkeley?"

"More than once."

Pete stood stock-still, letting Gwynn's words soak into the walls. "Are you a communist?" he asked. "You can tell me the truth, and it'll stop right here. I won't report you or anything, but I just want to know."

"Of course I'm not a communist. Why would you even think it?"

She stared at him, nodding her head. "Oh. I get it. I'll tell you why you think that." Her color was rising. "Because that's what you've been told to think. The same people who say that a man has to eat off a paper plate behind the cafe because his skin is black. The same people who won't eat off a plate that a Negro has used. There's some fine logic for you! The same people who think the earth is six thousand years old, while geologists who know better are finding the oil for them. Yeah, Pete. Around here you can get some first-class opinions from some real deep thinkers. No need to ask any questions when they tell you to kill and die in Viet-fucking-Nam, because anybody who questions it must be a communist!"

She stopped, tight-lipped and breathing through flared nostrils. Pete stood wide-eyed in the pregnant silence.

She started to apologize. "I'm sorr …"

"I never heard a girl say fuck before."

Gwynn snorted a laugh.

"You really don't like it here, do you?" he said.

"No."

"Sometimes I don't like it much myself."

Gwynn came around the kitchen table and took his hand. "Pete. You must stay out of the Army. It's not like the movies, all heroic action and all that. Some of my high school classmates have come back standing up, and one of them didn't. War changed the ones who did, and not for the better. The ones who've seen combat can't tell you why we're fighting this war."

"Is this about me registering at Panola?"

"That has to be up to you. I just don't know why you're ambivalent about getting to college. It's your ticket out of here, just like it's mine."

"Is here really so bad?"

"It's your question. You answer it."

Gwynn picked up a dish cloth, wiped at nothing on the countertop and, catching herself, threw it angrily into the sink.

"Pete, you know how much I like you. I don't want to hurt you. But I think you've been failing to understand something. I'm leaving Texas at my first good opportunity. Probably in December or January. My brother is getting out of the Army when his tour is up. We're both going to Berkeley, and maybe staying with our grandmother there. You and I are having fun, and I genuinely care for you, but this is temporary. I don't belong here. I'm not sure you do either, but that's not for me to say."

Pete put his hands on a chair back and hung his head. "Being right here with you is all I want."

"I know," she said. "That's not good. You know it isn't."

"All that stuff you said. Paper plates and Jesus."

"Pete, I'm sorry. It's just that …"

"No, listen. That stuff bothers me too. I never told anybody this, but I shared a chocolate chip cookie with Swat. At the wax plant. I mean, it was his cookie, and he broke it in two with his hands and gave it to me. I had to think about it, and I tried not to let it show that I was thinking about it. I reached out and took it and I ate it. My own dad would probably slap me for that. If he was alive, that is."

Pete turned away from her and went to the window and stood looking out. "Gwynn, I don't know anything that's worth knowing. Every single thing I know and believe is suspicious to me. I can't depend on any of it."

"Oh, Pete."

"I need to think, Gwynn. I don't know if I can think and

go to college at the same time."

Gwynn came behind him and put her arms around his waist. "Listen," she said after a moment. "I have to go to town. Bank, post office, groceries. Stuff like that. Why don't you go to the college and get the registration done? It's still early in the day. You can tell me all about it tonight. I'll get us a steak for dinner to celebrate. And some wine. I look forward to hearing about your classes and schedule."

"You make it sound fun."

"Pete, a year from now I'll be back in California and you'll be about to start your second year. You're going to meet so many new people. Girls. Give it a chance."

Pete opened his mouth.

"No, no, don't interrupt me. Yes, girls. They will be all over you. Your life doesn't hinge on me."

"Nor yours on me," he said with an edge of resentment. "There's something you don't understand. You've ruined me for other girls. There are no others around here that can compare to you."

"You don't know that, Pete. College isn't like high school. In a lot of ways college is easier. Sure, the coursework is more challenging, but it's also more interesting, and there's so much less bullshit. It lightens the load. Just you wait. And the people you meet! College weeds out the morons. And there won't be anybody there who knows about that time you wet your pants in second grade."

"I didn't wet my pants in second grade!"

"You know what I mean. You get a fresh start in college with new faces. People willing to find out who you are. Now."

"It was in ninth grade."

Gwynn punched him. "Will you be serious for a tiny fraction of a second? If you don't start college now, chances are you never will. It will never be easier than it is right now."

Chapter 31
A Different Official Version

Rake Connor stumbled into an opportunity he didn't know he'd been waiting for. He was in his office in the late evening when the phone rang. The dispatcher was in the bathroom at the moment, so Rake took the call. "Kickapoo County Sheriff's office."

"I seen something that just ain't right," a phlegmy voice said. "I figger I ought to tell it to somebody."

Rake rolled his eyes. It was probably just somebody whipping a dog or some such thing. "What is it that you seen that ain't right?"

"I'm out here at the Palm Frond Motel, you know where that's at? It's like if you was coming' in from Tyler and you ..."

"Of course I know where that's at," Rake drawled, almost mimicking the caller, "What is it you want to tell me that ain't right?"

"Well I was at the ice machine when this old car pulls in and a guy gets out, you see. A white guy it was. Well, I reckon that's just what you'd expect, bein' this here is a white establishment. Anyhow, this guy, he went and opened the door to the room and then come back out. So when he thought nobody was looking, he comes back to the car and opens it up and a nigger girl gits out and goes in the room with him. She had a scarf on her head, but I seen her. We don't allow that kind of carryin' on in Tallahassee."

"Who is this?"

"I'm just a concerned citizen from Tallahassee. I'm passing through headed to Albuquerque. But here's the thing. I'm pretty sure I heard two gunshots from in there."

"Gunshots."

"Yessir. I'm pretty sure. Two loud booms that sounded exactly alike. I don't think it was no hammer."

"Did you tell the night manager?"

"Not yet."

"Can you describe the car they was in?"

"It's a Chevy. A '58 I think. Green. And it was loud when it was runnin'."

"Do you see it now? Is it still there?"

"Yep, I'm looking at it."

"Can you read the license number?"

"I can make out some of it." The man gave him as much of the number as he could.

"And what's your name?"

"I ... I don't want to get mixed up in nothin'. I'm just tryin' to git to Albuquerque."

"Is it California plates?"

"Well. It might be. Looks different from the Texas plates."

"What room did they go into?"

"I don't know the number. It's the last one down at the other end from the office."

When Rake had the information he needed, he put the phone down and, after thinking for a moment, decided to go to the Palm Frond himself rather than dispatch a deputy. It might be better for the election if he personally showed up. He might get his picture in the *Herald.*

He went out to his cruiser and gave himself a head start before he radioed for backup, no siren, no flashers. Rake had been to the Palm Frond plenty of times to settle one kind of ruckus or another. Any place near a wet county line was like that.

Rake parked at the motel office and went in. To the night manager he said, "I got a call and have reason to believe that one of your patrons is a Negro. The folks in that green Chevy out there, what room are they in?"

The manager, wide-eyed and tight-lipped, said, "Yep. That Florida guy told me you was comin'. Number 6. I'll let you in."

"No you won't. You give me the key, and you stay put right where you are."

The manager squirmed and cleared his throat. "Don't you need a warrant?"

Rake glared.

"Or something? I'm just asking."

At first Rake gave him a look that said, *What kind of damn fool are you?* but then considered that he might soon need that man's vote. "I reckon this is a bit of an emergency," he said. "This might could save some lives."

The manager gave him the key ring. "Help yourself," he said. "It's the one with number 6 on it."

"I figured that." He took a step toward the door. "Thank you," he added.

Dease, the rookie deputy, drove into the parking lot about that time. Rake went out and spoke to him and then moved his cruiser to room 6, parked it parallel to the front wall and instructed Dease to stand behind it, weapon ready. Rake went to the door and planted his back against room 5. With an outstretched arm, he reached across to the door to room 6 and pounded. "Kickapoo County Sheriff. Open up!"

There was no answer. "I'm counting to three!" he shouted.

"ONE!" and kicked the door open and leapt into the room, firearm in hand.

"Damn," he muttered. He holstered his pistol and surveyed the room. "You can come on in," he shouted to Dease.

A small skinny body lay under the covers of the bed. A bloody pillow covered the face. The other body was sprawled in an armchair, the left side of the head mostly gone, much of it stuck to the wall opposite. A Browning .45 semiautomatic pistol lay on the floor on the right side of the chair. The room smelled of gun powder, blood, cigarettes and feces.

Dease came in, spun on his heels and went back out. Facing away from the motel, he shivered, collected himself and then went back inside. "Oh, man."

"Looks like we got us a crime scene," Rake said. "Go call for the coroner and them. We've got work to do."

Rake stepped outside and lit a cigarette. An idea forming in his head needed some incubation. He walked to the end of the motel and around behind unit 6. He looked off across a dark field beyond which he could just see a cluster of lights. An occasional plume of steam rose up in the light and drifted away. He was becoming more and more confident that this could work in his favor. Of course the coroner would rule it to be a murder-suicide, which is probably what it was. Any fool could see that. But what if it turned out to be something else?

He went back into the motel room and considered things. He stepped across the blood in the floor and checked out the bathroom. Sure enough there was a single window on the back side of the motel. He slid the window open as far as it would go. It was just big enough for a good-sized man to conceivably crawl through. For good measure he went back to his squad car and opened the satchel in the front seat. He took out an aluminum

35mm film canister which he slipped into his pocket. Back inside the motel room he wiped his prints from the canister and manipulated the prints of the dead man onto it. Then he dropped it onto the floor and slid it under the armchair with his boot. It would provide all the uncertainty he would need.

Chapter 32
A Likely Story

Rake's home life had been going seriously downhill ever since Rake Jr. left. He was losing the will to make it better. He often called home to tell Belinda that he had to work late. He knew that she knew he was lying, and that they both accepted the lie. It kept them both, temporarily, from having to confront the truth. Their marriage was already shaky, and Rake Junior's disappearance knocked out the props.

They still made joint appearances at church now and then. For Rake, attendance was necessary if he seriously wanted his hat in the ring come election time. But word and rumor had gotten around, and around again, more elaborate with each revolution. The sheriff's drug-using son had run away to become a godless hippie. He was, even now, traitorously demonstrating against our own brave soldiers and having indiscriminate sex with communists. When Rake and Belinda appeared at church, they were temporarily allies in a world that was indifferent to them at best.

When the election neared, Rake as always produced ads for local TV and radio. This time his usual self-assured and comforting voice fell flat. The bags under his eyes made him look depressed and tired. To make matters worse, his most senior deputy was running against him and had gotten the public support of the county coroner. In their own campaign they never made direct reference to Rake Jr.'s drug use, but they didn't have to. The *Riverbottom Weekly* did it for them with a feature article on the disgrace of drug-using unpatriotic war protesters, and insinuated that unfit parents were to blame. People were talking about the changes needed in the Sheriff's Office if Kickapoo County were to remain free of the kinds of trouble they were having in Chicago, Montgomery and elsewhere. There had already been trouble in Baton Rouge, across the Louisiana line.

Rake desperately needed something to boost his image, and he found it, or hoped he had, when the news put Sabine Gap on the map. The details were almost too sordid to mention in a family newspaper like the *Daily Herald*. But what the *Herald* left out, the *Weekly* was happy to fill in, if not outright embellish. It was a murder-suicide, perpetrated by a white male against a yet to be identified black female. Rake was familiar with that female, as was every other law officer in the county, and they had all seen her and the white guy together. Rake was also familiar with a relative of the black female, someone who might have a motive for murder. If he could "find" evidence that it was actually a double murder and then arrest the murderer, he might get some favorable headlines in the *Weekly*: CORONER BOTCHES INVESTIGATION: INCUMBENT SHERIFF FINDS NEW EVIDENCE IN DOUBLE MURDER. Rake would take glee in publicly pointing out that his opponent's main endorsement was from a sloppy coroner. He was mentally writing his speech. "If you like the way the coroner investigates a murder scene, you're gonna love his recommendation for sheriff."

Reports of the murder scene abraded the whole community's understanding of a proper world. A mixed-race couple.

The debasement of a red-blooded American veteran. Drug use. Rake could understand that a soldier, just returning stateside, would look forward to some pussy and booze, but he ought to do better than heroin and black snatch. This was all the same kind of nonsense that corrupted his own son. Rake could gladly shoot the troublemakers himself, and in fact already had shot a few.

In this case he'd be happy to let one Negro, who was forgetting to know his place, take the blame. If he failed to get a conviction, it wouldn't matter. He'd still get some good headlines.

For appearances he detained two suspects. One was the pimp at the Bottle and Glass who had certainly been providing drugs, but that arrest was just for show. The other suspect was the cousin of the dead girl, Prentice Waters.

It turned out that the pimp had a good alibi. He'd been sleeping it off in the drunk tank at the time of the Palm Frond murders. Waters had an alibi on the face of it, but it wasn't anything a resourceful law man couldn't work around. He had Swat brought in for questioning.

On a Friday morning at ten, Rake directed his staff to move the prisoner Prentice Waters from his cell to the interrogation room to stew for a while. At twelve-forty-five, Rake stuffed the last bite of his hamburger into his mouth, dropped what was left of his fried potatoes into the garbage and sipped his Coke. He stood from his desk and brushed off the front of his shirt and headed down the hall.

When Rake conducted an interrogation, he liked to take the prisoner by surprise. He stood outside the interrogation room and gave it a loud kick with his boot, then quickly jerked the door open, stepped inside and slammed it shut hard behind him. Then he slowly, as if distracted by some private thought, walked to the empty chair across from the prisoner. He turned his chair to the side, sat down and crossed his legs. He propped one elbow on the table and sat still for a moment.

"Name," he said without looking at the prisoner.

"Suh?"

"I am asking you your name."

"Prentice Waters, Suh."

"Your whole name."

"Prentice Haskel Waters Junior, Suh."

"Tell me, Prentice Haskel Waters Junior, have you served in the armed forces?"

"Yes, Suh. Seventh Infantry Medical Corps. Korea."

"You learned how to handle small arms, I imagine."

"Well, Suh, I …"

Rake cut him off. "Are you a violent man, Swat? That's what they call you, ain' it, Swat? Sounds better than Slap or Punch I guess. I'll bet you're kinda prone to violence. I'm sure you got used to that over there in Korea." He waited for an answer.

"Well, no, Suh, I …"

"No? You didn't encounter any rough stuff in Korea?"

"They was lots of fighting in Korea. I treated lots of …"

"Do you know this man?" Rake pitched a mug shot onto the table in front of Swat. It was Beulah's pimp.

"I probably seen him from time to time."

Rake slammed the flat of his hand on the table. "Don't get cute with me, nigger! I'm going to ask you again, do you know this man or don't you."

"I know him. Not his real name, but I know who he is."

"That's right. You know who he is. In fact you've seen him several times just in the last few months. Why don't you tell me about him."

Swat tried to bring his hand to his forehead, but his cuffed wrist stopped him. "I don't never see him on purpose, but he keep showin' up at …"

"Never mind about that. I know all about him. How are you related to the deceased woman, Beulah Waters?"

"She my cousin."

"When did you last see her alive?"

"I don't recollect exactly. Maybe a month ago."

"Where were you on the night she died?"

"I was at work out there at the wax plant on Goforth Road. Eleven to seven shift."

Rake leaned back in his chair as if he'd just thought of something. Swat meantime negotiated for comfort with his cuffed wrist.

"That's right. The wax plant. That gives you a pretty good alibi, don't it. Out there just working away." He put another photograph on the table. "What's this guy's name? Help me out here. You knew him." Rake waited.

Swat swallowed. "Henderson. Larry Henderson. I seen it in the paper."

"In the paper," Rake repeated. "Did you always call him Larry?"

"I never called him nothin', Suh. I didn't know the man."

Rake smiled pleasantly. "But you just called him Larry. The paper called him Lawrence. Why did you call him Larry?"

"I … I just heard Beulah say it a few times. So that's the name what come to mind whenever I thought about Beulah."

"Did you think about her a lot? Beulah?"

"Yes, Suh. Me an' everbody at Emmanuel Church. Everbody been prayin' …"

"It must have really pissed you off that she was, uh, *having relations* with that white man."

"Naw, Suh. It ain't like that. She been …"

"Yeah. I know. Using drugs. Turning the occasional trick.

I know all about that too. But I bet what really pissed you off was her always coming to you for money."

Swat was becoming rattled.

Rake continued. "I've got some very important questions here, and you'd better be very careful how you answer, Prentice Haskel Waters Junior. I know a lot of things already. Here's some of what I already know. Beulah didn't just want money. She didn't just drink and do drugs and turn tricks. She came out to where you work." He held his hands up beside his face in mock surprise. "At the place you work! Why, just having her come out there could have cost you your job. Nice job for a nigra by the way. Real nice job. And she didn't just want money. She wanted more heroin. Some of that white powder you been getting for her."

Swat's eyes widened and he sat up straight. "No, Suh! I never in any way had anything to do with no heroin."

"So you say. But let's talk about something else. Remember that night, I've got the date here somewhere. It was the night one of my deputies stopped an old green Chevy about two-thirty creeping down the road with one headlight busted out. Remember that one? Suppose you tell me how that headlight got busted."

Swat was frozen.

"Speak up boy. I asked you something. Would a sharp slap with this stick help you understand the question? How did that headlight get busted?"

"I busted it."

"You sure did. You busted it good. You busted Larry's lip pretty good too."

"No, Suh. I didn't hit him in the face. I gave him a gut punch, but I didn't have to hit him nowhere else."

"So you admit to hitting him? Committing assault?"

Swat sat shaking his head.

"Oh well, let's change the subject. Would you like to change the subject? Sure you would. Who owns that house you live in?"

Swat drew a breath. "That was my Aunt Minnie's house."

"But she died a long time ago. Whose house is it now?" Rake stood up and put his hands behind his back and looked up toward the ceiling. "Now that Minnie is gone?"

"Uh. I reckon it go to Beulah."

"Oh! To Beulah? Minnie's daughter, right. But wait! Now Beulah's dead too." Rake pinched the bridge of his nose. "I wonder ... I wonder who gets it now. Any ideas? Next of kin probably, huh? She can't take it back from you now, can she? Was she gonna kick you out?" Rake gasped and laughed as if he'd just understood the punch line of a joke. "Why, you stinker! That's YOU! Hummmm. Things are kinda looking up for you, aren't they. No more drain on your money. Own your own house. Good job lots of white men would like to have. So tell me," Rake said, making another abrupt change of subject. "At a fast walk, how long does it take to get from the wax plant to the Palm Frond?"

"Um. I ... I don' ..."

"Fifteen minutes tops, if you cut cross the creek and go through the woods to the highway. Thirty minutes there and back. It wouldn't be hard to slip away from the plant for that long. Not with that school kid the only other one out there. I bet he don't ask too many questions. Thirty minutes. Enough to get *Larry's* .45, do the job and hurry back. You could of done that easy."

Swat was breaking out in a sweat. His hands trembled. "Mista' Sheriff. I wouldn't do nothin' to hurt Beulah. She was like my sister."

"Sure. But you weren't above getting a little rough now and then, were you? Maybe you didn't mean to do it. Maybe it was even self-defense. Maybe things got stirred up after you got there. Got out of hand. They were too fucked up on the drugs that maybe you provided to them. Or maybe they didn't have the money to pay you, and you got into an argument. Maybe he pulled the pistol and you took it away from him. Maybe he shot her and then you shot him. There's a lot of maybes here.

"Let's say you confess and claim self-defense. You could get off with ten years for manslaughter. If you was to confess, I might even forget about the drug charges. My guys are searching your house right now, and when they're looking for something, they find it, know what I mean? So this could run anywhere from manslaughter to double murder. From ten years to the gas chamber. You help me out here, and it goes better for you."

"I ain't done nothin' to hurt Beulah. My hand on the Bible, I didn't do none of that."

Swat dragged his chained hands to his face, stunned, confused and afraid. He was starting to think that he might never again walk as a free man. He was very surprised at what came next.

Rake had slightly overplayed his hand. He'd already held Swat longer than he was supposed to. The judge wouldn't allow holding him longer without talking to the coroner. He wouldn't get his warrant until Monday morning at the soonest.

"I ain't charging you just yet. We'll see what evidence we find, and I'm going over that motel scene again with a fine-toothed comb. Don't leave town."

Later that afternoon Swat reclaimed his belongings at the front desk and walked out of the county courthouse into a world he'd feared he was seeing for the last time.

Chapter 33
A New Set of Wheels

The sheriff didn't offer Swat a ride back home, and Swat didn't ask for one. The walk from the courthouse to Tin Cup gave him a little time to think. The sheriff must have had a reason for letting him go. The only sense he could make of it was that the sheriff didn't want to arrest him. He wondered if he was being set up to try to run away.

By the time he reached Tin Cup, he knew what he had to do and that he had to do it immediately.

Minnie's truck stood out like a sore thumb, and most likely, every cop in the county would be on the lookout for it. If he tried to leave town in that truck he was sure to be noticed and followed, and probably arrested or shot.

He walked through the neighborhood at a brisk pace and got to his Aunt Minnie's house at a little after four. Normally at this time of day he would be waking up from his day's sleep. He would go over to Ruby's for his supper. "Normal" was a thing of the past. He went straight to his next door neighbor, stepped up onto Clifford's porch and knocked on the door.

Clifford leaned forward out of his recliner and tucked his undershirt into his pants. "Hey Swat, come on in. Get yourself on in here." He leaned and picked up a child from a nearby chair and set it, bewildered, onto the floor. "Sit down here,

Swat. Man! There's been the police all over your house. You doing alright? Oh man, Swat, we been worried."

Swat stepped inside but didn't sit down. He got straight to the point. "Clifford, I need you to drive me to Marshall."

"Marshall? Why Marshall? When?"

"Right now."

Clifford scratched his head. "What you gone do there?"

"I tell you 'bout it on the way. First though I got to go in the house and find something." He turned and went right back out. Clifford slipped his feet into some shoes and followed.

Swat entered his house through the side door. The place had been ransacked, but he took no notice of that. He got on his hands and knees in the kitchen floor and opened the cabinet door under the sink. The garbage pail that was usually there had been emptied in the middle of the room. Swat reached in and gripped the drain clean-out fitting with his bare hand and with a powerful twist unscrewed it and threw the plug aside.

Clifford in his anxiety could not stop talking. "What you doing down there, Swat? Cleaning out the drain ain't exactly where I'd start on this mess. Oh man, Swat. They done tore your house plumb up. Listen here, me and Lum, we'll come over and help you straighten this out. Lum, she'll bring Alice and them."

Swat gingerly pulled a slender olive jar out of the drain line. It was just slim enough to fit inside the pipe. He wiped off the muck with a rag that had been left on the floor and he held the jar up to the light. To his great relief, the two tight rolls of bills were just as he'd left them.

"Them police was here all morning making a racket. Lawd, didn't they make a mess! What's that?" Clifford said when Swat opened the jar.

"Your car got enough gas to get to Marshall?" Swat fingered out the first roll of bills and started working them flat. "If it don't, then you can take this and go fill it up and then come back here to get me." He held out a fifty-dollar bill.

"I believe it's got enough gas. Man, that's a fifty-dollar bill! Is all of them fifties?"

"Most of 'em's hunnerds. I'm gone lay down in the back seat until we get out of town."

"Lay down in the back seat? Who you hiding from?"

"If I try to leave town in Minnie's truck, the police gone take me in and not let me go this time."

Clifford nodded as understanding seeped in. "Well. I ... I reckon I need a minute to tell Lum."

"Go tell her. I be in the car."

"I'll put me on a shirt too."

"Do it."

While Clifford was out, Swat pulled a canvas U.S. Army duffel bag from a pile in the living room. He rummaged among his dumped-out belongings and retrieved some of his better clothes. His Sunday shoes. He grabbed some canned goods and an opener, a blanket and pillow. Some cheese and bologna from the refrigerator. There was still plenty of space in the duffel, so he stood a moment surveying the wreckage of what had been his home. All of his Aunt Minnie's trinkets lay scattered underfoot, their shelves ripped from the walls. His eye went to a small green glass figure lying on the floor. It was a tadpole about an inch long with tiny legs emerging from its sides. He picked it up and blew dust from it and held it up. If a tadpole could have a facial expression, this one had an aspect of serene wisdom. He closed his hand around it and held it for a moment before dropping it gently into his pocket. "This'll get me started," he said to himself.

They were on the highway when Swat asked Clifford, "Anybody

following us?"

Clifford checked his mirrors. "Naw. They ain't nobody in sight."

Swat peeked over the back seat and scanned the road behind them. "Okay, I'm gonna climb over into the front."

"So tell me what's going on, Swat. You got me plumb scared. You ain't killed nobody have you? Ain't robbed no bank?"

Swat laughed for the first time in days, but quickly got serious again. "The sheriff says I killed Beulah." Just saying the words brought tears to his eyes. He wiped them away.

"You don't mean it! Ain't nobody gonna believe that. How could . . ? What you gone do?"

"Don't nobody have to believe I did it for me to get the rap. The sheriff, he got his own reasons. But I don't know why he let me go. Maybe he just wants me to run off for some reason. All I know is, if I stay here another day, I'm likely going to jail and might not never get out. And if I get caught leaving it'll be the same thing."

Clifford thought for a moment. "We ain't even had Beulah's funeral yet. It ain't till Sunday."

"I know that. I can't go, Clifford. Y'all have to tell her goodbye for me." He put a hand on Clifford's shoulder. "Don't tell nobody you done this for me. But if the police ask you, then they already know. Just say my truck wouldn't start and you took me to meet a lawyer in the Safeway parking lot. Tell 'em I said I was getting another ride back."

Swat noticed that Clifford, in his anxiety, was driving faster and faster. "You better slow down," he said. "It wouldn't do for us to get stopped. Not with me in your car."

Clifford slowed and held the speed limit until they got into Marshall. When they got into town, he let Swat out of the car in front of the Safeway. "Good luck, Swat." His hands trembled on the steering wheel.

"I'll write to y'all."

"Do that. Lum can read it."

Swat dragged his duffel out of the back seat and stood back as Clifford drove away.

Swat wasted no time getting a newspaper. In the want ads he found a '61 Chevrolet Biscayne for $400. There were pay phones in a row at the front of the store, and he dialed the number. A white man answered. He said his name was Duncan, and that it had been his mother's car. He said it was a six-cylinder, standard transmission with 54,000 miles. It had air conditioning and was clean inside and out. Swat told him he had the cash and asked if he could drive it to the Safeway with the title, which the man did.

Swat paid him, and the man signed the title and gave it to him. Swat offered him a ride back home, but Mr. Duncan said that if he did, he'd have to do the driving and Swat would have to sit in back.

"Well," Swat said. "What do you want to do?"

"I'd appreciate the ride," Mr. Duncan said.

Mr. Duncan stopped the car in front of his house and got out of the car. Swat got out of the back seat and climbed behind the wheel. Mr. Duncan shut the driver's-side door and said, "Just out of curiosity, how come you didn't try to Jew me down from my asking price?"

Swat looked up at him. "I guess I ain't a Jew."

Swat filled up the gas tank at the first station he came to, and then went back into the Safeway where he bought an ice chest, ice and a stash of portable food. On his way out of the store he noticed that there was a flower stall, so after unloading his goods into his new car, he went back and bought one white lily and the entire bucket of daffodils that sat dripping on the counter.

It was nearly seven o'clock when he drove back into Tin Cup. Folks in their yards and on their porches looked up and followed with their eyes the unfamiliar car cruising their narrow street. He had the windows up and the air conditioner on, and nobody recognized him. He drove past his Aunt Minnie's house without stopping and a block later parked in front of the finest house in Tin Cup, a two-story with generous porches where Cora still lived with her parents.

Though Swat had been to Cora's house many times in the past, it had been a long time. Nostalgia swept over him as he went up the wide steps toward the front door. He and Cora had their first kiss sitting on those steps when they were both in high school. He walked bravely to the front door and knocked. He heard her sister, Mae, shout, "Cora, it's for you." He waited.

A moment later he made out Cora through the screen, smoothing her skirt as she emerged from the darkness of the house.

"Prentice. You lost your way or something, or do you sell flowers on the side now?"

"No, Cora. These flowers are for you. They needed some prettier place to be besides this bucket. So I brought them here to you."

Cora couldn't suppress a smile. "So, I'm prettier than a bucket, is that what you're telling me? Aren't you some kind of honey-mouth!" She accepted the daffodils and inhaled their fragrance. "Mmmm. They are pretty, Prentice. Thank you." She stood back, a little bewildered. "This is such a surprise, Prentice," she said. "Under the circumstances. It's been such a long time. And I'm so sorry to hear about Beulah. If there's anything I can …"

"Cora, I need to talk to you, and I don't have much time

to do it."

"Okay, Prentice. Okay. Is something wrong?"

Prentice took her two hands in his and looked into her black eyes. "I didn't want to do it this way. I just needed a little more time, but now I don't have any time. I have a lot to tell you, and one thing to ask you." He dropped one hand but held the other. "Come with me out to the Smokehouse. That joint out on the highway. We can get some supper and catch up. Please come with me."

Cora's brow furrowed. "But first you come on in the house and say hi to Daddy. We've all been worried sick about you. I'll find something to put these flowers in."

Swat stepped into the living room. "Good evening, Mister Nelson," he said. "How you feeling? I heard you were in the hospital last week."

"Oh, I'm fine. Fine. They just won't let me eat nothing unless it's either watery or tastes bad, one or the other unless it's both."

"That's terrible. Maybe me and Cora can get you some barbecue while we're out."

"Don't you be doing that!" came a voice from the kitchen. "He's got to cure that ulcer first."

"I guess we better wait." He leaned toward Prentice and cupped a hand to his mouth and whispered, "Wait till she ain't here."

Cora came back into the living room, her slender form now fitted into a pair of turquoise Bermuda shorts and a red blouse. Her toenails and sandals matched the blouse. "Daddy, we're going out for a while. I whipped up some ice cream and egg for you when you're ready for it. Mama gets off at nine-thirty."

"That's good, Cora. I'll be fine."

Swat and Cora both felt timid, almost as if they were high school sweethearts again. That had lasted until Swat dropped out of school and joined the Army. By the time he got back from Korea, Cora had gone off to New Orleans and Xavier College. Since then she'd been teaching at Dunbar High School. The whole Tin Cup community took an interest in the suspense between the pretty school teacher and her sometimes boyfriend. And none of Cora's siblings failed to anticipate Cora's bedroom coming up for grabs if she left.

"Daddy, can I borrow your car keys?"

Before Mr. Nelson could answer, Swat said, "You don't need to drive, Cora. I'll drive us."

"Prentice, I'm sorry, but I don't want to ride in that old truck. The passenger side door didn't even open the last time, and that was a long time ago."

"Look out front. You see any old truck out there?"

Cora looked out through the screen door. "Prentice! Is that your car? You devil! You come here with a bucket full of daffodils and driving a new car, and now you want me to go out for barbecue. Has something gotten into you?"

"Let's go. I'll tell you about it."

Cora took his arm as they went down the steps. At the car Prentice opened the passenger door but closed it again. Cora looked at him, puzzled. Prentice opened and shut it again.

"What are you doing?"

"Just showing you that this one has doors that work."

"It working is not any good until somebody gets in."

He opened the door wide. "Then we better make it work good."

"Cora, I have to be leaving." They were sitting in the Chevy behind the Smokehouse. The back service window for Negroes was busy, and they were eating drippy Cajun barbecue and watching people come and go, some of whom they recognized.

"What do you mean, leaving?" Cora said, already alarmed.

"Honey, the Sabine Gap law, they've got it in for me for some reason. They tore up my house. I'm afraid they're going to claim they found drugs. The sheriff already had me at the station all morning. He says he thinks I'm the one that killed Beulah and that white man she's been with."

"But that can't be, Prentice. The paper said suicide. At least for him. It's official."

"Baby, the sheriff has got something up his sleeve, and it's serious. The way he interrogated me this morning, he almost made me believe I did it. Maybe he just wants to scare me off for some reason. Maybe somebody wants my job, I don't know. But if I stay here, I'm going to jail, maybe for a long time."

Cora glanced around as if looking for help from somewhere. "What are you going to do?"

"I know this is a lot all at once. Just listen to me for a minute. I've been saving money ever since I got back from Korea. I wanted to wait a little longer until I was actually accepted."

"Wait. Accepted for what?"

"Nursing school. In California." He gave her a moment to let this sink in. "It isn't official yet. But I applied to a college there. I have the GI bill and nearly four thousand dollars saved up."

Cora's head was swimming.

"I wasn't going to tell you until it was official. I don't want to get your hopes up and then let you down ever again. I'm going to study to be a nurse. They'll let us do that in California. I have my Army medic experience. I can be good at it. Emergency room. They have a good …"

"Wait a minute," Cora blurted. "Wait just a damn minute! After all this time, you and me … you're just going to pick up and go to California? When had you been planning to tell me this?" She covered her face with her hands, breathing hard. "Take me home. Flowers, my ass."

"I was going to wait until you could go with me. I wanted

to have it worked out. But now … now I have to go in a hurry. Cora, will you marry me? I mean, when I have a place for us to live. And a job. You don't have to answer me right now. If I don't get into this college, I'll find another one. But when we can, I want you to marry me and come to California."

She stared at him, whether in horror or something else, he couldn't tell.

"But now I have to leave, Baby. If I wait another day, I'll be behind bars. They could be looking for me right now."

"So tomorrow? You're leaving tomorrow?"

"No, Cora. I'm leaving tonight."

"Prentice Waters! You have not called on me for nearly two years. Now you come with a bucket full of flowers, a car you just bought, asking me to marry you, and oh, by the way, you're leaving for California tonight because you runnin' from the law?"

She drew her palms over her eyes. "I understand all this in my head, but my heart is trying to catch up. What I don't get is why you have stayed away from me for so long. Was there somebody else? Explain that to me please."

Prentice stared into the floor of the car and spoke as if to some distant woman down there. "Cora, there has been nobody else. Not even when we were kids. But you've always been too high above me. Your whole family has been to college. And you're a school teacher now. Me, I never even went to school until my Aunt Minnie took me in. Even then I dropped out and joined the Army. I been wanting to get myself established so you could have a husband to look eye-to-eye."

Cora's face hardened. "Prentice, don't insult me. Do you think for one minute that I care more about that than I do about what's in your heart? Would you even want a wife like that? Don't you even know what kind of woman I am? You could have trusted me more than that."

Prentice considered her words, and he suddenly felt the loss of the past few years. He briefly imagined how it might have been between them if he'd been open with her. "I'm sorry," he said.

They were quiet for a moment. "Baby, it's a fact I have to leave tonight. I have not told a single soul except Clifford when he took me to get the car. But I couldn't leave without telling you. I had to see you. I want you to marry me, and I've been wanting that forever. Just say you're interested, and that you'll give me time to live up to my words. When I have a job and a place to live, I'll drive this car back to Sabine Gap and get you, and I'll sing to you all the way back to California."

When they drove back through Tin Cup to Cora's house, Cora muffled a yelp when she noticed a sheriff's cruiser parked on a side street in sight of Prentice's shack. "Did you see that?"

"I saw it."

"Are they looking for you?"

"They might be. But they don't know this car. He sure looks like he could be watching the house. I was pretty sure I wouldn't get far if I tried to go in Minnie's truck."

Cora's eyes were wide. "I don't expect that truck was going to make it to California anyway."

Prentice and Cora went quickly from the car, up the front steps of her house and inside. As they passed through the living room, Cora announced to all who were present, "Prentice Waters and I have some business to which we must attend. We are not to be disturbed." With that she led Prentice upstairs to her bedroom where she closed the door behind them.

Cora's father, couch-bound as he was, was too stunned to speak. He watched the two of them go up the stairs and disappear. "Ummm-ummm!" he said to himself. After a thoughtful moment he repeated, "Ummm-ummm."

It was a little before midnight when the two of them came out, Cora leading Prentice by the hand. Cora's mother had gotten home from work and she, with her husband and Cora's younger sister, Mae, were all pretending to be interested in something on television. Together they were passing the time as best they could, waiting impatiently for the "business-like" couple to come out and enlighten them about this "business" of theirs.

"Mama. Daddy. Y'all come in here in the kitchen. We got some things to say."

The kitchen was where all important family business was discussed. They all looked at each other with raised eyebrows and took their seats at the table. A folding chair was brought in so that Prentice could be seated next to Cora. Mae stood in the doorway until Cora said, "Come on, Mae. You might not be grown, but you're part of the family."

Mae rolled her eyes and with a half-grin took her chair to the table.

Cora began by explaining Prentice's predicament with the sheriff. She told them about the money he had saved and about his plans to enroll in nursing school. She finished by telling them, "… as soon as: number one, I finish teaching this school year; and number two: Prentice has a place for us to live, he's going to drive back here, and we're going to be married. Then I'm going to go to California to be with him."

Everyone's eyes went to Mr. Nelson. "You doing alright there?" Mrs. Nelson asked him.

"I'm fine." He straightened in his chair.

Cora explained all that she knew while everyone listened, occasionally casting glances at Prentice. When she stopped, her father was the first to speak. "Prentice, we've known you for a long time. I've wondered all along if you would be my son-in-law someday. We haven't seen much of you lately, so this comes as quite a surprise." He cleared his throat. "You've always been agreeable to have around, and I know you're hard-working. You've always been welcome here, and I've never wished you anything but well. But now you're planning to take my oldest daughter to California. You'd presumably raise my grandbabies there. This breaks my heart." He patted his wife's hand and went on. "This is oil-and-water news, Prentice. Happy news that breaks my heart."

"Mister Nelson. Missus Nelson. I never thought there was anybody for me but Cora. She was too little to be courting when I first fell for her. I always hoped I'd be bringing up our children here. Coming to this house on Sundays after church." He looked at the ceiling and back to Cora's parents. "I hope you believe me that I've done nothing wrong concerning the law. I certainly did not kill anybody."

"Oh, Prentice, Prentice," Mrs. Nelson interrupted. "We never for a minute thought that. We heard about you being hauled in. We had no idea it could get so serious. You were the best friend Beulah had, especially toward the end. None of those troubles were your fault."

"It has to be like this, at least for right now. Maybe things will change, and I can come back. Me and Cora have a lot to work out yet."

"Prentice, what if the law comes after you in California?"

Prentice chewed his lip. "I don't know. Just like I don't know why the sheriff thinks I killed Beulah. I don't even know if he even really thinks that. I'm just going to hope that coming after me in California will be more complicated than he wants to deal with. I hope that me leaving town will be enough to suit him."

"In the meantime," Cora said, "I'm staying here. The school needs me to keep my contract. I couldn't just walk out on them. So Prentice is …" Her voice caught. "He's leaving tonight."

"Tonight!"

"Yessir, Mister Nelson. My duffel bag is in the trunk. I've got some food in an ice chest. I need to cross the state line as soon as I can. If they get another chance at me, I don't know what would happen."

"No." Mr. Nelson was thoughtful. "There's no telling."

"And there's no telling the trouble that could come to you if they catch me here. I need to leave now before I bring trouble on everybody."

Cora's mother stood. "Prentice, you're not leaving until we fix you some things for your trip." She was trembling. "Mae, you slice up some of that ham in the refrigerator. And there's some left-over cornbread."

"Naw, y'all don't need to do that. I should go. We saw them watching my house when we passed by."

"Prentice, you won't get caught here. They don't know where you are. You take another step toward that door and I'll call the police myself. Now set down with Cora there and stay out of the way. We've got work to do."

She took Mae aside. "Here. Take this dollar bill and go knock on Ruby's door. Tell her … No, don't tell her nothing. Just say you've got to have half that chocolate cake she made this afternoon. Tell her you'll explain later. Just say Daddy's gonna have a fit if he don't get some cake. If you wake her up, tell her you're sorry."

Before Mae could get to the door, her father stopped her. "Mae, run up to the closet and bring me down that tin box from up on the shelf. There's something Prentice is going to need."

"Naw, Mister Nelson. I don't need no money. I saved up …"

"Hold on, hold on. This might be more important than money. It might save your life, and will certainly save you some trouble."

While Mae was trying to decide whether to slice ham, get cake or run upstairs, Cora said, "I'll get that, Mae. You go on over to Ruby's."

When Cora came back down with the box, Mr. Nelson opened it and took out what appeared to be a thick magazine and handed it to Prentice.

Prentice read the cover. " '*The Negro Motorist Green Book.*' What's this?" he asked, thumbing the pages.

"It's a few years old, but it ought to still be some good. It'll help you find places to eat and sleep. Get your car fixed if you have to."

"I've heard of this, but I've never seen one."

"You can send it back when you get settled. You might get a newer one before you come back for Cora. You got any maps?"

"No, I've been in such a hurry …"

"Here's Texas, but you want to get out of Texas. Which way are you going?"

"I figured straight up to Oklahoma. They'd be looking for me going to Louisiana because that's where I'm from. They don't know nothing about California."

"Alright, alright. Listen here. It's late already. I know you're wound tighter than a spring, but you're going to be real tired soon. I've got a sister in Texarkana on the Arkansas side. You cross the line up there. I'll call her and say you're coming. When you get to the Gulf station going into town, you can call. Them-all will come out and lead you to the house. But be ready for them to make a fuss over you, being Cora's intended and all. And don't eat too much of this here grub, because they gonna feed you again. It can't be helped."

He looked at Prentice for a long moment, deciding what to say and how to say it. "And Mister Waters."

"Yes, Sir?"

"I've been knowing you since you was stealing hubcaps and selling them at the junk yard." He raised his hands to stop Prentice from interrupting. "I know, I know. You didn't think anybody knew what you was doing, just like all teenagers think nobody knows nothing."

"Mister Nelson, I ..."

"Let me finish. You got a streak of daring in you. That's neither good nor bad, but it can be dangerous, especially for all us. You seen the news lately? There's upheaval going on, and the whites are getting jumpy. Keep a lookout. Don't take no unnecessary chances. I want to see Cora dressed in white for you. Not in black."

The commotion and planning went on for the next twenty minutes. While Mr. Nelson was on the phone, Mae came in with, not half a chocolate cake, but a whole one. She still had the dollar bill pinched between her fingers. "I told," she said.

They all rolled their eyes in dismay, but then they cut the cake, and they all had some. Cora and her mother kept finding more food items to add to Prentice's box. It was with a sense of despair that Cora realized that the preparations were almost done. It was near time for Prentice to go.

Before long Prentice stood at the door with a wooden apple box under one arm, the other around Cora. "Thank you, everybody," was all he could manage to say.

Cora said, "You can thank me enough by getting your black ass back here as soon as my school's out, if not before. It won't hurt you if you come back at Christmas."

They laughed together, if laughing was what you could call it.

Prentice kissed Cora, not for the first time that evening, but it would be the last for a long while. He turned toward the night and walked, as casually as his quivering legs would allow, to his new car, which now seemed dangerously conspicuous to him, big and white. Under the dome light he set his box of food on the floor, shut the door, started the car and drove down the street and out of sight.

He passed by the house he'd lived in for most of his life. Aunt Minnie's house. He saw a light on in Clifford and Lum's at this late hour. Probably something to do with a baby, he thought.

As he passed by where the squad car had been, it was not there. He checked his mirror. It was not behind him either. He headed south on the highway out of town. It was a little out of his way, but it was the quickest way out of Kickapoo County. He'd swing a few miles west and then head northeast to Texarkana.

Chapter 34
Nobody Home

Pete registered, paid the tuition and bought the books. He learned his way around campus, the names of the buildings and how to keep his schedule, but his mind was like a live frog in a frying pan. He could open a book to the correct page. He could write down what he read on a chalk board. He could stand up and sit down to the sound of a bell, but he could not care one whit whether a nematode had a peduncle or a contractile vacuole. He cared not whether "Teapot Dome" occurred under Warren Harding, Laurel and Hardy or a Pleistocene ice sheet. An algebraic equation was interchangeable with a French participle for all he was concerned. His mind was not his to command.

He was in love with Gwynn and he dreaded her leaving. He wanted to be with her every minute even though he often found their conversations disturbing. Gwynn's ideas regarding religion, race and morality were sometimes shocking to him.

"If there's no God, then how did we all get here?" he asked her. He'd bought their lunches at the Dairy Queen and brought them to her lake house. He was waiting there when she got home from the Streamliner.

"Until you can say how God got here, that's a pretty silly

question, isn't it?"

"But God has always been here."

"Yeah, sure." She rolled her eyes. "That explains everything."

Pete closed his algebra book and put it down on the table.

"Really," he said. "It's different, isn't it? If you're talking about God. If you're talking about the creation or the Creator."

"How's it different? Look," she said. "I'm not saying there's no god. Maybe there is. But this whole idea of an overlord who wants to burn you in fire for eternity if you don't get your beliefs just right? Even if you've been trying really hard? That makes no sense to me. Certainly not a god I can think very highly of."

Pete nearly swooned at those words so casually spoken. The combination of simple logic and blatant heresy ricocheted in his head like unexploded cannon balls.

After a while he said, "What made you start thinking that way?"

"What way?"

"You know. Not afraid of Hell. Casual about religion. Having sex without being married. Having unpatriotic ideas. All that stuff."

"Oh, I don't know, Pete." She was sitting across the table from him with a copy of *Newsweek* open in front of her. "I guess I was never made to feel afraid. When I was in junior high I just decided that the stuff in Sunday school didn't add up. I just sort of wrote it off as fairy tales. Not that there's not some good lessons. Kindness. Charity. Do unto others. As for sex, I don't want to get pregnant. I don't want to pass any diseases around. And I don't want to get hurt or hurt anybody. Including you. But all that morality stuff; that's mostly a property issue, as in, a married woman is the property of her husband, and no other man is allowed to trespass." She started to go back to her reading, but stopped and looked up. "And as for unpatriotic ideas: when I see my country making a huge mistake, it would be unpatriotic not to speak up."

Pete considered the state of Gwynn's soul. He leaned back in his chair and watched her, intent on the article she was reading. So lovely. He saw an eyebrow raise slightly and there was a small twitch of her lips. He imagined her in Hell, screaming in pain. Eternal and irreversible torment. "I need to go for a run," he said and stood up from the table.

"Where are you going to go?"

"I don't know. Down the road, I guess. I just can't stay sitting here."

"What about your algebra?"

"Sure. What I need is algebra. I've got to go."

"Are you mad at me?"

"No. But right now I don't think I would know it if I was."

Pete went out the back door, through the carport and up the driveway to the road. The leftward direction was the way from which he'd always come, and he'd never been past Gwynn's driveway. He went to the right this time and settled into his pace.

It was getting late in the afternoon, and the air was cool. The road dropped down and bridged a creek and went up steeply on the far side. On the uphill stretch, he increased his speed, feeling gravity yield its hold on him. The exertion felt good, and when the road leveled out, he extended his stride. He felt like he could run forever.

The woods grew close to the road and large oaks spread a canopy overhead. In places it was like running through a tunnel. Small creatures startled in the grass as he went by, and one rabbit sped off into the underbrush. After a couple of miles he encountered a clearing on the left side of the road. There stood a small clapboard church, white against the darkening woods, its steeple no match for the trees around it. He stopped and faced it. The wide steps up to the decrepit paint-peeled doors. The handrails on each side were of plumbing pipe. "Lord's house," he said to no one, for no one was there.

He went up to the door and found it unlocked. He stepped inside and peered into the gloom. Everything was just as he would have expected. A center aisle to the pulpit. A glass-fronted baptistry at the far end up behind the choir loft. Hymnals in the pew racks. He walked down the aisle and took the two steps upward to the pulpit and turned to face the pews, his breathing slower now. He stood still, imagining a congregation on Sunday morning, people in their shabby finest, looking toward him. Smiling. Waiting for his words. He stood there a long while, feeling that he should say something, but his breath became short and rapid. His eyes filled. He started to weep, quietly at first.

He choked out the words, "This is never going to happen." A raw laugh burst from him, and he shouted it. "This is never going to happen!" He stood there at the pulpit and sobbed his confusion, his rage and his terror. Confusion about belief. Rage that he'd been given a false God. Terror of what his future would be in Its absence.

"God! If this is Your house, why isn't anybody home? Knock, knock!" His knees buckled, and he knelt near the pulpit and cried aloud. With his head and elbows on the floor he heaved such deep sobs that he thought he would retch. He wanted to vomit but could not. He wanted to vomit every hateful lie, every false and foul doctrine, every putrid belief out of his mind. He stayed there, fetal, until he was weak and empty.

It was growing dark. He drew himself up and laughed and went down to the pews where he found a church bulletin and a stub of pencil. He wrote in the margin, *Dear Lord, I stopped by, but nobody was home. If You ever get this, give me a call. You've got my number.* He took it back to the pulpit and left it on the lectern for someone else to find and puzzle over.

He left the place, and leaving, could not at first bring himself to close the door behind him. He went down the front steps and stood on the ground looking back. Fresh-fallen leaves stirred at his feet. "I should shut it," he said aloud, and went back up and looked into the darkening sanctuary and then gently closed the door.

The sun was below the horizon, and the dampening air smelled of autumn leaves. Pete ran without vigor, but with purpose in the direction from which he'd come. At Gwynn's driveway, lights from the kitchen illuminated the carport. A more lovely light he'd never seen.

Gwynn was opening a can of some kind of vegetable when he came in. He looked at her there under the kitchen light.

"I want to make love," he said.

"Now?"

"As soon as possible."

"But you're all sweaty."

"Yes."

"Well." She wiped her hands on a towel. "Let's shower then."

Gwynn was watchful of Pete. He had a more solid presence than she had seen in him before. He was less boyish. Something had come over him that she hadn't seen before. Over the summer she'd come to care for him and trusted him, and his love-making was always tender. She was willing to accommodate him.

They undressed and went into the small shower stall. They stood together under the shower head. "Pete, you're trembling. Are you okay?"

"I don't know what okay means right now."

"Did something happen?"

"A lot has happened lately."

"Do you want to talk?"

"No, not now. I need to fuck you first." He knelt and wrapped his arms around her and pressed his face to her belly. She stroked his head and bent to kiss him as the water ran over them.

Chapter 35
Baby, Don't Go

Not long after the fall semester started, Pete was in the library dutifully enough, hoping to find material and perhaps inspiration for a paper he was supposed to write for freshman English. He managed, with great effort, to almost stay focused on the task at hand. But as he searched the stacks, divining the ciphers of the Dewey Decimal System, the spine of a book caught his eye. *Nature, Man and Woman.* It was a title that promised enlightenment on the one subject that most had his attention. He glanced up and down the row to see who might be watching, pulled the book from the shelf and held it close to his chest. He opened it furtively, expecting some grand insights regarding the nature of sex. He stood there in the dim light and scanned the table of contents. He was disappointed at first that the book didn't seem to be about sex at all, but nevertheless, the chapter titles were intriguing. Spirituality and Sexuality. The World of Ecstasy. Consummation. He began to read. Forty minutes later he realized that he hadn't moved from the spot. He self-consciously took the book to the checkout desk.

When he got the book home, he was careful to keep the spine turned away from his mother's not-so-casual glance. He could not stop reading. Every page lifted his spirit and expanded his soul. He'd never imagined that reading a book about Buddhism could shed such light on the Gospels. Reading it was more like being born again than getting saved had been. A year ago it would have been nonsense to him, but now it offered a way to think about recent experience.

"It's good to see you studying so hard. You're probably going to have some good grades."

Pete covered the heading of the page with his hand and turned to his mother. "Yeah. We'll see."

"Well. Keep up the good work." She went on by him carrying an armload of clean towels for her beauty shop.

Pete tried to act normal, control his breathing, not turn red. He knew that she would likely yank the book from his hands if she knew what he was reading. He also knew that his grades would not be good, and that, if she thought they would be, she was in the same state of denial as he was. The recognition frightened him, that his mother was evading the truth. A child depends on adults to be grounded in reality, and when they're not, the child has to be.

He sat looking at the open page, but was no longer reading. He could hear his mother in the next room folding the towels and putting them in the box she used. In a few minutes she would tell him, not ask him, to carry them to her car. He would obediently do so, and his obedience would be the assurance she needed that her world was in order. Severely damaged, but still in order.

His grades would not be good, nor would they be better the next semester, and he knew it. He simply didn't have it in him. At best he had a little time to make a plan for that failure. Gwynn had completely convinced him that the war in Viet Nam was an utterly inglorious cause.

His best idea was to join the National Guard, which would

satisfy his military obligation while allowing him to stay stateside.

The local armory was only a few miles from town, and he drove out there one afternoon to take the first step. The place was all but deserted; just one Chevrolet was in the parking lot. Pete found the door unlocked and went in, temporarily sun-blinded in the cavernous gloom. "Hello," he said into the dark. At the other side of a wide expanse, he made out a partially open doorway to a lighted room, and walked toward it, his footsteps echoing from the high walls. He rapped lightly on the door and stepped into the light.

A man in uniform sitting behind a clean metal desk looked up at him without speaking.

"Hello," Pete said.

"What can I do for you, son?"

"I, uh, wanted to find out about joining the Guard. Sir."

The man, without adjusting his posture, simply said, "Son, is your daddy a senator?"

"No, Sir, my daddy is dead."

"Then that's a shame. There ain't nothin' I can do for you."

Pete stood for a moment assessing the finality of the statement.

"Will there be anything else?" the man asked.

Pete said, "No, Sir," and turned uncertainly. He walked, straight and erect, through the cavernous building and emerged into the blinding sun.

He tried the Coast Guard, but they were full up and not accepting applications. The Air Force was taking only those who could qualify for pilot training, and that required a college degree. He considered the Navy, but with dread. Confined spaces gave him the horrors. The semester would end soon, and he had to think of something.

Pete began to cling more tightly to Gwynn. She was the only one who kept him sane. Hers was the most liberated mind he'd ever encountered. Sometimes he thought about consulting Brother Deckert about how he should go into the future, but he didn't have the stomach for the repetition of scriptures that he already knew.

The only other person he could think of who he trusted was Swat. Swat had been in the Army and been to war. He had an uncommon view on how the world worked. But Swat had disappeared. They told him at the plant that Swat had stopped showing up for work. Griz said he was going to fire him if he ever saw him again. Nobody knew what had become of him. Pete even dared to go into Tin Cup to the Negro church to ask about him. The pastor there was friendly enough, but very guarded. His answers to Pete's questions were ambiguous at best. Pete felt that the man knew more than he was telling, and he left there even more perplexed.

In the end he had no one but Gwynn to whom he could truly connect. She alone had a coherent perspective on the broader world. He redoubled his efforts to entice her into his world, and particularly loved bringing her to the outdoors. He strove to show her some of the places he knew. On a free day he once drove her to Lake O' the Pines to enjoy the autumn colors. They packed a picnic and ate it at the spillway of the new dam. He showed her where he and his dad used to spin their casting nets out over the turbulence and draw them in laden with shad, which they froze in milk cartons for bait. There was another place, a ditch, really, where they had seined for crawfish. Pete enjoyed Gwynn's disbelief at such things and took some pride when she admired the landscape. He could name most of the trees: black cherry, chinquapin, buckthorn and others. It was a cold day, and they stayed mostly in the car.

It was weeks later, on a sunny day in December that he and Gwynn were in the woods below his house. He wanted to show her where he lived and the woods where he'd spent so much time growing up. His mother was not at home. The path wound through thick woods, deep dry leaves rustling underfoot. They held hands and more than once stopped to kiss.

"I used to hunt squirrels down here," he said.

"No. Don't tell me any more!" she said, then couldn't help asking, "What did you do with them when you caught them?"

"*Killed*, not *caught*. Ate them of course."

She gave a *what next* kind of sigh. "And I suppose they taste like chicken. Everything supposedly tastes like chicken."

"Dark meat," he said.

"Yeah, sure."

As they walked Pete pointed out little things of note. "One night I came out here in the dark. I wanted to see how close I could get to a whippoorwill that was making so much noise. I didn't turn on my flashlight until it sounded like the critter was in my pocket. And it nearly was. I could have almost touched it."

"What did it look like?"

"Just a stumpy-looking brown bird. Kinda ugly really."

"What did it do?"

"Nothing. Just moved out of reach. It went into some thick underbrush and that was it. Oh, and those vines over there, by the way, are poison ivy. You allergic?"

"I have no idea."

Gwynn turned serious. "Pete, I have to tell you something."

There was something in her voice that told him that this wasn't something he was going to like. He felt his knees weaken a little. He'd felt this coming. She'd been more distant lately, like her mind was far away. She was sometimes less than enthusiastic when they made love. He stopped walking and turned to her.

Gwynn gently grasped both lapels of his jacket and turned her face up to his. "Pete, I'm going back to California. I'm going next month."

"Why?" he said flatly.

"You know why, Pete. This has never been a secret."

Pete's eyes filled immediately. He looked away from her and wiped them. "Why so soon?" he said in a voice that he held steady.

"I'm going back to Berkeley. I've already re-enrolled. I've already told my Daddy too."

"And you just now thought to tell me."

"Pete, don't. I wanted to have things worked out. I couldn't tell you when until I knew when, and I had to work those things out with my family. With things settled now I can tell you."

"Settled for you. Not for me."

"This is not something for you and me to negotiate, Pete. My brother is getting out of the Army. I thought he might come here to see Dad, but he said no, maybe later. He and I will be staying together in California at my grandma's house. That's still to be worked out. We will at least be family to each other there. He's thinking of going back to college."

"I don't want to hear about your brother or your dad or college or anything else that takes you away from me. What am I going to do here? You think I can just go back to holding hands with the girls at church? That'll be just hunky-dory. We'll spend hours talking about the homecoming queen. Now that I've known you, Gwynn, I don't even fit in around here anymore."

"So what do you think I'm going to do, Pete? Put down roots here in Sabine Gap? I fit in around here even less than you do. It looks like the only choice for a woman here is to join a Bible-thumping church or be a slut. You're either in or you're out. Taking you for a lover has branded me here, but I don't care about that." She stamped a foot to the ground and walked a few steps away from him. "Dammit! Why are we even talking like this? I'm going to leave, Pete. I will miss you dearly. I truly care for you, but I will start classes, get busy, make friends and move on. Maybe you and I will keep in touch. Remain friends. Pen pals. That remains to be seen. But moving on is exactly what you need to do too, or you'll just sink into the mud. We will miss each other. We will. You've changed me too, you know. It hasn't been all one-way. You've treated me with a rare kind of respect. From now on I will never settle for less, and I thank you for that." She stood facing him, her arms hanging limp at her sides. Tears rolled down her cheeks. "Pete, hold me. No more talk right now. Just hold me, please."

Chapter 36
Another Line to Cross

Pete had time to kill, and he was hungry. He put his suitcase into a bus station locker, memorized the nearby landmarks and struck out into the heart of Seattle. Looking for promising directions, he crossed Pike Street and from there looked down the hill toward a bay, seen in glimpses through the fog, as were the seagulls that cried in the iodine air. He met a middle-aged man walking impossibly swiftly up the incline, looking as if he could do it all day. "It's a foggy one," the man said to him as he passed.

"Where can I find some breakfast?" Pete asked quickly before the man was gone.

He stopped and pointed. "Block down on the right. Gay Nineties. In the hotel there. Folks here call it the Gray nineties. There's more way down there at the market."

"Market?"

"Yeah, Pike Place Market. Six blocks down. You can't quite see it for the fog, but it'll burn off pretty soon. I hope." The man went on his way, leaning into his stride up the hill.

Pete shrugged deeper into his inadequate coat. Even the nearest place to warm up was too far away to suit him. He found the Gay Nineties at the corner of Seventh and Pike and went in. Three steps up took him to the level floor.

A moment later had him sitting at a small window table with steaming coffee in his hand. Stronger coffee than what he was used to, but it was good.

Three pancakes and three eggs later, Pete, out of curiosity, walked down Pike Street toward the market. He still had two hours before his bus north.

The market was a labyrinth of stalls, stairs and hallways. The fog persisted and smelled strongly of fish. Pete soon discovered why. Shouting men dumped huge trays of iced creatures with strange appendages into display cases and arranged them for appeal. There were sea-things with suckers, legs and pincers that Pete had no name for. "I guess people do eat that stuff," he said to himself.

He came to a stall tended by a woman near his own age. She sold brightly colored woolen goods, some woven from cords as thick as pencils.

"Hi," she said. "You need a hat."

Pete allowed that perhaps he did.

"We raise the sheep just outside Olympia. Spin the wool, weave the fabric. I make the dye from berries, beets and things. We do it all, start to finish."

Pete instantly loved the girl. He bought a knit cap in one of her more subdued colors and went on his way with warmer ears.

At a phone booth he spread his nickels, dimes and quarters on the steel shelf. He fished a strip of paper from his wallet and flattened it over the coins and then spun out the phone number Gwynn had given him of some Unitarians in San Francisco. As instructed, he fumbled coins into the slots and waited.

"Hello." A girl's voice.

"Hi. I'm trying to reach Todd Jefferson."

"Oh." There was a pause. "Uh, he's not here right now. I can get him to call you back."

"No, I'm at a pay phone. I need to get a message to him. My bus leaves Seattle a little after one. I'll be there tonight. They told me in San Francisco to call this number."

"Okay. That's enough. You never know who's listening. Don't even say your name. I'll tell him." She hung up.

At one-thirty in the afternoon under steady drizzle, a Greyhound bus pulled out of the Seattle terminal and swung its wide turns onto city streets, making its way to the I-5 on-ramp headed north. It was December and, at that latitude, evening starts early. The day had never really gotten started, and now it was already perceptibly ending. Views of the city rolled across the windshield while the driver pulled at the wheel with large confident motions. Pete caught glimpses of the city and its several bodies of water.

Soon after gaining the interstate the bus crossed Seattle's ship canal bridge, the highest and longest span Pete had ever seen. He looked down as if from an airplane, where hundreds of feet below and to the left stood a smaller bridge counterbalanced at an upward angle. Traffic on both sides of the canal waited while a tugboat pulled a long raft of logs seaward. The bus landed on solid ground on the north side of the canal and picked up speed. Every minute was another mile away from everyone and everything he'd ever known.

It was a little after three when the Greyhound crossed the Stillaguamish River, according to the sign. The bus climbed over a great rise and, a few miles later, descended again into a river delta. Now the Douglas firs and steep hills gave way to open flat farmland. It was raining and appeared to have been raining for days. The fields were sodden. Gray light reflected off the broad puddles in plowed furrows far into the distance. Flocks of birds, ducks of some kind, foraged the water and mud. Then more birds, large and white. Someone aboard said, "Are those snow geese or trumpeter swans?" No one knew.

A gust of wind rocked the bus, and Pete glanced forward through the windshield. The headlights of opposing traffic reflected off the pavement. The enormous wipers made their authoritative sweep across the glass. The bus yielded nothing to the buffeting wind and spray. Eventually it slowed. The driver announced, "Mount Vernon." It was the last stop before Pete's destination further north.

Pete watched the town come into view. An incredibly steep hill rose to his right. It sprang out of flat land to a steep promontory in the span of a hundred yards. The bus crawled the narrow streets until it came parallel to a wide and vigorous river, churning between its broad earthen dikes. Pete had never seen so much water in one day.

It was nearly dark, but shops and businesses were still open. People were on the streets and sidewalks. He checked his watch and was surprised that it was not yet four.

The bus stopped in a gravel lot near a cafe. People got off and claimed their luggage from below his window. People greeted each other and loaded into cars and went away to their own purposes. Some stood next to their luggage and gazed at the street, waiting for what was next. The driver came around to the steps and punched the ticket of a bent old man in a plaid flannel shirt and knit cap. The man boarded the bus and shuffled past Pete without acknowledgement, smelling of wet wool. Then the driver climbed in, gave someone a wave and settled into his seat. The door closed, the transmission grumbled, and the bus moved forward again. "Next stop Bellingham," the driver said.

The bus crossed the river on a steel girder bridge. Pete looked down on the water where drift logs clung to the pylons of the adjacent span. Then he could see no more. Pete brought his gaze inward and let the heaving of the road be his world.

After a few miles the road tilted upward into a mountain range. As they gained altitude the rain became slush and then snow. The highway was still wet and bare, but the roadside was white. The driver was busier now, negotiating turns and pitch and yaw. Pete watched cut-rock walls pass by his window, seeming no more than inches away, glimpsed briefly in the headlights.

The highway levelled and rounded a bend where city lights came into view, a city that sprang full-formed out of the darkness. Bellingham, Washington. A few minutes later they stopped on State Street. A fellow passenger, presuming him to be an arriving student, pointed out that the college was just up the hill. Pete kept his seat while the bus emptied. The finality of his decision was closing around him.

He was the last to claim his suitcase at the sidewalk beside the cargo hold. He took it into the terminal and opened it and drew out his sheet of paper. He unfolded it and found the phone number written in Gwynn's hand.

Pete heard the car before he saw it. An ancient VW Beetle. It parked across the street, and a heavy bearded man climbed out into the rain and walked toward the station. Pete stood and gripped his suitcase and advanced toward the door.

"You must be Pete Loucas," he said, holding the door while Pete came out.

"You must be Todd Jefferson," Pete said.

"Not my real name," he said, presenting a high-five to Pete's offered handshake and clumsy recovery. "It's what I go by these days. A wanted-by-the-FBI thing. I guess I got a little too rowdy in the SDS back East. A lot safer for me here. This is one far out town."

"Far out," Pete mused.

Todd was about 5-foot-10 with a thick chest and muscular

build. He wore decorated bell-bottom jeans and a string of beads that looked like a combination of glass, chestnuts and bone. He smelled like spices of some kind.

Once in the car, Todd lifted a tiny pipe from a holder on the dashboard, filled it from a pouch and tamped it with his little finger. "You haven't eaten for a while, I bet."

"I had a late breakfast in Seattle." Pete eyed the pipe while Todd lit it.

"I know just the place. You got any bread?"

"Bread? Well, no, I had some crackers and …"

"Money. You have any spending money?"

"Oh. Yeah, and some travelers checks. Enough to get by for a while."

"Far out." Todd took a heavy pull from the pipe and offered it to Pete.

"No thanks."

"Different strokes," he said and started the car.

They drove a mile or three southward along the bay to a run-down part of town. Todd turned right onto a steep downward slope, the first brick-paved street Pete had ever seen. They parked across from what looked like a bank, and indeed, had a sign reading The Bank Bookstore. People were everywhere, and they were all similar in appearance. Long haired men. Women in colorful long skirts. Thick woolen hats and work boots. People gathered in sheltered doorways. Someone was playing a guitar somewhere and singing loudly his objection to bombs and war.

Todd led Pete toward the Bank, but instead of going up the steps, steered him down a narrow outdoor stair below the sidewalk. "Toad Hall," he said. "Best pizza on the planet."

The dingy concrete stair opened into a large basement room. It was lively with people in tropical fish colors sitting on benches at heavy hand-made tables. The smell in the room was wonderful. Long-haired servers in long skirts carried rounds of thick, complicated-looking pizzas on whole wheat crusts.

Todd ordered and Pete paid.

They ate as much of the pizza as they could and wrapped the remaining slices in napkins and put them in their coat pockets.

"You gotta get you some threads, man," Todd said when they climbed the stairs to street level. "First thing tomorrow."

"Threads?"

Todd shook his shaggy head. "Clothes. You need a parka. Stompers too." Seeing Pete's expression, he added, "A warm coat with a hood. And some boots. Maybe you and Dennis can go to Yeager's tomorrow. You don't look ready for the climate. Matter of fact, you don't look ready for much of anything."

Slightly offended, Pete said, "Whatever *anything* is, I'm as ready for it as I can get."

"Far out, man. That's deep. Outta sight, man. You're getting yourself out of this fucked-up war. That's the main thing. Calls for a beer. Follow me."

Todd led up the hill and took a left. Pete kept up as best he could, his smooth shoes slipping somewhat on the wet pavement. "Stompers," he said.

"What?"

"Nothing. Where are we going?"

"The Kulshan. Freaky tavern. Everybody's expecting us. I told them I'd bring you."

"I'm not twenty-one. I can't go into a tavern."

"You can go into this one."

The Kulshan was jammed with people, mostly students from the college and a few of their professors, Todd told him. Lively conversation filled the room. Pete felt conspicuous in his unadorned jeans, button-up shirt and short hair. He didn't have so much as a mustache. His nylon jacket was completely un-suitable for the rain. He saw a few people give him a second look and turn away to say something to someone who flashed a brief third look.

A beautiful long-haired girl left a bar stool and came to Todd and flung her arms around him. They stood in a long embrace, their pelvises snug against each other. Todd muttered something into her ear. She burst into bawdy laughter and let him go with a punch to the shoulder.

"Judy, meet Pete Loucas, the one from Texas."

"Far out, Pete," she said above the noise. "Sweet Pete re-peat," she said, and replicated her recent embrace, this time against Pete's body. He wasn't exactly comfortable, but he didn't exactly mind either.

Over the next two hours they drank schooners and shout-ed conversation into the smoke and noise, the smoke carry-ing overtones of the pipe Todd had lit. At one point a man, apparently a professor, called for silence. For the next few minutes younger people at his table took turns reading poetry they'd written. The crowd was rowdy and specific in its praise and ridicule. Pete was utterly lonely and perplexed, and yet he could think of no other place he'd rather be.

Unaccustomed to the beer as he was, the new faces and names, sights, sounds and smells, spun in his head. He fell in love with a petite brunette named Kirsten or Krista or some-thing, who had a sweet face and a low-cut blouse. She was from Chicago and seemed to want to know everything about Texas. He told her everything he knew and then some. She looked into his eyes while he talked, and his eyes watered in gratitude for her attention.

Todd indicated that it was time to go. He summoned Judy, and the three of them went out to the VW and climbed in onto the cold seats, Pete folding himself into the back. They drove further up the hill and turned into a steep and rutted alley. At a tall unpainted house they climbed out of the car and went inside.

From upstairs a record player howled in a language almost Biblical. Pete's eyes widened.

"Babylon has fallen," Todd said.

Pete shrugged.

"Hendrix. You know? The album?"

Pete did not know. They both gave up on the subject.

"Anyway, the bathroom's there," Todd said, indicating a small room directly off the kitchen. "And through this way you can crash on the floor behind the couch there, or on it if you want to, but it's lumpy and probably too short."

During the night, in a process invisible to Pete, an Arctic wind swept southward out of Canada and collided with the wet air in Bellingham. The temperature dropped into the mid-twenties, and a heavy snow began to fall. A foghorn sounded on the bay.

When Pete awoke it was very cold in the house and completely dark. He'd slept in his clothes, including the damp nylon jacket. He wanted to sleep some more, but he was too cold. He got up and poked about for another blanket or even a loose rug for cover, but found none. He shuffled into the kitchen, turned on a light and lit a burner on the stove, not yet knowing what he would put on it. He warmed his hands. At the back door he looked out upon a darkness that seemed to be in motion. He flipped on a porch light and was astonished at the swirling whiteness in the opaque air. He could see nothing more and turned off the light.

He heated water in a pan and found a cup which he washed at the sink. He pulled a chair to the kitchen window and sat drinking hot water and looking at nothing. He checked his watch. Six forty-five.

He heard a sound from upstairs, and soon a red-bearded man appeared. He said his name was Dennis, and he behaved more like a host than Todd had. He made coffee and brought oatmeal and granola out of glass gallon jars, and honey from a cupboard. He sliced bread from a heavy loaf, the sturdy likes of which Pete had never seen. Dennis buttered the bread and toasted it in a cast-iron skillet and offered it to Pete, who gratefully accepted it.

"How long have you lived here?" Pete asked.

"About two and a half days," he said. "I don't really live here. I'm from Chehalis, Oregon. Came up this week on my way to Canada."

"The draft?"

"Yeah."

Pete leaned back in his chair. "Yeah, me too."

"I've got money from picking apples last fall," Dennis said. "I've got to get me some warmer clothes. Wouldn't hurt to have a sleeping bag. You too, looks like, if that's all you've got," he said pointing his chin toward Pete's suitcase."

"Yeah, same here."

"Well, I'm going into town. Want to come?"

Outside there was gray light. The snow had stopped, and a stiff wind was pushing clouds off to the west. Patches of brilliant sun flashed from the islands. It was very cold.

Dennis and Pete went together in the VW to the north end of Bellingham where they found Yeager's Sporting Goods. They bought wool socks and long underwear. Pete bought a pair of waffle stomper boots, gloves and a Coleman sleeping bag. From there they went to Goodwill where Pete got a wool coat of approximate fit and a navy watch cap. Dennis got a quart of oil for the Volkswagen.

They found a place on Holly Street that served hot lentil soup and heavy brown bread that was so unlike the white bread he'd always known that he thought there should be another name for it.

They sat at a steamed window, and Dennis wiped a dry spot with his sleeve. Through the opening they could see whitecaps on the bay.

"At least the wind is carrying the mill smell away from town," Dennis said.

"Yeah, what is that?"

"Paper mill. Georgia Pacific. It covers that whole area down by the water."

"Does Todd know we've got his car?"

Dennis laughed. "That's not Todd's car. It's mine."

"When are you going to cross the border?" Pete asked.

"I dunno. I keep putting it off for some reason. Once we go, we can't come back. Ever. There'll be prison if we get caught coming back."

"You ever think about just doing the prison time and getting it over with?"

"Fuck that!" Dennis said. "It ain't me that's in the wrong here. This war sucks from one end to the other. I'm not going to prison to satisfy some asshole idea that this cluster-fuck is anything but a crime. It's not my duty to justify this thing."

"Yeah."

"I'll miss my family. My sister's in college here in Bellingham. My little brother is in tenth grade in Chehalis. My dog... I won't ever see Stinker again."

"Stinker," Pete said with a straight face.

"How 'bout you? When are you going up?"

"Nothing stopping me. I left everything and everybody in Texas. Home is already so far away that crossing the border is like just another county line. Maybe I'll feel different when the time comes. Right now I just feel like I'm already gone, so ..."

Dennis took a deep breath. The waitress refilled their cups. Outside fine snow swirled up in the wake of passing cars.

"Tell you what," Dennis said. "Give me one more day to see my sister. Day after tomorrow you can ride up there with me. We'll go across together."

"Shit," Pete said. "Right now you're the best friend I've got. How could I say no?"

They toasted with their coffee cups.

Pete spent the next day killing time. Todd's house was too dark and claustrophobic for comfort, so he went out for a walk in his new clothes. The Fairhaven neighborhood, at one time a town in its own right, was mostly run-down. But the hippies and students gave it life. Tibetan prayer flags flapped on porches in the cold wind. God's-eye weavings spun on their swivels. Tie-dyed fabrics covered windows and whimsically painted cars crept by on the snow. On Harris Street people greeted him with peace signs. Antiwar sentiment was evident in bumper stickers and window signs.

Much of the pavement was packed into a hard sheet of ice. Pete walked gingerly into a food co-op just to see what it was. Bins of orange spice–Darjeeling tea, lentils, mung bean sprouts. Alfalfa sprouts. "They eat hay," he said quietly. He bought something called a bagel with lox and cream cheese. It was the first salmon he'd seen that wasn't from a can. He envied the people who seemed to know all about such things. Herbal medicine. A poster for an alternative school and another that announced a planned rally and sit-in.

He walked the three miles north to Bellingham proper and up to Garden Street and the college campus. He found the student union building and went in to warm himself, and fantasized about enrolling, imagining a life in such a lively and beautiful place. He sat on a bench to watch the people. People who knew each other and had business in common. Watching them brought his loneliness too much to mind, so he stood and went out and walked again.

He crossed a brick-paved plaza where students conversed in small groups, carrying their books. He stood still for a moment, watching.

He made eye contact with a bearded fellow who carried a sign on a stick. "YE MUST BE BORN AGAIN," the sign read, "John 3 Verse 7." Pete speculated that, not so long ago, he himself might conceivably have carried such a sign, and he was bemused at his own reversal. His current rebirth.

The man took their eye contact for an invitation, and he turned and walked toward Pete with an expression of pained sincerity. When he was within conversation distance he said, "Hello, Brother. Are you saved?"

Pete looked at him for a moment, searching his own insides for a true answer. "No," he finally said, and he laughed. "No. I'm not saved." He laughed again facing the blue sky. "Matter of fact I'm like a frog dumped out of a tow sack. Completely bewildered."

"What?" the man said, not knowing whether to be encouraged by this confession.

"That's it exactly," Pete said louder. "But I tell you this much: I AM born again. Yep. Born all over again." Pete nodded his head in self affirmation. He nodded and turned away from the man toward his own journey, striding over the frozen bricks. He threw up his arms and shouted aloud his own new public profession of faith, so that everyone on that plaza took notice, "I AM A FROG DUMPED OUT OF A TOWSACK," he hollered. "BUT I'M BORN AGAIN! BY THE GRACE OF FROG, I AM BORN AGAIN!"

He went away toward he knew not what, weeping and re-joicing, and bearing within himself a fresh and trustworthy uncertainty. A knowledge of little substance except that he was not who he'd been before. Old things had passed away. All things become new.

The next day he and Dennis loaded their belongings into the VW. Pete squeezed himself into the passenger seat and lifted his feet from the ground. The closing of the door rang in his heart like a liberty bell. When he next opened it and put his feet on the ground, he would be in Canada.

The two of them spoke little during the forty-minute drive to the border. The sky was clear and the air was very still. Along the route, they noted the several red-tailed hawks perched on the wires. Dennis wept briefly. Coming into Blaine, the bay stretched out before them in a wide low-tide mud flat. At the checkpoint Dennis brought them to a stop behind a flat-bed truck driven by a Sikh, known by his beard and the turban he wore.

Dennis turned to Pete. "Well, Cowboy, it may be a while before your next plate of cornbread."

Pete, feeling dizzy, forced himself to breathe and say, "Yeah. A while."

The truck ahead of them drove on through and away. Dennis shifted into gear and pulled forward to the booth.

Epilogue

Eleven years later, in January of 1977, President Jimmy Carter granted amnesty to the men in Canada who had gone there to avoid the draft. Peter Loucas was thirty-one years old and a Canadian citizen teaching history and metal shop in a Vancouver high school. He and Ruth, his wife of seven years, had two daughters. Ruth was a yoga teacher, a ski instructor and a volunteer at the Natural History Museum.

Down south in the United States the Jim Crow laws were dismantled. At least legally. Schools were desegregated. There were no longer Whites Only signs on restrooms and water fountains. Doctors offices now had one waiting room instead of two. Most churches remained as they had been.

Sheriff Rake Connor was no longer alive. He had lost an election and taken a police job in Baton Rouge, Louisiana. He was killed there in a head-on with a speeding drunk.

Belinda hadn't gone with him to Baton Rouge. After the divorce she stayed briefly with her sister and brother-in-law in Atlanta before finding an apartment in nearby Stevenville. She worked in a law office there and married a junior partner two years later. Rake Jr. came to live nearby. He sometimes travelled in Europe with Belinda and her husband. It would be years, though, before they included R.J.'s male partner.

Brother Deckert was no longer in the ministry. He completed his Ph.D in theology and took a post at Southwestern Theological Seminary. His Biblical scholarship led him to a more open and inclusive spirituality which sometimes conflicted with prevailing orthodoxy, but he found kindred spirits where he could.

Prentice and Cora Waters bought a home in Sabine Gap proper, though it was fairly near the old black neighborhood of Tin Cup. Cora was principal of the elementary school, and Prentice was a trauma care nurse at Good Shepherd Hospital in Longview. Their son, Luke, was five. Luke's grandparents and his aunt Mae spoiled him enthusiastically at every opportunity.

Gwynn had gone back to Berkeley to major in journalism with a minor in international studies. She graduated with honors and, after a short internship, took a job at the *Washington Post.* She went to El Salvador to report on the war there. Afterward she reported from Beirut and Iran and elsewhere. In Morocco she met and married a French novelist of some repute with whom she settled near Domme, in an old stone house with a view of the Dordogne River. She bore a son and a daughter. Gwynn for many years wrote a monthly syndicated column on race, gender and ethnicity which circulated widely in the English-speaking world.

Lavena's health had begun to fail, and she showed signs of early-onset dementia. She was bitter and strove with Satan. She left the church she'd belonged to in favor of an angrier congregation led by an angrier preacher. She built a protective wall of scriptures around her pious delusions and waged war with all the evils that plagued the world.

In their kitchen in Vancouver and with the amnesty in place, Ruth and Peter Loucas considered making their first trip to Texas to introduce Lavena to her grandchildren, girls five and three. The summer break would come soon, and they could perhaps take Lavena to the beach for a few days in Galveston. In the end they decided that Peter would go alone.

To save a little money Ruth and the girls drove him to Seattle for his flight to Dallas. As fraught as Peter's border crossing had been eleven years past, this crossing, which would have gotten him arrested just a few months earlier, seemed to have no import at all. At SeaTac Airport Peter kissed Ruth and the girls at the gate and boarded his plane. From Dallas he took an American Eagle DeHavilland to Gregg County where he rented a car and drove, unannounced, to Sabine Gap.

Even though the weather was quite cold, Peter drove with his window down to breathe the East Texas air. The smells of grasses, pines and crude oil thrusted him into a nostalgic melancholy. His old dreads seemed to peer out at him from the woods. He could almost feel Satan following him beneath the ground. Coming into Sabine Gap he drove past the church where he'd been baptized. It seemed to have shrunken with age. He went to the cemetery and stopped the car a few yards from his father's headstone. He killed the motor and sat for a moment. The wind rocked the car slightly.

He opened the door and stood, stiff and bleary from his flight. He strolled past headstones to the one he sought. It was pink granite and small. A brass plaque at the foot read, Pfc. John Loucas, 508th Parachute Infantry, 82nd Airborne. He wondered if his father would have ever forgiven him for dodging the draft. It would not have been an easy conversation. "I still miss you, Daddy," he said. He stood there for a while, waiting for something of substance from a world beyond. There was nothing but the wind. The sounds of traffic and oilfield commerce. His father was neither there nor anywhere that could be known.

He got back in the car and drove out to the Streamliner and went in for lunch so as not to arrive hungry at his mother's house. Chicken fried steak, cornbread and red beans were not to be found anywhere in Canada that he knew of.

He finished eating and paid the black waitress, and with a sigh, headed out, dreading meeting his mother. Their correspondence had never been encouraging. He procrastinated further by visiting the site of the wax plant. The state had built a spur around Sabine Gap that included an overpass at the railroad. There was no sign of the plant. Only the overpass and its on-ramps. Peter stopped the car on the shoulder and studied the landscape, trying to piece it together into something he knew. His vision and his memory could gain no purchase on it.

The cattle guard sounded its familiar rumbling chord under the tires. The driveway was in poor repair and the front yard overgrown. Peter parked in front of the house and went to knock on the front door. Lavena opened it and with little affect said, "So, you've come back."

"Not moved back. I've just come to visit."

"Well come on in." She turned her back and walked to the kitchen. Peter wondered if she even realized that he'd been gone for nearly a dozen years. He spent the next several days arranging for her care. His mother spent the time trying to preach him back to Jesus. On his third day he drove her to Longview for the chest X-ray as required by the care home they'd chosen. When they passed by the First Baptist Church, Peter noticed a bus in the parking lot. Young boys were milling about with their luggage, being hugged and instructed by their parents and boarding the bus. He took a deep breath and wished them well. He wished he could save them from all horrors.

His mother saw them as well. "Praise God," she said. "I hope they come out better than you."

He flew home later than expected, landing in Vancouver, hungry for the feels and smells of the Pacific Northwest. Jubilant to smother himself in Ruth and the girls. With luggage claimed and loaded into the front of their Volkswagen, ice cream was called for in celebration. Daddy's home.

Heading toward English Bay, Peter broke into a song he made up on the spot:

> I'm back with my girls
> And I'm smiling at their curls.
> I got one in the front seat
> And two in the back.
>
> We're getting ice cream
> And it isn't just a dream
> And I couldn't be happier
> If had a Cadillac.

A sweet voice shouted from the back seat, "Sing it again, Daddy."

THE END

Acknowledgments

The first person to make me feel proud of something I'd written was Mrs. Hood, my ninth-grade English teacher in Kilgore, Texas. I wish I could lay this novel on her desk and hear her laugh.

I want to honor all the fellow writers who have tolerated, supported, praised, ridiculed, critiqued and demanded that I carry on. A special mention to the late Tom Villa-Lovoz, whose enthusiasm for story and whose wonderful humor still ring in my ears.

I would like to especially thank the women in my writers group. I could not have written a credible female character without them. Special thanks to my editor and friend Susan Z. Witter. Thanks also to Catherine O'Mara Wallace who did the painstaking work of formatting this novel for print. It's been quite an education for me.

I am grateful for the Chuckanut Writers' Conference, which has given me opportunities to meet and learn from great writers, as well as to rub elbows with crowds of people enthusiastic about developing their craft.

Finally, I thank Jane Elizabeth DeBrock, my wife. Her love and tangible support, her understanding of me and this story, her pride in me and her willingness to tell me the truth have made me a richer person and made this a richer story.

L.D.

About the Author

Leslie DeBrock grew up in the piney woods and oil fields of northeastern Texas in the 1950s and '60s. He graduated from East Texas State University with a B.A. in English and taught high school English in the small town of Hughes Springs. In 1972 he left Texas and made his home in the Pacific Northwest and made carpentry his career. He lives in Bellingham, Washington, with his wife of 40 years, Jane Elizabeth DeBrock. They have a daughter and a son.